In Between Dreams

IMAN VERJEE

ONEWORLD

A Oneworld Book

First published in North America, Great Britain &
Australia by Oneworld Publications, 2014

This paperback edition first published in 2015

ISBN 978-1-78074-620-3 (Paperback)
ISBN 978-1-78074-397-4 (eBook)

Text designed and typeset by Tetragon Publishing
Printed and bound in Great Britain by Clays Ltd, St Ives plc

Oneworld Publications
10 Bloomsbury Street
London WC1B 3SR
England

To my Father: For his wisdom
To my Mother: For teaching me how to dream big
To my Sisters: For their love and friendship

1

St Albert, Canada. April 1992

I keep running even though I know there is no one behind me. I like the strength of my feet as they hit the mud, still drying from yesterday's rain, bringing up brown flecks that hit my ankles. The tall field bends at my outstretched fingers and above me extends blue sky, miles of it.

I know I'm close when the ground begins to dip. When its smoothness turns bumpy and surprising and I slow my pace as, all of a sudden, it is upon me. The track that leads up to it is jagged and uneven from disuse and I struggle to get down it with my bare feet. Small stones dig into my heels and stay there, sending pinpricks of pain up my legs every time I take a step. I reach the end of the path as it drops down to the mouth of the cave, dark and wet with waiting. Using my hands and feet, I follow it, pausing to unhook my skirt from where it has snagged on an upturned root. I land on the slippery moss and hold onto the opening of the cave, inhaling its ancient, wild smell. *Back again,* I hear it say in its deep, booming tone and I smile and hold up my shoes, laces looped around my fingers like a greeting to an old friend. Or an angry God.

I go in surrounded by echoes of my breath and tired footsteps, allowing my vision to adjust to the cave's particularities; the smooth, inviting roundness as you enter, the jutting structure as you go further in that has caught me unaware several times. Now that I am used to the cave, a part of it even, blending into the walls and feeling for my body prints as I go along, I move in it with ease. It feels good to be back.

A bag full of books and a torch lie in a corner, next to a bean bag I dragged here from home. I fall into it, feel the hard earth beneath me, and smile. I have become so accustomed to this pillow that it's difficult to sit on anything else without squirming. I don't reach for the bag. Today it won't help me.

I discovered this cave a few weeks back, having stumbled upon it accidentally when I was skipping school. There was something about its secrecy, the musty, enclosed space of it, that made it feel like it was alright to be alone—like being lonely was something special. But now, the darkness is too pressing. I tilt my head back and force out a scream and the resounding noise just reminds me of my isolation. I scare a bat out of its sleep and though it dashes manically about, swirling the air above me, it doesn't come when I call it.

There is a pain in my gut; the kind that doesn't hurt but whose presence is annoying and it has been there for days. My muscles are exhausted and my legs suddenly seem longer than I can ever remember them being. I have tripped and crashed through the entire week, hoping that tonight I will fall asleep and tomorrow will pass me by. That it will come and go and no one will notice that I have turned fourteen, that my mother has thrown me a party and no one has come.

*

It's only when the sky begins to fall into the blue hour of twilight that I decide to make my way back home. The road stretches ahead of me but my house comes into view too quickly; the sprawling, dirty whiteness, the sprinkling of lights indicating the busyness going on inside. I know she is making preparations; probably last-minute changes to the menu or hunting the neighborhood for the perfect dish for the cake. I step into the driveway and reluctantly press the doorbell. My father's umbrella has not been dropped into the basket on the porch and I consider coming back later, when I know he will be home. But it's too late. She has pulled open the door and is smiling at me. My annoyance at her has ceased to surprise me. It started weeks ago and the time and fast-approaching fact of tomorrow has only made it grow stronger.

'Finally, you're home.' She gives me a quick kiss and ushers me in. 'There are still so many things we need to do.'

'I told you I didn't want a party.'

'Nonsense. It's your birthday,' pushing me further inside. 'You'll thank me one day.' There are gift bags stacked in a corner and decorations have already been strung in every available space with a big 'Happy Birthday' banner swinging in the entrance between the living room and dining area.

'You told me you weren't going to make a big deal out of this,' I say, pulling off my shoes.

'Where have you been?' she asks, frowning down at my dirty socks. 'Take those off. I just cleaned the floor.'

I ignore her question and repeat mine and it's only when I have removed my socks, rolled them into a small ball and pushed them into my shoe, that she answers.

'All your friends are going to be here,' she says. 'I have to make it special. That reminds me,' she moves into the kitchen and gestures

3

for me to follow. When I reach the door, she is leaning against the counter and holding up a stack of invitations. 'I thought you said you had given them out already.'

My heart jump-starts in my chest but I am prepared. 'No one gives invitations anymore,' I say. 'That's lame. Where did you find them anyway?'

'You left them lying by your bed. You told your friends, didn't you?'

'Yes.'

'How many?'

'Too many to count,' I can't help but say.

'Frances.'

'Alright.' I pretend to count in my head, judging the pile in her hands but there is only a clear, perfectly round zero swimming in my mind. 'Around twenty.'

I don't know what will happen when she finds out I haven't told anyone. That I have no one to tell.

'Perfect.' She is like a little girl, intertwining our arms and dragging me toward the oven. 'I wanted it to be a surprise, but I'm just too excited.' She points to the cake she has made and for the first time there is a small, horrible spark in me that wishes the day could turn out as it already has in her mind. It has two layers and the white, flake-shaped icing is soft and perfect, reminiscent of a bright and thick winter morning. The warmth of the kitchen smells like sugar and bread and I have to stop myself from reaching out to it.

'It's beautiful.'

Her face glows and my rush of irritation comes back.

'Can I go to my room now?'

'But we still have those gift bags to do—'

'I have a test next week that I have to study for.'

The words die in her mouth and she turns back to the cake,

nodding slightly. 'Okay, whatever you want,' and I pretend not to hear the dropping tone. I leave her standing in front of the cake, her hands twisting tightly around the plate and setting it in the corner near the window, where she can be sure no one will touch it until tomorrow.

When I hear his voice downstairs, everything in me bursts into flight and the swift cheerfulness of it dissipates the nerves in my stomach that have been bothering me all week.

'Where's my birthday girl?' The words dance themselves up the stairs.

I am out and rushing down to collide into them, throwing myself into his arms where he catches me tightly to him.

'It's not my birthday yet,' I say, but can't help the shift in my emotions; the high color in my cheeks and the warm, circling pleasure in my stomach.

'Then I guess you don't want this just yet?' He holds the present high over his head and I jump for it.

'What is it?'

'You'll just have to wait until tomorrow, now that you've reminded me.'

'No!' I start to tickle him around his waist and he doubles over, laughing into my hair. His breath is hot against my scalp and he smells wonderfully familiar, peppermint, and instead of grabbing the gift, I put my arms around his neck and press my face to his cold cheek. He holds me there for a long moment before we hear footsteps and he shifts away. I take the opportunity to snatch the box from him and eagerly start to unwrap it.

'What's this?' My mother comes over and kisses him quickly on the lips and I try not to look. I still feel the stinging roughness of his stubble against my forehead.

'Just a small gift for my daughter.' He wraps his arm around her narrow shoulders but she looks strained.

'You never said.'

'It's just something I picked up on my way home from work,' he answers quickly.

I pull out a square, blue box with silver writing on it and toss the cover aside. I suck in the air around me. It's a delicate, gold necklace and the charm that hangs from it is a long key. Nothing has ever felt so wonderful in my hands. It's weightless and beautifully heavy at the same time.

'Will you put it on for me?'

'Of course.' He lets go of my mother and comes around me, lifting my hair. When his fingers graze the back of my neck, I glance swiftly at my mother to see if she has noticed. But she is distracted, chewing her lip with her arms crossed tightly over her chest. He fastens the necklace and lets the hair drop back down around my shoulders. The chain is smooth and cold against my throat and I play with the charm.

'It's beautiful,' I say, bringing his face down to kiss his cheek. 'Thank you.'

'It suits you,' he lays a hand on my cheek. I start to dance out of the room but he stops me. 'It's from your mother too,' he calls out. I pause, turn to her, but don't go any closer.

'Thank you.'

'You're welcome, darling.'

As I move out of the foyer, I hear her turn to him in heated whispers. The angry sounds settle warmly in my chest and although I love the necklace he has bought me, the pleasure of it gets lost in the knowledge of her aggravated eyes and tight lips; slight yet significant actions that are just that small bit more wantingly beautiful.

2

St Albert. April 1992

He wakes me early the next day and I rouse to his face, blurred and close to mine. His finger is pressed against his lips. *Ssh. Come on, let's go*, and for the first time, in the slanting darkness, as I struggle to pull on my pants through sleep-blind eyes, with him laughing and assisting me, I am excited that it's my birthday.

He takes my hand and leads me quietly down the stairs, and when we get to the door he helps me with my coat and pulls my hat down low and close to my ears. He bends, a strand of blond hair falling, as always, into his left eye and he kisses my nose.

'Happy birthday, beautiful,' and then we are outside, into the chilly, rain-coated morning with my hand securely in his, the warmth of his body warming mine. We walk hard and fast, basking in the absolute silence around us; the limitless freedom it provides as if all of it—the wet, gray street, those trees shiny with dew, the birds tilting their heads back to the lavender morning light—belong exclusively to us. We laugh and skip and hold tightly to each other, allowing everything to fall away behind us, seeing nothing but the pale pink fingers of sunrise creeping up ahead over the horizon, calling us forever forward.

*

He takes me to the park, which is always at its most beautiful in the spring. Everything smells young and fresh; reborn after a harsh winter, eager to please. Once we reach it, our footsteps slow to a leisurely swing and we walk in comfortable silence with the occasional shared smile. As we turn the corner toward the small lake, he bounds a little ahead of me. *Come here, I think I see a duck,* and he looks brighter, sharper, surrounded by all this loveliness. His hair is a magic carpet of colors, sunflower blond with a chestnut tease, sliding into sophisticated silver whiskers at his temple. A throat that rises from the collar of his blue sweatshirt, stretching infinite and golden. He moves with such an assured grace that a part of me is jealous. Long, sturdy strides, arm outstretched behind him, calling to me. But I ignore him, wanting to watch him from a distance. Trying to figure out if the way I see him is the way other people do as well.

He drops down, balancing steadily on his heels, and extends his palm to call the bird to him. Pushing through the brackish water, the bird flaps its wings noisily and approaches my father, cautious and staying just a little out of reach.

'Aren't you a pretty little thing?' he says in that low-down voice, measured and slow, and the sound of it, the chuckle deep in his throat as the bird pushes its beak forward into his fingers, draws me to him. He wraps his arm around my waist as I approach and I lean my hip against his shoulder. For a long moment, the world falls still and smiles. I feel his eyes roving my face and my skin prickles in acknowledgment.

'Fourteen years old,' he shakes his head. There is a slight tremor along his upper lip and he gathers it between his teeth. 'Time goes by so fast, doesn't it?' And he stares out into the spreading water, rippling in the wind. The sharp nub in his throat moves as he swallows hard. 'Before you know it, you'll be all grown up and forget about me.' He stands up, dusts the dirt off his knees.

'That could never happen,' I say and my words are urgent. 'We're going to stay together forever.'

He laughs at this but after glancing down at my face, he turns serious. 'You shouldn't say that.'

'But it's the truth.'

He tucks a strand of hair behind my ear and smiles a little sadly. I hold his hand and he brings my fingers up and kisses my palm. When he lets my arm drop to my side, I can't read his expression. 'Come on,' he says. 'Let's walk.'

She is waiting for us when we get back, standing in the doorway and tapping her foot anxiously. She smiles as we get closer and holds out her arms.

'Happy birthday, honey,' gathering me close, pressing her cold and dry lips to my cheek. 'I wish you had told me you were going out, I would have come with you.'

'It was so early,' my father moves behind her, kissing the top of her head and winking at me from above it. 'I thought you might want to rest a little before the party.'

At the mention of the party, my happiness from this morning turns sour. I had forgotten all about it.

'Let me make you some breakfast,' my mother says, pushing us inside and taking my coat. 'What do you feel like? Pancakes?'

I shake my head. 'I'm not hungry.'

'I can make it with the chocolate stuffing you love. We haven't had that in a while,' she continues, moving toward the stove.

'I said I don't want anything.' The stiffness in my voice causes an awkward silence to fall over us. She stares at me and then, before she can speak, my father clears his throat.

'Chocolate pancakes sound good, Annie,' rolling up his sleeves.

'Let me make them. You've been working so hard.' He kisses her temple and cranes his neck back to look at me. 'It's not too late to change your mind, Fran.'

I can't help but smile, unable to refuse him. 'Okay, just one.'

I sit down at the dining table and it's only then that I notice my grandmother, silent as ever, hunched over three balloons, struggling to tie them together.

'Let me do it, Bubbie.' I pry them gently from her old fingers and she pinches my chin, planting a wet kiss on my cheek. 'Where do you want them?' I ask, after I'm done. She points to the door. 'You want me to hang them on the door?' She shakes her head, thrusting her hand in the direction of the window, pointing out to the street. 'Outside the door?'

It has become easy to read her gestures; I don't remember how we used to communicate before she stopped talking. At her nod, I get up and stick them to the outside of the door. One unties itself from the bunch and floats down the driveway. I let it go. *It's not like anyone is going to be looking for this party, anyway.*

I wonder what I will tell my mother; how long it will take for her to realize that all her hard work has gone to waste. Tears prick the back of my eyes when I think of the embarrassment I have yet to face, all the explaining I will have to do. And then I hear him calling my name, *first pancake's for the birthday girl,* and I move back inside, into the direct line of his smile and it no longer matters that no one else is going to show up. As long as he is with me, nothing can go wrong. I kick the door swiftly with my foot, despite my mother's repeated pleas not to do so, hearing the resolute slam as it shuts us away from the rest of the world, just as the first of our neighbors are beginning to stir and yawn awake.

*

I have never really noticed the nature of silence before today. The mugginess of it; how uncomfortable it can sometimes make you, pressing down on your ears and your chest. How unbearably noisy it is.

My mother goes to the window and leans out. 'I don't see anyone coming.'

Bubbie is staring at me but I refuse to meet her eye. My father has gone into his study, grinning as he left, saying, 'Don't want to be in your way, ladies,' and I wish that he had stayed.

'I'm sure they'll be here soon,' I say, trying to keep the nervousness from my voice, hating her as I say it. Hating the way her black hair falls thick over one shoulder as she stretches further out, the shine of excitement across her cheek. The way her foot taps impatiently on the hardwood floor. 'Stop doing that,' I say irritably.

She turns to me. 'Don't talk to me that way, young lady.' Her voice shakes; she is still unused to my recent behavior.

'Sorry.'

She sighs and falls into a chair, glancing up at the clock. It's one thirty. 'Are you sure you told them twelve?'

'Yes.' I know I should just tell her. The longer I prolong her anticipation, the worse it will be. But I can't bring myself to say the words and I wish that she would just give up, leave the table and never ask me about it again.

At two fifteen, I pop one of the balloons that has drifted down from the corner of the 'Happy Birthday' banner. My father came out of his study twenty minutes ago and now he leans over the table, his fingers intertwined, trying to catch my roaming eye.

'There's something you're not telling us.'

'Maybe I got the day wrong.'

'You forgot when your birthday was?'

I look around the room. This morning, it had been beautiful. My mother had pushed back the heavy curtains in the dining room, letting the long, wide windows stand open, the clear, afternoon sun spilling through in a golden spotlight, warming everything it touched. The table was tastefully set; a new, white tablecloth and colorful plates and cups with matching napkins. An impressive crystal bowl held a large volume of bright pink punch in the center. The radio, having been brought down especially for this occasion, sat blinking red and quiet. There were balloons everywhere.

But now, hours of waiting has caused the whole place to sag. The streamers are unpeeling from the walls and falling messily to the ground. My father helped himself to the punch and dropped some from the silver ladle, leaving a loud stain on the cloth. The house spreads, empty and wide. It has never seemed bigger.

'Frances,' my father says again, breaking through the cloudy fear in my mind. 'Tell us what's going on.'

I play with the hem of my skirt. I am so nervous, I am close to tearing it apart. A million excuses fly through my mind, but none sits long enough to form into a possible story. In the end, I have to tell the truth. My mouth has gone dry and itchy.

'No one is coming.'

'What do you mean?' My mother sits up straight, uncrosses her legs. 'How do you know?'

My face jerks up to hers and the look in my eyes makes her blink and turn a little away.

'Because I didn't ask anyone.'

My confession sits heavy in the air; no one is sure how to react. Finally, she speaks.

'You didn't ask anyone.' She repeats my words, letting each of them sit on her tongue for a prolonged moment.

'Yes.'

'I don't understand.' I have never heard her voice so hard; nor seen the bright color of anger in her face. 'Why not?'

I can't bring myself to tell her the truth. I can't bear to hear it said out loud. 'I told you I didn't want to have a party, didn't I?' I am slightly shocked at the blankness in my voice; at the easy way I meet her eye while saying this. There is a small glint of pleasure that rushes through my body at the sight of her falling face.

'How could you do this to me?' Her voice rises; it becomes high-pitched and unsteady. 'This whole week, you could've said something.' She takes a deep breath, shakes her head. 'You lied to me.'

'Marienne.' My father puts a hand on her shoulder. 'Calm down,' but she ignores him.

'I don't know what's gotten into you lately,' she says. 'I don't know what I've done to make you want to be so cruel.'

At this accusation, with him watching me so closely, I desperately wish I could tell her the truth, but it's too late now and she might not believe me. Besides, I don't want her pity.

'I'm going upstairs,' I say.

'You're not going anywhere.'

I push the chair noisily away. 'You can't stop me.'

My father catches her arm as she stands up. 'Let her go, Annie.' He isn't looking at me; his eyes are trained on my mother, even though I am trying to catch his gaze. I need him to come with me but I know better than to ask.

'What about all this food?' She turns to him. 'And the cake? What are we going to do with all of it? Do you know how long it took me to make it? I can't just throw it away.'

13

He thinks for a moment, pulling her down next to him and holding her hand. I don't want to watch them but I can't drag my eyes away.

'Call the neighbors,' he says. 'Tell them we had a small party for Frances and there's a lot of food left over.' He gets up and starts to take down the decorations. I should be happy that this ordeal is finally coming to an end, but the absence of any friends has hurt me more than I expected and the act of him pulling everything down is like a tight pinch in the corner of my heart. 'Melissa is always complaining we don't invite her home anymore.'

'Okay.' She nods and starts to help him. 'That's a good idea.' Their backs are turned to me and I have never felt more alone. I glance at Bubbie and she is sitting as calmly as always, her cool eyes upon my face. She is the only one who watches as the tears finally escape my chest and spill from my eyes. I clamp my hand down on my mouth to catch the sob bursting through, turning to run up the stairs before I give myself away.

When he finally comes, it's later than usual and I turn on my side, pretending to be asleep. I feel the light graze of his fingertips on my back, the hot air of his whisper. His breath is sweet and thick and the commotion of people from the dinner party they had without me is still fresh in his veins.

'Are you awake?'

I want to ignore him but the muscles in my neck move alone in a slow nod. *Yes, of course I am.*

He lifts the covers and slides into the space I have left for him. His body curls around mine, his arm going around the entire length of my waist. He kisses my neck quickly but warmly and my body exhales into his chest. I try to turn and face him but he holds me firmly in place.

'First, tell me what happened today.'

Hot tears form in the corners of my already burning eyes and block my throat. From my position, I can make out the dark image of us in my mirror. His long leg thrown over mine, the perfect arch of his foot reflecting in the moonlight, smooth as bone-china. My head nestled against his chest, in between his wide, accommodating shoulders. Having him so close makes the truth easier to handle.

'I didn't ask anyone.'

'I know that.' His voice is soothing, low and sinking into the darkness. 'Why not?'

'Nobody likes me.' My few tears have turned into full-fledged sobs. I can hardly breathe. It's a pain so acute; such a deep hole of loneliness, that I can never imagine getting over it. 'I didn't ask them because I knew they wouldn't come.'

'What about Kylie? She used to be over here all the time.'

'We're not friends anymore.'

'Why not?' There is an edge of concern in his voice but he hides it well.

'They all say I'm strange. And they made her believe it too.' Here, I stop myself. I cannot tell him what really happened. A quick memory of that hazy afternoon flashes through my mind and I blink it away. I turn in his arms and this time, he lets me. He rests his chin on top of my head.

'When did this happen?'

'I can't remember,' I answer. 'It's been a while, I guess.'

'You know it's not true, right?' His hand runs under my hair and rubs in slow circles down my back. 'You know how lovely you are.'

'Then how come you didn't defend me today?' I look up at him, pushing against his chest. 'You just stood there and let her shout at me.'

He doesn't answer. Instead, that familiar, agonizing look comes across his face and his fingers slip into mine. The pillow beneath me falls silently to the floor and the events of the day become insignificant.

I feel the roughness of the sheets tangling around my feet, the slick heaviness against my skin that I missed all day. The long sighs of the night, so close and loving in my ear, fill my heart with blood and happiness. I see, from the corner of my eye, the luminous glow of my fake galaxy above us; watch as it expands and blurs, finally bursting into infinite space. There is a shot through me; I gasp. Nothing more needs to be said.

When it's time for him to leave, he kisses my nose lightly. His bare feet hit the floor with hardly a sound. 'Goodnight, darling,' and the door closes just as silently behind him. I roll into the warm valley his body has made in the mattress, and miss him so much, it hurts everywhere.

3

St Albert. April 1992

After my father tells my mother the real reason for me not inviting anyone to the party, she insists on dropping me to school the following Monday. She parks the car and we both sit in silence, watching as the students swarm by, giggling and shoving one another. One boy slams into her window and she jumps in surprise, letting out a little shout. I can't help but laugh.

'There's Kylie,' she says, pointing to a brown-haired girl hoisting her backpack further up her shoulder. My mother shouts her name before I can stop her. The whole student body seems to stop moving as pale green eyes search the crowd, finally falling upon us. Kylie gives a meek wave, not meeting my eye, and then someone beside her says something and her face breaks out into a mean, little laugh. My heart constricts and I turn away. 'She didn't even come and say hi.' My mother sounds hurt. 'I really should tell Heather to teach her daughter some manners.'

'I told you, she isn't talking to me anymore.' I unlock the door. 'Can I go now?'

'Maybe I should come in and talk to the principal.' She is chewing her lip thoughtfully.

'So he can force Kylie to be my friend again?'

'I'm sure there's something he can do,' she shrugs helplessly.

I get out of the car, slamming the door and then leaning in through the window. 'Please, just go home.'

'I want to know what happened, Frances.' She leans forward, puts her cool hand on mine. Her gold bangles dance and shimmer in the sunlight. 'I'm worried about you. I just want to make it better.'

'Right now you're only making it worse,' I snap. 'I'll see you this evening.'

'Frances, listen to me—' she starts to say.

'Bye.' I throw myself into the moving mass outside the car, getting lost in it.

At the top of the school stairs, I turn to see her green sedan slowly reversing out of the parking lot and, with a sharp swerve, it turns the corner and disappears from view. I wait for a few moments to make sure she isn't coming back and when I'm certain the coast is clear, I run back down and slip out of the gates, hiding among the numerous students coming in, heading fast back in the direction I came.

I am stopped in my tracks when I spot Kylie and one of her new friends. They are hiding out in the field; her friend is attempting to balance on a fallen log, her arms outstretched and circling her body like a falling helicopter. Her eyes look up and see me.

'Hey, Ky, isn't that your old friend?' She stops walking and grins at me; her teeth are broken and brown. Kylie turns and I see that she has a cigarette tucked between her fingers. She throws it down when she sees me and her face closes up in embarrassment.

'What are you doing?' I ask.

'Who are you, her mother?' The girl on the log sneers.

Kylie looks at me and those green eyes I know so well cause me to cast my look downward in shame. We had been friends ever since childhood and it still surprises me how abruptly it all came to an end; that I was the one to blame.

She had come over to my house a few weekends ago and we had been lying on the bed, talking about something that is now lost in everything that happened after. The sun was in her face, casting her features into beautiful shadows. I don't know what it was that made me lean in and kiss her; what terrible force grabbed my hand and moved it up to her chest. Recently, the impulse to touch someone, not only her, but other people too, had become too strong for me to resist. I couldn't always wait until night time and even then, sometimes, he never came.

'What are you doing?' One minute she had been lying beside me, and the next, she was standing at the edge of my bed, clutching her arms around her.

'Come on.' I had been so brazen, so full of something hot. 'It's fun, I promise.'

'How would you know?'

I met her eye and refused to answer. She grabbed her bag, not looking at me. 'I don't know what's gotten into you recently, but I think they're right.' Her voice trembled and there were tears in her eyes.

'Who?' I sat up straight, narrowing my eyes.

'Everyone at school. They all warned me about you—said how strange you were.' She was going for the door. 'I should've listened.'

'Wait, Kylie,' I protested weakly, not really caring at that moment if she stayed or not, because despite everything she might have thought, she wasn't the one that I wanted.

Now she stands in front of me, picking up her cigarette and blowing the dirt off it. She puts it back in her mouth and inhales with a dry cough. I can't help but think how ridiculous she looks.

'What do you want?' she asks.

I don't want to tell them where I am really going; I don't want anyone else discovering my secret cave. 'I followed you to apologize,' I say instead. 'I really miss you, Kylie.'

'We all know how you feel about Kylie,' the girl on the log snickers, stepping down. I notice how heavy her foot is in her black boot; the way it slams down on the ground and brings the dust up around it.

'It's none of your business,' I snap back, horrified at the thought that Kylie has told her what happened.

'Actually, it is.' She puts an enormous arm around Kylie and I think I see Kylie shrink a little away. 'We're friends now.'

'Kylie, about what happened,' I decide to ignore the other girl. 'It didn't mean anything, I promise.'

'That's funny.' The huge girl comes forward and before I can react, she grabs the hair at the base of my neck and tilts my head so far back that I feel the pressure of it in my eyes. I stay perfectly still. 'Because usually when you kiss someone, it means a lot. When you touch someone,' her eyes fall to my chest, 'there, it sure as hell means something.'

'Well you would know,' I retort, refusing to show her how frightened I am. But there is something about this scenario that also excites me. 'I heard you're into that kind of thing.'

She yanks my hair and throws me to the ground. My arm scrapes painfully against the dirt; I feel specks of it drag along my exposed nerves and I cry out despite myself. I attempt to push myself up but she kneels down and shoves me in the chest so that I end up sprawled once more on the reddish mud. I'm not sure how I'm going to explain the rust color of my socks to my mother. 'Get lost,' she says in a low growl. 'Kylie doesn't want to speak to you anymore, got it?' Then she turns to my old friend and gestures with her head. 'Come on, before they notice we're missing.'

I meet Kylie's eyes once more and the coldness in them hurts more than anything. 'Leave me alone, Frances,' she says quietly, dropping the still burning cigarette at my side and stepping over me. I shut my eyes against the hot sunlight and when I open them again, they're gone.

I make my way home early; the cut on my arm is burning now and has turned into an ugly purple bruise along its edges. My mother's shift starts at two o'clock so I leave the cave at that time, knowing she'll be gone by the time I get back and that Bubbie will not say anything.

My grandmother is making beans on toast when I come through the door and I lean against the kitchen doorframe, watching her poor and bent body, the lugging motion of her feet, and I wonder what has happened in her life to make her so sad. She turns at that moment and I hold up my arm, shrugging and trying to laugh.

She motions for me to come in and reaches into a cupboard for our medicine box. Then, she points to the seat next to her and I slide in. She picks up my arm and studies it closely.

'Gym class,' I lie. 'We were playing soccer outside and I fell.'

She doesn't say anything to me, instead, pouring a generous amount of antiseptic onto a cotton swab and before I have time to think, she rubs it against my torn skin and I try to pull away in pain. But her fingers are like thirsty roots that anchor my hand in place. She pauses, looks up and shakes her head firmly, so I stop struggling.

When she is done, she applies a cold, soothing cream and covers it with a bandage. I sag against my chair, exhausted. She notices my socks and then holds out her palm. I give them up gratefully.

'Thank you.'

She gets up and presses her wet lips to my forehead, cradling my head against her and my arms go around her bony waist. Then she draws her head back and in that one second of silence, with nothing but the light chirping of birds outside, I know she is getting ready to tell me something. Her mouth starts to move but I can't tell at first if it's a twitch from old age or if she is trying to form words; because some things need to be said out loud. They cannot afford to be miscommunicated. Her fingers tighten their hold around my neck and a dark urgency draws across her eyes. There is a deep strange gurgling beginning in her throat and her eyes dash from side to side, as if she is no longer in control of her body. The noise, odd as it is, reminds me that I have missed the sound of her voice; that she used to sing me to sleep sometimes, but I also have an inkling of what she wants to tell me and I don't want to hear it.

'Are you making beans on toast?' I ask, jumping down from the stool and going to the stove. 'Because I'm starving.'

She stares after me a little forlornly, dazed by the passion that consumed her seconds ago. Then she nods and moves slowly to the pot, making a spooning action with her hand and then pointing at me. I smile, relieved to have her back.

'Yes, I'd love some.'

She goes back to stirring and the moment is lost.

That night, I clutch to him tighter than ever. I tell him what happened and he listens with his cheek pressed to mine. I check the time to see how long we have until my mother comes back from work; it's only nine o'clock, which gives us two hours. But hospital work is unexpected. Sometimes, she comes home as late as early morning, rubbing her bleary eyes, still glowing from the excitement of an emergency. When I was younger, I used to wait out on the step for her, holding my eyelids open to fight off sleep. But now, I find myself hoping for a bus collision or a premature birth—anything that will keep her busy.

Bubbie is already asleep. We can hear her gentle snoring coming under the door, assuring us that we are safe. His hand trails down my arm, passes lovingly over the bandage as I talk. I am not even sure if he is listening.

Finally, he turns to me. 'I have a mind to go and talk to the principal about that girl.' My heart soars when I hear the angry undertone of his voice.

'I'm okay,' I say, curling up into his arm and thinking that for right now, this is all that matters. I feel his chest swell beneath my cheek, quiver for a moment and then he lets it go with a long, rapid *whoosh*.

'You,' he looks at me tentatively and I see the worry in his eyes. 'I wanted to ask you—you haven't told anyone about,' he stops again, lowers his voice to barely a whisper. 'Us?'

'Of course not.' I shake my head vehemently. 'You know I wouldn't do that. You asked me not to.'

'Good.' He gives me a small kiss but he is distracted. He turns away, lost in thought. 'Because you know, people just won't understand.'

'No,' I reply, marveling at how special our relationship is; how the secrecy makes it all the more exciting. 'I guess they won't.'

4

St Albert. May 1992

The blood comes late and with the end of spring. The rain looks blue through the tinted window above the bathtub. I always forget to draw the curtains and I don't do it now because I am too busy staring down at my stained underwear. *What an ordinary brown.* I had hoped my insides would be beautiful; wet, shiny and ruby red like my mother's lips. This brownish, chipped stain doesn't make me feel like a woman. I rub my fingers against it and then hold them to my nose. I like how it smells; like something old, full of the women who have come before me and those who are still waiting.

I call out for Bubbie because she is the only one home. My mother is at one of the neighbor's houses, after promising to help them prune their roses, and I'm glad I don't have to share this with her. I stretch toward the door knob, pushing it open and settling back when I hear the quiet shuffling of her feet. I feel wings of nervous excitement pound against my chest and I can't help but smile widely as my grandmother peers through the door. Her gray hair falls loose and surprisingly thick over her thin shoulders.

'Come in,' I mouth the words, so used to her silence that I sometimes stop talking around her. I point giddily with my hands and when she comes closer, I thrust my finger downward. 'Look what's happened.'

Bubbie stares at me through her curtain of silver and her mouth twitches and her eyes jerk up to meet mine. My heart vibrates in silent anticipation. *Welcome, Frances! You're finally here.* Instead, she begins to cry; slumping against the sink and holding her head in her hands.

'Bubbie!' I am alarmed, thinking that perhaps something has gone wrong—that this isn't what I thought it was.

She grabs my cheek and turns it sharply upward. She says something and, at first, I am too distracted by the foreign sound of her voice—reedy and unsure—that I don't hear what she says.

'You tell your father about this, sweetheart, you hear?' She knocks me gently on the chin. 'The pads are under the sink.'

My grandmother, talking for the first time in three years; her words are rusty and seem to belong to the past. They bounce uncomfortably off her tongue. She makes a move to say more and I lean forward, but then she is backing quickly out, anxious eyes darting everywhere, terrified of the ghostly reverberation of her words.

When I emerge fifteen minutes later with thick cotton between my legs and an ache for her to refer to me so affectionately once more, I find that her voice has receded into the pinkish depths of her throat and I know it's never coming back.

I decide not to follow Bubbie's advice, so my first few days of womanhood pass in a whirlwind of secret-keeping; a memory that is entirely my own. To my parents, I am still their little girl, but away from them, in school, I grow and swell and burst open. I love feeling the blood against me; it's warm and thick and sometimes it pushes forward with such intensity that I have to cross my legs in an effort to contain it. It transforms me from *freckled-nose Frances* into someone resembling my mother. I begin to walk like her, hips swaying, and sit like her, one leg crossed over the other. I catch people staring at me the way they look at her; with a mixture of awe and desperation in their eyes. I steal her sunglasses and wear them during lunch, sprawling my new body over the sweet-smelling grass. Love notes have started to slip into my locker, *you are a red-headed goddess; be mine, Frances McDermott; you have sexy legs.* Boys whistle as I walk by and even girls, wanting to benefit from my new position, shyly offer up gifts of lipsticks and chocolates.

I fall in love with myself in front of the mirror, brushing my hair and smiling. *You're beautiful, you know that?* Almost overnight, my features cross the line from awkward to pretty and my body settles into an easy gracefulness that people seem to admire.

One lazy lunchtime, I am lying on the school quad, feeling the sun burn through my skin. It plays games behind my eyes, forming confusing red images that streak and tease the insides of my lids and, no matter how hard I try, I cannot figure out what they're supposed to be.

'Hello.'

A shadow comes across my face and my eyes flicker open. I hold up my palm to shield my gaze from the light and I see a big smile and a head of dark, curly hair.

'Hi.'

'I'm Tom.' The boy falls down next to me. He tries to cross his legs but they are too long so he ends up sprawling them in front of him. I know who he is; Tom Porter, the over-confident and charming senior that every girl has her eye on. What I don't know is why he is talking to me.

'Frances,' I say.

'Nice shades.' The way he is grinning at me makes my body stir pleasantly. It reminds me of someone else.

'Thanks.' From the corner of my eye, I see Kylie coming down the path and I sit up, leaning closer to Tom, wanting her to see me. 'You can borrow them anytime.'

He laughs warmly and, as I hoped, Kylie's ears prick at the sound and her eyes shoot toward us. For a moment, our gazes meet and I smile in triumph before turning back to Tom. I know that she has liked him for a long time. We spent countless nights talking about the way his hair fell perfectly to the side in a thick wave. The length of his body and how it made everyone and everything around him seem small and insignificant. Rather, Kylie did and I listened, wondering if she felt the same way about him—the heady, painful joy that I had only recently discovered myself. I am glad I have this opportunity to hurt her, after what she has done to me.

'How come I've never seen you around before?' he asks, leaning back on his elbows and tilting his face up to mine.

'Maybe you weren't looking.'

He laughs again and Kylie rushes down the path, her pace angry. We lapse into silence after that. Now that there is no longer someone to put a show on for, I have lost interest. So I settle back down and close my eyes. I can feel him watching me closely.

'What are you doing on Saturday?' he asks.

'I don't know. Why?'

'Do you want to come to a party with me?' There is a sliver of doubt in his voice and it is pleasing to think that he is nervous around me. I stare at him through the dark lenses for a long time. A part of me wants to say yes. To hold his arm and go to this party. To feel everyone's eyes on me and have them take notice and be envious of what I have. But it also feels like a betrayal. I know my father won't like it and the thought of him being angry with me makes me shake my head.

'I'm sorry, I'm busy.'

'You just said you weren't sure what you were doing.' There is a whiny note to his voice that irritates me. I shrug, getting up and dusting the grass off my skirt. His eyes linger for a second too long and a hotness starts to spread down to my knees. 'I just remembered I have some family stuff going on. Sorry.' I throw the bag over my shoulder. 'See you around, Tom.'

I feel his eyes bearing into my back as I walk away from him. My body takes on a form and gait of its own; straightening up and sliding into an unabashed confidence I have never had. I have never felt more powerful.

When I get home, I find Tom sitting at the dining table with my mother. He gives me a wink as I come through the front door.

'I was just telling your mother about the party on Saturday night,' he tells me.

'Sounds like fun, darling,' my mother says, blowing a cloud of smoke in front of her eyes. She reaches her arm out to stub her cigarette in the ashtray and Tom's eyes follow her movements; keenly watch the fingers twist the butt around and around to make sure it is completely out; see the way they turn up in gleeful surprise to the curve of her chest, suddenly exposed because a draft of wind comes through the open window and blows her hair back.

'Yes,' I say, wanting him to look at me that way instead. 'Yes, it does sound like fun. Of course I'll go with you, Tom.'

'Really?' At first, he sounds doubtful, but then he clears his throat and his face is shining with a smile again. It really is a lovely grin.

'I'll pick you up at eight then.' He stands up and straightens out his polo shirt. 'Great to meet you, Mrs. McDermott.'

'Likewise.' After her cigarette, her voice is husky and slow. If I felt powerful before in front of Tom, now I am just a little girl thrown into shadow by this startling woman blinking her long lashes expertly. I don't look at her when he leaves and when she says to me, 'Lovely boy, isn't he?' I sneer at the ground.

'Don't you think he's a bit young for you?' and then I turn and stalk out before she has a chance to answer.

When my father comes home, he is angry.

'I don't want a boy like that with my daughter. For God's sake, Marienne.' I watch him from the top of the stairs, as he paces angrily back and forth, pushing his hands through his hair, pausing to stare at her. 'What were you thinking?'

'It's about time she started making some new friends.' My mother stands calmly in front of him, unaffected by his anger. 'I'm just doing what I think is best for our daughter.'

'So you're letting her go to some party with some...' He throws his hands up in the air, waves them around, lost for words. 'Some cocky sixteen-year-old?'

'He seems like a sweet boy,' she replies. 'Besides, there'll be a chaperone there.'

'I don't have to go,' I interject from my position, staring down at them. I don't want to upset him.

'You're going,' she calls up firmly, turning back to my father. 'She's going, James,' she repeats, placing a hand on his upper arm before turning to come up the stairs. When she passes me, she reaches out to stroke my hair but I move away from her. He stares up at me for a long time, something tight in his jaw, and when he comes up, he goes by me without a word and slams the door so that I can't hear them anymore.

My mother finds out about my period when I leave a mark of red on the cream chair.

'Honey?'

I turn to look from the chair to her hopeful face and I feel happy that I get to ruin this moment for her.

'I already know.'

'You know?' She is visibly shocked; she looks at me as if she can't really see me; as if I don't belong to her.

'I've had it for four days now.'

'How come you never told me?' she asks. 'How did you even know what to do?'

'You weren't home,' I shrug. 'So I told Bubbie and she helped me. It's not a big deal.'

'Bubbie?' My mother's face crosses with confusion. She turns to my grandmother, who is sitting in her rocking chair by the T.V., staring at the blank screen. When she notices us watching, she turns. 'How did Bubbie help?'

I want to tell her but there is a look in my grandmother's eyes, a slight shake of her head, that stops me.

'Elsie?' My mother calls to my grandmother but is met with a resolute silence. Her old back turns to us once again. 'Did she talk to you?' she asks me.

'No.'

'Frances, if she did, you have to tell me.'

'Look, I figured it out myself. It wasn't hard.'

My mother walks to the sink and takes a dish towel that is neatly folded on the drying rack and puts it under the tap. She stays there for longer than necessary, allowing the water to run down her arms and splash against the metal sides of the basin. Then she wrings out the towel and dabs it gently at the chair.

'You should have said something to me,' she says finally.

'Sorry.' I resist the urge to smirk at her. After the incident with Tom, I am angrier with her than ever. Last night, my father had sat in the chair at my desk, not moving or talking, just straight and serious, staring at his own reflection. I was too self-conscious to ask him to come any closer; too afraid of being rejected. After thirty minutes, he stirred and I sat up straight.

'I guess you don't need me anymore,' he said and left, even though my mother wasn't due back home for another three hours.

Now, she stands close to me, rubbing the seat too hard. 'These things—they're important to talk about.' She pauses, falters slightly. Then she looks at me and blinks hard. 'I'm your mother, Frances.'

'I'll remember that next time,' I say.

'Good.' She drops the towel onto the chair, leaving it to soak into the material which I know will only make the stain darker. She holds out her arms and I have no choice but to walk into them. 'I'm really glad, sweetheart,' she says. She sighs into my ear and I can feel her smiling against it. Maybe she thinks things will change between us now—that it will go back to how it used to be—but if there is one person my new state has made me dislike, it is my mother. I become aware of how beautiful she is; the perfect angles of her face and the wonderful slopes of her body—how different she is from my freckled paleness. I see the way she strokes my father's thigh and whispers in his ear, her full lips grazing his skin. When she tells him my secret, I hate her. When she says, *maybe she's too old for story time now,* I am sure she is punishing me for not telling her. When he stops coming, I am convinced I will die.

Tom picks me up in his father's sky-blue Chevrolet. I feel my father watching me as I rush toward the door in my new white dress and it makes me smile.

'Don't be late,' he calls out to me. His voice is stern and strong and it's all I can do to keep from shutting the door and locking Tom out.

Tom has sprayed the inside of his car with cologne and he apologizes every time I sneeze. The party is at Ian Davy's house. His parents are out of town and the chaperones are his eighteen-year-old cousins. Tom grins at me from the side of his face. 'Do you think your mother bought it?'

'I'm here, aren't I?' I answer and his smile quivers, unsure of what my tone means. So I smile reassuringly at him and he turns back to driving.

'I feel bad lying to her about it, though.' He squints through the darkness in front of us. 'But I'm glad you came.'

We drive the rest of the way mainly in silence and join the party in the backyard with a swimming pool and the full moon. A tide of girls greets me as I come through the back door. *Frances, let me get you a drink. Frances, that dress is amazing. Frances, you're so lucky you came with Tom,* girls I have never met before, those ones who have previously snickered behind my back, are now all vying for my attention. It feels a little uncomfortable, after all these months spent being unnoticed, to suddenly being liked; to be wanted by almost everyone. I see Kylie and her friend standing in a corner. They look at me then turn to each other in whispers and I shift my gaze from them and don't look back for the rest of the night.

I notice that the pool is in the shape of a whale and that a barbeque pit sits right at the tip of its tail, where most of the boys and Ian's older cousins are standing. The garden is surrounded by a fence covered in thick vines of purple flowers that curl upward and make me feel as if I am in a soft, closed off world, away from everything outside.

Tom hands me my first drink and I choke on it. I have my second and the hot liquid forces my eyes and throat to close. After my third one, my world descends into a tornado of bliss and by the fourth, everything has sunk into a haze except the solid feel of Tom's hand through the thin material of my dress. Someone shows me how to smoke a cigarette and then teaches me how to get rid of the smell by running perfume-laced fingertips through my hair. Voices blend together and stretch out around me but Tom's voice is steady and sure in my ear. *Come with me, Frances*. He joins our fingers together and leads me through the house. Past the glass coffee tables and the white couches in the living room. The dining area with its long mahogany table and eight chairs, even though Ian is an only child. I wonder if they have dinners here with those same cousins outside; if they have a large, extended family that comes over every Sunday for barbequing and smoking. I wonder if he is as lonely as I am. Through the kitchen with its French windows and spacious island, yellow daises in a black vase sitting on its top.

We climb the stairs into Ian's room and I don't have time to breathe before Tom's mouth is on mine. I feel his tongue pressing against the roof of my mouth, the sides of it, forcing and unkind. His breath isn't soft but labored and erratic. He sounds like a stupid animal. My name escapes his lips but it doesn't come out right because he doesn't love me. He takes my hand and puts it to his trousers, breathing through his teeth. A part of me is excited by this, but mostly, I just want him to stop and I try to pull away, but his fingers keep my head locked where it is. His hand finds its way to the band of the elasticated underwear I stole from my mother and I try to stop him but it's too late. I feel his fingers pushing up inside me; his legs are forcing mine apart. *Get off, get off.* I bite into his shoulder and he shouts before shoving me away. The hole is beginning to rip my stomach to shreds, screaming out his name. Tom tries to reach for me again but I snap at his fingers, my teeth grazing his skin.

'You're fucking crazy,' he says and he is gone. I fall to the floor, hugging my knees to my chest.

You're the only one that I want.

Tom drops me home and hands me a breath mint without looking at me.

'I don't want your mother thinking I'm a bad influence.'

I slam the door, running up the porch steps as I hear him drive away. My father is waiting up for me, sitting in almost complete darkness. The only source of light comes from the houses opposite and from passing cars that shine triangles of gold through the spaces in our curtains. They stroke his throat, caressing his perfect, pear-shaped Adam's apple, my favorite part of him.

He hears me come in and I see his back tighten at the sound.

'Did he do anything to you?' he asks and his voice is full. I shake my head, stepping into his view. 'Don't lie to me, Frances.'

'I promise, he didn't.'

He stands up but doesn't come near me. He looks away. 'Go to your room.'

'Will you come?' It is the first time I have ever asked him. I can see the shock on his face.

'No, Frances.'

I start to cry and he is beside me in an instant. *Hush baby, it's okay.* His arms are bigger than Tom's and fit around my entire body. 'I'm sorry, but we can't do this anymore.'

I take his hand and put it under my dress, amazed at my own boldness. His strong fingers slide into me and I let my head fall against his shoulder. *The days have stretched on forever without you, but now you are here and they have stopped and become full.* He tears his hand away and steps back. His blue eyes are wide with horror and his chest rises and falls too quickly. I smile at him even though he refuses to meet my eye. I turn and leave slowly. After a second or two, he turns off all the lights and follows.

5

St Albert. May 1992

The notes have stopped filtering into my locker. Although I still get offers from boys to meet them behind the bleachers or to let them drive me home, my status has been diminished, reduced to *that weird girl from the party—you didn't hear what she did?* and once again, everyone leaves me alone. It doesn't affect me much; being alone has become a natural state for me and I don't mind it any longer. I am too busy always thinking of him, itching to be back home where I know I will only have to wait a couple of hours before he is sliding out of his coat and smiling at me. And only a few hours after that, he will be in my bed and he will touch me and everything else will be forgotten.

Every night except Wednesdays.

'Let's go to the movies,' she says, her eyes hopeful and excited. 'We haven't done anything as a family in so long.' She looks at the three of us expectantly.

'Okay.' His smile is uncomfortable and he ends up licking his lips nervously. He tries to look at Bubbie but she is quietly pushing food around her plate.

Last night I made a sound. He clamped his hand down tightly over my mouth and I tried not to giggle.

'Sorry,' I whispered, throwing my body back on the pillow. 'It couldn't be helped.' As I did this, I caught a reflection of myself in the mirror and had to blink twice to make sure it was me. The person staring back didn't look like a girl anymore.

He got up quickly, his eyes darting around the room like he didn't know where he was or what had just happened. He crept to the door and pressed his ear against it and then, all of a sudden, jumped back.

'What was that?'

'What was what?'

'I heard something.'

'You're just imagining it—there's no one there.'

He opened the door slowly and I started to stop him but he looked so determined, so frightened, that I didn't. 'I'm going to bed now,' he whispered. 'Goodnight.'

Now, his eyes are searching her old and empty face, trying to gauge if she heard us, but she keeps her head down, piercing her food with her fork.

'What do you say, Mom?' he asks. His voice trembles and he stops, annoyed. 'Do you want to go?'

My mother and I look at him. *Why are you asking her? She won't answer you, you know that.*

Bubbie shakes her head slowly.

'What was that?'

Silence. His chest flares.

'I didn't hear you. What did you say?'

My mother puts a hand out to stop him. 'James, what are you doing?' but he brushes her away.

'Speak up woman. Marienne asked you a question.' He stood up and leaned over the table at her. 'It's been three years since you've said a word and I'm sick of it. All I'm asking is for a simple yes or no. You want to go or not? It's as easy as that.'

Bubbie sits back in her chair and closes her eyes. He bangs his fist down on the table so that everything hops up noisily and then clatters back down. I press my knees together to stop the flooding in my stomach. His eyes are a lovely dark color when he is angry.

'Say something, for God's sake!' he shouts. 'Anything. Don't you have something you want to say to me?'

She straightens up and her lips begin to move. For one, awful moment, I think that she will say something. His jaw slackens and his eyes drop and she turns back to eating.

'James,' my mother glances apologetically at Bubbie. 'Stop it. Just stop.' She rises and puts a hand to his cheek. I have to contain myself in my seat. 'It was only a suggestion.'

He pushes his plate away. 'No. We're going. She doesn't have to come.' He looks at me and there is something attractive in the way his lips are held tightly together; something desirable in the way he addresses me so harshly. 'Get your coat, Frances. Let's go.'

He bends down to Bubbie on his way out of the dining room. 'What's the point of you being here?' he asks quietly, 'silent as a statue? You might as well be dead.' Then he stops, reels back from his own cruel words. She looks up at him and when he starts to apologize, she holds up her hand and shakes her head.

We leave in such a rush that no one sees her raise her eyes to us. No one hears her croaky sound, except for me. She says two words and her eyes are incredibly sad. It's crisp and short and final.

'I'm sorry.'

There is only one cinema in our town; a small, dilapidated build-ing surrounded by an enormous parking lot that is a common hangout for students. But today, although it is full of cars, there is no one drinking beers hidden in brown paper bags or sneaking a kiss behind a fogged-up window. We make our way to the busy, loud building and as soon as I open the door, laughter and voices come over us in a rush.

'Popcorn?' he asks and I grin.

'Salted?'

'Sounds good.' He chuckles and rubs my hair.

'I'll get the tickets,' my mother says and leaves us alone.

While we are waiting in line, I wrap my arm around his waist and hug him tight. I slide closer to him and my hand begins to rub against his shirt. He unwinds my grip and steps a little further away. After a few seconds, my hand finds his and I intertwine our fingers. I can't seem to stop wanting to touch him; I will never stop marveling at the way it makes me feel. He pulls his hand away and glances quickly around the room, turning to see if there is someone behind us but there isn't.

'Frances.' His voice is so soft, only I can hear it. 'Stop it.'

'Why?'

He seems surprised that I could question him; I have never done it before. 'Because I said so. What's wrong with you?'

I feel the tears pressing up against the back of my eyes almost immediately. 'Fine.' The embarrassment of being refused chokes me. 'Fine, I'll never do it again.'

He sighs, almost irritated. 'Come on, you know that's not what I meant.'

People are starting to filter into the movie and from the corner of my eye, I see my mother making her way to us. I grab the popcorn he has ordered and refuse to look at him. Guiltily, he tries to reach out for me but I step away.

'Everything okay?' My mother looks at me with concern.

My father takes her arm, kisses her hair and whispers something while doing it. Then he clears his throat and says out loud, 'Everything's perfect. Come on, the movie is starting.' They walk ahead of me and I notice with bitterness that his fingers crawl into her palm and intertwine themselves with hers.

In the darkness of the theater, he sits between my mother and me. She is leaning against his shoulder, glowing in the movie light and they are still holding hands. But I no longer mind because his other arm hangs loosely by my knee, the side of his hand grazing my thigh purposefully so that I can't pay attention to the screen and all I feel is the slow warmth of him working his magic.

When we get home, it's completely dark and the silence, when we call out for Bubbie, is louder than ever.

6

St Albert. June 1992

A couple of weeks after Bubbie's funeral, my mother slides an application form under my door that reads, 'Academy of the Holy Family' written in bold letters at the top. I rip it into as many pieces as I can and leave them in her ashtray. She doesn't mention any of it to my father and even if I had wanted to, he wouldn't have listened. The empty spaces Bubbie has left behind; the tall-back chair at the head of the table, the pink-pillowed rocking seat just beside the television, occupy all of his attention. I see him look up in between bites of his casserole, as if he is getting ready to talk to her before realizing she is no longer there.

Unused to being ignored by him, I have a sudden urge to remind him of me so I slip off my shoe and slide my foot up the length of his leg. His muscles strain beneath my toes and I have to put a spoon in my mouth to keep from making any noise. He pushes me away without glancing up.

No one has used her bathroom since the day we went to the theater, when we came home to find Bubbie floating in the bath, looking so peaceful that, at first, I thought she had fallen asleep. There was an empty bottle of sleeping pills that had dropped from the corner of the tub, the cap having rolled close to the door, making it stick so he had to shove it with his shoulder before we could get in. After the ambulance had left, the blue-red of its sirens still flashing in our minds, my father reached into the bath and pulled the plug and we heard the water draining in the backyard. He locked the door and keeps the key under his pillow or in his pocket and sometimes, I catch him playing with it, as if his fingers are searching for her in its bronze scratches.

He comes past my room at night and each time he passes, darkening the doorway, my body rises to meet him. But then his footsteps drag on and the floor creaks as he sits down against the banister, facing the bathroom. I crouch beside my door, pressing my ear to it, but I can't hear a thing. Something holds me back from going to him. He doesn't want me right now. I only hear him again when the sun comes up and he has to go to work. Another sleepless night spent apart goes by.

Two days after I found the form, I walk into my room to see a completed one sitting on my bed, propped up against the pillows, alongside the green rosary Bubbie used to wear around her neck when her wrist grew too thin. *Tear it up all you want, my darling. I've already sent it in,* my mother's writing taunts. I sit at the windowsill, burning holes into the paper with a lighter I find downstairs. I keep it flickering against the line that says, 'provide young women with a strong sense of Christian values.' When the paper begins to crumble in my hands, I toss it out of the window and watch as the embers fly away and die on the pavement. I turn the flame to my wrist, waiting for my blood to catch on fire. My skin prickles to its defense and when I take the heat from it, I find a scattering of soft, white lumps. I press my fingers to them, one by one and then all at once. The pain shoots from my arm to the middle of my chest and floods my mouth, making it numb and sweaty. *She can't make me go. I'll run away and take her husband with me.*

I look around my room; at the glow-in-the-dark stars he helped put on my ceiling when I was seven and at my desk, under which I have carved our initials. Thinking of him pushes me toward the bed as my body begins to crave and ache, forcing me down on my stomach. He is alive in the hand that slides down in between my legs. My dress rubs against my blistered wrist and the pain of my skin eroding away is excruciating. I sink my hand into the mattress and my waist lifts up; I reach inside myself—I can't reach far enough. I thrust my body forward, pushing it into my fingers and stroking; everything at the same time, the arc of my thumb rubbing over it again and again, forcing my breath to hiss out and making me clutch the bedcovers, crying out his name into my pillow. *Don't let her do this to us. Don't let her do this, James.*

That night when I don't hear him come past my room, I slip out and creep toward his. I hear them talking quietly and I fold my body into the door. Her voice is soft; his is softer. For a while he says nothing but *okay.* She keeps giving explanations even though he keeps giving in.

'I'm sorry I didn't discuss this with you before,' she says. 'I know Whitehorse is far away, but I think the distance will do her some good. And it's only two years—she can come back here to finish high school.'

'Okay.'

'I don't know what's gotten into her lately,' my mother says. 'She's become so rude, so distant—and all that lying about the party.' Her voice becomes full and she stops talking. 'It really shocked me. I don't understand what's happened.'

'I was surprised too.'

'Sending her away to a boarding school was your mother's idea.' At that, I can feel him stiffen. 'She was so adamant about it and at first I couldn't bear the idea of Frances not living here.' Her voice lowers and I stop breathing, scared she might have heard me listening. 'But with the way she's been acting recently, having all those problems in school, she needs a fresh start.' She pauses. 'What do you think?'

At first, he doesn't reply. I hear the familiar, comforting sound of his clothes falling to the floor and the wood closes around me, warm. I wait for him to say something, anything that will make her change her mind. I imagine him storming out of the room, threatening never to speak to her or touch her again if she sends me away. The idea is so strong in my mind that I almost miss, and don't quite believe, what he says next.

'Maybe you're right. Maybe it's a good idea.' He becomes loud, unrecognizable. 'With everything that's been going on—maybe she does need a change of scenery. New people, a new place.' He sighs. 'This place can be suffocating.'

I bite down hard on my fingers, twist them in my mouth so they can't hear me crying.

'I've spoken to some people who know about the school,' my mother says. 'They say it's a great place. The Head Nun is a real disciplinarian—I think she can really help us.' The sound of sheets being pulled away drown out my mother. 'And we need help. I just want what's best for her and I don't know what else to do. I can't see any other way, after what happened on her birthday...'

There is a brief silence and then she speaks again, somewhat fearful. 'Do you think she knows—' There is a catch in her voice that is impossible to miss and for a brief moment I wonder what she means, but then I hear him and everything else is forgotten.

'No,' he says quickly. 'She can't possibly. I'll talk to her tomorrow,' he offers.

She smiles. I can hear the satisfying stretch of it; the way it causes her body to relax and shift against the bed. She falls silent when the space between them is taken over by him; overwhelmed that for the first time in a month, he is sleeping in their bed instead of spending the night on the carpeted corridor outside Bubbie's room. 'About your mother—' she says, trying her luck.

'I don't want to talk about it,' he says, almost coldly. 'I don't want to talk about her.' Silence. And then, 'She didn't even have the decency to leave a note.'

'We have to sort her things out.'

'No.' I know he is shaking his head, his lips are tightening. I wanted him to defend me this way. 'I can't do it, Annie. I can't clean her things out. It's all I have left of her. Please, don't ask me to do that.'

I want to bang on the door; hammer on it until the wood caves and drives into my fist.

'Okay, honey. It's alright—I know how much she meant to you. Whenever you're ready, just let me know.' Their lights turn off. She has won.

I wait for both of them to leave the next morning before taking the key from under his pillow and opening the bathroom door. The stench of Bubbie roars at me even before I am inside. She has seeped into the cracked tiles and she is dripping from the walls; powdery and full. Her perfume bottle still sits on the sink and I spray some of it onto my neck before pulling off the top and spilling the rest of it into the bathtub. I have brought up my mother's cleaning supplies and I pour the blue fluid all over the bathroom, the scent of ammonia filling the back of my throat and spilling poisonous tears down my cheeks.

I throw away Bubbie's creams and lipsticks and her favorite hairnet, which smells of talcum powder. I hold it to my face for a moment and the scent of it sends an electric shock of memory charging through my nerves. I throw away her floor mat because she has touched it and I throw away her soap because it has touched her.

I move into her bedroom through the connecting doorway and pause. I had never realized how close she had been to me this whole time; separated only by a thin wall. I blush, though I'm not sure why. Then I continue the process. I fold her clothes and push them into dark bin bags, watching as her memories fall away like dust from their creases. I find a picture frame hidden in the back of her closet, made from dried-up pasta and holding tribute to a smiling family of four. There he is, grinning across at his father who is staring back out at me. There is a baby cradled against him. I am suddenly angry that there is a history to my father's life that I am not and can never be a part of.

I work slowly and steadily throughout the morning until there is no trace left of my grandmother except for the faint smell of roses that comes from one of the incense sticks I keep. Making sure the bags are tied tightly and securely, I gather two in each hand and leave, sneaking out the back door and into the startling brightness of the afternoon.

I drop the bags down heavily, their contents shaking and causing loud echoes around me. During my brief stint of popularity, I had forgotten about this cave and now I touch the walls of it, feel the wet moss underhand and I'm happy to be back.

I drag the bags to the farthest corner, where the light never reaches, and then I stand back and say goodbye to my grandmother's remains. It is the first time I have allowed myself to think how sorry I am that this has happened and the strength of my feelings make me immediately guilty for what I have done; allowing her to rot and die away in a damp cave where no one will ever find her. I kneel down in front of the bags. The hard floor digs into my knees and the pain feels good. I put my fingers to my lips in a long kiss and then touch one of the bags. I whisper that I'll miss her. I say how much I wish I could have heard her talk one more time before she left, because I have questions. Did it hurt, all those swallowed pills releasing their slow poison into her blood? When all she could feel and taste and see was water, did she suddenly change her mind only to be met with the terrifying conclusion, as her lungs popped neatly one by one, that she no longer had a choice?

When I get back home, I change into a new nightgown and the material is loose and cool against my exhausted skin. With the curtains drawn, I sit with my head resting on raised knees until the clock strikes five and the sounds of distant conversations and bells of bicycles rise and greet the falling evening. He will be home soon and I take another of my grandmother's incense sticks and light it. I move around the house, the trail of a hundred flowers following me, taking up residence in our curtains and carpet and pillows. I walk up and down the stairs and around his room until I am dizzy. I throw the key onto his bed, not minding when it misses his pillow and hits a picture of him and my mother instead. Then I go into my room, pack my bags, and wait.

7

St Albert. July–August 1992

He can't look at me—he hasn't for days. I sat cross-legged on my bed, waiting as he walked into Bubbie's empty room. After a small silence, the bathroom tap began to run and I heard his deep grunts as he splashed water on his face. I came out of my room and walked to the edge of the bathroom door. His hands were clenched around the ceramic sink, watching the water circle downward, and he paused for a moment when he heard me. Lifting his eyes, he met mine briefly in the mirror before he swung his foot back and kicked the door shut. When he was done, he went past my room and into his own. *She's a monster. How could she do this to me?*

My mother came into my room and we both pretended we hadn't heard him say it.

'Honey, we know you're upset, but really, this is too much.' She didn't know where to sit. Nowhere was far enough. Her eyes showed how bewildered she was by me, the shake of her hand as she ran it over her mouth. 'Just tell me where you put all of Bubbie's things and we can figure this out. You know how much they mean to your father.'

I turn away. *Leave me alone, just go away*, refusing to say anything—to tell her that we were only minutes away from most of it, sleeping and decaying in the old cave.

Now I try everything to win him back. I wear makeup around the house, even while I am sleeping. My clothes are a size too small for me, hugging at my breasts and clinging to my curves that have formed to his fingers. Yet he continues to ignore my attempts to apologize and love him again. My suitcase sits by my bed and most of the time I simply lie down beside it, trapped in a strait-jacket of memories. Seconds pass like hours; minutes drag on for years, sluggish through the summer heat. I can only count down the days until I am gone and he will begin to miss me.

My mother doesn't comment on the state of me; on the dirty residue that is growing slowly and thickly under my fingernails, or the husky scent that slips from my mouth whenever I speak, or that assaults her each time I lift my arms.

'We should go shopping,' she says a few days later, coming into the living room and standing before me. I ignore her, pretend to be asleep under the arm that is thrown over my eyes. I feel her staring down at me, biting into the apple that is balanced carefully between her long fingernails, no doubt leaving lipstick marks on the wet flesh inside. 'We have to buy you some new clothes before school starts.' She reaches over in an attempt to push the slick hair from my face and I swipe at her hand more forcefully than I intend to. Her apple goes skittering across the coffee table. She bends to pick it up, and I can see she is trying not to cry. 'Would you like that honey?'

I take my arm from my face and look at her, wondering at her insistence. It's so easy for her to love me, so effortless when she is glorious, supreme in her victory of having won the Main Man,

49

the Big Cheese, the Silverback of our small family herd. I stare at her and then say, 'I told you I'm not going and you can't make me.' Then I turn on my side, closing my eyes and letting my hair fall in my face. Her fingers flutter at this barrier between us but then she pulls away and walks out without a word.

He closes the door behind him; so softly that I don't hear him until he is kneeling next to me, his arm thrown over the back of my chair, the rough bristles of his stubble rising to rub against my cheek.

'Frances.' I stop my fingers moving underneath my desk but I don't turn around. His breath smells of fresh mint and I open my mouth a fraction to breathe in the cool particles. I don't look at him because then he will see how much I have missed this; the light grazing of his arm hair across my exposed skin, the sight of his shoulders stretching on endlessly and strong. 'Are you going to look at me?'

His fingers reach into my hair until they find and hold onto the bone of my neck. I turn against his grasp so that my back is fully facing him. 'Frances, come on. Look at me.'

'Why should I?' I rub my eyelids. I attack my lips with a fury, becoming aware of what I look like and I wish he could leave so I could comb my hair or put on some of my mother's stolen perfume. 'Why should I when you haven't said a word to me in over a week?'

He presses his face into my shoulder blades and his breath is heated and slow through my clothes. 'You know how upset I was. You really hurt me, Frances.' His teeth bite into the creases of my shirt. 'Come on, please.' His mouth moves with my body as it gives in to him, coming up and around and fixing wetly on my collarbone. *Darling.* A long, sweet murmur. I stand up and he rises with me, his arms sliding naturally around my waist and pulling me near.

We move toward the bed and I find his mouth and he lets me stay there for a while before pushing me away.

'You don't love me anymore,' I say and I can't look at him. I play with a fray in his pants. 'You hate me.' His hands push at my temples, tilting my head back until his face is over mine.

'Of course not. I could never hate you.' He lets me go and the loneliness that has filled the past few days comes falling at me. He holds my hand and puts it in his lap, playing with my fingers. He runs his fingernails across their lines, forgetting me.

'I'll give it back,' I tell him. 'All of Bubbie's stuff, I can give it back to you. I'm sorry I took it.'

He puts his forehead to mine. 'Thank you, baby.' He strokes my hair the way I like it best; starting from right at the temples and pushing roughly downward. 'You understand why you have to go?'

'No.' I push my face into his neck but he draws back. 'Please, I said I'm sorry. I told you—you can have all of it back.'

He sighs into me. 'All of this, Frances—everything that has happened recently,' his thumbs streaking along the bones of my rib cage, lulling me into a daze, 'it's not good for you.'

'I can't leave you. Please don't make me leave you.'

He laughs but it sticks in his throat and I feel him stiffen. He stops touching me. 'It's only for a year.'

'Two years.' My hands are on his chest, gripping and pulling at his unwilling waist. 'She's sending me away forever.'

'I'll talk to her,' he whispers, giving in to me. 'Just a year, honey.' I push back to look at him, but his eyelashes cover his eyes, dark and wet.

'You promise?'

'Yes. Only a year—how can I do without you for longer than that?' He falls against me and my legs stretch out and bend around his waist. 'You'll do this for me, won't you?' His face sinks into my shoulder and I don't want him to stop, so I nod.

'Yes, but only a year and then it'll go back to being normal, right?' Breezy kisses against my nose and gentle bites to my cheeks and earlobes. I tilt my head back and close my eyes.

'Yes, darling. You do this and when you come back, everything is going to be alright.'

Goodbye St Albert, hello open, empty space; if I could, I would take a winding train through your green, daffodilled grass all the way to the world's edge with my body hanging out of the window and the soft air in my face. I curl up in my seat, trying to get as far away as possible from the old lady sitting beside me. I try not to stare at the gray fuzz above her upper lip or the lipstick smears on her teeth and chin. I lean my head against the window and the soft vibrations lull me into a sort of half-sleep. My mother dropped me to the station that morning and tried to kiss me goodbye. *We'll visit as often as we can,* the joy in her words as she drove away, her small sedan struggling against the wind, her arm waving, discarding me like the old vegetables she sniffs and throws away, uneaten.

'You going to eat that?' Wrinkled fingers point at the sandwich next to me, still wrapped in its silver foil. I press harder against the window and shake my head.

'I'm not hungry.'

'Well, I'm just going to then,' she reaches for it, 'if you don't mind.' Eager eyes, a quivering throat as I push it toward her. I watch with growing distaste as the jam squeezes through the bread, slimy in the spaces of her teeth, covering what the lipstick has missed.

He left early this morning without a goodbye and through the mist I caught a glimpse of the slightest slant of his skin against the upturned collar of his brown coat. I chased after him, my bare feet soundless on the tarmac. I shouted his name, screamed it until its sharpness tore my throat apart, but he never heard me.

'Got anything else?' the voice, having been fed, swelling with hope. Blue eyes just like his.

'Please leave me alone.' I turn away and she moves down the carriage, grumbling and pulling empty wrappers from under peoples' feet, picking up a discarded juice box from a still warm seat, sucking at her winnings with large smacks of her lips.

We travel through the night and I toss and turn in the small bed provided, my mind full of empty dreams that gather me up in their darkness and wake me with a start. Toward the evening of the following day, a white sign flashes by, 'Welcome to Whitehorse' and the distance I have traveled suddenly seems too far to ever go back. The train grinds to a stop. *This is the end of the line, folks,* the train conductor making his way through the carriages, ushering people off, shaking their hands and slapping their shoulders. He comes toward me once the train is empty, having checked on me several times during the journey upon the request of my mother.

'Alright there?'

My throat is full and hard with tears. *Can you take me home again?* He helps me with my suitcase, hoisting it down and dropping it into the dust. He smiles; a quick, friendly streak of light. 'You have someone picking you up, have you?'

'Sister Ann.' He is gone, disappearing back into the cool darkness of the train before I finish saying it. I pull out a small slip of white paper from my pocket. *Ask for Sister Ann when you reach Whitehorse. She's coming to get you.*

I push my way through the crowd; talking and laughter and the whistling of trains all coming together too loudly, reminding me that I will never feel safe again. Finding an empty seat, I sit down and can't keep my eyes open any longer.

'Frances?' A gentle voice. I nod and start to cry. Cool fingers at my forehead, patting my shoulder. 'Take her bags will you, Joseph?' A tall shadow leaning over and picking up my suitcase. *I'll go and get the car.* Sister Ann sits down beside me, holds my hand and I can feel her watching as the tears curve down my cheeks and fall into my collar. I bend over my knees, the stiff, cold air of Whitehorse only suffocating me more. 'Just breathe, honey.'

The tears become silent and in their silence, more painful. I open my eyes and see her. Pointed chin, pointed cheeks; slim, half-moon lips. She is smiling down at me and I am taken aback by how young she is. 'You are Frances—Frances McDermott?'

'Yes.'

'I'm Sister Ann, from the Academy.'

'Yes.' My breath isn't capable of sustaining more than that one word.

'You're a long way away from home, aren't you?' *Inhale, exhale,* gathering myself together, straightening my clothes and hair, reminding myself of why I already dislike her.

'The train ride was alright.' I pull my hand away and she lets me. 'I'm not going to be staying for very long.'

She stands up and I copy her without meaning to.

'Well, while you're here, how about we go back to the Academy and get you something to eat?' I don't protest because there is a low humming in my stomach and I let her arm go around my shoulders and lead me out into the foggy heat of the car where a tall, dark man sits ready to steal me away.

8

Edmonton, Canada. July 1965

He had never smelled anything like it; sleepy heat, sour and warm. When she sighed close to his neck, her breath spreading milkily against his throat, James felt himself grow, filling all the spaces within him reserved for adulthood. He put his face to her fine hair and noted, with fearful surprise, how delicate her skull was. Soft and unformed still, he could crush it in his grip. So he kept his hands at her waist and held on tightly.

'I'm tired.' Her tiny, musical voice.

He watched in the window as her eyes drooped heavily forward, her mouth slightly open as she rocked against him. He bent forward, as if to look over her shoulder, and in the process, pressed her closer to him.

'Just a little longer,' he said. 'Don't you want to finish the book?'

'Okay.' A stretching yawn; the inside of her so shiny and pink. The newness of it took his breath away.

'Go on, then,' his voice low and encouraging. 'Just a few more pages.' And as her sweet voice crawled over them, he closed his eyes and swayed softly, allowing the girl to melt and fold against him. He had imagined this for so long; a blurry, expanding need that had grown inside of him and he hadn't been able to identify until now. This perfect body curving exactly into his own, the softness and smallness of it that made his heart race. It was a while before he realized she had stopped reading. That her head had fallen against his neck and she was fast asleep. His hand traveled down the side of her cheek and she gave a small murmur.

At six years old, her hair was a shiny blonde that he knew would sadly fade out by the time she became a teenager. Her skin was rosy white, unblemished and astonishing. He was at once disgusted and elated at the sensations she caused within him and he leaned down to whisper in her ear, 'Ssh. It's okay, I'm here,' thrilling in the dead weight of her.

Stretching his calves, lifting his torso, his hand falling to still the swinging chair because all he wanted was to feel the motion of the child. He held his jaw shut, grinding his teeth together so that the sound of him wouldn't wake her, but he couldn't help the small gasp bursting from his mouth. The air tasted of his exertion. When he could finally move again, he kissed her gently on top of her head, marveling at the fact that she was still sound asleep, and carried her carefully to her bed. As he tucked the blanket around her, he felt the first inkling of bewilderment crawl in.

'Well, isn't this a sight for sore eyes?'

The noise startled him and he turned toward the door where Nina was standing, leaning against the doorframe and smiling at them. Her voice had made the world real again and James didn't like what he saw. He stood on trembling legs, feeling the shame burn in his throat.

'I was just putting her to sleep,' he said.

'I can see that.' Nina came up behind them, twisting Donna's hair around her finger. 'She's beautiful when she's sleeping, isn't she?' She's so beautiful, James wanted to say. I'm so sorry for what I've done.

'I should be going,' he said, moving toward the door.

'I haven't paid you yet.' Nina reached into her purse but he held out his hand, appalled at the idea of taking her money. At the same time, his eyes darted wildly around the room to see if he had left any clues, certain that she would notice something, that she would call his mother as soon as he had left. But her face remained jovial.

'Please, don't worry about it,' he said.

'I insist. After you coming here on such short notice—you just can't rely on some of these girls in the neighborhood.' She pushed the notes into his hand. 'Thank you so much, James.'

He took the stairs two at a time, out of the door before she could see the disgust take a hold of his face.

A week later, Nina called to ask if he would babysit again.

'Donna absolutely adored you,' she said, and in the background he could hear the young girl crying. The sound filtered through the receiver, ribbons of temptation rubbing against him like the softest Chinese silk, tugging teasingly between his legs. It would be so easy. He hung up with a quick, 'I'm sorry, no.'

'I thought you enjoyed babysitting Donna,' his mother said. 'You were happy, I remember, when you came home last week.'

It was true. He had returned that night after babysitting with excitement brewing inside him; he hadn't been able to sit still. For the first time in his seventeen years, he understood what being alive meant. Everything had seemed to grow around him, charged by his own exhilaration. When his parents had gone to bed, he had sat alone for a long time, with that feeling inside him, searching in its chaos to find its starting point. When the memory had been used up, it left a residual discomfort, like a rotting tooth somewhere in him. He was afraid and almost went to wake up his mother but stopped himself at the last minute.

Now, he watched as his mother rubbed her stomach and smiled up at him. 'You should go again. It'll be good practice for when this little one comes along.' The reminder that there would soon be a baby in his house, that it might grow into something as enticing as Donna, terrified him with excitement. What was it Uncle Roy had said when he came to visit them last month? 'Giving into temptation is how sin is born,' shaking his beer can in James's face, forcing it down his throat. James's father had laughed, smiling down at his son.

'You're preaching to the wrong person, Roy,' he said, his eyes bright. 'Not a bad bone in this one.'

James knew that he had no choice but to outrun the monster that had leaped up at him that evening in Donna's nursery, among the blue walls and painted animals. He bought a poster of Greta Garbo in an almost transparent white dress from the boy next door to prove to himself there was nothing wrong, but in the next two days, it lay crumpled in his trash, unused.

That summer, the rain forgot to end but he was endlessly thirsty. There was Tamara Wilson on the bus, sliding into his lap, offering her lollipop to him. He stared at the slick candy, shiny with spit, and his tongue ached. He shoved her off and walked the rest of the way home.

'Why are you home so late?' his father called out to him as he came through the door.

'I missed the bus,' he said, running up the stairs in search of Greta, grunting over her and pretending it was her face he was thinking of. Again, a few weeks later, sin was mewing in his arms in the form of his young cousin, Gabriel, a scent like honey upon his whispered breath. He pushed the child into someone else's waiting arms.

He watched with rising terror as his mother grew larger every day, already feeling the now familiar plunge within him at the sight of her swollen belly. His mother noticed him staring one day and took his hand in hers.

'I know it's going to be a big adjustment,' forcing his hand in full, slow circles over her stomach. 'But we're going to be a perfect family.' Her eyes were closed so that she never saw what was happening to him. He almost pried them open and begged her for help.

Her tongue was in his mouth; he could taste the sourness of her gum somewhere in the back of his throat. He tried not to touch her, not to feel the way her waist dipped and curved, its youth lost, fully ripened. She pushed harder against him. 'Tell me what you want, James,' her lips, her words, slimy in his ear.

The day before, James had run into Travis in the Moscovitz's store, pushing condoms into the pockets of his faded jeans.

'There's a party on Suicide Hill tomorrow,' Travis had explained. 'Have to be prepared, you know what I mean.'

'Sure,' James said, though he didn't. It was as if he had skipped a step ahead of all the other boys in his class; somehow missed a crucial crossing point and had got lost. He watched Travis for a moment before turning to leave. He was almost out the door when he stopped and turned back around. He checked to see what Mrs. Moscovitz was doing behind the counter. She was on the telephone, the blue receiver cradled between her shoulder and chin, her stooping back toward him. He walked back to Travis, grabbing a handful of condoms, not caring in his excitement when a few scattered around his feet.

'I'm going to need some myself,' he said and Travis smiled at him. It was an easy smile and for the first time in a while, James felt the pressure lift from his shoulders and he was innocent once again.

'My girlfriend's sister is coming with us, if you're interested?' Travis had suggested and James couldn't nod fast enough.

'Thanks, yeah.'

'Anything to help out a friend,' a sly wink, 'see you at eight?'

James had waited for Travis to sneak out and disappear around the corner before he reached back into his pockets and pulled out the foil-wrapped condoms. He kept only one, safely tucked in his jacket.

The following night, James had picked up the three of them in his father's station wagon and they drove up to Suicide Hill. The party was already in full swing and someone had started a bonfire. James walked toward it, kicking away empty coolers and beer cans. The heat curled pleasantly against him, crisping his face.

'Shall we go back to your car?' an arm going around his waist, sliding into the back pocket of his jeans. He followed her down the winding road until the glow of the fire was as small as the corner of his eye. No one could see them. It couldn't have been easier. *Tell me what you want, James.*

'Cry.' He whispered it. The word shivered in the night air, evaporated in the steam of her kiss. 'I want you to cry.'

'What?' She sounded amused and his heart rocked in his chest. He saw the monster rise up in front of him but this time he was playing its game, following its rules. 'If you can't outrun a bully, outsmart him instead,' his father had once said to him. James felt his teeth tremble in anticipation. It wasn't too late to stop but it was too hard and he didn't want to.

'It doesn't have to be loud, just—if you could just try.'

She settled back on his knees so that she could see his face. She took the gum out of her mouth and twisted it around her finger.

'Crying?' She pouted, widened her eyes, blinked a couple of times, forcing them to water. 'Like this?'

He pressed his hands into the flesh of her thighs, buried his face in her neck. She was repulsive to look at. 'Make a sound.' In his desperation, he became loud, aggressive. 'Please, anything.' She threw back her head and so tight and helpless was the noise that came out of her throat that he felt himself involuntarily buck beneath her. He thought about skin so soft, a body still so new, it couldn't help but depend on you. *Don't stop Hayley, don't stop, never stop.* He kept his eyes shut so he wouldn't have to see her, kept his hands on her thighs so he wouldn't have to touch any other part of her, just listening. When he pushed himself into her, the relief was so acute, he whimpered.

Afterward, he sat for a moment, enjoying the buzz of a body almost completely satiated until he opened his eyes. Saw the girl sitting in front of him, not a girl at all but a woman. He pushed open the door and vomited.

9

Whitehorse, Yukon, Canada.
September 1992

There is a long, tarmac track that juts off the main road about thirty minutes from the train station. It winds and teases through the thicket of pines that close behind us like a curtain the further we go down it. The fading day follows us; an occasional golden burst in my eye. There is music playing lightly in the front and Joseph's fingers drum on the wheel as he sings softly along. Sister Ann turns to look at me from the front seat.

'Not long now,' she says and then points to the left. 'The river is down that way. Sometimes, when the weather is nice, we all go there for a picnic.' I follow the direction of her finger and don't see anything but dark green. She looks through the rearview mirror at me. 'You're going to love the Academy,' she says, 'it's beautiful,' and then leaning forward, she squints her eyes. 'There it is.'

The trees have grown more scant, as if opening up a secret world, and in front of us lies a wide open field and a rising stone building that resembles an old castle. It's partly lit up from the west, a burned orange from the sunset, and even I have to admit it's spectacular. Long French windows decorate the entire face of it and its roofs are blood-red, pointing straight up to the sky. The building is split into three wings, the center one rising above the two adjacent, and bordering the school are the last of the summer flowers, bright purples and pinks, and a smell like honey hangs thick in the evening air. It seems to be smirking down at me.

There are yellow lights beginning to be switched on from some of the windows and I see shadows pass behind the curtains. My heart constricts in my chest and my breath turns shallow. Sister Ann squeezes my arm.

'It gets easier,' she promises. 'Pretty soon, it'll start feeling more like home than home does.'

I continue to stare up at the gray building, lit up fully now, and don't reply.

You can hear everything from the main foyer of the Academy. Its large circular floors and high domed ceilings are designed to catch and hold even the softest, most hidden sounds. I can hear girls upstairs; laughter and overlapping voices are chased down the winding staircase by half-whispered gossip and hurried footsteps. I wonder if they have been living here for so long that they have forgotten this secret or if they no longer care that they are being watched, carefully listened to.

'It'll be dinnertime soon,' Sister Ann tells me, glancing at a large clock that sits on the high wall near the front door. 'How about we get you something to eat and then I'll show you to your room?'

I nod because there is nothing else I can do in this foreign place except follow the instructions given to me.

'Joseph?' There is something about the way she says his name, with just the slightest modulation. But then she turns crisp and formal again, and the feeling I had, the inclination of something I can't quite grasp, is lost. 'Would you take Miss McDermott's things up to the third floor?'

Joseph, who up until then has been standing motionless in the dark, moves forward and I jump. I had forgotten he was there. We stand at the base of the impressive staircase and watch as Joseph, the clockwork movement of his muscles just visible under his shirt, takes long and sturdy strides up the wide stairs, not once pausing to rest under the weight of my life.

'Shall we go in, Frances?' Sister Ann asks, cutting through my thoughts and I pull my eyes away from the figure moving upward, losing itself in the shadows and grooves that my gaze cannot reach. 'Yes, okay.'

She leads me to a doorway on the left side of the staircase. The movement is neither on the tip of her toes or the soles of her feet, but floating on the curved arch. She walks as if she is used to being quiet; practiced at being invisible. A door is pushed open and I am guided through it.

I have to hold my hand over my eyes for a moment when I step into the mess hall. The light is too bright and yellow; obnoxious compared to the low, dim welcoming of the foyer lamps. When my eyes adjust, I see rows and rows of benched tables, starting from close to the door and leading up to two large windows looking into a cluttered kitchen. The walls are an aged white, moving up into a sagging ceiling that is a patchwork of brown from countless leaks.

'Why don't you sit by me today?' Sister Ann suggests, taking a seat at the first table, facing away from the kitchen so that she can observe everything. The smell of food behind me is strong and digs further into the emptiness of my stomach, reminding me that I haven't eaten all day. It fills my mouth so that I can't do anything except shrug my consent and tuck my skirt into the crook of my knees so that I don't feel the splintered bench cut into my thighs. We sit for a moment in silence and I watch Sister Ann; see the words of what can only be a prayer start in her cheeks, move down into the willing cave of her mouth. Her face is calm; devoid of any emotion except for a betraying vein in her slim neck, sneaking up to her jaw, clenching and unclenching with every word, reaching high up over her buttoned collar.

I sit pressed to the wall and that is where I see it. Small writing done precisely with the tooth of a fork. A small message engraved into the stucco wall; *if God doesn't exist, then anything is permitted.* It is encircled by a series of waves and curves; aimless, thoughtful scribbling. I am not sure why it makes me pause; draws my eyes to it to read the words over and over again. Perhaps because it is so out of context, here in a place that I have been sent to so that I can remember Him, so that I can remember how to be good. It's a flash of comfort, sharp and swift, before the clock strikes six o'clock and everything bursts into noise around us.

Sister Ann finishes her prayer just as four women in stained aprons and hairnets enter the kitchen. They call out simultaneous hellos to us and Sister Ann waves and greets them back. I notice her movements because it's hard not to. Everything about her is simple and graceful, as if she is moving through water. The women turn on the stoves and two of them slam down large, silver pots on its top and stir the broth noisily with long, metal serving spoons. Sister Ann sits perfectly straight, her hands folded neatly in her lap, unfazed by the commotion behind us. Yet in her stillness I sense an undercurrent of energy and she seems too young and full to belong to a place like this.

Then I feel, before I hear, the soft vibrations caused by the footsteps of so many girls coming down the stairs together and I am overcome by a sudden nervousness. A low aching begins in my palms and they start to sweat. I rub them up and down the cotton of my skirt. My heart stirs and jumps painfully, forcing against my rib cage in its panic, desperate to get out.

'Don't be nervous,' Sister Ann touches my shoulder and speaks softly. 'You'll fit right in.' Some of the girls wave at her and, seeing me beside Sister Ann, smile quickly before sliding into their seats. Once they have all settled down, Sister Ann stands, her hands sliding off her rising lap and clasping behind her back. She calls for silence and then says a name. *Madison Rivers.* From somewhere in the sea of faces, I see a blonde head emerge. Madison is saying something but I can't hear her and it's only when Sister Ann repeats it softly, near my ear, that I realize she is saying Grace. *Bless us O Lord and for these gifts we are about to receive, may the Lord make us truly thankful. Amen.* As she settles back down, the girls cross themselves and kiss their fingertips before rushing up and coming toward us. Most don't notice I am there, even as they pass us to get to the food.

'Someone different says Grace every night,' Sister Ann tells me over the sound of plates and cutlery. 'You can say it however you want.' *What if you don't want to?* I resist the temptation to ask.

I am no longer hungry but force down the soup I am given. I also take a slice of bread and tear it into small, square pieces. I dip them, one after the other, into the steaming broth and allow them to grow soggy. They fall apart and drop into the soup, soft and inedible. I spoon one out and let it sit on my tongue for a few seconds, feeling it sear through the tender, purple muscle. My tongue protests, jerking in my mouth, trying to push the food down my throat, and when I swallow there are tiny bumps and raised ridges left behind. I press my teeth down on them and run them along the roof of my mouth and the pain instantly comforts me. Sister Ann asks if there is anything else I want to eat; there is a slice of meat pie with my name on it, she says, but I shake my head. I am so engrossed in my own activity that I don't notice the hall slowly starting to clear out. Girls are scraping the remaining food off their plates and into large buckets placed beside a table near the door before exiting.

'You didn't eat much,' Sister Ann says, and I look down at my half-eaten bowl of soup; the grayish, tepid liquid has grown thick and green from the circles of oil that have floated to the top.

'I wasn't hungry,' I say. 'It's been a long day and I'm tired.'

'Let me show you to your room, then.' Sister Ann pushes back her chair, and as if I am bound to her, the legs of my seat scrape along with hers. My body rises at the same time and in the same manner; a little pull of our calves, a quick roll of our necks. If she notices, she doesn't show it. I go through the same motions as the other girls did, pouring out the soup and watching as it splashes against the tall, plastic sides of the basin.

We enter the main foyer again and everything has quietened. The last remaining girls move by us in pairs or small groups, linked by their elbows, heads bent together.

'Hurry up, girls,' Sister Ann speaks softly but they hear and listen to her. *Yes, Sister.* They rush past us and up the stairs, disappearing behind closing doors. Sister Ann tells me that it's time for the girls to do their homework.

'We follow a strict schedule here,' she says, as if warning me. 'Dinner is from six to six forty-five followed by an hour and a half of homework.'

I want to ask her what happens if I'm not hungry at that time or if I finish my homework before eight-thirty and if I am allowed to call my father before I go to sleep every night?

We reach the top of the first floor and there is barely a stirring around us. It's as if I have dreamed up dinnertime, as if the horde of girls I have just seen was nothing but my own over-active, tired imagination. We keep climbing up, past a similarly soundless second floor and then onto the highest level. It's more shadowy here than anywhere else in the building. There are long, elegant windows on either side of the corridor, covered in heavy velvet curtains that cast a teasing, clandestine darkness over the rooms.

'I hope you don't mind staying at the top—I know it can be quite a climb.' Sister Ann smiles at me as we carry on down the long hallway toward a room at the end. She knocks before opening the door with a master key that sits in her pocket attached by a string to her belt around her waist. She steps back and lets me through. The first thing I notice is the size of the room. It's small, much smaller than my room back home and the angled ceiling slopes downward on one side, making it seem even more cramped. There is a bed on either side of the room, attached to its own desk. A long rectangular window runs along the front wall and the patterned curtains—a poor attempt at making the room feel more homely—are carelessly drawn, allowing in cracks of bluish moonlight. One of the beds has been made immaculately, its blankets tucked in, corners perfectly folded out. The other is unmade. A single sheet and a thin, woolen blanket are folded and lying on top of the spring mattress.

'I told Judy—that's your roommate—to do her homework in the library tonight. Give you some space to settle down before tomorrow morning,' Sister Ann says. That's when I see my suitcase neatly placed in the corner beside the closet.

'Where should I put my things?' I ask.

'There are some drawers under the bed and here,' she points and opens the cupboard. 'That should be enough space for you.'

'I don't have that much,' I say. 'Like I told you, I won't be staying for very long,' I can't help but add and then oddly feel as if I am betraying her kindness toward me.

Sister Ann sits at the edge of my bed. She takes my hand and holds it in both of hers. Her fingers move against my skin as they would against the beads of her worn-out rosary and I wonder if it has become a reflex now, if they always move like that, even when she is sleeping.

'I know it's difficult, Frances,' she says, 'and I'll be there to help make it as easy for you as I possibly can, but you're going to put in a little effort as well. Do you understand?'

When I nod, she stands up, leaving my hands to fall at my sides, grown alive at her stroking touch, and she pats my hair. 'Good. The bathroom is down the other way—would you like me to show it to you?'

'I'm sure I'll find it if I need to.' I want her to leave now. 'Thank you. I'm just really tired.'

'Of course. You must be, with all that traveling.' She glides back to the door. 'We wake up at six-thirty sharp. A general alarm will go off on the floor and the prefects will come around to make sure everyone is awake.' She pauses, her body part-shadow from the moonless corridor. 'Sweet dreams, Frances.'

'Thank you.'

She leaves and I turn off all the lights. I step out of my sticky clothes, slowly, until I am left standing on the stained carpet in nothing but my underwear and the thin vest I wore all day under my blouse. I walk to the window and push back the curtain. The room overlooks a wide, neat field and in the distance I can make out the blurred, night-edges of another stone building, smaller than the one I am in and less imposing. I wonder what it is used for but I am too tired to care. The darkness has cooled my frenzied skin. It has slowed the pace of my terrified heartbeat and left me drained. I throw my clothes into a corner and fall back onto the creaking mattress. I wrap the sheet around me and the blanket on top of it, the hard threads poking through and irritating my already sensitive skin. It has been an endless two days and I can hardly believe where I am. I push into the corner, only taking up half the bed, leaving as I always do just enough space for him. Sister Ann's words ring in my ears.

Sweet dreams, Frances.

10

Edmonton. Winter–Spring 1966

January would remain in his mind as the month his life was saved. He wanted to think it was because that was when he met Marienne for the first time, struggling up the snowy hill, tugging at her wet jeans and pushing her hair away from her face all in one movement. He walked carefully behind her, hoping she wouldn't hear him, but when she dropped her satchel and caught his eye, he felt he had no choice but to catch up to her.

'Need some help?' Even as he said it, he wished he could snatch the words back, swallow them whole before they reached her. She smiled gratefully, pausing to hold out her hand. He shook it, drawing his fingers back the moment they touched hers and curling them into a fist in his pocket.

'I'm Marienne,' she said and her voice was high and girlish.

'James.' The name came out broken, nervous. 'I live down there.' He pointed toward his house and realized for the first time how isolated it was.

'Looks nice,' she said politely as he picked up her fallen bag, slinging it over his own shoulder. She started to walk, checking to see that he was following. He didn't speak but listened to the breath straining in her throat; saw the way the effort of pushing through the frozen slush caused the blood to thicken in the veins of her cheeks, pushing red against her skin. She tightened the hood of her jacket around her ears and when they reached the top of the hill, he hoped to leave her there in view of the main pathway. Yet she never asked for her bag back and fell into step with him as if they had been walking to school together for years.

'You're going to William High, aren't you?' she asked with a wide grin and when he nodded, she said, 'Just checking.'

He had to slow down his pace to let her keep up with him. When she tried to talk to him, he pretended not to hear her over the wind rushing at their faces. Walking with Marienne made him aware of how secluded he had become after the incident on Suicide Hill. Her banter, which expected to be met with an eager flirtatiousness, was too loud; her movements beside him too distracting that they caused him to stumble once or twice. So when they reached the school gates, he pushed the bag into her hands and started to move off, when her voice stopped him.

'Maybe you could show me around?' She saw the startled way his eyes grew wide and hurried to add, 'just for today, at least.' Then she stared down at her glitter-laced loafers, right heel crushing the toes of the left. The childish gesture, so heavy with anticipation, touched him and left him unable to say no, although he desperately wished he could leave her there and not have to think of her again.

She told him she was from Toronto, staying with 'Dolly,' her mother's eccentric third cousin and when he asked where her parents were, she waved her hand in the air and said, 'Oh, you know. In New York, waiting for The Beatles.' He didn't ask if she had wanted to go along because when she looked up at him and blinked hard, he had his answer. She asked about his family and he responded with the standard answers, *mother, father, only child,* his eyes falling at the last one, feeling hugely resentful of her. Her new-student status, made infinitely more interesting by her strange bob and colorful clothes, constantly drew attention to them throughout the day, dangerously allowing countless eyes to fall upon them; eager gazes he felt sure would see right through him and know what he had done.

During lunch, when she leaned against the stone-wall entrance and pulled out a foreign-looking packet of cigarettes, he moved further away from her. He didn't like how it looked on her; a big town girl too large for this small city. When she began to blow perfect, smoke-shaped circles into the frigid air, James felt the curious eyes of every passing student scrape against him as cold and grainy as sandpaper.

So it was a relief to leave her at the bottom of the hill that evening; to turn away and head toward the crusty sunlight hovering at his house windows. With every furthering step, his body slid and settled back into its familiar silence and, as he crossed the doorway, Marienne slipped away from him like the melting snow from the soles of his boots. She was the farthest thing from his mind when he sat down at his desk, pretending to do his homework but instead straining to hear his parents' soft whispers. He didn't think of her all night until the next morning when he happened to glance out of his window and saw a slim figure waiting where they had separated the previous day.

He paused and pressed his forehead against the cold glass, confused at his jogging heart that pushed out a small smile to fog the window even as he wished she would go away. He watched as she rubbed her hands together, blowing on her exposed fingers and stamping and spoiling the fresh snow and he dressed quickly. It took him a while to find something to eat for breakfast. The kitchen cupboards were bare and he tried to remember the last time his mother had left the house, to do the shopping or anything else. He found an almost empty box of cereal and poured the remaining flakes directly into his mouth. He ate hurriedly, standing in the stooping darkness of their small kitchen, and when he finished he left a note for his mother before closing the door quietly behind him.

Pretending not to see Marienne, he walked with his head down until he drew close enough and she handed him her bag with a blushing laugh.

'I'm not very good with directions,' she told him as they began to walk. 'I know I would just get lost in all this snow.' She paused to gauge his reaction. 'You don't mind, do you?'

He shook his head, feeling a slight tremor of pleasure in his stomach. As much as her attention made him uncomfortable, it felt good to be acknowledged. It made him feel solid—enclosed warmly in her gaze. He gestured toward the hill and watched as she trekked up ahead of him, pulling her collar around her and tucking soft, black strands neatly behind her ear.

He had English period just before lunch and he sat at the far back, blending into posters explaining volcanic eruptions, the workings of the solar system and a sad poem about someone's dead dog. He saw her come in, felt what her new presence did to the boys around him. They shifted and nudged and grinned. No one looked at him. He had left her by her locker that morning and now she was flanked on either side by fast-talking girls, *sit here, sit there,* eager to have some of the attention deflect off her and onto them. Eventually she sat just where she wanted, in the middle of the classroom, catching and holding his eye as she settled in. She smiled and the room held still. He thought everyone paused to follow and contemplate that look, tried to understand what it meant, and how did she possibly know him? Then he looked away and the noise started up again. A half-crumpled ball of paper whizzed somewhere over his head. A low whistle, *what's your name, doll?* and laughter all around.

'Okay, okay. Quieten down everyone.' In a waft of chalk dust and coffee, Mr. Simon closed the door loudly behind him and came to sit down on the desk, hitching his left pant leg up while the right foot tapped impatiently on the floor. 'I know it's just before lunch and you're all hungry and eager to be outside—please don't think I feel any different, but let's just get on with it, shall we?' regarding the still noisy classroom, 'and maybe we can all leave a little earlier.' Immediate silence at this empty promise. He picked up a book. They were reading *Great Expectations* and James had already read it twice over the break. It was his mother's favorite. He felt a slight clenching of his gut and ground the pencil into the desk. The wood broke around it and he felt a momentary thrill of satisfaction.

'Hal, let's start with something easy, shall we?' Mr. Simon's eyes trained on a boy sitting near the door, his backpack still on the desk, hiding his face. 'Put the bag down, please.' A low, reluctant thud. 'Good. Now, what's the name of the house where Miss Havisham lives?'

'Who?'

Quiet sniggers, relief that they weren't the ones being picked on.

'Miss Havisham.' Mr. Simon pronounced it slowly, the *sh* a whistle in his throat, giving the boy time to reflect on the answer. The name was met with bemused eyes, a rapid, panicked blinking. Hal opened the book and flipped uselessly through it. Then he looked up and shrugged. 'Sorry, sir. I don't remember.'

Mr. Simon sighed. 'You don't remember or you didn't read it?'

Silence.

'Satis House.' Slight musical intonation, soft and tentative, the answer raised in slight question at the end, as if she wasn't entirely sure of it.

Everyone turned to look at Marienne. James couldn't see her face but from the way her hands were twisting themselves under the desk, he could only assume she was blushing under the attention.

'Miriam, is it?' Mr. Simon checked his attendance sheet.

'Marienne, sir.'

'Marienne. Right. And why does she wear a wedding dress every day of her life?'

'Because she was abandoned by her fiancé on their wedding day after she realized he had duped her.'

'That's right.' He turned to Hal, who was now whispering to someone beside him. 'Hal.' A breath through the nose. 'Mr. Parker, I find it interesting and slightly disturbing that Marienne, who has just joined us today, knows more about this book that I gave you the entire holiday to read, than you do.'

'Sorry.'

'Of course you are.'

'I read it at my old school,' Marienne said apologetically to Hal as he shifted around to glare at her.

'Okay, well then let me ask you this,' Mr. Simon paused, a glint in his eye, 'what does Miss Havisham come to realize toward the end of the novel about her actions?'

Marienne glanced around the room; she might have turned to James but he was concentrating on making black holes in the wood.

Then she answered, almost guiltily, 'She realizes that instead of achieving any kind of personal revenge, she has only caused more pain and has broken Pip's heart the way hers was broken.'

'Something like that, yes. Good. Very good.'

She sank back in her chair but Mr. Simon stopped her. 'I have one more question for you.'

'Okay.' She sounded wary, anxious for him to turn his attention elsewhere. But he was enjoying this too much; a student who had actually read and understood the book was too valuable to let go.

'One of the main themes of the novel is social class,' Mr. Simon started, stopped, and then asked, as an afterthought, 'do you agree?'

'Yes.' Her voice tripped, unsure.

'Good. How does Pip's attitude toward social standing change throughout the novel? What does he come to learn?'

The class watched her, waiting to hear what she would say. It seemed to be a judgment; a collective voice saying her answer would tell them whether or not she was worthy of being their friend. She sat straight and tall in her seat and it was only the nervous tapping of her foot that gave her away. She didn't have a clue.

An answer was forming on his lips and his heart began to flutter, pounding in his mouth. He never spoke in class, and now he tried to practice how to string the words together, not sure if they would make sense once they were out. But he felt them starting up in him, eager to be heard, eager to help her out.

'I'm not sure,' she said.

'Try,' Mr. Simon prodded. 'Come on, I'm sure you can think of something.'

'I really,' she shook her head helplessly, 'I really don't know.'

'I think that the theme of social class is central to the novel's plot and to the ultimate moral theme of the book.' His mouth moved on its own and for an absurd moment, he looked around just like everyone else to see who was talking. It was only when the teacher dragged his eyes away from Marienne and fixed on him that James realized it was his own voice filling up the classroom.

'Mr. McDermott.' Mr. Simon sounded surprised. It had been a long time since James had done anything to draw attention to himself. The teacher looked back at Marienne who was now fiddling with the hem of her skirt. 'Care to elaborate?' he asked.

'When he falls in love with Estella, he wants nothing more than to become a gentleman, a part of her social class. He thinks that this will make him happy, and when he does receive a benefactor, he shuns his old friends and his old life.' The words were rushing out of him; how did he even know how to say this? Was he even making sense? He spoke with speed, wanting it to be over quickly. He wasn't sure why it had started—only that he had felt responsible for her. A film of sweat began to tickle his upper lip and he resisted the urge to wipe it away. He kept his eyes trained on the chalkboard at the front of the room. 'But when he comes to admire Magwitch, he realizes that wealth and class are less important than loyalty and inner worth and that being wealthy does not necessarily mean you will be happy.' He finished in a breathless flourish, something pulsing in his throat. His head felt so light that he thought it might float away. He put his hands under his thighs so no one would see how they were shaking.

Mr. Simon cleared his throat. Students shifted in their seats, someone shouted *nerd* and was told to be quiet. The teacher stood up. 'That's very good, James. Excellent.' He started to write on the board, and eventually all eyes followed him. Except hers. Her neck craned backward, she stared at him until he was forced to look up. Her eyes were too bright.

'Thank you,' she mouthed. He felt exhilarated, empowered and inexplicably protective over her. He thought he smiled back but felt so disengaged from his body that he couldn't be entirely sure if he did.

Somehow, she managed to escape from her new friends and found him at lunch. He looked up and the bread of his sandwich turned dusty on his tongue. He washed it down with a sip of water.

'Hi.' She pulled nervously at her ponytail.

'Hello.'

'I just wanted to,' licking her lips, 'say thank you.'

'What for?' he asked, although he knew what she was referring to.

'For helping me out like that in class.' Blood pooled in her cheeks and her lips seemed to fill with it. They grew soft and large, more like a young girl's than a teenager's. It was that—the sweet childishness she seemed to embody without meaning to—that had made him want to help her in class. He took his eyes away and shrugged.

'You did it for Hal, didn't you?'

'Yes.'

He started again, tried to be more generous. 'Mr. Simon has a tendency to pick on people,' he explained. 'He gets a little carried away sometimes.'

The words found and presented themselves; he didn't have to search for something to say. He hadn't found it this easy to communicate with someone in a long time, let alone a girl of his age. It was something her unhidden interest inspired in him; she made him feel less self-conscious and a little flattered.

'I can see that,' she grinned. 'You don't know how relieved I was when you jumped in. That was brave of you.'

It was his turn to blush. 'It's not a big deal. It's one of my favorites, so I know it pretty well.'

'It was still very nice of you to come to my rescue.' She was jovial now, pulling out a chair to sit opposite him. 'You're my knight in shining armor.' She said it, saw his face and blushed. 'Sorry, that was a stupid thing to say.'

'No.' He fiddled with his food, rearranged the items on his tray and tried to keep his face neutral. 'It wasn't stupid at all.'

The bottom of the hill became their ritual morning meeting place and each time Marienne would hand him her satchel and they would climb the snowy slope and walk the fifteen minutes to school together. He knew she could have made other friends if she had wanted to. There was something endearing about her indifference to the people around her that made them want to reach out to her, as if to shake her and remind her of their presence. Yet, day after day, she would wait for him by his locker or seek him out at lunch, always ready with a story about Dolly or a letter from her parents.

She would remove the crumpled item from the pocket of her navy parka, pushing at it with the heel of her palm to drive the creases from it, and then read it out loud. Sometimes, she would re-read particular ones, closing her eyes at the parts she had memorized. *Dear Marienne, we wish you were here with us. Annie, New York is unbelievably beautiful in the winter time. Ann, what did we tell you about behaving at Aunty Dolly's house?*

At first, James would listen quietly, neither with encouragement nor dissuasion. He had slowly grown used to Marienne's company and had started to think that her voice was quite pleasant and so he didn't mind listening to its throaty, wistful lisp. But as winter dragged on into an even colder and bleaker February, which disappeared with a spring burst in March, she started to pause between lines and ask for his opinion, listening to him with a wide-eyed trust, as if everything he said must be true and adhered by. He thrived on this attention; it reminded him of the feeling he had discovered that previous summer, though not as clear nor as strong. The sense that he was needed made him feel grown up and right. James often caught himself, in the husky silence of his home, craving Marienne's speedy, stumbling questions or the particular way her accent snatched up the ends of her words.

Sometimes, when he wasn't ready to go home in the evening, he would walk Marienne to her house and Dolly would invite him in. He would be greeted by the muddy, unmistakable scent of marijuana that always left him mildly dazed as Dolly took his coat and kissed both his cheeks. When she fell asleep on the couch, as she was apt to do whenever he was over, saying, 'Can't see a thing with my eyes closed, kiddos,' the two of them would climb up to Marienne's bedroom.

One time, as they lay on her bed together—after much coaxing, she managed to move him from the chair near her desk—passing a stolen joint between them and counting the ridges of her ceiling, James felt ready to tell her everything. To confess so that she could carry his secret for a while and he could remember what it felt like to be clean.

'Alison had dark hair just like yours,' he said. His eyes flickered shut and for a moment he forgot where he was, and when he said her name, he allowed himself the impossible hope that perhaps he had dreamed it all. Marienne turned toward him and he felt her warm breath on his nose.

'Who's Alison?'

'She was—' he stopped himself just in time. 'She was just some-one I used to know.'

'What happened to her?' There was an edge of jealousy to her question that flattered him and he stared at her for the briefest of moments. He touched her button nose and told her how cute it was. She rubbed it.

'It's a baby's nose,' she said, scrunching her face, and he thought she was pretty when she did that. 'Doesn't fit in with the rest of my face.'

'I like it.'

'What happened to her?' she asked again, wouldn't be deterred.

'She got really sick,' he said and sat up straight. 'People just do, right?' he spoke pleadingly, as if he were trying to convince himself, and Marienne sat up next to him and stroked his back. James swallowed the lump in his throat and felt a little better.

'I'm sorry,' she said, and when she started to lean into him, he slid off the bed.

'I should go now,' he said and pretended not to see the way the disappointment curled her features.

As he walked home that evening, though he hadn't told Marienne the entire truth, he felt better than he had in a long time. It had felt good to say Alison's name; to feel its young, rounded letters on his tongue because it made him believe that perhaps he hadn't been to blame after all.

Each day he was with Marienne, the past summer became a little less clear; the edges of its memory increasingly blurred until he could play with it, sometimes even pretending none of it had ever happened. No longer did he feel cornered by the looks cast toward them in school. Instead, he began to respond to them with a quick nod; the familiar, lost grin of the playful boy of twelve they had all forgotten. This unanticipated return to teenage normalcy, his desire to cling to whatever part of it he could, brought him closer to Marienne. When she leaned down to whisper in his ear while people watched, James felt a spark in his chest that fell to his gut and ignited a tickle of pride and happiness. He was grateful for her friendship; for her ignorance and adoration of him, for the relief her company gave him because it allowed him to be normal again and that was greater than any respite his previous isolation had ever provided.

It was during a reading of her parents' newest letter that Marienne tried to kiss him. They were sitting cross-legged on the bleachers of the auditorium, their lunch on their laps. Her mother had sent the lyrics to a Beach Boys' song and Marienne was singing it softly, 'Barbara Ann' floating away from them and filtering out into the empty court below. Somewhere between *rockin and a-reelin*, James felt the cherry-tinged muscles of her mouth against his and her eyelashes frozen against his cheekbone. The tactile sensation reeled him. No one had touched him so gently in weeks and now Marienne was moving through him in a steady vibration that made him pull away, more out of surprise than anything else. She watched him, putting a hand to her lips as if she was just as shocked as he was.

'I'm sorry. I just thought…' Her eyes were wet with embarrassment. 'You do like me, don't you?'

He tried to speak but his windpipe had been licked clean and nothing but the fruity scent of her chapstick rose from his burning mouth. He wished he could reassure her. He wanted to lean down and put his forehead to hers and explain to her that it wasn't her fault, something else was wrong. But he couldn't shake away the image of an impossibly still, dark-eyed baby from his mind.

'I really should go.' Before he stumbled down the stairs, it almost broke his heart to see a tear slide down the curve of her cheek, collecting in the gentle dip that joined the end of her nose to the tip of her trembling mouth.

The next morning, the silence weighed down on him as he made his way up the muddy tracks alone, his left shoulder straining to feel the weight of Marienne's satchel. The nerves in his mouth were wide awake and while they called up the memory of a warm, swaddled body, a small fraction of them ached for Marienne. The sensation of her on his mouth had been pleasant, had satisfied a little bit of him, and now he missed her constant, noisy presence; the way her hand would brush his and she would leave it there, thinking he wouldn't realize she had done it on purpose. The loneliness her absence had unexpectedly cast him back into was disconcerting and he stopped to greet unfamiliar faces bobbing by him in the hallway, whispering a hello into the air just to hear the sound of his own voice.

He didn't see her until lunchtime and it was a relief to find her sitting alone in the cafeteria. He wasn't sure what he was going to say to her, only knowing that he had to make things right. She watched him approach and he stumbled, unsure of what to do. When she gestured to the seat in front of her, a smile drew gratefully across his face.

'Harry asked me to the dance,' she said, even before he had sat down. His neck jerked up.

'Harry Miller?'

'Yes.'

They hadn't talked about the Spring Formal and although he hadn't wanted to go up until that moment, he knew Marienne had been waiting for him to ask her. The thought of being so quickly replaced, forced back into inky silence; to know that someone else would hear her read those letters he had come to love, made his stomach churn. He had the inexplicable sense that she was someone he should not let go of. She scraped back her chair, hesitating for a moment, as if waiting for him to say something.

'I said yes, James.'

He continued to look down, his vision blurred blue by the tray in front of him. When he eventually forced his eyes up, the cafeteria had emptied out and the *cling-clang* of plates against metal forks reverberated around the empty walls, petering out into soft echoes that loudly mocked his sore heart.

James left school immediately, sitting on the cracked steps of the cemetery they passed every day on their way home. The jealousy that had pooled in his stomach was foreign to him, but once he recognized what it was, he welcomed it eagerly. It would help him fight for her. He stared down at his watch, the thin silver fingers of its dials crawling toward and slipping past the designated time and he worried that Marienne had taken a different route home.

He drummed his fingers absently on the stone step until she came up the pathway, ten minutes late and not alone. A deep voice had tangled itself in hers, laughing and flirtatious. James considered hiding but she saw him before he could move. He stepped through the iron gates, disappearing around the corner where he could still hear them talking.

'I'll be alright from here,' she told Harry. 'Thanks so much for walking me.'

'I'll see you in school tomorrow, then,' Harry's voice grew thinner the further he went from her and, several moments later, Marienne was staring down at him.

'Hi,' he said.

'You were waiting for me?' she sounded pleased. He came out from behind a forgotten tombstone, accidentally crushing some old roses that spread around it.

'Can I walk you the rest of the way home?' he asked. She put her small, gloved hand into the crook of his elbow as a response and followed him out onto the path. 'I missed you today,' he said, staring down at the stones crumbling beneath his feet, startled that he could say it so easily and even more so at the truth of it.

They walked slowly to her door where she extracted her arm from his. Not wanting to leave her just yet, he pushed his toes into the ground and said, 'I guess I'll see you tomorrow, then?' slowly stepping back. She caught his wrist as he moved away, tugging at it with such force that he stumbled into her.

'Are you going to kiss me or what?' she said and so he did. The coldness of her tongue felt good. The fact that she didn't mind when he fumbled and paused, calmed him. The sensation of her leaked into him slowly but surely, washing away the ugliness inside him and leaving him empty. It was a good kind of blankness. She pulled away with a shiver, her skin glowing. He wanted so badly to feel the same way, for his body to ring with the thrill of waiting for and finally getting her—to feel the need to put his mouth to hers once more, but if she never kissed him again, he wouldn't mind. It was the security her company gave him that he craved; or perhaps it was the hope of something more, that caused him to hug her close and keep her there for a long time.

And when Marienne had disappeared into her house, James walked home with a slow assurance to his footsteps. He felt settled and cheerful; the strain in his rib cage relented and he was able to breathe easily the cool, sweet air, allowing it to spread through his body. The night seemed sharper to him now. The black-navy of the sky and the silver edges of the stars had never seemed so clear, smiling down at him. It was because, when he looked for it, the hazy fear that had clouded his life for the past half-year was nowhere to be found.

He wanted to believe that; to be certain of the fact that it had been that moment that had brought him out of the terror of the previous summer. The way Marienne tucked her fingers into his afterward, smiling into his shoulder, looking just the way people their age were supposed to feel. But it wasn't. What had saved him was Alison and the fact that, at barely four months old, his younger sister had died, swiftly and suddenly in her sleep just as the town drank and kissed to the start of a bright and shiny new year.

11

Whitehorse, Yukon. September 1992

When I wake up the next morning, I can still feel his fingers intertwined in mine, pressing against my bones, crushing them under his weight. My ears are wet from his breathing and my throat hurts from struggling to keep all the noise within me trapped inside it.

'Hey, hey. Come on, wake up.' The sound is new; it doesn't belong in my crimson thoughts and neither do the insistent hands on my shoulder, shaking me awake. I sit up with a start, pulling the sheets against me. I am confused because he is not with me; disorientated because the shapes of my room are all wrong. It comes at me again. 'Nightmare?'

A tall girl is leaning over me and as I sit up, she moves back to sit on her bed, smiling sympathetically at me. 'I...' I try to speak.

'Don't worry about it. We all get them from time to time.' She stretches out her large palm and I take it, watching as my own folds and disappears into her fleshy skin. 'I'm Judy, by the way.' She smiles widely and her teeth are charmingly crooked; too big in the front and smaller everywhere else. 'I would have introduced myself last night but you were fast asleep by the time I got back.'

'Frances,' I say, as I struggle to sit up, pushing myself out of the tangled sheet and blanket that have tied themselves around my feet. 'I'm Frances,' I repeat, trying to shake my vocal chords awake.

'You slept right through the alarm,' Judy says. 'That might be a problem.'

Everything is slowly becoming clearer and I worry that I might have said something in my sleep; something that I don't want Judy to know.

'I was really tired, I guess,' I say. 'I'm usually a light sleeper.'

'Here's your uniform.' She hands me a stack of perfectly folded, starched clothes. 'I ironed them for you but you're going to have to start doing that yourself.'

'I don't iron my clothes.'

'Suit yourself.' She grins some more. 'All the other girls are already downstairs for breakfast,' she looks down at me, 'but you look like you could do with a shower.' She talks fast, all her words running together.

My mouth feels dry and acrid and when I run my tongue along my teeth, I discover a thick, overnight fuzz. I like the way it feels. I have never forgotten to brush my teeth. I was always prepared, in case he came.

'Come on,' she says. She doesn't wait for me, already out of the door, and I grab yesterday's clothes, tripping into them and hurrying after her.

I have never been in a shower room before so I don't know what to expect. It's cold, despite the leftover steam hovering around us, trapped between the air-vents in the ceiling and the floor. The stark granite of the shower recesses stand sharply angled against the wet cement floor and it smells faintly of urine and cheap soap. I can't imagine feeling clean here after showering with so many girls.

'You'll get used to it,' Judy says, as if she can tell what I'm thinking. Perhaps she had the same thought when she first came here and stood where I stand, surrounded by the streaked white tiles. 'There're some showers back there that have curtains, but they don't work very well.'

'Thanks,' I say gratefully. 'I'll use those.' I don't want anyone else seeing my body; seeing what only belongs to the two of us.

'Don't say I didn't warn you,' she calls after me but I don't hear her as I rush toward the back. 'I'll see you downstairs for breakfast. And try to hurry up otherwise you'll miss it.' She leaves me in the watery space. There is nowhere to hang my clothes so I lay my skirt down like a carpet on the damp floor and put my uniform on top of it, out of reach of the shower. I turn on the water and it takes a while before it eventually comes spitting out and although I stand under the jumping stream for over ten minutes, it never warms up. The water feels uncomfortably oily and eventually I give up and turn it off. I forgot to ask Judy for a towel in my rush to follow her, so I stand against the cool wall, waiting for my skin to dry off. I am ice cold but I enjoy the sensation. It sinks into my brain, freezing over all of my thoughts and worries and all I am able to think of, be aware of, is the hard cement under my curling toes and the smooth white tiles spreading across my bare back. Knowing that I should hurry, I pat myself half-dry with the shower curtain and then put on my uniform and old underwear, making a mental note to unpack before tomorrow morning.

After throwing my wet skirt onto my bed, I rush downstairs, hoping I haven't missed breakfast and I get to the dining room just as the last girls are leaving. My stomach protests loudly; a low, gurgling sound when I see that a black metal grille has been pulled over the kitchen windows.

'Frances!' Judy calls to me from the back and she is sitting alone, waving me over. Sister Ann isn't here and I wonder if I will see her today.

'I got you some porridge.' She pushes a bowl toward me and I thank her. I spoon the lumpy liquid into my mouth while I am still standing. It's cold and tastes sour but I don't mind. Even when it's finished and there's nothing left, I keep scraping the spoon against the sides and sucking on it.

'I'm sorry I didn't get you any more.' Judy is watching me with an amused expression and I blush.

'No, that's okay.' I let the spoon drop and it swings against the curved inside of the bowl before settling down again. 'Thanks for keeping this.'

We get up together and I place my bowl into the bucket near the door, hearing it crash and slide into the other dishes. I am already accustomed to one of the rules of the Academy. I glance at the time above the door. There are the same clocks in every room; a constant reminder of the rules and regulations I must now follow. It's only seven thirty. He will be going to work now; will he pass my room on the way out, pausing to look into the clean emptiness of it? It thrills me to think that we are dreaming of each other simultaneously.

'What happens now?' I ask as we go back upstairs.

'Assembly is at eight o'clock and classes start at eight twenty.' Judy is collecting her books, placing them, one at a time, into her open satchel. 'We have to walk across that field, to get to that building.' She gestures out of the window. I kneel beside my suitcase and unzip it. I lean into it, waiting to smell something that reminds me of home but it offers up nothing. My mother went shopping for me a few days before I left. *I can't let you go with nothing but these old clothes,* she had said. She tried to persuade me to go with her and when I refused, closing the door in her eager face and saying, 'The brochure said we have to wear a uniform. Maybe you should have read it before deciding to send me away,' she went alone. She came back with no clothes but had bought a pile of stationery instead. Pens of every color, pencils of all types. A long ruler, a short ruler, a ruler with a wavy, ocean edge, all packed into a new, purple pencil case. She had placed it in my bag, on top of everything else, with a little note tucked inside it. I find and unfold it now. *Remember me every time you use this. That means you'll think of me every day, just as I am always thinking of you.* I want to tear it up with my teeth and rip it with my fingers, but I am aware Judy might be watching, so I crush it in my hand and let it fall to the floor.

'Are you ready?' Judy is waiting by the door, impatiently shifting from one foot to the other. 'We can't be late.'

I don't have a bag, so I carry the pencil case tucked under my arm. 'Yes. Let's go.' As I am leaving, I step on the disfigured note and feel a mean pleasure go off in my spine, one spiteful spark at a time.

St David's. I discover the name of the building I saw last night from my window and it's where all the classes and daily assemblies are held. It's also where most of the staff sleeps, Judy tells me.

'Not the teachers, of course. They sleep in the same building as us.' She grins sideways at me, and her breath frosts in the chill morning air. 'I mean the kitchen staff and cleaners.'

The grassy wetness gathers beneath my feet, collecting in the hem of my socks, making my ankles itch. A shiver works its way up my legs and makes the hairs on my neck stand up. The white shirt is too thin to keep me warm, even in this easy cold, and the blue cardigan that Judy gave me is the same material as my woolen blanket and just as rough against my skin. I unbutton it and tie it around my waist.

'I wouldn't do that if I were you,' Judy says. We come up to the building and that's when I hear the singing. Judy reaches out and undoes the sweater from around me and hands it back, telling me to put it on. When she sees the quick irritation pulse at my face, she shrugs and says, 'Trust me.' I put it back on reluctantly and she pushes open the heavy oak door by its ringed, metal handle. 'You'll get used to it,' she whispers, as I knew she would. *Don't worry, Frances. You'll get used to being without him.*

The singing welcomes us in, rising higher and louder until it reaches and would surpass the ceiling if it weren't for the stained glass keeping it down. The morning light filters through the glass pattern in gold, green and yellow particles that fall upon the immaculate rows of girls that have formed, drifting and floating above the strong, firm choir. Judy leads me to the second-last row and we join the end of it. She starts to sing and I envy her because I cannot. I don't know this hymn and yet there is something magical about the group of voices coming together; accommodating and forgiving of each other's flaws; up, down, sideways and into each other, creating something that goes far beyond the meaning of the words they form.

I look around the open, spreading hall. The teachers are standing along either wall, straight and still as statues, none of their backs touching the dark oak behind them. They are staring over us, hands folded neatly to their bodies. When I find Sister Ann, I stare at her and want her to look back and acknowledge me, but she doesn't. She is the only teacher not looking at us; her eyes are closed and her fingers hold up her rosary that shimmers in the light. The singing finishes too soon and there is a second or two of inspired silence before a woman walks up onto the stage in front of us. She is dressed in a black habit and she is so large and broad-shouldered that the podium she stands at seems to shrink in her presence. She begins with a prayer which the girls follow in perfect unison.

> *Direct me now, O gracious Lord,*
> *To hear aright thy holy Word;*
> *Assist thy Minster to preach,*
> *And let Thy Holy Spirit teach,*
> *And let eternal life be found*
> *By all who hear the joyful sound.*
> *Direct us now, O gracious Lord.*

The simple and silly rhyme makes me want to laugh; small tickles of sound that I struggle to hold in. My ears fill with it so that I can't hear what the woman on stage is saying in her rough voice, but it also makes me angry. They finish off the prayer with a quick crossing; *forehead, chest, left shoulder, right shoulder, hands together.*
    Amen.

The students leave the assembly; everything here is done in straight lines and rows and small groups. I hang back in the crowd but I am pushed forward and jolted out into the now sunny morning. My pencil case drops from under my arm and I lose it in all the feet going by me. I start to reach down for it but stop. I think about all those pencils and rulers getting crushed, splintered into small pieces that will be easier to throw away.
    'I believe this is what you're looking for?'
    The crowd has faded, spread away into another door in the building and the tall man from last night stands in front of me. He is holding the still intact case and he smiles, his teeth a row of stars

against his dark skin. I try to remember his name, *Joseph,* and when he moves to hand me my case, his scent is unfamiliar and inviting; a mixture of grass and soap. I notice some of the girls looking my way before disappearing back into the building.

'Yes, thank you.' I take it from him while staring down at the perfectly polished wing-tips of his black shoes. My eyes move slowly up long legs in navy wool, round a thin belt on a surprisingly slim waist and finally resting on the white shirt rolled up to reveal his forearms and a gold gleam at his finger. He is too smartly dressed; too clean and combed. I tell him this without realizing it, *how come you look so fancy for a driver?* He laughs at me and puts a light hand on my shoulder, lapsing into a seriousness.

'What's your name?'

'Frances.'

'Well, Frances, do you know what my mother always told me?' I stare up at him, waiting. He continues. 'There are only two things that make a man; his clothes and his manners.' He laughs again but I'm not sure at what. He has crouched down so that he can look in my eyes and now he straightens out my sweatshirt and dusts imaginary creases off my shoulders. He glances up at someone over my head and his eyes crinkle in the corners as he rises back to his full height.

'And that goes for ladies too.'

I turn my head with his gaze and see Sister Ann standing behind me, her hands joined at her waist. She is smiling at him and then looks down at me.

'Good morning, Frances.'

'Good morning.' My eyes and ears are still full of this laughing man with the confident, comforting charm, sunlight glimmering at his back.

'Hello, Joseph.' Sister Ann's hands are on my shoulders, gripping them too tightly. He tilts his head to the side and grins down at us.

'I guess I better be going then.' He points to my case, now held like something precious in my hands. 'Careful with that now, Frances,' and he is gone, gracefully striding down the field, his shirt billowing out behind him like a balloon. Sister Ann turns me around and we start to walk in the other direction.

'Frances, we follow a timed schedule here,' she says to me as we reach the door, 'and it's important that you respect that. Do you understand?'

'Yes.' But I am hardly paying attention and as she walks in front of me, I look back quickly, hoping to catch one last glimpse of him bounding across the grass.

12

St Albert. November 1973

Proposing to Marienne was the arc that completed the cycle of a terrible adolescence; those four, defiant words bringing it to its end in adulthood, providing him with the final assurance that the goodness he had been brought up with still resided strong within him. He was so relieved, he couldn't finish his sentence.

'Will you—' he didn't have to. She saw the ring he held out to her and fell on top of him with a heated yes.

'Of course, yes. Took your time, didn't you?' Marienne, with her dark eyes, her every kiss a promise to bring him out of this nightmare and lift him into the white picket-fenced, flower-gardened life he knew they were heading toward. Just the two of them.

A few weeks before, under the influence of a strong wine and the unusual warmth of that particular November night, Marienne had told him she never wanted to have any children. It had become a habit of theirs, to talk about their future together as if it were a certain thing. As if they were only waiting, prolonging the moment of their youth, before they made the commitment.

'Why not?' he had asked.

'I had the worst kind of parents,' she reminded him. 'Not like yours, James. You're very lucky.' The wine had stained her feelings and her words were punchy and fast. 'I mean, what kind of people abandon their daughter for a group of singers? I never want to turn out that way.'

After spending a few months in New York, her parents had decided to settle there permanently. He still remembered when she had got the news. More than halfway through her first year in Edmonton. It was a phone call rather than a letter and she played with the wire, twisting it within her hands. She was silent for most of the conversation and when she did speak, it was with a low tremble accentuating her words—a nervousness he was unused to hearing from her.

'I've forgotten how to talk to my parents, can you believe that?' she had said to him afterward. 'I thought my mother was a stranger. A loud, obnoxious woman I wouldn't want to speak to again if I met her on the street.'

'Are you going to go?' he had asked.

'To New York?'

'Yes,' he said, his anxiety making him impatient.

'It sounds exciting, doesn't it?' She brought her knees up to her chin and hunched her shoulders, her sweater large and enclosing around her small frame. 'All that life and noise—sometimes I miss it. It would be nice to have something else to do apart from going to Millie's Milkshake or Suicide Hill.'

'You never seemed to have a problem with it before.' He had bristled, despite her neutral tone.

'It's not that I have a problem,' she explained patiently. 'It's just,' shrugging, 'sometimes, I get it—what my parents are doing. There's a whole world out there to see, you know what I mean?' She picked at her fingernails, flakes of blue paint falling into her lap. 'So many opportunities. I always wanted to be a singer.'

'You would be a great singer.' Something sick was closing over his heart. He hadn't known she thought of those things; that there could be something he was holding her back from.

She watched him carefully. 'Would you be sad if I decided to leave?'

'I would be heartbroken,' he said simply.

She flushed with pleasure, kissed him and took his hand, putting it under her shirt.

'No.' He was across the room in a fast moment. 'Not now. I told you, I want to wait.'

'Sorry,' she sighed, chastened but not suspicious. 'To answer your question,' her voice was loaded with meaning, 'they said I can join them if I want after I finish the two years here and visit over the holidays in between, so I'm staying exactly where I am. With you.'

'I'm okay with that.' They smiled at each other and he went back to doing his homework at her desk.

After several moments of silence, she asked, 'Don't you want to know why I'm staying?'

'Why?'

'Because I'm in love with you.'

'I love you too,' he said and in a way, it was true. It had scared him, how easy it could be to lose her. How much was at stake if she walked out of his life and that made him more grateful to her than ever.

By the time, close to a year later, that Marienne's Aunt Dolly, drug-free and love-ready, got married to a dairy farmer and moved away to lead a 'simple and quiet life' as she put it, Marienne and her parents had become so absorbed in their separate lives that she no longer felt the need for their support. Instead, they had continued to communicate sparsely, and even less so in the last two years, through letter and lyric.

She had moved in with James and his family by the time they were nineteen, looking after his parents when he went away to college. They accepted her eagerly; their dead daughter in another form.

That winter night, the snow and cold suspended temporarily, he said to her, 'You would never turn out that way. I think you would make a great mother.' She was his best friend and he didn't want to see her hurting and it was at times like these, when he had something to offer, that he thought he might one day feel something stronger for her.

'What about you?' she asked. 'Do you want children?' The question, posed so innocently, made his breath turn airy and come out in light, shivering whispers.

'I never really thought about it,' he lied, taking a quick sip of the lukewarm wine. 'No, I don't think so.'

'I guess that won't be a problem for us then,' she teased lightly, but he stayed quiet and the wine clumped in his stomach, making him queasy.

He asked her again the next morning, just to make sure, and when she gave him the same answer, 'Yes, I'm positive. It's just not something I want or think I'll ever need,' he had almost laughed out loud at his outrageous luck.

So, made bolder by the fact that there would be no future obstacle in the form of his own child, he asked Marienne to marry him. Terrified she might meet someone who offered to give her what he could not, or even worse, that he would allow his doubts and conscience to creep in, he persuaded her to marry him within a few months of his proposal and she was more than happy to oblige. As James left the church with his new bride, he saw his parents look at each other and he knew they were thinking, *at least we still have our son.*

They moved into their first house within the next few weeks, the deposit being a guilty gift from Marienne's parents for not making the wedding.

'I don't know how they have any money left after all the fucking drugs they use.' It was the first time he had heard her speak that way.

The house was a pretty, off-white squarish structure that sat on the outskirts of town and as Marienne filled their home with matching plates and paintings and perfectly ironed sheets, James planted a sapling. A cherry-blossom tree, which in its prime would bend over the fence facing the street; it would grow to drop its folded flowers on passers-by, gently boasting the happiness contained within the four walls just beyond.

They settled quickly and easily into their roles as husband and wife and James found a job at one of the local tobacco companies as an assistant accountant. The title made him proud and he carried his business cards around in a small, silver case that Marienne had given him, always held in his breast pocket.

Marienne made friends almost instantly with the women living within the square. They flocked to her, this delicate, plump-lipped woman with no family except for a silent husband who looked more like a young boy. They offered to help her in any way they could and every day there would be another fresh-faced housewife, or a seasoned veteran in James's kitchen, teaching Marienne the tricks of their trade. He watched as she starched his shirts before washing them, used a solution of warm water and vinegar to remove the stains from the cotton and if that didn't work, she tore the shirts into strips and used them to scrub the walls and floors, reaching into places he assured her no one would ever look. They taught her how to make dishes guaranteed to 'drive him crazy' and, within a month of their marriage, James began to come home to the crisp scent of an apple pie or a cold bottle of beer as they waited for Marienne's meatloaf and garlic mashed potatoes. Her natural talent in the kitchen landed her on the weekly rotary of dinner parties held around the square and James would watch as she smiled and served her guests.

On their wedding night, as she had pressed close to him and slowly unbuttoned his shirt, he hadn't recoiled at the touch of her fingers. It wasn't difficult because she was small; tiny and straight and he just closed his eyes and pretended. Afterward, he couldn't look at her because she was slick and gleaming with fulfillment while his stomach ached with emptiness; it craved a release it hadn't quite reached and he felt something close to jealousy spark at his cheeks. He wanted so badly to feel a fraction of what she had felt in the moment after; to be real and present and sure in his own mind. But he cared about her and was guilty of not being in love with her, so he couldn't begrudge her this. It got easier over time, the horrible nothingness he felt, even as she pushed so close to him, they could have been the same person. After weeks spent watching her derive the kind of pleasure he ached for, he learned to steal a little bit of it, watching her face and movements closely, trying to recall what it felt like.

But he tried not to linger on things he couldn't have. He was lucky to have found her; to have a life that kept on growing and which every day, he found easier to fit into. A few weeks after they had moved into the neighborhood, they had a picnic in a nearby park to celebrate someone's birthday. He lay across the red-and-white checkered cloth, a beer in one hand and his wife tucked under the other, her body resting against the length of his. Discarded paper plates lay scattered all around him, with pieces of crumbling black forest cake, the icing melting and sticky in the sun. Half-empty glasses of wine balanced precariously on the grass, threatening to spill over at the slightest movement. Behind him, where the trees gave way to an open, flat space, some of the men had started up a football game.

'You coming or what, McDermott?' one of them had shouted.

'In a bit,' he had answered, not turning around, closing his eyes against the soft breeze that lifted his shirt off his back, cooling his skin. He inhaled the scent of his wife's hair; for as long as he had known her, she had always smelled lovely. 'I just want to stay here a moment longer.'

'You can stay as long as you want,' she had murmured and her words made her body purr. She held tightly to his elbows and pulled him tighter around her. He smiled, feeling her friends watching them; they always were. He knew how they must look to other people; he wasn't oblivious to how beautiful his wife was, nor to the amount of attention he was careful to pay her. He was always holding her hand or playing with the collar of her shirt, his guilt, still fresh, making him restless. Her friends were jealous, she would always say to him with a proud, little laugh. 'They never stop telling me how lucky I am.'

'And what do you think?' he would ask and she would stare at him, and sometimes her eyes would fill.

'I think they're right,' leaning in to kiss him. 'I don't know what I did to deserve you,' and that never ceased to make him sad.

'I think I'll go and play some football,' he had murmured to her that day at the picnic and she nodded her consent, pouting cutely.

'If you must,' and he slid his arms out from under her and stood up, tilting his head slightly forward at the ladies gathered around him.

'You don't have to go,' one of them, a pretty brunette, not much older than Marienne, had said.

'I'm leaving so you can all gossip about what a wonderful husband I am,' he had teased right back and they all giggled and he felt a wonderful surge in his chest. Winking one last time at his wife, he made his way over to the men.

'You sure do have a way with them,' George Comack said, throwing the ball hard at him. He caught it and it smacked loudly against his palm. 'My wife is always telling me to steal a page out of your book. I've never seen her so smitten.'

James laughed. 'I'm happy to give you any advice you need,' he had replied, throwing the ball back. Evening was tiptoeing in, the sun was glinting down through the trees and pretty soon it would be completely dark. 'Do we have enough time to play?' he had asked, squinting up at the sky.

'Five minutes and then we can all go back to my house,' George had answered. 'What do you say? This day has been too much fun for it to end so quickly.'

He stood, staring at this man; so ordinary, almost plain looking, but he had never felt so grateful to anyone. 'Agreed,' he said and jogged down the grass to take his position.

After that, it stopped feeling like he and Marienne were only children playing grown up, simply going through the motions of a married couple, hoping that eventually it would suit them. Like all things practiced, it soon started to feel like something natural and he couldn't remember what their lives had been like before it. And as the laughter and friendship continued to fill his house, lining its walls with a thick barrier of contentment, the fear which still stuck to his gut slowly dulled until the face of the tormented teenage boy he saw so often in his dreams was now only the face of a stranger he no longer cared to know.

13

Whitehorse, Yukon. September 1992

The day is difficult for me; I am not used to it being so full. Back home, I had started skipping classes, hiding out in the girls' bathroom, or if I could, leaving and going down to the cave, using my time how I wanted. There is no freedom here. Everything is planned out for me and I have no time to think about anything except what is taught to me. Algebra and English followed by an afternoon of Home Economics and Music; corridors full of noise that stop as soon as the girls enter the classrooms. Each lesson is taught by a different nun in the same manner; cold and abrupt. There are no lingering giggles, no whispering or note-passing. The girls sit with their legs and arms drawn close to their desks and speak softly and only when called upon. The rooms are kept cold and bare, with one or two posters pinned perfectly straight on the dark pin-up boards and a few other incentives such as 'Student of the Year' and a 'Gold Star Race' chart. I am given six new notebooks with crisp pages that make loud sounds when I turn them and come with a warning; *we do weekly inspections, so keep them neat and tidy.*

God is everywhere in this stone building—an overwhelming presence that some of the girls might find reassuring but I find suffocating. Every lesson begins and ends with a quick prayer and I am given a new Bible with a hard cover and soft, black writing. *You can read it if you want. We don't force anyone to do anything they don't want to do.* Yet, I still feel as if He is being quietly enforced on me, just as the team of voices this morning pushed the prayer onto me. I am told to memorize this prayer by tomorrow morning. *You don't want to start the day off on the wrong foot, do you, Frances?*

Judy has already been here for two years and, at sixteen, she takes me under her wing, speaking to me as one would to a younger sister. With her help, I fall into the routine grudgingly but without much trouble. Her quick chatter and constant, bent smile make me feel less alone and she doesn't mind how quiet I am or ask me any questions. She points out rooms and people and pictures, stating little facts about each that I forget as soon as we move on. She is a big girl with a loud presence and mostly everyone seems to know and like her.

At five o' clock, the classes end and the girls are allowed to do what they want. Mainly they just go back to their rooms, but Judy takes me outside, around the building, where we have to cross the field once more to get to a small pavilion.

'It was an old football stadium,' she tells me, which explains the bleachers that surround it, 'when this used to be a boys' school, but none of us are really interested in playing sports.' She jumps up onto a bench. 'So now we just use it to hang out. It's the one place the teachers don't really come to inspect. It's too far out for them.'

'This used to be a boys' school?'

'Up until fifteen years ago. Then Sister Margret took over,' she holds her hands out and laughs, 'and the rest, you can say, is history.' As she is talking, a group of girls is coming toward us.

'Oh look, it's the girls.' She cups her palms around her mouth. 'Hurry up, Frances is dying to meet you!'

'Hello, Frances,' the girls climb up all at once and the bleachers shake with the weight of them. *We saw you in class. Where you from, anyway? Is that your real hair?* So many questions are thrown at me that I simply stare at them in a daze. Six girls all looking at me with interest and I start to think that it felt better to be ignored.

'Of course it's her real hair you idiot,' Judy gives it a hard tug and I cry out. 'Oh, sorry.'

'It's fine,' I murmur, massaging my head and trying to suppress the annoyance I feel.

'She's just jealous of it because she has none,' a drawling voice comes from behind us and we all turn to see a tall shadow coming in from the back entrance. When the girl steps into our sight, I see that she walks with a slight, natural swing of her hips and even the uniform, shapeless as it is, complements her curvaceous body. Her face is full and round, a stark contrast to her lithe body, but I think it's charming.

Judy pats her hair and I see her smile disappear for the first time that day.

'What do you want, Victoria?'

'You don't own this space, do you?' she asks and when Judy is silent, she smirks. 'No, I didn't think so.' She holds out her hand to me and her fingers are full of rings and a multitude of colorful bracelets twist around her wrist. 'I'm Victoria.'

Before I have a chance to answer, Judy interrupts. 'On your way to meet Leo, are you?' she asks.

Victoria turns to her. 'What would you know about it?'

'Word gets around,' Judy retorts. 'You better be careful; you know what would happen if Sister Margret found out.'

Black wavy hair is tossed over a shoulder, red lips curl into a snarl but then relax into an almost smile. 'See you around, new girl,' Victoria calls over her shoulder as she saunters out and disappears, and I feel sorry that she has gone.

'Stay away from that one,' Judy says and all the other girls consent with a burst of murmurs and I am too afraid of being thrown out of this new group to admit that there was something about her that I liked.

By the end of the day, at dinner, I cannot stop thinking about him. He has been on my mind all day; and I remember him in small pieces. His long, sharp nose. The natural, clean-cut of his eyebrows and how he used to raise them playfully at me across the table when I was younger and everything was perfect. After I have finished eating, I am desperate to talk to him.

Sister Ann is on dinner duty again today and I wait for all the girls to leave before approaching her. She smiles when she sees me coming.

'Hello, Frances.'

'Hi.' I slide in opposite her.

'How was your day?' she asks. 'Are you settling in okay? I know it can be a little hard.'

I nod. 'I'm okay, thanks.'

'Can I help you with something?'

'I was just wondering if I could call my father—it's just that I haven't spoken to him since I've been here and I just want to let him know that I'm okay.' I've been practicing the words in my head, worried she might sense something strange in my obvious desperation; that she might say no and that would be even worse.

'I'm sorry, Frances, but phone hours aren't until next week.'

'Phone hours?'

'Yes. Phone hours are every Monday, between the last class of the day and dinnertime. You can call your parents then.'

'No one told me about phone hours.' She can see how upset I am and starts to apologize but I interrupt her. 'I just want to let them know that I'm okay.'

'They already know,' she says. 'I spoke to your father last night.'

My face clenches. Everything stops moving in me; even my blood seems to pause. 'Why didn't you tell me?' I lean forward and my voice rises. 'You could have called me down—I wanted to speak to him.'

'I'm sorry. I thought you were tired from your journey and I wanted to let you sleep.'

'So I can't call him today?'

'No, I'm afraid not.'

'Tomorrow, then?'

'Not until next week, Frances.' She starts to get up. 'It's almost six forty-five—you have to start your homework.'

I stand up and push the chair back so hard that it almost falls over. 'What if I told you it was an emergency?'

'The phone is in Sister Margret's office and it's locked now.' She has turned firm and her easy features take on a stern edge. 'Like I said, you can talk to your parents next week.'

I don't wait for her to finish, I turn around to rush into the empty hallway. At the door, I almost bump into a girl bending over the bucket and she straightens up, throwing her long hair back over her shoulder.

'Whoa.' It's Victoria. She is grinning down at me as she twists the bracelets around her hand. 'Phone hours,' she pats me sympathetically on the shoulder, 'what a pain in the ass, huh?' and then she throws her plate down and goes slowly up the stairs, leaving me to my loneliness.

After homework is done, the group of girls I met earlier in the pavilion allow themselves into my room. They don't knock; they simply place themselves anywhere there is space. Someone comes to sit by me on my bed, patting my knee and smiling. Another girl sprawls, stomach down, on the carpet and one even pushes my books to the side and perches herself on my desk, swinging her legs back and forth.

'That algebra was a nightmare,' she says. 'I had to copy most of it from Amanda.'

The black-haired girl on the floor twists her bubblegum around her finger and then pulls it in between her teeth. 'We're totally going to get caught, you know that right?'

'Who cares, it's just Sister Bea anyway.' She turns to me, unaware that the edge of my book is being folded underneath her. 'You're not going to tell, right?' she asks.

'Come on, Dee, of course she won't.' Judy smiles at me from across the room. 'She's our friend now, right Fran?'

I don't like the way she shortens my name without asking; it's what he calls me and it sounds almost like a threat from her.

'Frances,' I correct her.

'Of course.' Her voice stays level but her eyebrows rise in quick surprise.

'And no,' I say, softening my tone and trying to smile. I should be happy to be surrounded by these girls, after what happened at my old school. But there is something suffocating about being with them, and my chest feels heavy and homesick. 'I'm not going to tell on you.'

'I might.' We turn to see Victoria leaning against the doorframe, legs crossed at the ankles. She is examining her fingernails and she glances up quickly at me and winks. 'What a naughty girl, cheating on her homework.' Her laugh is loud and condescending and the girls prickle around me.

'What do you want, Victoria?' Judy asks. 'I don't remember anyone inviting you.'

'Actually, I came to speak to the new girl,' she replies. She looks at me and tilts her head toward the corridor, slowly swiveling her body around. 'Want to come out here for a moment?'

'She doesn't want to speak to you.' Judy looks annoyed.

'It's fine,' I say quickly. I try not to smile as I step over Amanda and close the door behind me. When it's fully shut, I lean against it and blow out an exasperated breath.

'Exhausting, isn't it?' Victoria says and her face looks softer than before, pretty.

'What?'

'Being around Little Miss Priss.'

'Kind of.' There is something about her that inspires trust and we giggle together.

'I should know. When I first got here, we were best friends—did everything together. But two years around her has driven me crazy.' She clears her throat. 'Anyway, you got a boyfriend or what?'

'Excuse me?'

'Earlier,' she waves her hand impatiently in the air. 'I saw how desperate you were to use the phone.'

'Right.' I shake my head. 'No, actually, I wanted to talk to my father.'

'Your father?' her forehead wrinkles and I realize my mistake too late.

'I'm just kidding.' I force out a laugh, trying to cover up, but something uncomfortable sticks in my throat and makes my cheeks burn. 'A boyfriend,' I speak in a rush, almost a babble.

'What's his name?'

'Tom.' It comes to me almost immediately and I'm a little taken aback at how easy it is to lie.

'Cute?'

'Gorgeous.' I think of that angular face, perfect in its proportions, the way two of my hands fit into one of his.

'There's a way, you know,' she lowers her voice.

'A way to what?'

'We're not far from the main street. You could easily sneak out and go use a payphone or something.'

My palms start sweating with excitement. 'Don't they lock all the doors?'

'There's a window, in the library,' she explains, 'that leads out onto the veranda. Just climb out from there.'

'Have you done it before?' I ask.

She laughs and straightens up, her voice loud again. 'I don't know you all that well yet, new girl.' She squints. 'What's your name, anyway?'

'Frances.'

'Well, Frances, I'm just saying, if you want,' she shrugs, raises an eyebrow and starts down the hallway, 'there's a way. Just be careful not to get caught.' And she gives a small wave before going back into her room.

The encounter with Victoria leaves me lightheaded and grinning, though I'm not entirely sure whether it's because of the facts she has just given me or if there was something about her smile, so inviting and friendly, that makes me almost giddy.

When I get back to the room, everyone is quiet and staring at me.

'What did she say?' Judy asks and her voice takes over the room, demanding.

'Nothing,' I answer, sliding back onto my bed. *It's none of your business,* I want to add but don't. Instead, I lean back against my bed frame and ignore all the curious looks until they turn away from me and go onto a different subject. They stay in the room for over an hour but I don't pay attention to them, not even when Judy pointedly tries to add me into the conversation by asking what it was like to go to a co-ed school.

'I wouldn't get anything done,' Amanda had giggled and I stared blankly at them.

'It wasn't that exciting,' I said, and turned back to my racing mind. The thought of being able to speak to him makes me fidgety. I almost tear my blankets to shreds.

'You really should make more of an effort, you know,' Judy says to me once the girls are gone. 'I was trying hard to include you.'

'I'm sorry,' I say. 'It's just taking a while to get used to everyone, that's all.'

'Just remember, you're going to be here for quite a while.' She climbs into bed and places the Bible in her lap. 'So be careful who you mix with.'

14

St Albert. January 1976

The restlessness crept into their lives, swollen and rude. It occupied all of the space in their kitchen, forcing Marienne to pace the corners of the linoleum floor as she waited for the steamy whistle of the kettle or the snap of oil from a burning pan. It fitted itself comfortably into their private life, pushing her from the bed in the middle of the night. James would slide out with her and wait as she straightened out the sheets, pulling the duvet over and tucking it roughly into the corners of their mattress. He would look at her; she would stare at him until he fell back into bed with turned shoulders, pretending not to feel the butterfly touch of her fingers and tongue. He knew what she wanted; had known it ever since fat and shiny Lynette Waters invited herself into their home. James had stood, tense and wary against a neglected enemy, hardly daring to watch as Lynn lowered herself hugely onto their divan. 'Oh!' the sofa sinking softly beneath her, 'my poor ankles!' smiling up at him, happily massaging her bloated calves. James grunted a reply into his beer can and avoided Marienne's warning glances. He watched from a safe distance as his wife tucked her feet under her knees, leaning down to press her ear against her friend's belly, smiling to hear the gentle, teasing murmur of life.

'How does it feel?' Marienne asked.

Lynn looked at him and smiled. 'Why don't the two of you find out for yourselves? It's about time, don't you think?'

When James looked over at Marienne, it was with a wry smile that made it clear he thought Lynn was joking. He blinked in surprise at the look in Marienne's eyes. She was looking longingly from him to the bump under her traveling hand. His chest constricted. In the two years they had been married, they had never brought up the subject of having children. Even in the past six months, when it seemed that everyone they knew were starting their own families, Marienne had never approached him with the idea nor even hinted at it being something she was thinking about. So when Lynn's drawling voice and motherly glow were gone, leaving a dark, hopeful seed to germinate in their wake, deep and strong in the organs of his wife, James was dismayed to find Marienne bent over a dirty teacup, her hand caught beneath her shirt, absently stroking her stomach.

When he reminded her of her vow never to have children, she told him she hadn't expected her body to change her mind. It was widening, she said, creating space for a family. All it needed was something to fill it.

'Imagine,' she whispered to him one night as they lay close together; having her in his bed had become a needed comfort and now he slept with his body curled around hers, pulling her close into the curving arch of his stomach. 'It'll be all ours, James. Just imagine.'

He asked her to wait, trying to keep the rising panic from his voice, hoping that she would remember he had been enough for her once. He pretended to keep busy at work. A promotion had moved him into his own office, allowing him to stay in the building long after most of its lights had blinked off. Sometimes, he would catch his broken reflection in the window, tracking it as it blended into black trees, moving quick and low between slanted roofs; coming back closer and more unclear than before.

At times like these, he would allow himself to think of what it would be like to give Marienne what she wanted. Although he had been happily married for two years, that stirring need inside him had not vanished and he felt it yawning now, rousing to the sound of his friends' expanding families. He found these new babies to be a cruel invasion into the small, easy world he had built for himself; a reminder that no matter where he went, there was something inside of him that would always follow.

When Lynn finally had her baby, Marienne had insisted they go over to congratulate her. He had hovered over the clean lawn, his finger barely on the bell. He was glad it was dark so that Marienne couldn't see the expression on his face. She pushed his finger aside and pressed down hard on the bell. When no one answered, the sound of his heart racing with relief made his head ache.

'Maybe they're not home,' he suggested hopefully. 'You can come back another time.'

'She said they would be here when I called.' Marienne frowned and when she tried the door, it swung open.

'We can't just walk in,' he snapped.

'I can hear voices,' she said. 'Come on. There must be other people already here.' When she took his hand, he wanted to pull away but at the same time, grasped her fingers tightly. The foyer was clean and empty.

'What did I tell you?' he tugged at her elbow. He felt like a sulky child; he almost stomped his feet and wanted to carry her out of there. 'Come back during the week.'

'Hello?' Marienne called, ignoring him.

'Marienne.' His heart sank when Lynn's voice came from around the corner. 'We're in the living room, come on in.' A sound flushed with joy.

Marienne followed the noise, leaving him standing alone near the messy rows of discarded shoes and an overnight bag she must have taken to the hospital. A series of *oohs* and *aahs* and *he's so beautiful,* slipped out from under the door Marienne had opened, and she must have been holding the baby because the crying started up almost immediately, sharp and sweet and taking him by surprise. It broke something open in him; an idea, a long-lost dream of a beautiful family filled with pink ribbons and bicycles dropped carelessly by the porch steps; running laughter and small, excited bodies that never stopped moving. A soft hand he could put his lips to. Fleshy cheeks that would be hot and sweet beneath his fingers. He tried to take a step; backward, forward, anywhere, but the sound and its images held him firmly in place and all he could do was clench his fists and breathe. He heard Marienne calling for him.

'James? I swear he was just behind me,' he heard her say before turning around and rushing out of the door, walking hard and straight for the pink shadow of his tree, welcoming him home safe.

When Marienne got home an hour later, she stood at the door of their bedroom, her arms crossed and waiting for an explanation. She wasn't angry; he didn't act that way often enough for her to be upset.

'I don't want to talk about it,' he said, his voice muffled by the pillow. He was on his stomach, the blanket pulled up to his chin.

'I don't know why you're so upset,' she said, slowly undressing and padding over to the bed, clicking on the bedside lamp. He shut his eyes tighter against the glare of it. 'I'm only asking you to try. That's all I want.'

He bunched himself up on his side of the bed. She touched his shoulder but he shrugged it away. 'Please, not now.' He felt like crying; not out of fear but because he felt alone. Desperate. He thought of how unfair it was that he should be denied something he needed—and resented Marienne for her easy life and simple feelings and for all the things being with her meant he could never have.

So he knew it could never be done; he couldn't give Marienne what she wanted without ruining everything else. It made him sad and angry to realize how little choice he had in the matter. He tried to distract her by taking her into the city; hoping to drive some of the impatience from her eyes with the thrill of young life; the promise of a marriage filled with a certain kind of freedom—to do what they wanted whenever they wanted to do it. Chocolates, earrings and bracelets twisted into necklaces, countless hours spent kissing and loving her so she wouldn't have to think of the space flourishing inside her, tightly waiting.

But she didn't want those things anymore. When they would come home after a night out, his mind buzzing with city life and a few glasses of scotch, she would carefully navigate her way around his body, undoing his shirt and pulling down his trousers. He often got lost in her movements because that was when she came back to him as the girl he had married; easily pleased and dependent on him for something. But as soon as she pushed herself on him, he sobered up instantly and pushed her away.

'I'm tired.'

'You didn't seem it fifteen minutes ago.' There was a whiny edge to her voice he had never heard before, loaded with a disappointment fully aimed at him.

'I'm sorry. Maybe tomorrow.'

He was afraid to touch her; certain she had a trick up her sleeve to get pregnant. He had seen her talking to Melissa Comack and that was how she had done it—by getting her husband blind drunk and then climbing on top of him when he couldn't think fast enough to stop her. That was the story anyway, as told by George during one of the barbeques, while the wives were in the kitchen and the men gathered in James's living room. George sat, miserable and tired, with his wife shouting at him from the other room, asking if he had remembered to pick up the diapers from the store.

'You can't trust them,' he had said, flicking the edge of his glass with his forefinger and thumb. 'Even after you've been married to them for years, they still do exactly what they want without even considering you.'

'But now you have a son, surely you've forgiven her?' James had asked.

'I love my boy, don't get me wrong,' said George, swirling his drink in his glass, taking a long and final sip. 'It's the wife I'm not sure about anymore.'

The paranoia that had been instilled in James from that conversation made him vigilant against his wife. Whenever she spoke to him, touched him, he would flinch away, terrified that this was some game she was playing, manipulating him into giving her what she wanted. The less they touched, the more they refused to communicate what was really troubling them, and the further they drove each other away until one day, he sat down at his kitchen table and hardly recognized the hopeless, worn-out woman in front of him. When he came home one night to find her crying in the bathroom, squeezed into the small space between the bathtub and the toilet, he made one final and desperate attempt to save them.

15

Whitehorse, Yukon. September 1992

I lie on my back and trace my fingers against the low ceiling. I can hear Judy breathing; soft, girlish snores that won't let me sleep. My finger pricks against a splinter and a hurried pain runs down my arm and settles around my face, relaxing it just a little. I try to think of him but he has already become unclear and the hazy image I have only makes me feel worse. I hold onto a pillow, my arms grasping at its softness, but its weight is all wrong.

Getting up slowly, I maneuver around the desks until I am pushed up against the cold window pane. I put my forehead to it and my breath lets out, steaming up the glass. My fingers move against it and write his name in the circle of heat. Slowly, I open the window and it creaks. Judy is still snoring, having turned on her stomach, her face buried in her pillow and away from me. I push at the window until it's almost fully opened and then I lean out. The air is sleepy and warm. Sounds like crickets and a dog somewhere far off are coming into the room, causing Judy to shift in her sleep and I know that soon the noise will wake her up. I make one final sweep of the field, just a hard, black carpet of neatly trimmed grass, and I'm satisfied there is no one around. I close the window and climb back into bed, waiting for her to settle down again into the irregular pattern of her dreams.

Then, without allowing myself to dwell on my plan, I take off my pajamas and dress back into my uniform. I pull the thin sweater around my shoulders and push my pillow into my bed, tucking the blanket around it so that in the dark, and in a sleepy state, it could be mistaken for me. I slip out of the room and tip-toe down the hall.

The house is asleep but I feel the floor waking up beneath my feet as I go down the stairs, hearing them strain and creak behind me. It's almost completely dark except for a small light in the foyer. I pass through, open a door on the right and find that I am in the library. Shelves line the walls, spreading across the floor and grazing the top of the paneled roof. They are packed full of books, whose natural smell fills the room. I walk through the narrow spaces of the desks, following a path lit up by a hint of moonlight coming through the curtainless window that faces onto the veranda. It's heavy and difficult to open, making the house groan with the weight of it. At first, my heart drops and I think that Victoria has tricked me into this; that it is just a cruel joke, but then with a sudden click, it pushes outward. I don't want the noise to wake anyone, so I squeeze myself out through the thin space, balancing carefully on the ledge and sliding down, one leg at a time, onto the wooden floor of the veranda. I stay crouched against the wall until I'm sure no one has heard me and it's all quiet. When I start moving again, I don't stop.

It feels good to be outside. The late summer air is cool against my cheek; a relief from the stifling atmosphere of the Academy. I walk quickly. Judy might wake up at any moment and, seeing me gone, tell someone. I reach the perimeter of the building and stop. Victoria never mentioned the gate; iron and tall, it surrounds the entire space of the Academy and it's locked. But now that I'm here, I cannot let this stop me. I wrap my hands around the metal, feeling it dig pleasantly into my skin. I push myself upward over the fence and my ankles burn for some time after I reach the ground. I need to hear his voice. Even just a breath would be enough. I jog down the winding track, until I come out at the main street, but even that is deserted. I hadn't realized how secluded the Academy was, tucked into its own little space, away from houses and other people; a masquerading prison. I keep walking straight and watch the road stretch invisibly and forever in front of me, wishing I had asked Victoria for specific directions. I look for the twinkle of lights, a payphone, or even a bus-stop—anything that will bring me closer to him.

I look back and can no longer see anything I recognize. The darkness is still full and pressing; I am not getting any closer to any houses. I know it's hopeless. Eventually, I will have no choice but to turn around and go back to the school, but still, I keep on walking. Every time I come to a change in the road, a dip, a small bend, my heart lifts and I think that soon I will talk to him and stop feeling empty.

I hear a low rumbling and see a silver-blue car pulling up toward me. I slow my pace so that it will get to me faster and stretch out my hand, signaling for it to stop. I don't know what I will do once I am beside it, but I wave my hand and even shout, hoping it won't miss me. The window rolls down and Joseph is leaning out, one hand on the wheel, eyes straining in the dark.

'Are you lost?'

My first instinct is to stay hidden in the shadows, to turn and run, but the idea of a week stretching out ahead of me without speaking to him, forces me into the golden glare of the streetlight.

'Frances?' his eyebrows rise in mild surprise. 'What are you doing here?' When I don't answer, he pushes open the passenger door. 'Come on, get in.' He waits until I have settled down before speaking again. 'What are you doing out here?' he repeats. I don't answer, so he continues. 'Does anyone know that you've left?'

'No.'

He starts the car. 'Let me take you back, then.'

'No—wait.' The car is still running beneath us, purring and moving through my legs in insistent waves. 'I just need to make a phone call first.'

He laughs. He thinks I am joking—perhaps delirious from walking the empty streets half-asleep. He stops when I keep looking at him and my face doesn't change.

'And why couldn't you have done that in school?'

'Phone hours are over.'

'Well then, maybe you can make that phone call tomorrow?'

'It's only once a week and I need to do it now.'

He turns off the car and allows me to sink deeper into the seat, giving himself time to think.

'And who do you need to talk to so badly that you're wandering around alone at eleven o'clock at night in a place that you barely know?'

I consider lying then change my mind. 'My father.'

'You really shouldn't be out here alone like this.' He tilts his head slightly toward me. 'I'm sure if you ask at the school, they can make an exception.'

'I have and they won't. I just need to speak to him today—please.'

'You won't find a phone anywhere around here, Frances.'

'Then take me to your house.'

My bluntness shocks him and this pleases me. I want to stay in his car, surrounded by the tired smell of leather and artificial heat. I want to talk to my father and now that I have this chance, I refuse to let it slip away so easily.

'I don't think that's a very good idea.'

'Please. It'll only be for five minutes—I promise, I'll be quick.'

'Okay. But only because I live just ten minutes down the road and if I drop you back you'll probably just sneak out again.'

'Thank you.' The words speed out of my mouth before he has a chance to change his mind.

We start to move and that is when it occurs to me; he remembers who I am. He hasn't forgotten my name and the realization makes me grow hot, my smile steaming up the already clouded car.

His house is warm and full of noise. He lets me in and I can hear a child shouting, and rising above it, the laughter of a woman. *Go on. Look who's finally home.*

A young boy runs down the cluttered corridor and Joseph is ready for him—arms open wide to catch him and throw him squealing into the air.

'Hello, Alex.'

I stand pressed against the piles of discarded shoes and some toys and I watch as he covers the boy's face in playful kisses before setting him back down again. Alex starts to run off but Joseph grabs him lightly by the shirt and tugs him back. 'Aren't you going to say hello to our guest?' Dark eyes look up at me from behind Joseph's thigh. I stare back, equally afraid. Joseph places a hand on Alex's head and pushes him forward. 'Come on, now. Where are your manners?'

'Hello.' The way he smiles makes me certain that he is Joseph's son. Identical, small white teeth. The brazen stretch of his lips as if his face doesn't know how to be any other way.

'Hi.' I look up at Joseph but he isn't looking back at me. He is holding his son by the neck and grinning down at him, eyebrow cocked and a glow in his cheeks. I hadn't expected him to have a family and I don't want to be here anymore.

'What are you doing up so late, anyway?' he asks his son.

'The new babysitter just left,' a woman comes out behind me and I sink further into the coats. 'She said she had trouble putting him to sleep and I just got home.' There is a crossness in her voice but she is still smiling. 'He said he was waiting for you. He wanted to show you what he drew in school today.'

'Is that right?'

The boy nods proudly and holds up a crudely drawn picture, crumpled in his small fist. Joseph takes it and unfolds it.

'Genius!' he exclaims loudly even before it's fully opened, tickling his son until the boy is on his knees, laughing and trying to get away. Clearly, he has been waiting for this all night. 'This is absolutely genius!'

I can't make out the picture but I spend time looking at it anyway, the sticky crayon lines, so that I don't have to think about how sad I suddenly am.

'And who might this be?' the woman asks. Joseph walks over to her and kisses her lightly on the mouth.

'This is Frances. She just joined the Academy.' His wife gives him a quick look which he responds to with a reassuring grin.

'Hello, Frances. I'm Nova.'

'Hi.' What am I doing here, on one side of the corridor, faced with this happy family? I feel more miserable than ever.

'She just needed to use our phone,' Joseph says. He is moving back into a room and gesturing for me to follow, so I do, treading wearily, as if the ground is filled with hidden traps.

I go into a small room where the blue glow of the television burns my eyes and I can hardly make out Joseph's outline near the steep staircase. When I reach him, he clicks on a small table lamp and hands me the receiver, telling me he is going into the kitchen.

'Take your time,' he says and leaves me in the quiet darkness, the sounds of their family coming through the door and pricking my chest.

'Hello, darling.'

She is supposed to be at work. I check the clock hanging on the wall above the phone to make sure I have the time right. She comes in throaty waves through the receiver. I had been so sure he would pick up and an acute eagerness moves in me, making me shake so that I have to hold the phone with both hands. When she answers instead, I snap at her.

'I thought you were supposed to be at work.' It doesn't matter how this makes her feel. I want to speak to him.

'I have the night off. It's Wednesday, remember?' Her tone recoils, injured, but she carries on talking. 'How are you, sweetheart?'

'I hate it here.' And surrounded by this sudden disappointment and the cheerfulness in the other room, I really do hate it. 'I hate you for sending me here.'

'Frances—'

'How could you do this to me?' My voice is rising and I don't try to lower it. I let it carry up everything. 'Do you have any idea what it's like here? What I'm going through? I hope you're happy.' I start to cry somewhere in the middle. 'Please, let me come home.'

I picture him sitting in that favorite chair of his, glasses resting on the bridge of his nose, chewing thoughtfully on a pencil as he attempts to do a crossword. Every so often, his eyes will rise from the page and he will smile at me and we will think of our secret, but I am missing all of it. 'I promise, I'll be good. I can't stand it here anymore.' She stays silent and I give it one last fight. 'Please, Mom.'

She sucks in her breath and the word hovers between us, growing larger the longer our silence extends. *Mom*. I know she can't remember the last time I called her that because I don't remember it myself.

'I'm sorry, Frances, but I can't do that,' she says. 'You have to trust me—we know what's best for you. Besides, your tuition has already been paid for the year.' The finality in her tone stops my tears.

'Just give him the phone. I don't want to talk to you anymore—I don't want to talk to you ever again.' I am sure that I can convince him; that he misses me just as much as I miss him and he will come and get me if I ask him to. I imagine him coming through these doors and sweeping me, laughingly, into his arms, just as Joseph did with Alex. *Hello my best girl. I've missed you.*

'He's not here.'

My heart falls, drops down and leaves a crater in my chest. 'Don't lie to me.'

'I'm not. He's gone round to one of the neighbor's houses.'

'Well can you go and get him? I'm sure he wants to speak to me.'

'How about I tell him to call you tomorrow?'

'Don't bother,' I say and drop the receiver back onto the cradle without saying goodbye.

I sit on the carpeted stairs, drained and listening to the now quiet sounds coming from outside the room. I can't hear what they're saying and when I step outside, I see Joseph and Nova standing in the corridor and they stop talking when they see me.

'Did you speak to him?' Joseph asks. I nod but don't reply because the only thing that will come out is a resigned sadness. They look at each other:

'Would you like something to eat? Some tea, maybe?' asks Nova. My stomach is packed with anger but I don't want to go back to the Academy just yet.

'Yes, please.'

Their kitchen is small but clean and there is already water boiling on the stove. I can hear the soft bubbling of it, rising above the slim orange flame. I sit down at their table and my knees come up right to the edge of it. It is a table made for children and pretend tea-parties. Joseph has to sit sideways, his legs extended outward and crossed at the ankles. Alex climbs into his lap.

'You should be in bed now, young man,' Nova says from the stove and the boy smiles sleepily at her.

'What's ten more minutes?' Joseph winks down at his son, stroking his forehead.

'Here you go.' Nova puts down three mugs of tea and goes back to the cupboard for a plate of cookies. She sits down and stares at me over the dim lights. She is a tall woman, with strong shoulders and sloping, almond eyes. In the darkness, with her jutting cheek-bones and graceful limbs, she looks more like a feline; an animal protecting her territory. She takes Joseph's hand and holds it in her own. Their fingers come together effortlessly, as if his hand has been molded especially for hers to sit in.

'Have one,' he says, pushing the plate toward me. 'Oatmeal and raisin—Nova's special recipe.' It is soft and perfectly crumbly and I chew down on the sticky pieces of fruit, pulling them apart between my teeth. My leg stretches out and accidentally grazes Joseph's. She can't see what I am doing and I let my knee sit there, barely resting against him.

'So where are you from?' Nova asks.

'St Albert.' The tea is sweet and milky; just like a mother should make it. I drink most of it in a few gulps.

'What are you doing all the way here?' She speaks softly, in a friendly tone. Politely curious.

'I came for school,' I say.

'Surely they have schools in St Albert,' she says.

'Nova, stop interrogating the girl.'

She looks at Joseph and then gets up, asking if I would like some more tea.

'Yes, please.'

She pours Joseph and me some more tea before picking up Alex. He opens his eyes and then falls straight back asleep. 'I'll go and put him to bed.' She leans down to kiss Joseph, then whispers something in his ear that he nods at. His hand lingers on hers at his shoulder and then lets it go at the last minute, only when he has to. 'Goodnight, Frances. Good luck with school.'

I thank her again for the tea and then it's just the two of us. There is no more talking; all I hear is the quiet crunching of biscuit in his mouth and all I see are the taut muscles in his cheek working as he chews. I drink slowly to prolong my leaving, and pick the crumbs off my skirt and put them in my mouth. When he is finished, he pushes his mug away from him.

'So was it nice to talk to your father?'

I nod. 'Yes.' I think of him at one of the neighbor's houses, not knowing how sad I am or how much I want him; how angry he will be with my mother when he comes home and finds out that I have called.

'I'm sure he misses you very much,' Joseph says. I press my leg further into his and this time he notices my weight and shifts away from it. I follow him without knowing why, so now our toes are touching. 'Is this your first time away from home?'

I chew down on a cookie, only half-swallowing so that some of it lodges in my throat and blocks off my tears. 'Yes.' I finish the tea and let the last sip sit in my mouth and burn my gums.

'Frances, you know that I'm going to have to let the Academy know what happened tonight.'

'Why?' I pull my leg away. I know she has told him to say this. This is what they were talking about in the hallway.

'It's my responsibility. And if anyone was to ever find out and I haven't said anything—'

'They won't. I'll keep it a secret.'

'I can't take that risk. I'm sorry, but I have to let them know.' He pats my hand. 'Don't worry, you won't be in any trouble.'

It occurs to me then that perhaps I will be. Maybe they'll kick me out and my mother will have no choice but to let me come back home.

'Okay.' I try to look sorry. 'That's okay, I understand.'

'I knew you would.' He stands up and ruffles my hair, as if he has been doing it my entire life. 'Come on, I'll drive you back.'

I watch the road speed by, picking up signs and cues that I might need should I ever want to come to his house again. A broken streetlight. A pub with a loose sign hanging outside; the picture of a rearing black horse swinging in the night wind. *The Barn.* Around the bend and climbing up a steep hill that will be easy to run down. It doesn't take us long to get back to the school and he parks the car, looking up at the locked gate.

'How will you get back in?' he wonders out loud.

'The same way I got out,' I answer.

He turns to me and laughs. 'And how is that, exactly?'

'I climbed the fence.'

He turns serious. 'I'm not letting you do that.' He starts to get out of the car. 'I'm going to get someone.'

'No, please. Just wait until tomorrow before you tell anyone.'

He stares at me, pauses, and sighs. 'Alright. I'll help you.'

We stand at the edge of the iron fence and he blows in his hands and rubs them together. 'Come on, then.'

I start to climb but freeze when I feel his hands on me.

'What's the matter?' he asks. 'Are you scared? I can still go and get someone to open the gate.'

I shake my head, but all of a sudden I am afraid and I don't think that my legs will help me because my muscles have turned to liquid. I step down and then feel too light, like I'm falling, when his hands leave me. He snaps his fingers.

'Hold on a second.' He goes back to the car and fumbles for something in the glove compartment. He pulls out a set of keys and grins like a boy who has found treasure. 'Can you believe it—I forgot I had these?' We walk over to the gate and he tries a few keys before finding the right one and we hear it slide and click into place. He keeps up a constant chatter, maybe to make up for my sudden silence or because he is afraid that he is doing the wrong thing. 'They gave them to me a month back when I had to bring someone in late at night. I haven't used them since.'

The gate stands wide open between us and he looks up at the building, his arm loped around one of the spikes. 'How are you going to get back in?'

'I'm going to go through the library window.'

He stares down at me. 'And I'm going to pretend I never asked you that.'

I don't want to leave him but it's late, although he is too polite to rush me. I start to walk through the gate but he catches my wrist and kneels down beside me so that our faces are almost level.

'Hang on,' he says. 'I don't want to see you walking down these streets alone again. You need something, ask. I'm here to help.'

And then suddenly, my arms are around his neck and I am hugging him, feeling the bones beneath his shirt. He laughs quietly and gives me a formal pat on the back, trying to move away, but I won't let him go. I press my face into his neck, craving the physical contact of someone else. 'Frances—' I don't hear him. My lips open up against his skin and I feel it on my tongue, the sharp taste of salt. 'Frances—what are you doing?' He struggles backward and his face has changed. It is no longer relaxed but creased with shock. His smile has gone but his eyes are still kind. I look up at him for a moment and when he opens his mouth to say something, I start to run. He doesn't shout after me but I feel him looking until I am lost in the darkness and he can't see me anymore.

16

St Albert. March 1976

The colors of Stolleri Hospital were red, purple and yellow; a smiling building that was dimly lit and cold inside. The vast foyer filled him with an inexplicable sadness, so complete that he wondered if it had been growing inside him all this time and he had just failed to notice. It wasn't because of the sickness that hung in the air, smelling of cheap disinfectant. It wasn't even because he had slipped out of his house early that morning without telling his wife where he was going, what he was planning on doing. It was because he saw, near the glass entrance, just beyond the stretch of morning light, a man sitting on a concrete bench facing the parking lot. His son was standing in between his knees, gently tilted against his chest. The boy's waves were gathered in his father's fist, held loosely at the base of his neck as if it were the most natural position to be in. This innocent display of love, ordinary to everyone except him, made James ache in a way he never had; somewhere deeper and more painful—a pinch he couldn't locate and whose evasiveness only made it seem larger.

He had taken fatherhood for granted when he was younger. It was something he had convinced himself he could do without in his early twenties. But now, knowing the finality of what might happen in the doctor's office, he was tempted to call Marienne and tell her just how much he wished they could have a baby.

'Mr. McDermott?' A nurse stood above him, holding a clipboard to her starched, uniformed chest.

'Yes?'

'Follow me, please.' As he got up, he looked around quickly, sure that the people sitting near him could sense the selfish cruelty of the simple action of moving from his chair to the closed, tinted doors of the doctor's room. The office smelled of furniture polish and a sweet, aniseed smell he couldn't quite place, a welcome change from the cold cleanness of the waiting area. When the doctor heard them enter, he held his arm toward the seat in front of him.

'Sit, sit,' he said. 'Please do have a seat.' He reached for the nurse's clipboard and she left them, closing the door behind her and letting it shut with a loud click. James ran his tongue over his lips, facing the small, shifty-eyed doctor who was staring at him, waiting patiently.

'I—' James started but didn't know how to finish.

'You called in to ask about the vasectomy, didn't you?' The word was weightless in the doctor's mouth. It rolled off, unforced and pleasant, as if he were talking about something easy and inconsequential—a decision most men made without consulting their wives. He realized then that he was the spouse George had warned him against; he was exactly like Melissa.

'Yes.'

'Right, right.' The doctor spoke in a quick, mumbling tone and James had to lean in closer, pressing his hands to the oak desk that seemed too large for the other furniture; a giant stranger in the room.

'I only wanted to know what the procedure involves.'

'Well, it's a very straightforward operation. In fact, I often do it in here.' The doctor gestured around the cramped room. 'It should only take about forty minutes.'

Forty minutes could be a meeting. It could be time spent stuck in conversation with someone he had met on the way home. Forty minutes could be covered up, painted over, easily lied about.

'And the recovery?'

'Well, it's usually about a two-day recovery period. Three days at the most and there won't be that much pain but you'll have to take it easy for a while.'

'And will there be any scarring?' He got right to the point.

'A small one.' And then, as if he knew exactly what James was thinking, the doctor said, 'But you won't be able to notice it unless you know it's there.'

James leaned back against his chair. It seemed to be the perfect solution; quickly done and even quicker to forget. She would never know and wouldn't blame him anymore for not trying. Yet just as he was about to say, 'That's great, when can I book an appointment?' the words hid from him, getting lost somewhere in the forest of other words and thoughts that stuck in his throat. The doctor watched James carefully, his fingers forming a pyramid under his chin.

'Before you decide whether or not you want to go through with this, I'm going to have to ask you a few questions.' The friendly tone was gone, disappearing into a slow seriousness.

'What kind of questions?'

'Mr. McDermott, do you understand that this surgery is irreversible?'

'Yes, I know that.'

'Right.' The doctor paused, taken aback by the sting in James's words. 'And are you married?'

'What does that matter?'

'Given the impact of this decision, we usually like to talk to both partners involved. To make sure you understand the consequences and are alright with the choice being made.'

Caught off-guard, James fumbled and stammered. 'We made the decision together,' he said, collecting himself. 'My wife is busy, so I came alone. She'll be here if we decide to go through with it. You can ask her then.'

'Of course.' An uneasy smile; a quick darting of the small, black eyes. 'I'm also going to have to ask you your reasons for wanting this surgery.'

He could have let the truth out then. Watched as the doctor's weak shoulders shrunk back in horror and his small, rounded mouth trembled in disgust. He might grab the picture of his pretty daughter off the desk and slam it into his drawer. He might call the police. Or perhaps, he would take matters into his own hands and force James down on the oak desk itself, shiny with the reflection of his determined face, and do the surgery at that very moment.

'That's my private business, Doctor.'

'I understand that, of course. We just recommend that you don't make the decision if you are going through a big change in your life or if you are under any increased pressure from work or other areas in your life.'

'Is that all?' The doctor's questions were throwing James further into a doubt he hadn't expected to feel. He thought about the father and son he had seen sitting outside; how peaceful they had looked. Was it possible that in two years, five years, he would be able to feel that same way? That he would be able to look at a child of his own and love it how he should? Then came the whispering desire, stronger than anything else, and it helped him find the words he had been looking for. 'I have to think about it.'

The relief on the doctor's face was evident. 'I think that would be wise.' The easy smile pressed deep lines across his jaw, leading up to his cheeks once again. 'You just never know how you're going to feel in the future.'

He entered the house quietly, holding the door and closing it with the softest click. He hoped to sneak back into bed so she might not realize he had been gone.

'You're back?' Her voice surprised him and he let out a small, stunned shout, spinning around. She was sitting at the dining table, watching him. She looked tired; she always seemed spent these days.

'Yes.'

She nodded, waiting for him to say more.

'I just went for a walk.'

'In those shoes?' She looked pointedly at his work shoes. He stared down at them for too long.

'I couldn't find anything else and I didn't want to disturb you.'

'Is there something you want to tell me?' she played nervously with the tablecloth, not used to accusing him of anything.

'I wanted to apologize,' he said. 'For the way I've been acting recently. You don't deserve that and I'm sorry.' He sat down beside her and put his hand on her knee. Felt the hard edge of bone beneath her skirt. 'I don't want it to be like this anymore.'

'How can it not?' she asked. 'We both want different things now.'

'But you said—'

'I know.' She was gentle, patient. 'I know what I said but I've changed my mind. I was young and I didn't know what it would be like. You've seen all our friends—you've seen how happy they are. I want to be like that. I want to have a family with you.'

'And if I say no?'

She was silent. He knew what the answer was.

'I want to make it better.'

'Are you willing to try then?' she asked.

His hand slid off her leg. He sunk his fingers into his hair and pulled at the roots. He answered without thinking; only wanting to make this moment better, to make her better. He said it without imagining the consequences, telling himself that he could deal with it if it ever came to that. 'Yes.' The relief on her face was evident and he felt a surge of power, knowing he had caused that. For the time being, that was what he wanted most. 'Yes, we can try.'

17

Whitehorse, Yukon. September 1992

Sister Margret's office is cold and uninviting; as if it were a part of her that had extended outward and separated itself, then grown into the room that she sits in. Sister Ann is beside me, quiet and girlish in the presence of this large woman.

'This sort of behavior is completely unacceptable.' Her voice isn't the same as it was yesterday when she was reading the prayer. Today it is hard and crisp, missing the loud passion that had projected it across the hall, although it is just as forceful—aggressive almost. She doesn't even acknowledge that I am there. Her dark eyes are fixed on Sister Ann who is sitting still and nodding. 'How could you let this happen?'

'I'm sorry.'

'I don't want to hear it.' Sister Margret leans forward and her eyes narrow. 'What if something had happened to her? What would I have told her parents?' Her hands fall to the desk and everything freezes—even the metronome on her desk seems to stop, skip a beat and start again. 'She's been here for two days. Two days and she's already causing trouble.'

'It won't happen again.'

'You better make sure that it doesn't, Ann.' They look at each other, as if there is something they understand and have left me out of. 'Now, I want to talk to Miss McDermott alone.'

Sister Ann stands up. She doesn't look at me as she is leaving, closing the door on her way out. I watch after her, angry at her passivity, annoyed that she could let someone talk to her so harshly and take the blame for something that wasn't her fault.

Sister Margret turns her enormous gaze on me and I meet it straight on. *Tick, tick, tick*, my mind clicks with every beat of the metronome and I stare so hard at her that she begins to blur.

'Do you have anything to say to me, Miss McDermott?' I blink and when I open my eyes she is clear again and leaning over her desk.

'I know you want me to apologize.'

'That would be the right thing to do, yes.'

'Well you can't tell me what to do,' I say. 'Or stop me from doing anything.' It feels good to be so angry. There is a reservoir inside me and it's tipping over.

'We're not here to do that. You can ask if you want something and we'll do our best to accommodate you. If you miss phone hours one week, then you can do it the week after. It's as simple as that.'

'No one had told me about phone hours and—'

She holds up her hand to silence me, closing her eyes as if in pain, and then stands up. She walks toward me but doesn't kneel down. My neck hurts from looking up at her but I refuse to break her gaze.

'I don't know how it was in your old school but here, I make sure that my students are disciplined. That they follow the rules. Otherwise, how else would I run this place?' She pushes her arms outward and gestures around. I look at her hands; notice how big they are and flinch. She laughs—a short, barking sound. 'I don't use violence, Miss McDermott. That's not how we do things at Holy

141

Academy.' She goes back to her desk and slides into her chair, pulling off her glasses and setting them down beside her. She looks at me expectantly. 'So I'll ask you again. Is there anything you would like to say to me?'

I let my hand fall on a pile of paper, intentionally dragging them over the desk as I stand up. They take the metronome with them and it falls noisily near my feet but doesn't break. It lies on its side, among the scattered papers, and I see its thin, black needle shiver and swing in protest to this unexpected aggression. My blood skips in my veins in small, excited hops.

'I'm sorry,' I smirk.

Her lips curl in a twisted smile that bares her teeth at me. I want her to get as angry as I am but her face stays perfectly still and her voice remains low and steady. She doesn't look down again at the mess I have created, even when I shift and step on a few papers.

'This will be your first and last warning. I assure you, the next time something like this happens, there will be severe consequences.'

I want to say more but the bell sounds somewhere far off and she puts her glasses back on and looks at me over them.

'Classes are going to start soon, so I suggest you hurry.'

The Academy is a place of rituals. A place of order and rules and obedience and in two days I have become a kink in that perfect chain—something that has gone wrong. So when I become an outcast that morning, something to be ignored and forgotten so I don't ruin the whole thing, it's not unexpected.

When I sit down beside Judy in class, she avoids my eye and moves to whisper in another girl's ear, their eyes coming up together at me. It's childish and cruel and I meet them with a smile, as if I am in on the joke and they quickly look away. It doesn't take long for me to become used to the girls' whispering as I pass them, at the smirks and little sparks of nervousness in their eyes when I catch them looking at me.

Victoria stops me in the hallway before lunch, taking my elbow and dragging me into an empty classroom. She shuts the door and starts laughing loudly, craning her neck back and shaking her fist up at the ceiling.

'Brilliant!' She grabs the sides of my face and gives me a hard, exaggerated kiss on the cheek. 'I can't believe you did it. How did you manage it?' There is a curiosity in her eyes, a twitch of her chin, and I realize what has happened.

'You tricked me.'

'What?'

I stand up and the desk gives a shudder. 'You didn't know whether or not I would find a phone, did you?'

'Look—' she starts but I interrupt her.

'So you thought you'd let me go first, see if it was worth taking the risk.' It's her fault that I am no longer part of a group; that I'm isolated and alone once again. And I didn't even get to speak to him. That hurts more than anything.

'No one forced you into anything, Frances.' I turn to leave but she catches me. 'Hey, come on. It's not a big deal—it's not like you were expelled or anything.' I keep quiet and she walks backward until we're face to face again. The smile is back; her lips are crooked, the top one leaning toward the right. I feel myself softening. 'How was it, anyway?' she asks. 'Bet he was fucking excited that you called.'

'I didn't get to talk to him,' I say, pulling my arm out of her grip. She has reminded me of my disappointment; of my anger at my mother and of how desperate I am to leave this place. 'This is all your fault. You know, Judy tried to warn me about you.'

'I'm the only one still talking to you.' She is angry now too. She leans in close. 'I'm the only friend you've got here. You can't really afford to be saying things like that.'

'I don't want to be your friend,' I say, pulling open the door. 'I don't need any friends. I'll be out of here soon enough.'

'Look, I'm really sorry,' she tries again but I shake my head firmly.

'Don't,' and I re-enter the throng of girls moving toward the lunch hall. 'Just don't.'

I expect him to call that evening, and when he doesn't, or in the days after, I try again the following week but no one picks up. I stand in Sister Margret's office for a long time, just dialing the numbers over and over again until I can do it without looking. *Pick up, pick up—just please, pick up.* The dial tone dances around in my head, gathering speed and volume as it passes through my ears, filling me with fear. Fear that something could have happened to him, but more than that, I am afraid he has forgotten me. I want to pick up the phone and throw it against the wall, through the window, but instead, I slam my fist down on the table repeatedly after every missed call, yanking the cord and screaming in my head. *I hate you. I hate you. I fucking hate you.*

The next morning, I hear the alarm but I don't get out of bed and Judy doesn't bother to wake me up before leaving. There are so many girls in the school that I worry no one will notice I am missing. I dress slowly, rolling my shirt and twisting it between my hands before pulling it over my head. I crease it some more. I take a pencil and lick the nib before rubbing the wet charcoal into my palms and smearing it onto my shirt. I tie my sweater around my waist and smudge some lipstick onto my lips. When I am satisfied with my appearance, I leave the abandoned building and stroll across the field. I time it perfectly so that everyone is leaving the assembly just as I am arriving. The girls watch as I approach. Some trip over their shoes—others collide with each other, all whispering frantically and with wide eyes. I spot Victoria; she looks at me and shakes her head, laughter twisting her lips. I let them stare as I fall into the back of the now messy line-up. Sister Margret is the last to leave and she grabs my elbow, pulling me to a standstill.

'Keep going, girls,' she calls out. 'You don't want to be late for classes. Straight lines, please.' She waits for everyone to disappear before speaking to me.

'Put your sweater on, right now.'

'I'm not cold.'

She stands before me and I see a vein flicker, thick and alive, down the side of her face.

'I said, put it on, Frances. You're just embarrassing yourself.'

I untie the sweater from around my waist and hold it up to her.

'Well if you're so concerned, why don't you just put it on for me?' I am heady on the words shooting out of my mouth and the thrill makes me unsteady on my feet. Sister Margret's thin mouth stretches over her teeth and I think again of how she resembles a caged animal; how dangerous, and it only excites me more. Then I see Joseph coming up the walkway and he spots us. I don't want him coming any nearer; for some reason, I don't want him to see me this way. The thrill diminished, I pull the sweater over my head in the hope that it will satisfy Sister Margret and I can escape. Joseph glances at us once more over his shoulder before disappearing around the back of the building.

'Good.' She grabs my arm and pulls me toward the classrooms. I let her drag me, throwing my full weight against her, allowing her to be as rough as she likes. When she pushes me into the building, I start to laugh. It echoes off the empty corridor walls and breaks into little pieces of sound that sneak under the doors and reverberate off the high ceilings. Sister Margret grabs a tissue from the pocket of her habit and reaches for my face. I jerk my neck away but she takes a hold of my chin roughly, gripping it tightly so that I can't move away. She could break my neck so easily and the idea of that happening, of being gone and missed by him, makes me almost wish she would do it. She spits into the tissue and rubs it hard against my mouth. It smells sour and I don't like the feel of her on my lips and teeth but I smile when I see the red streaks come off. Her hand is shaking and she leaves it in her pocket. Annoyed to have lost her composure, she breathes heavily through her nose, still holding onto me. Then she releases my face and lets out a long, wheezy exhale. 'Get to class. Right. Now. You're late.'

'Well, I wouldn't be if you hadn't stopped me.'

There is a barely contained anger that colors her face but she doesn't say anything more. Instead, she takes my arm again and walks me to my classroom, opening the door louder than I know she intended to. The class stops and all heads turn at the same time, like a pack of trained monkeys. I sneer at the idea and want to say it out loud but she doesn't give me the time. She directs me to a desk at the front and I hope I still have some lipstick on my lips. She speaks to the teacher in soft tones and then turns to the class and smiles widely.

'Sorry for the interruption, girls. Please continue.'

'Yes, I'm so sorry,' I say loudly. The sound of my voice, almost manic, unnerves even me and it makes everyone squirm in their seats, watching to see what Sister Margret will do. No one looks at me except for Victoria, sitting in the corner, her black eyes trained almost enviously on me.

'I'll see you in my office at lunchtime.' Sister Margret leans down and speaks to me alone. 'Don't think you're getting away with this.'

'I wouldn't dream of it.' As she is leaving, I crane my neck backward and call to her large, retreating back in a sing-song manner. 'See you at lunchtime then.'

My room is checked and my belongings are cleared of anything that might be regarded as something to cause trouble with. I am made to sit by myself at meals, and during our free time I sit in the library under the supervision of a teacher or prefect. The solitude suits me fine; it gives me the space to think of things I want to dream about without interruption, though under such close watch, it is difficult to be troublesome. Sister Ann comes to my room every morning and watches as I get dressed and then accompanies me to the assembly to make sure I am on time. This continues for two weeks, during which I don't get a single phone call from my father and I can't call him because as a part of my punishment I am not allowed to use the phone. Sister Margret hopes that this will make me give in; that I will realize I have no choice but to blend into the order of the school and start behaving, but I won't give up that easily. I refuse to do my homework, spending the hour doodling in my notebook instead. When I am called upon in class, I pretend not to hear my name and if it is insisted upon, I say I can't be bothered to know the answer. I call the teachers by their names instead of addressing them as Sister *This* and Sister *That*—I even call one of them a fat cow but nothing seems to work. Sister Margret is as intent on molding me into the woman she has promised my mother I will become as I am of leaving. She gives me every punishment she possibly can; washing the dishes after everyone has finished dinner, cleaning the floors of the foyer, using a toothbrush to scrub the scale off the underside of the toilet seat—everything except what I want her to do.

I become increasingly frustrated as I start to run out of tricks and then one day, Judy provides me with the opportunity I have been waiting for. They are sitting in the pavilion during the morning break and I am heading back to my room, having been sent to fetch my notebooks by one of the teachers.

'Look who it is,' I hear her call out and I stop and turn to face her.

'What do you want?' I ask.

'All alone, I see,' she comes toward me, the girls moving behind her like a pack. 'You can't say I didn't warn you.'

I enter the pavilion and go closer to her. She falters for a moment but doesn't stop moving until we're face to face.

'I hope he was worth it,' she says. 'Because of him, your time here is going to be very lonely.'

'I don't care,' I say. 'I don't need any of you. I'm going home soon anyway.'

She seems amused by this statement. 'What makes you say that?'

I keep my eyes trained on her but my mouth stays shut.

'You think you can just leave whenever you want?' She touches her satchel lightly and I see her Bible sticking out from beneath the cover. 'You need to be here more than any of us, Frances. I can see why you've been sent here.'

'You don't know anything,' I say. 'Just because you carry that thing around with you all day and read it at night, doesn't make you an expert on anything.' I laugh. 'It just makes you a fool.'

Her eyes flash and she stands up straight. 'We'll see,' is all she says and then turns back to her friends. As I am leaving, I hear her say it softly. If I had been two steps further, I might have missed it, but the wind carries her words and they pierce my ears and make me grow wild. *I bet her parents are glad to have gotten rid of her* and before I know what I'm doing, I have slammed her against the wall and her back hits it with a thud. Her body jerks forward as she lets out a bewildered cry. She stops breathing for a moment before I shove her back. Her body makes satisfying contact with the wall and the sound of it fills me with an odd sense of pride. There is a sudden release in my chest, as if it is collapsing, just as her shoulders fall under my hands.

'What did you say?' my voice is a low, mean growl. 'Try and say that again.'

Her eyes are wide. 'You're crazy and I'm not surprised your parents didn't want you anymore.'

My hand comes up and I'm about to strike her. One of us shouts but then strong arms are pulling me back and all her friends suddenly swarm around her, protecting her from my flying fists. Joseph is behind me and I am held tightly to his body and I hear her crying and all I can say is *I hate you. I fucking hate all of you.*

Someone comes to get me at lunchtime from my room, which I have been secluded in since that morning.

'Frances, you're wanted in Sister Margret's office.'

I stand up. There is a dull ache in my arms and it pulls and sharpens when I roll my shoulders. I smile at the nun as I walk by and she shrinks away from me. I am certain that this is enough to get me out of here. Surely I am going to be told to pack my bags and I can't wait to show Sister Margret my suitcase, already packed and ready to go. But when I get to her office, she is standing outside it, waiting by the door. Her eyes flash at me and her mouth curls into a different smile this time. She tells me to go inside.

'You have a phone call,' she says.

I go in and she closes the door behind me. I pick up the large receiver that has been left lying on a pile of papers on her desk and when I hear him, everything inside me springs awake. The past two weeks' events, this morning, the feel of Judy's body giving in to my strength and anger; all of it disappears and becomes inconsequential. This is all I need.

'Hello, Frances.' His voice is slow and deep and snaps me back into myself. The world tips and dances for a moment and when it straightens out, everything is in its place.

'Oh God, I've missed you so much.'

He is silent. I think that the call has been disconnected and I panic. *Hello? Are you there? Please be there—hello?*

'I'm here.'

'Why haven't you called me? How could you forget about me like that?'

'I haven't forgotten you.' He sounds irritated. 'It's been less than a month since you left.'

'I know and every time I've tried to call, you never answer.'

'I've been busy, Frances.'

'Busy doing what? We both know you never go anywhere.'

'I told you, there's a reason why you're there.' He is almost shouting now. 'Why are you causing such a scene? You almost hit a girl in the face, for God's sake!'

'But I only thought that—'

'Don't you think people will wonder?' He is rushed and quiet and speaks over me; doesn't want to hear what I am saying. 'Don't you think they'll find it strange, you sneaking out at night to call me? Find *you* strange?'

I hold the receiver away from me and stare at it. He doesn't sound the same. He sounds distant; like a disgusted stranger who doesn't want to talk to me. I want to be at home more than ever; to hug him and kiss him and bring him back to me. He carries on talking. 'You were almost expelled today. Do you have any idea how hard it was to persuade Sister Margret to keep you there?'

'You did what?' I try to shout but my words are lost—trapped in the short, half-breaths of my disbelief. My lungs narrow and I have to sit on the floor, dragging the phone down and holding it between my crossed thighs. I bite down on the cord to keep from screaming. 'You told her...' *breathe,* 'you told her—oh my God.' A wave of nausea hits me hard. 'How could you do that to me? That's what I wanted! Do you know how hard I've tried? I want to come home so we can be together.'

Again he is silent.

'Answer me. Hello? Answer me!'

'You need to be there, Fran. I told you, you have to get some distance from everything that has happened here.' His tone softens into the sleepy, loving one that I know. 'I need you to be strong and listen to me when I tell you it's only for a year and things are going to get better.'

'And if I get expelled?'

'You aren't coming home, Frances.'

'But—'

'I don't want you here.'

I knew those words were coming. I had felt them so many times; seen them in his eyes for so long and now they are out, they hurt, but they are also, in some strange way, a relief. I don't have to wait for them any longer. In one moment, everything has turned to nothing. A long, soft wail escapes my lips; it's deep and guttural and doesn't sound like me. I don't feel like myself anymore.

'Why?' I ask. 'Why are you doing this to me?'

'Please don't cry. I'm sorry. You're my daughter and I love you and that's why you have to stay there.' His desperation is too much to bear. I don't want to hear it—I don't like the way it makes me feel about him.

'Do I have a choice?'

There is no answer. I lie down on the floor and think of my packed suitcase, waiting eagerly for me by the door. I think of everyone who hates me and how there is nothing for me here. I let the tears fall into my hair.

'Frances?'

I push down the lump in my throat and force my response through it. 'Okay.'

'Okay?'

'I'll stay here. Only for a year and then I'm coming home and you won't be able to stop me.'

'And you'll behave?'

'Yes.'

'And try to make some friends?'

I don't say anything.

'Frances?'

'I'll try and make some friends.'

'Good. Thank you.' He clears his throat and his breath has deepened and slowed down. 'That's my good girl.' He has regained himself and is calm but he also seems astonished at his power over me. The way I can't seem to disagree with anything that he wants.

'Can I call you at least?' I hate myself for asking. I hate that I still want to hear his voice, hear it again even as I am talking to him. That I can feel myself slowly breaking under those words; *I don't want you here.*

'We'll call you,' he says. 'I'll call you very soon, I promise.'

*

When I finish with the phone call, I wipe away my tears and clear my throat. I smooth back my hair and make sure it's neatly tied. I tuck in my shirt and walk to the door. Sister Margret is still waiting outside.

'I'm sorry for the way I've been acting,' I say. The words come out dead but she has been waiting for a victory and this seems to satisfy her. 'It won't happen again.'

'You're going to make a formal apology at the assembly tomorrow,' she says. 'And also, personally, to Judy. She says she's afraid to stay in the same room as you and I want you to assure her that nothing like this will ever happen again.'

'Okay.'

'And you will continue with your chores until I am convinced you have learned your lesson.'

'Yes.'

'I don't want to see this kind of behavior from you again, is that clear?' She glares down at me and today I don't meet her eye. 'I'll be keeping an eye on you, Frances.'

I don't hear anymore as I start to walk out into the foyer. The mean, final ring of the dial tone continues to trail behind me, screaming in my head for the rest of the day.

I sit alone that evening during our free time. It's raining so most of the girls are inside the library or upstairs in their rooms. The rain makes everything smelly and wonderfully gray. It brings out all the noises and the scents and they assault me until my brain grows weak and drunk off the rhododendrons that are crawling up the metal arc around me. His words become mixed up in all of this. I want to cry but feel empty because I know it will be no use. My stomach has opened up and everything is falling into it but nothing ever seems to go anywhere.

'Hi.' Joseph is coming toward me, moving fast out of the rain and stepping under the low veranda. His skin glows and I see drops of water shine at his cheek. They run down his chin and slide down his neck, collecting in the same spot my mouth found so many nights ago; near his Adam's apple. He runs a hand through his short hair and shakes the water from it. He sits down but far away from me. My father's words come at me again. *Don't you think they'll find you strange?*

'Hi.' I pull a red flower off the vine and start tearing at its petals, my eyes following their floating trajectory as they fall into a puddle at my feet. I wonder what it feels like to be that way; to have nothing inside you that hurts even as someone slowly picks you apart.

'Are you alright?' he asks. I think he might say more; mention what happened that night he dropped me home, but he sits there patiently, waiting for me to answer.

'I'm fine.'

'Do you want to talk about what happened this morning?'

'What do you mean?'

He looks shocked at my question. 'With that girl, in the pavilion.'

The day has gone on for so long that I have forgotten about everything that happened that morning. Now I recall how the violence exploded inside me, the taste of it as it came up to the roof of my mouth. 'There's nothing to talk about.'

'She thought you were about to hit her.'

'I was.' I pull another flower and it resists before breaking off with a quiet, sad snap. I start to curl the petals downward and up over the end of the stalk—something Bubbie taught me how to do.

'Why?'

'She asked for it.'

He slides a little closer to me, taking the flower and letting it lie in his large, open palm. The color is stark against his skin. I look up at him. His wrist drops to hand me back the flower but I don't take it so he lets it fall into my lap. 'What did she say?'

'It doesn't matter now.'

'I know how difficult it can be to make friends in a new place,' he tells me.

I slide the flower up the side of the metal structure and let it grow soggy from the rain that is running slowly down, watching the petals tear and fall away. 'It's not that,' I say softly but he hears me.

'You miss home.'

'Yes.' I'm glad for the drops on my face; he won't be able to see me crying.

'That's natural,' he says gently. He puts a hand on my shoulder but then reconsiders this, and it ends up draped across the back of the bench. 'Can I give you some advice?' He leans in a little closer so I nod. 'You're a sweet girl. You just have to give them a chance to see that.'

I don't like the way he is invading, presuming to know me. The way he is coming in without asking first. He doesn't understand that something has happened to me; that I am different now, strange, and I will remain that way forever.

'Look, it's none of your business.' I stand up so quickly, he has to move away so I don't hit him. 'Why are you so interested anyway? It's not like you care about me. No one does.' I run down the slippery stairs and I think that he might follow. But for the second time, he only sits and lets me go.

18

St Albert. June 1976

When they first got the news, a couple of months after his visit to the hospital, James sat facing the doctor, holding Marienne's hand. The doctor's words moved slowly over the desk, taking so long to reach him through the fractured silence and even when they did, he wasn't sure how to feel about them.

'But it was just an infection,' Marienne tried to argue. 'That's what Dr. Banes told me when I went to see him.'

'Mrs. McDermott, Dr. Banes referred you to me for a reason.' Calm, unmoving gray eyes reaching out to them, preparing them for something neither of them had expected to hear. 'He thought he saw something abnormal in your tests and I'm sorry to say—'

Marienne shook her head, stopping his words. 'Well, do the tests again,' she said. 'Do them again because I know you're wrong.' She pulled her hand from James's grip, clenching her fists together on her shaking knees, her knuckles growing white and hard.

'It must be quite a shock, I know,' a sympathetic pause in breath, 'but sometimes these things happen. I'm very sorry.'

Those words must have been repeated a thousand times by this doctor, changed up and reused with so many other young, hopeful couples. But no matter how you spun them, or what order you chose to place them in, the message was always the same. It still caused the same anguish, the same relief.

'Look, I know what I'm feeling,' Marienne said, leaning forward. 'There's nothing wrong with me. I feel fine. My body is perfectly fine so I'm asking you to do the tests again. I'll do as many as you want.' She stopped, closed her eyes and whispered, 'I'll do anything you want.'

Dr. Grayson pushed back his chair and stood up, pulling his glasses off and rubbing his palm against his bearded chin, reaching up to pinch the sharp hook of his nose. He walked slowly to the small, rectangular bed by the wall, absently smoothing out the white sheet with his fingers. The short moment before the doctor turned to them allowed James to process the information given to him and the room thickened with his anticipation. He hoped Marienne wouldn't sense the relief that pulled a sigh from him, causing him to sink back in his chair. Dr. Grayson leaned loosely against the bed frame, his arms crossed over his chest. He chewed down on the arm of his glasses, clicking it against his teeth before he continued.

'Our bodies can be very tricky,' he said slowly; a man carefully assessing his situation and planning his words accordingly. 'Sometimes they can make us believe that they're alright and everything is functioning as it should be.' He came back, sliding into his chair. He wiped his glasses clean before putting them on again and tapping his hand on a large, brown envelope that lay beside him, pressing a fingertip to Marienne's name that had been thoughtlessly scribbled across its center. 'But these tests tell a different story.'

'Then we'll go for a second opinion,' Marienne said. 'And a third and fourth one if we have to.'

Dr. Grayson, accustomed to the anger that tripped and weaved through Marienne's fast-flowing speech, extended his arm across the table to stop her.

'You're more than welcome to do that—in fact, I would recommend that you did.' He was still holding the envelope and now he pushed it toward them. 'I know this is all very overwhelming, so if you would like, I can explain what I found in your tests before you leave. It might help you understand the situation a little better.'

'You just want to convince me that you're right,' Marienne said.

James put a hand on her wrist and she paused, midway off her chair, glancing down at him in surprise.

'Just listen to what he has to say, Annie.'

She sat back down and they waited as Dr. Grayson pulled out a small chart from the bottom drawer of his desk. He laid it out in front of them and when Marienne saw the title, 'Main Causes of Female Infertility,' she chewed down hard on her bottom lip and pulled at her fingers.

The chart was divided neatly into two columns and several rows of different colors highlighting the various causes of infertility and what they meant. James was surprised to see how easily organized and defined the problem was; color-coordinated according to the severity of each category, possible causes and symptoms added to further help the patient understand their diagnosis. It made him wonder if all problems could be as cleanly categorized and explained; their roots as systematically analyzed and solved.

'You have what is called Premature Ovarian Failure,' Dr. Grayson began, pointing at a purple row near the top of the chart. 'It's caused by abnormally low levels of estrogen, and to put it quite simply, it means you've stopped producing fertile eggs.' The cold, smooth science of the doctor's explanation, the half-relaxed posture and authoritative tone it inspired in him, hinting at the sureness of his diagnosis, broke the rigid stance that Marienne had taken up when they first entered the office. Her shoulders fell forward as she leaned heavily into the desk. As she stared down at the chart, something registered in her body, tightening as she asked in a shaking voice,

'Does that mean I was at some point?'

'Was what?'

'Producing eggs. Do you mean that if James and I had tried earlier for a baby, I might have become pregnant?' James felt his breath catch in his throat. 'It's important for me to know.'

'There's no way to tell that,' Dr. Grayson said, 'but usually the onset of POF is at a very early age.'

James followed Marienne's eyes to the chart, hypnotized by its glossy writing; its smiling curves and teasing loops.

'It says here that five to ten percent of women with this condition can spontaneously become pregnant,' James read. Dr. Grayson's lip twitched a little with annoyance but his eyes and voice never lost their sympathetic composure.

'That's right,' and sensing Marienne had lifted in her chair, he continued quickly, 'but I don't want to get your hopes up unfairly. The possibility of that happening to the two of you is very low, probably non-existent.' He paused, giving them time to digest this information, folding up the chart, ready to leave them with their loss. 'I'm very sorry to be so blunt here but I think it's important to be realistic in a situation like this. To know what you're up against.'

'Which is what, exactly?' James pushed him to say the words, wanting to hear them in the same straightforward, clean manner in which the doctor had offered up his diagnosis, so that there could be no mistaking what was being implied.

'I'm afraid the chances of you never conceiving are very high and I would say it's extremely unlikely that the two of you will ever have a child together.'

She was silent as James drove her home but as they passed as signboard that said, 'Happy Faces Daycare: *where we look after the most important little people in your life,* she started to cry and said, 'fuck.' He stroked her hair but she slapped his hand away. 'If we hadn't waited,' the words turned soggy from her tears and he struggled to hear her. 'If we had tried earlier, maybe it would have been okay.'

They had begun trying for a baby soon after his visit to Stolleri. He'd had no other option; he knew Marienne would have left him if he had refused and that would have been worse than anything. So he bore his trepidation well; the idea of a child still seemed like a faraway thing and it was easy not to be afraid of only his wife's simple hope. So he watched her wait and pray for weeks, followed by days of her disappointment and his relief.

'I don't know why it's not happening,' she said to him once, after. 'Everything feels right—ready. We have to keep trying. These things take time, right?'

'I guess they do,' he had replied, lost in his own thoughts. Despite not wanting to have a child, he couldn't help but wonder what it would be like; to have something so closely linked to him. A daughter as lovely as his wife, with dark hair and the sweetest eyes. Or a son he could teach how to play baseball; whom he could form into a good man. A better man than himself.

'It'll happen,' she said, rolling back on top of him and kissing his neck. 'We're going to make it happen, no matter what.'

Two months passed in this manner until she contracted a urine infection and had gone to see Dr. Banes. She told him about her difficulty getting pregnant and he had referred her to Dr. Grayson. *You will never have a child together.*

'I'm sorry, honey.' He gladly took the blame for her infertility, sick with guilt because he was free now and she was trapped within the confinements of her deficient biology.

'That's not going to make it any better,' she said, getting out of the car and leaving the door swinging open. 'A sorry isn't going to make us a family.' He followed her into the house where she went straight to the living room, bending over the coffee table and pulling out a pile of magazines. Babies. Babies. Babies, mother-hood, family. Her desperation hit him too hard and he fell into his armchair, watching as she tore pages from one magazine and threw others at the wall. 'He must be wrong,' she said. 'He has to be wrong.'

James fell to his knees beside her, catching her frantic wrists, forcing her to stop. 'I was so sure…' she gave up then, growing slack in his arms and he stretched out his legs, leaning against the couch and pulling her onto his lap. She brought up her knees, curling into him.

He rubbed her back and whispered in her ear. 'We're going to be alright.'

'I have nothing,' she said, as if she hadn't heard him. 'I'm nothing now, James. Everyone—all of them—they have families. What do we have?'

'Don't say that.' His breath was hot and angry. 'I don't want to hear you say that again.' He kissed her face, collecting her tears with his mouth. There was a slow, snaky happiness expanding in him. The guilt was only a tickle in his chest and he could live with that, knowing everything had turned out for the best.

*

They visited three more hospitals after that first meeting with Dr. Grayson. They spent long, tired minutes in three different rooms, all with the same stinging smell that stuck to their clothes and lingered in their noses for days after, before Marienne decided not to do any more tests. All the doctors produced the same results, found the same shriveled womb grown old too early. All three were extremely sorry to say but Dr. Grayson's initial diagnosis had been correct and Marienne was unlikely to ever have children of her own.

On their last trip, having seen all the doctors in and around town, they drove three hours to Calgary to meet with a doctor that Lynette had suggested. They left early in the morning, the flat greenness and occasional signposts simmering and flashing by them in the solid heat that had already covered the road by ten o'clock. Her hope seemed stronger that day, as if by driving so far and trying so hard, she was entitled to get something back.

'I have a good feeling about this one,' she said to him, leaning in to nibble on his neck. She was light and young again and he wanted to drive on forever. 'I'm telling you, this doctor sounded really positive.'

So when they got the disappointing, yet bitterly expected news, she took it harder than the last times. They left almost immediately and she fell into an angry silence as they drove slowly and tiredly through what seemed like a different landscape from the one that morning. Dusty pink creased the fading blue of the sky, folding it into a darker purple, and the air had turned thick with the promise of a steamy evening thunderstorm. The fields they had passed dozing in the morning sun now stood erect and, having cooled down, swayed slightly in the humid wind. They stopped at a diner whose neon sign announced that they were open and a bell rang loudly overhead as they stepped through the door. Once they had settled in a booth in the almost empty place, James tried to console his wife.

'Are you okay?' It was a pointless question and the look she gave him told him he should have known better than to ask.

'What do we do now?' She sidestepped his concern and moved onto hers. She picked up a napkin and began to shred it; hard rips that tore it into clean, neat strips. He drank his lukewarm coffee, dark rivers of liquid leaking through the slight cracks of the already stained mug, sticking to his fingers.

'There are still two more doctors we can see and we'll find others—' he started but she shook her head.

'No.' She crumpled the frayed strips of napkin into a ball and pushed it into the space between the booth and the window. 'I can't do those tests anymore. I can't face any more doctors.'

He heard the bell in the front of the diner go off and watched as a young couple, not much younger than him and Marienne, when he thought about it, walked past them, whispering to each other; bleary eyed and so happy.

'I'll do whatever it is you want me to do,' he turned back to her but she wasn't looking at him anymore. She was staring out of the window and into the almost empty parking lot.

'Bet that's their car over there,' Marienne said, referring to the couple who had now taken a seat at the far end of the room. Their loud chatter, ringing with occasional laughter, seemed heartless and he wished he could tell them to stop. Marienne gestured with a tilt of her head to the dusty car parked outside. Their bags were pushed up against the backseat windows and the ones that hadn't fit were sat on the roof, carelessly tied down with cheap rope.

'We have other options, Annie,' he said. There was a long pause as she continued to stare out at the darkening sky. As she let out a long sigh, he wondered why he had said it; he couldn't have asked for an easier way out than this, yet her world had fallen apart around her and picking up the remains of her happiness seemed more important than anything else.

'No, we don't.' She took his cup and sipped at the coffee, although her own sat just beside her elbow. She stayed that way for some time, coffee mug to her mouth, her eyes turned outside. When she finally put the cup down, he saw that her chin was trembling. 'You don't get it. I want it to be mine.' He followed her eyes out to the car. The couples' unhinged license plate faced the diner, revealing how far they had come.

'All the way from BC,' he said, to fill in the silence. Exhaustion overcame him so that it hurt to even pick up his mug. The fear and anxiety of the past few months were now running out of him, pooling down at his feet and when she said, 'I can't believe we're never going to have a family,' he felt the last of it drain away from him. He saw, just within his grasp, those happy, easy days on which his marriage had thrived.

'I wonder where they're going,' he murmured, not to her although she heard him.

She leaned her body against the wide glass, looking through him. 'I guess we can do that now, if we wanted.'

'Do what?'

'Just pack up and leave and no one would care.'

The rain had started to fall; long, silverish droplets, cold and steady, streaking down the window and leaving sad stains behind. The kind of stinky rain you get only after an incredibly hot summer day. Marienne craned her neck upward to watch it fall, as if she could hear it through the glass. 'There's nothing keeping us at home any longer.'

*

After they returned from Calgary, she told him again she didn't want to see any more doctors.

'I won't be poked and prodded again,' she said. 'I can't do it.'

'The chart said—'

'I know what the chart said, James.'

Although she refused to go to any more hospitals or talk to any friends about their situation, she was adamant that they keep trying and went about it with a grim determination. It was emotionless and quick and he didn't like it. Over the two years of their marriage, he had grown used to having her body beneath his. The boyish, flat canvas of it. The burnished, olive skin and her black hair that sometimes smelled of butternut, especially at night, tickling his cheek as he pressed down close to her. It was never something he longed for, but he enjoyed giving it to her; watching her face and body writhe beneath his hands, her short breaths steaming the crevices of his ears. It helped keep his desires at bay. He could close his eyes with Marienne beneath him and imagine he was elsewhere, with someone else. Only for that small window of time and it was never a betrayal because he would be back with her soon, sprung into reality by the convulsing of his own body and it would be over, and most importantly, no one would be hurt.

Now, she took no pleasure from him and in turn, he could take none of it for himself. It was frustrating to see her trying fruitlessly, each night a reminder of what she was incapable of, each first day of her period, a stark and terrible insult.

She had never been particularly religious, but she prayed all the time in those hard months. Before they went to sleep, when he would wake up, she was on her knees, her elbows resting on their bed. *If you give me this, if you could only give me this, take anything else that you want.*

'It's not going to work,' he said to her one day, stirring to see the morning light at her back, the tiny hairs on her arms like spun gold. She squeezed her eyes tightly closed and continued. He reached out, the covers slipping off his naked torso, prying her fingers away from each other. 'Stop it, Annie. You'll just end up disappointed.'

'This is all I can do,' she snapped, rising from the floor. 'And a little support from you wouldn't be so bad.'

He knew how she felt because he had been that way once. A young boy begging for the thing he wanted the most; a guilt-ridden teenager bargaining with a God he had to believe in because it was the only thing obscure enough to give him hope. *If you could only make me stop feeling this way. Just make me normal, like everyone else. I'll give you anything you want.*

She would figure it out eventually, though for her sake, he hoped it wouldn't come too soon. There was nothing so hopeless as coming to terms with the awful simplicity of it all; she could pray as much as she liked, for as long as she felt was needed, but what was the point when there was no one there to listen?

19

Whitehorse, Yukon.
October–November 1992

It's a strange, new kind of loneliness without him. My body seems to lose its balance, as if missing a limb or some vital organ. I stumble through the corridors in school, blind and unsure of my movements. Sometimes, when I am called upon in class, I open my mouth and he floods my senses and nothing comes out. I have forgotten how to do everything; pushed it all out in an effort to create more space for him—filling every pocket of my mind with his images. I miss him so fully that I can't imagine he doesn't feel the same way.

When he doesn't call for two weeks, and then four, I convince myself that he sits by the phone all day, picking it up and putting it down. Dialing the numbers and then replacing the receiver. It's unimaginable that he has gone on living while I am stuck in the same moment, with those same five words racing through my mind. *I don't want you here.*

I spend a lot of time looking at myself, trying to make sense of what I see. A slim face and a mouth that is too full for it, but he has always liked that. His sea-like eyes and eyebrows, strangely dark for someone with my hair color. Perhaps I got that from my mother.

'You look like a swan,' he told me once, his nail scraping tenderly down to the place where my collarbones stick out. 'I don't think I've seen anyone with a neck as long as yours. It's something amazing,' and when I touch the taut, sensitive skin there, I find that it isn't mine; he claimed it long ago.

'There's just something—I can't figure out why I don't like her.' I overhear someone saying this about me as we enjoy the last of the summer heat in the garden. The warmth has stayed well into October and it's made us all lazy; most of the girls are lying in the grass, their hair and skirts splayed around them. It's evening, just before dinner and the birds are starting up and the air is just beginning to cool. A wind carrying the traces of distant poplar trees makes us all heady with dreaming.

'Why do you think she's here?' I heard another one ask.

'She probably had an affair with a teacher.'

Excited giggling all around. They couldn't have imagined how close they were grazing to the truth. 'Maybe she threatened to kill his family if he didn't leave them for her. She looks the type to do something crazy, doesn't she?'

I keep tidy and stay silent. I grow invisible, disappearing into the structure of the Academy and this is even worse than being hated. I do it because he has asked me to and I don't want to disappoint him anymore. In the first few days after the phone call, I make up a calendar for the year. I scrawl down the remaining days in large, red numbers on a writing pad I find and each night I cross out the day passed. Every time I slash an end to those long, empty hours— for the few seconds it takes the marker to cross from one end of the page to the other—I allow myself to hope. In a year, it will be over. In a year, everything will go back to how it used to be and I can forget this ever happened. I retreat into myself, get lost in the sleepy world I created long ago for the two of us, the place where I am the happiest, and pray for time to pass quickly.

I watch out for Joseph more now, compelled by something outside of myself. Some late afternoons, I even sit on the veranda, hoping to see him striding down the gravel with the silver keys shining at his fingers. I don't want to speak to him. When he approaches, when I see the glint of his polished shoe, or the white of his smile, I let his eyes rest on me before I turn around and walk the other way. His gaze puts a temporary stop to the emptiness in my stomach. It's direct and always kind and I make space for it—but that is all I want from him.

One evening, he appears around the side of the building unexpectedly. I see that his hands are soiled, black streaks down to his elbows, and he takes a green rag from his back pocket and starts to clean himself carefully. He swipes it across the back of his neck then pushes it once more into his pocket. He is too close and I know that if he spots me, he will come over to talk to me and I'm not ready for that. So as soon as his eyes meet mine, I turn and nearly run down the hill that leads from the back of the Academy into the forest, in the direction of the river. Once I reach past the line of trees, I pause to catch my breath, holding onto my knees and sucking in the potent smell of forest. I hear a rustle and then a sob; long and loud somewhere to my right. Making my way down toward the river, I catch a flash of a blue-and-red plaid skirt—the school colors. Two long legs covered up to the knee in navy socks, and black hair that is falling free from a loose ponytail.

'Victoria?' I say her name softly at first, and then louder when she angles her face toward me and I'm certain it's her.

'Leave me alone,' she says, wiping hard at her face.

'What's the matter?'

'Like you care.' She tries to breathe but her nose is blocked and her eyes are puffy. 'You said you didn't want to be my friend, remember?'

'I'm sorry.' I say it sincerely because ever since I have been forced to stay here, I've been lonely and looking for a way to apologize to her. I promised him I would make friends here and she is the only one still willing to speak to me.

'I was angry that day and I didn't mean it.' I pat her shoulder awkwardly, unused to comforting anyone. 'What happened? Was it Judy?'

She laughs, a short bark. 'Of course not.' Then her face slackens. 'It's Leo.'

'Your boyfriend?'

That laugh again. 'He's not my boyfriend.'

'So what's the problem?'

'That's it,' she turns to me, suddenly heated. 'That's the problem. He didn't show up today and I've been waiting for hours.'

'They didn't notice you missing?' I ask.

'I pretended I had cramps,' she shakes her head. 'I can't believe him.'

We stand side by side, leaning against the rough bark of a tree. I push my toes through a pile of dead leaves and kick them into the air. The crickets are beginning to sing, a horrible hum that fills my entire skull. I look up to see the sun fading and my chest constricts. It's in the evenings that I miss him the most and already I feel it; that stretching emptiness in my abdomen that makes me want to double over and scream.

'Have you ever been in love?' she asks me so directly, so eagerly, but I feel like she is accusing me. 'Like really in love, when it just makes you feel like shit, and everything, a book, a song, even this ugly tree, reminds you of him?' She grabs the roots of her hair and groans. 'I haven't slept in fucking years.'

I want to tell her yes. I want to share my secret with her because at her words, it's beating in my chest, ready to take flight, straining to be acknowledged. Because I miss him so much and talking about him might make me feel better. Instead, I shake my head.

'That sounds terrible.'

'It is.' She sighs but I can see that she is enjoying some part of it; it makes her feel grown up and I want to tell her that I understand. I hand her a tissue from my pocket and she takes it gratefully, blowing her nose. 'I hate him,' she declares loudly. Then she takes my elbow and links her arm through it. We start walking back to the school.

'Does he come every day?' I ask.

'He tries. Sometimes it's difficult because,' she hesitates. 'Well, he has a girlfriend,' she finishes in a rush, looking at me and biting her lip. 'Does that make me a bad person?'

'No.' We are more similar than she thinks and I feel an instant closeness with her.

'You know,' she changes the subject. 'I've never seen Judy hate someone as much as she does you. I've never been able to get that reaction out of her, even after she caught me making out with her brother during parents' day.'

'You did what?'

We look at each other and laugh until our stomachs hurt. When we stop, Victoria wipes her tears from her eyes and asks, 'So what happened between the two of you?'

I tell her about the time in the pavilion; the way I slammed Judy into the wall, brought my fist up and saw the tremble of fear in her face. Victoria leans in closer to me, puts her head on my shoulder and the intimacy of it makes me physically hurt. I feel her laughing against it as she says, 'Where have you been all my life?'

The moon is the color of eggshells and it sets a strange spell over the forest. For one, crazy moment, I think that Victoria's plan might work.

'Do you have it?' she whispers when we meet outside her door.

I hold up a candle I found in Judy's drawer. 'I hope she doesn't notice it's gone.'

'Who cares. Come on, let's go.' We creep down the stairs and once again out of the library window. As we run down the hill toward the forest, Victoria lets out a loud *whoop*, pumping her fist in the air.

'We did it!' then she grabs my hand, 'Come on, let's hurry.'

We walk for quite a distance into the forest and when she finds a small clearing, she stops. With her foot, she draws a large circle and then throws down an old white sheet at the center of it. 'We'll do it here,' she decides, dropping down, cross-legged, and pats the space beside her.

'Where did you find this anyway?' I ask, pointing to the paper in her hands.

'One of my friends sent it to me last week. She said it helped her.'

'Have you ever done anything like this before?'

'Never had to.' Her mouth is set in eager determination as she lights the candle and hands it back to me. 'It's supposed to be red but I don't think that matters much.'

I want to ask her if she really believes that a love spell will make Leo leave his girlfriend but she is so hopeful that it seems unfair of me to doubt her.

'You ready?' she asks.

'Yes.'

'Okay. It says I have to close my eyes and think of him really hard.' She squeezes her eyelids shut and despite my reservations, I do the same. I think of that morning in the park on my birthday and I see him, kneeling beside the pond, his arm outstretched for me, his face turning back to make sure I am coming.

'Open your eyes.' Victoria's voice interrupts my thoughts. 'We have to do a chant now.'

'Okay.'

It no longer seems funny to me that we are out here, praying to the moon, hoping that it will spark something in the people that we love, making them love us back. It seems like it's the only thing we can do. And so when Victoria spreads out the piece of paper on the blanket, underneath the flickering candle, I chant it with her, using all the force I can manage.

> *Diana, Goddess of Love*
> *I ask that you hear me*
> *Please let him*
> *Send love towards me*

Then she blows out the candle and puts my hand above the rising smoke and places her own palm on top of my fingers.

> *Make you think about me day and night.*
> *Night and day, day and night.*

And we sit there, in the silver darkness, lost in our own thoughts for a little while. A dog howl somewhere far away jerks us both back to awareness.

'Do you think it worked?' she asks.

'We'll have to wait and see.' I can't help but feel excited; to feel certain that now my plea is out there, floating in the skies, he will sense it and come for me. I get up and brush the dirt off my knees. 'We should get back before they notice us missing.'

She rolls up the blanket and then turns to me, catching me in a hug. 'You're a really good friend.' She pulls away and her hair hides her face. 'I've never really had any proper friends, you know?'

'Yeah,' I say impulsively grabbing her hand and linking our fingers together. 'I do.'

And as we say goodnight, breaking out into unrestrained giggling, hushing each other as we do it, I notice that the ache in my belly has dulled and as I walk back to my room, there is a lightness to my step that I have not felt since I left home. The year doesn't seem so endless anymore—I can see it flash past in days like this, spent with Victoria, and it occurs to me that after all of it is done and I'm home again with him, there might be something left at the Academy that will be worth missing.

20

St Albert. September 1976

The snowstorm caught them all by surprise. They weren't strangers to heavy weather, but this was different. Although the lowering temperatures had warned them of the encroaching winter, it had been unseasonably dry, so this sudden white storm was unexpected. The clouds had hung low all day, pregnant with frozen rain, and a biting, merciless cold had descended upon the town, settling in a thousand falling flakes. He had to call Marienne and tell her that he would be late.

'The roads are all suspended, covered in ice.'

'You only work ten minutes away.' Her voice sounded like it was coming from some distant place. 'And you're walking.'

'I can't see two steps ahead of me.'

'It's just going to get worse—it'll be better if you come home now.'

He hesitated. There was no way to hide it. He looked around the bar. 'I'm not at work.'

'Where are you then?'

'I'm at a meeting.' A cold blast of wind hit him as the door swung open to let someone stumble in. A shout went up from the table beside him, welcoming the stranger, and he cringed.

'What was that?'

'We're at a bar. I had to meet a client here.'

'Since when did you travel to meet clients?'

'It's an important one, Annie.' He wasn't used to her interrogating him and it set him on edge. 'I should be grateful I got this opportunity at all. We were supposed to meet here to go to his office but the storm started.'

'Just let me know when you're leaving.'

'Okay, I love you.'

'I love you too. Be safe.'

He went back to his table, feeling guilty and annoyed for having been forced to call her. He wasn't there to meet a client. He was alone and he climbed back into his seat and took a sip of watery beer. He had started coming here a few weeks ago, straight after work. The thought of going home had become an uncomfortable, threatening prospect. The constant disappointment and stress of failing to produce a baby had changed Marienne. She stopped cooking and cleaning the house—took up smoking again and listened to music all day instead. When he tried to talk to her, engage her in the life that was moving on without them, she barely listened, always interjecting with another new remedy proven to boost fertility, or complained that perhaps they weren't trying hard enough, sometimes even walking out of the room, leaving his words tripping and limping after her.

The first time he had come to the bar, it was with a few friends from work and when he eventually made it home, nothing seemed as bad as it had that morning. And so he came back; he never drank much, only enough to coat his situation in an easier light and Marienne never noticed, and so he kept on doing it. He liked the dimness of the place, the soft music playing in the background against the loudness of its patrons.

Today, however, there were more people seeking its shelter than usual; women and their families, looking for a place to pass the storm. His heart stopped when he heard it; the full sweetness of the laugh. He would know that sound anywhere. His eyes darted quickly through the dark room, a chill, not from outside, pricking his neck and making him break out in a cold sweat. He finished his beer in one gulp, wiped his mouth clean and stood up to leave. It was too hot in here and Marienne was right; the snow and wind would only get worse. It would be much better for him to go now.

'You're not leaving in this weather, are you?' A smooth, husky voice behind him. He turned around.

'Gina.'

Gina was a friend of Marienne's—or friend being too loose a word—an acquaintance. She lived close to them and when she had been married, had often come to the barbeques and picnics they had held. He had never taken a particular interest in her except to notice that most of the women didn't like her. And of course, her hair; a deep, burned shade of red, always pulled neatly from her face and allowed to fall in loose waves. Even he had to admit, it was lovely to look at.

'Nice to see a familiar face in this dump.' She looked around distastefully and sat down at his table.

'Sorry to disappoint you but I have to get going.'

'I can't let you. It's not safe.'

'I'll be fine.'

'A strong man. I like that,' she teased and when he didn't respond, she pursed her lips and twitched her head toward the speaker in the corner of the ceiling. 'Listen.' The radio was on. He could only catch bits of sound. *Worst storm to hit us in over twenty years. Stay where you are… Die down, but safety comes first.* She sat up straight and smiled. 'So you see, it's my duty as a fellow neighbor to see that you don't make a rash decision. And it's yours, as a man, to make sure I'm safe in this hole.'

He looked outside. It was darker now and the wind was banging against the window frames, the high whistle of it rolling by. 'I guess I'll stay for a while then.'

She clapped her hands. 'Great. Let's get you a drink.' She snapped her fingers for a bartender and ordered them both a whiskey. 'I hope you don't mind. That's what I'm having.' He shrugged off his coat once more. The laughter had stopped. Perhaps he had imagined it—that happened a lot these days.

'That's fine, thanks.'

'What are you doing here, anyway?'

'I had to meet a client.'

She scoffed. 'That's what my ex-husband always used to say. You men seriously lack in creativity, don't you? Always lazy—can't even be bothered to think of a proper excuse.'

He blanched. 'I don't know what you're implying.'

'Oh, nothing.' She saw the hard set of his mouth, the way his eyes fixed on hers challengingly. 'I'm sorry. Just because Kevin was a cheating asshole, doesn't mean all of you are.'

'I wouldn't do that to Marienne.'

'Of course not.' She smiled. He had never liked the taste of whiskey, it was too strong and left a numbing sensation on his tongue. 'How is she, anyway?'

'She's fine.'

'I heard the news. It must have been sad to find out.'

'We're dealing with it.' He put down his half-full glass. 'Look, I really should be going. Marienne will be worried about me.'

'She'll be more worried if you get lost out there.' She pushed the glass back at him. 'Come on, finish your drink at least.' He didn't know why he was compelled to listen to her. Her voice was demanding, leaving no option but to follow its direction and take back the glass. The drink was warm as it went down his throat and that was when he heard it again. Closer this time and he almost choked.

'I love your ring.' The absolute innocence in it that no adult sound could produce; curious and pure, nowhere and everywhere at once. It shook him to the core and he put the glass down. He saw her standing in front of him looking at Gina, but the whiskey had made his sight unsteady and he wasn't sure if she was real.

'Thanks honey,' Gina grinned at the illusion. 'Do you want to try it on?' She slipped it off her finger and gave it to the young girl, standing on her tiptoes to reach the high table they were sitting at. He simply stared at the girl as she played with the too-big ring, twirling it around her thin fingers. He stared at her polka-dot dress, the swaying skirt as she pirouetted, hand out and giggling. The small feet covered in ballet shoes, and her brown-gold hair tied up with a barrette: he felt the twitch and jump low in his stomach and he thought he would be sick with wanting.

'Candice.' Someone calling her, her eyes squinting into the darkness.

'My mom's calling me,' she said and looked up at him. Her mouth a perfect, pink oval. He cleared his throat, tried to say something to keep her there, but only strangled air came out.

'Well, you better go then,' Gina held her hand out for the ring and reluctantly the child gave it back. 'Bye.'

She gave a small wave and skipped back into the corner, where her parents were sitting. She jumped on the woman's lap and giggled as the arms encircled her, a face was pressed into her cheek.

'Are you alright?' Gina followed his eyes.

'Fine.' He cleared his throat. 'I'm fine.'

'Thank God I never got stuck with one of those.' She rolled her eyes and then winced. 'Yikes. Sorry, that was insensitive.'

'It doesn't matter.' The last of the whiskey left the glass, although he knew he should stop. Those small feet danced around in his mind, trod on his reservations and broke them into shards.

'Are you still trying?' she asked.

'Yes.'

'Any luck?' She played with the rim of her glass, trailing her long fingers over it. He couldn't help but think how sensual the action was. The shock of seeing the girl had disrupted his previous calmness and everything in him seemed to be on fire.

'No and I don't ever think it's going to happen. Marienne is just having a difficult time accepting it.' He knew he shouldn't say more; he understood the way gossip spread in this town, but he had to have something to distract himself.

'That must be hard for you.' Her hand fell to his knee and stayed there. The smooth band of the ring pressed into his pants. He felt her fresh skin on it; the excitement she had experienced wearing it, radiating into him. It loosened up the knot in his stomach and so he let Gina's hand sit there.

'It is,' he admitted. 'It's hard to see her so upset all the time.'

'Puts a strain on the marriage, doesn't it?' She squeezed his thigh when he started to move away. 'I'm not intruding. It's just that I've been through something similar.'

'With Kevin?'

'I need another drink.' She signaled for the bartender and ordered two more. James didn't protest. From the corner of his eye, he could see her, cuddling up to her mother, her dress hitched up now above her knee. The smooth leg half lit up by the poor bar light, swinging back and forth; the ballet shoe off now, toes barely grazing the floor. He could stay here forever and watch that movement, it was so beautiful. He took the whiskey that was handed to him and downed half of it in one sip. Gina continued talking. 'We just reached a point where we wanted different things, I suppose. Where we stopped paying attention to each other and let the small stuff get in the way.'

'I never saw that happening with Marienne and me,' he said. 'She told me she never wanted a baby. We agreed on it and all of a sudden, she changed her mind.'

'I'm sorry.' Gina's hand inched further up. He didn't know if she was doing it intentionally, but it was keeping him distracted. Usually the cravings died after a while, but with the alcohol, the girl glinting in the corner, and Gina's hand on his thigh, he could see only one way of expelling it.

'You want to get out of here?' His voice was gruff; the words not his. Her eyes widened in surprise and then she finished off her drink. He might have changed his mind if she had offered up the slightest resistance.

'Lucky for you, my cousin owns the motel two doors down. Why don't you go and get us a room and I'll come in through the back. Get the key to room 204.'

He left his half-full glass, took one last look at the girl, now sleeping on her mother's shoulder, opened the door and was engulfed into the wet, cold world.

21

Whitehorse, Yukon. December 1992

The Academy looks different when it's wearing snow; a grand and elegant old woman glittering under a cold chandelier of sun. I get out of bed, the frost coming from under the window panes rousing me and I hit the thermostat twice with my fist before it whirs into motion. Judy is already downstairs and I dress quickly, washing my face in the small sink just outside our room. The water freezes my fingers and I have to slap them against my upper arm, kept warm from my sleep, before I can feel them again.

Victoria is waiting for me at our usual table, where just the two of us sit, side by side, as she points out a new girl each day and makes fun of her.

'Heard she peed her bed the first night she got here.' She points to someone a couple of tables in front of her, not caring if anyone hears her or not. 'Is that lame or what?'

'Totally.' I've learned to agree with everything she says because I love the way her face lights up when I do, the way she looks at me in that secretive way.

'Listen,' she leans in closer than usual, lowering her voice. 'Leo's coming today. He says he has something to tell me.'

'What do you think it is?' I ask.

'I think it worked, Cee.' That is her new name for me, and I never get tired of hearing her say it. 'That spell we did. I think he's going to tell me he loves me.'

At first, I don't know what to say. I haven't heard from my father since the phone call over a month ago and it seems unfair to me that Victoria is getting what she wants and I will be left with nothing. She shakes me.

'Will you come with me? I'm so nervous.'

'Sure,' I shake myself from my thoughts. 'What time?'

'Same time, at four thirty, after classes?'

I can't look at her; her face is too bright and happy and she has become the stranger I knew before we held hands and chanted in the forest. 'Okay. Yeah, I'll meet you there.'

We leave the dining room; I throw away the rest of my porridge, and toss the bowl into the bucket, hardly knowing what I'm doing. I can no longer think straight and I realize that I've been harboring the secret hope that the spell is doing its magic and soon it would work. But now that I know Leo is here to see Victoria and I haven't heard one word from my father, I remember how silly the whole thing had seemed to me at first, and I know I will not see him for another seven months.

'It's really going to happen,' Victoria is still speaking, almost running up the stairs. 'I can't believe it actually worked!'

He is waiting for us as we make our careful way down the icy slope toward the forest. The pine trees are full and beautiful and catch the snow within their needles; velvet green spotted white. He is wearing a leather jacket that fits his large torso perfectly and from the back, I see that his hair hangs long and flicks at the base of his neck.

'He's so hot,' she whispers to me, pausing to fan her face dramatically. 'How do I look?'

'Perfect.' She slaps her cheeks silently to get the blood flowing and then tosses her head forward and flips her hair, pushing it up with her fingers. 'Okay. Stay here, I'll be right back.'

She saunters up to him, touching him on the shoulder and he turns around, crushing her in a hug. I step behind a tree so he won't see me.

He kisses her and her hands slide up the back of his jacket and when they break it off, she presses her face to his chest.

'You really kept me waiting,' she says.

He is quiet, stroking her hair and then pulls her back and holds her by the shoulders. 'I did it, Vick. I told her that it's over.' He pauses and even before he says it, I know he will, and I almost shove my fists in my ears because I don't want to hear it. But I have to. 'I love you.'

It is said with such earnestness, such passion. Perhaps I am just angry, or it has been such a long time since I have heard those words spoken to me, but Leo's declaration seems more real than anything I have ever heard from my father. Though they carry a thousand meanings, the words coming from Leo are unburdened. He smiles when he says them, they make him throw his arm around her neck and laugh loudly, and looking at him, I realize that my father never looks like that when he says it to me. Those three words make his eyes stormy, his face look older and sad. They weigh him down while lifting me up.

I back away from the tree, stumbling down further, heading in a direction I have never been before. I just want to move away from my thoughts; eventually, Victoria and Leo are lost and I have come to the edge of the river. It's wide and travels down in the direction of the town. I know that in the summer it's not a clear blue, but shines a strange shade of green, emerald almost, though today it's covered in a thin sheet of black ice and I can see the water struggling beneath it. I touch my foot to it, hear the strain it causes, and pull back. I step on it again, in a different spot, and this time the ice carries my weight. I inch further along, placing a second foot on the ice and let out a frosty exhale when it stands strong. I hardly know what I'm doing.

There is something exciting about being in danger; it wipes my mind clean of anything and all I can do is concentrate on keeping my balance, fully aware that my next step might crack the ice and I will fall through. I don't think of what that could mean; I simply enjoy the thrill, throwing my arms out and tilting my head up to the tall, stretching circle of trees around me. *Why?* I shout silently up at them. *Why have you given this to her?* I spin around, slowly at first, but the air feels so wonderful in my face and the trees are such a stark, mossy green, that I get lost in them and don't hear the warning sound of the ice beginning to give beneath me.

It occurs so fast that I don't know what has happened until the water reaches my chest and the breath blows out of me. I kick desperately but the water is violent and frozen around me. I scream, tilting my head above the water and letting the sound carry itself. I shout for Victoria, for Leo, even though I don't know him, but they don't come. My jacket is weighing me down and I attempt to pull it off but I can't do it without sinking under, so I leave it and go back to trying to slide onto the ice. I manage to haul myself up half-way, my legs are still in the water and my whole body is numbingly cold.

'Help!' I yell. 'Please, somebody, help me!' I start to cry, my tears creating steam that rises off the ice. 'Daddy,' I mumble into my scarf. 'I need you to help me.' My muscles have stopped working and even though I am clawing at the ice, I don't seem to be coming

185

any further out. The water, happy to be free of its icy cover, splashes hungrily around me; it burns my eyes and spills into my mouth and I choke. 'Please. Victoria, where are you!'

I hear a loud bark, followed by three consecutive quick ones and I see a golden retriever standing at the edge of the pond, hunched on its front paws, barking out at me. I am closer than I thought to land and I reach my hand out. It cannot be alone, there must be someone with it. 'Help.' The water fills my mouth and the word gurgles. 'Help me, please.' I cough it out but that only lets more of it in. I am so tired and my body has finally frozen over. I miss him already, even though I am not yet gone, and Bubbie springs to my mind. *So this is what it felt like.*

And just before my eyes close, I see a flash through the trees. Someone is sprinting down, sweeping in and out of branches, shouting, 'Hold on, hold on,' and I recognize the voice. When Joseph finally comes into view, I almost cry with relief. He sees me and grabs the dog, unpinning the leash from around his neck.

'Frances, just stay calm, okay.' His voice is as careful as his footsteps and he tries to step on the ice but it starts to break under him. He quickly returns to the edge of the river. He lies down on his stomach and slides a little closer to me.

'Am I going to die?' The breath freezes in my lungs before it comes out but I have to know.

'You're going to be fine.' He sounds so sure and confident. 'Look at me—try to keep your head above the water.'

I try to nod.

'Now, I'm going to throw you this leash and I want you to grab a hold of it and swim out.' He makes it sound so simple and easy and a little of my anxiety starts to die away.

'Okay.'

'You can do that, right?'

I nod, finding the strength in my neck.

'Good girl.' He throws the leash at me. It's a stark red and sturdy enough for the large dog it's intended for. He keeps his hand wrapped around the other end, tied around his palm. I reach for it and miss. I try again, and still my frozen fingers won't grab it. I start to cry.

'I can't do it.'

'Yes, you can.' He slides a little closer. 'I can't come there and get you because the ice will break. So I need you to grab onto the leash, okay? Don't be scared.'

I try again and this time I manage to hold onto it. 'I've got it.'

'Good.' He starts to pull. 'You need to swim now, Frances.'

'I can't.' I'm sobbing and it's making breathing more difficult. 'I can't feel my legs.'

'I know it's hard but just try. Kick your legs out. I've got you.'

I start to kick, the ice separating and letting me through. I think of my father; of his body so close to mine, the solidness of his chest so wide and safe, and I keep kicking. 'There you go, come on.' Joseph sounds closer now and then he lets go of the leash and his hands are grabbing me under the arms and pulling me out, dragging me onto the snowy ground. His jacket is off and around me in an instant. 'I've got you.' And it's his heat I feel and the rapid pacing of his heart that I hear and nothing has ever felt so good. He falls back and I fall beside him. The dog is back and licking my face. 'Stop it, Benson. Shoo.' Joseph is leaning over me, pushing the dog away. 'You're safe, it's okay. You're safe with me, now.'

22

St Albert. September 1976

He was heartbroken, lying in bed with a woman he never wanted to see again, craving one he knew he was making unhappy. Gina leaned her head against his chest, her arm wrapped around his upper body. It had been almost a month since she had found him sitting in the bar; when they had snuck into her cousin's motel, his blood boiling with whiskey and need. Afterward, perhaps due to his guilt, or the drink, he had begun to talk about Marienne.

'How could she say she never wants children and then just change her mind?' He was talking more to himself but it felt good to have someone to direct his words to. 'And even if she did, how can she expect me to just go along with it?' He hardly noticed Gina's hand in his—twisting, unfamiliar fingers. 'We're wasting our lives, our time, on something that will probably never happen.'

She called him two days later at his office and although he didn't care to see her again, he needed someone to listen to him. To say out loud to a witness everything that had been troubling him since the whole thing began. So he agreed to meet her on the weekend, and the weekend after that, always under the pretense of meeting a client or having a sudden load of work to finish. The third time they met, it was at a different motel, somewhere outside of St Albert. The red velvet décor had made him infinitely sorry he had said anything to her in the first place. But then she put her hand on his and asked if everything was alright and he felt a compulsion to say again what he had said to her that day in the bar.

'I love her. I really do, but this obsession with having a child is taking over our lives. She barely speaks to me anymore.' The way Gina had turned up her lips in understanding and nodded her head to these words had filled him with such gratitude because if she believed him, he would have to believe himself. He had leaned in to kiss her cheek but she turned her face at exactly the same moment so he met her mouth instead. The shock of it; to do something so indiscreet in public, where someone might see him and then real- izing he was safe, had sent a momentary thrill ringing through his head, so when Gina had said the following weekend that she had taken the liberty of obtaining a key from the concierge and asked if he wanted to join her, he hadn't hesitated to say yes.

Marienne had stopped sleeping close to him; she found an old teddy bear he had given her a long time ago and began sleeping with that instead, wrapping her body around the silky material, pressing it firmly to her abdomen. If he tried to touch her, she would move further away until eventually he could stretch his entire arm out and feel nothing but empty space. He missed the comfort of another body close to him; the warm, solid heat only another human's skin can give.

Now, lying in another room smelling of too much use, two weeks later, he didn't know how to say no to Gina anymore and even though he wasn't attracted to her, and didn't particularly like her, he missed the physicality of his and Marienne's relationship, searching for it in Gina instead. She was an outlet, an escape, and he couldn't make himself stop.

'I wish we could do this more often,' Gina said, arching her neck up to look at him.

'I have a wife, Ginny.' He slid out from under her as he said it, swinging his legs over the bed and pulling on his jeans.

'Don't remind me.' Her scornful laugh made him want to turn around and slap her. 'If only she wasn't at home so much.' Gina sat up behind him, leaving wet kisses across his shoulders and he tried not to move away.

'Where else would she go?' he asked, shrugging on his shirt. He checked his watch; still early enough to say he had been caught up at work.

'It would be easier if she had a job,' Gina mused. 'Something to keep her occupied so I can have you all to myself.'

She said this casually but the thought stuck with him as he pushed his feet into his shoes, using his index finger to stretch the heel so they slipped in easily. It might not be a bad idea for Marienne to have something else to concentrate on. He knew all about the power of distraction; its effectiveness. He wondered why he had never thought about it before.

'That might be a good idea.'

'I was joking, baby.' The endearment turned sour in his ears. Gina took a sip of the cheap wine he had brought along with him. 'She's a housewife. What kind of job could she possibly get?'

From his position on the bed, he could hear the sounds of the end-of-day traffic in the street below. The deep, loud drone of waiting cars relaxed him as did the far-off voices, a church bell somewhere. He could imagine the huge mass of bodies moving in between and around each other. All the noises rose and fell in a murmuring rhythm, creating a hole in his stomach that stretched and widened as he stayed sitting on the edge of the bed, listening to the traffic of humans, vehicles and voices, all of them headed in the same direction. All of them going home.

'Maybe you could help her get a job at the hospital?' Evening was falling into the room in playful shadows and he was grateful for it because it blurred the lines of her face, making it easier for him. He stood up and pulled on his jacket. 'I mean, you are the head nurse. It wouldn't be hard.'

'Let me get this right,' pulling at the lapels of his jacket, running her teeth against his lower lip. He half pulled away. 'You want me to work with the woman whose husband I've been sleeping with?' She was incredulous, laughing at him. He pressed his lips fully to hers. A part of him enjoyed these motel meetings because they allowed him to drive away the murkiness that weighed him down, that would have sat inside him and made him weaker. But he missed Marienne and was convinced that a job would be a good idea; that it might allow her to be happy once more.

'What better way to make sure we don't get caught?' he said. After a moment, Gina smiled, pulling back to look at him. She ran her sharp fingernail against the dimple in his chin.

'You're a genius, baby.'

They waited a few more days before Gina ran into them in the local supermarket. He had told her exactly what to say.

'I don't want Marienne becoming suspicious,' he had said. 'I don't want her to start guessing at anything.'

Gina laughed, seizing his chin and kissing him roughly. 'I love it when you get all worked up,' and then seeing the way he looked at her, she sighed. 'Okay, okay. I'll be careful.'

They had planned it perfectly. Marienne followed an unchanging schedule when it came to doing the shopping. She liked going on the weekends, when everyone else seemed to disappear; had gone fishing or picnicking with their families. She enjoyed the time it gave them to spend together, uninterrupted by anyone else. He told Gina to meet them early on Sunday morning, ignoring the way she trailed her teeth down the flap of his earlobe, saying, 'I can imagine a hundred other things I'd rather be doing with you on a Sunday morning.'

Now, walking through the cold, gray aisles of the almost empty supermarket and seeing the anticipated flash of red hair around the corner, James looked down at his unsuspecting wife and felt guiltier than ever. He took Marienne's hand and held onto her delicate wrist, massaging it between his fingers. She turned to him in surprise. It was an unexpected display of affection after so many days spent keeping a certain distance from each other, moving carefully and silently around the spacious house, each lost and lonely in their own worries. When her lips turned up slightly and she brought his hand up to kiss his knuckles, he pulled her toward him and hugged her tightly.

'Well isn't this a surprise.' Gina's voice was a rude shock and he looked up to see her coming toward them, walking quickly and empty-handed. He held onto Marienne, feeling a fast jerk of anger skip along his jaw. Marienne pulled away from him silently, leaving him off-balance.

'Hello, Gina,' Marienne said and she sounded loud, happy. 'Funny running into you here.'

'I had to pick up a few things.'

He wished those green eyes would look anywhere other than directly at him and he shifted under her hard gaze. Then she released him and turned back to his wife.

'Did I interrupt you two lovebirds?'

Marienne laughed, slipping her arm around James's waist, fitting perfectly against him and, despite the situation, he had a sudden urge to lean down and whisper in her ear how much he adored her.

'No, you didn't. Not at all. It's good to see you.'

He finally lifted his eyes to Gina and she met his stare, bright with jealousy. She was waiting for him; for a gesture or an acknowledgment that they were in this together and when he stayed silent, she gave them a small wave, her bracelets dancing under the cheap, fluorescent lighting.

'Well, I guess I'll be going then,' she started to move away. 'I'll see the two of you around.' She was testing him, seeing how much she meant to him.

James let go of Marienne, calling after her, trying to control the annoyance in his voice, concentrating on making it sound as ordinary as possible. 'How's work?'

She stopped and spun around on the high-heel of her shoe. She tilted her head at him and her body shivered with inaudible, mean laughter. She was enjoying this; playing with him and his wife, carelessly toying with his marriage because she had already ruined her own, wanting to spoil everything he loved.

'It's good, thanks for asking.' She came back toward them, walking with a deliberate, slight sway.

'I hear it's really busy over at the hospital.' He was prodding her, guiding her into the words he had told her to say.

'Is that right?' She smiled at Marienne before twisting her gaze back toward him. 'Who'd you hear that from?'

'I can't remember.' He said the words slowly, so they wouldn't shake with his irritation. 'I just heard.'

'It's hectic,' she finally admitted. She had gone too far and seeing him angry had caused her face to relax. 'Actually, Marienne, I'm glad I ran into you.'

Marienne, who up until then had been listening to their conversation with a polite indifference, wrinkled her eyebrows. 'Really? Why's that?'

'I was wondering if you would be interested in working at the hospital for a few weeks.' The words fell into the open air, hanging, waiting to be received. They watched Marienne together, their breaths caught up in each other's, each with something different at stake.

'Me?' she asked and when Gina nodded, she said, 'But I don't have any qualifications.'

Gina shrugged, waved her ringed fingers in the air. 'Oh, it's a reception job. Really easy, really straightforward,' she assured Marienne. 'One of our night receptionists had a family emergency and it's impossible to find someone at such short notice.' Marienne began rearranging items in their cart and he knew she was getting ready to say no.

'I can imagine how busy it gets there,' he interjected before Marienne could speak. The words were stiff and unnatural on his tongue and he spoke slowly, afraid of making a mistake. The fact of his affair with Gina hovered over them, ready at any moment to slide into the practiced conversation in the form of a slipped-up word or an unconscious gesture.

'It sure does,' Gina replied.

'I'll think about it.' Marienne pushed her hair behind her ears and tightened her hands around the handle of the shopping cart. 'Would that be alright? Like I said, I don't have any experience.'

'I'll be there to show you how everything works.'

'I'll call you next week,' said Marienne, hinting that she wanted the conversation to be over, and when Gina looked at him, he gave her a small nod.

'Of course.' Gina leaned in to kiss Marienne's cheek, and as she did, she gave him a slow wink. He pretended not to see it. 'Give me a call and we can discuss it.'

'Okay,' Marienne said, and James wrapped his arm protectively around her shoulder, saying goodbye to Gina. She was gone in a tinkling of jewelry, the space she occupied smelling strongly of perfume, leaving her empty basket on the ground and he was angry at her carelessness. Marienne didn't seem to notice as she straightened out the items in their cart, arranging them in clean, neat categories; food-stuff on the left and everything else packed to the right.

'I think it might be a good idea,' he said.

'Really?'

'Yes. It'll only be for a little while, in any case.' The words sped into the air, spurred on by how close he was to getting what he wanted. 'I think it'll be good for you to get out of the house.'

She stopped moving the shopping around. 'I'll think about it, okay?'

He knew not to push her anymore and they began walking, their heads bent close together. He pressed his face into her hair and the smell and feel of it was so familiar that the extent to which he had missed her hit him hard.

'I'm sorry I've been distant lately.' The words burst from his mouth. He had to say it because when he did, it soothed the soreness of all the lies he had told.

'It's okay,' she smiled up at him, pressing his hand. 'Let's talk about all that later.' Like him, she was hesitant to ruin the moment;

they had avoided each other for so long and it felt good to be close again. She pushed the cart away from her and leaned into him. He recognized the look in her eyes; the dark, swirling need that had nothing to do with children, but only the two of them. 'Forget about shopping,' she murmured. 'Let's go home.'

After a few days of thinking it over, of James nudging her toward the decision he needed her to make, Marienne took the job and James thought he was in the clear. She would come home, her mind soaked in the tragedies and joys of other people, too preoccupied with their problems to be worried about her own.

'It puts everything into perspective, doesn't it?' she said to him. 'We have each other, we're still trying. Nothing's been lost yet.'

After five weeks at the hospital, she hadn't wanted to leave and no one asked her to. So she continued and each day, their relationship began to mend itself and although Marienne's desire to have a child didn't go away, it began to fall asleep in her mind. She could go for several days, sometimes weeks without mentioning it. He treasured each smile over the dining table, the slight brushing of her fingers here, a quick goodnight kiss there, taking them to be light, tentative steps back into their old life.

James spent a few last weeks with Gina, waiting for Marienne to leave for her night-shift before cutting through the neighbors' gardens and moving invisibly through the darkness, meeting Gina at the back door of her house. She would be waiting for him; a slim figure lit up by the small, green light coming from the lamp on her dining table, leaning against the wide open doorway. As the nights went on, she started playing nervously with the blue curtains or sometimes stepping out of the house when he was late. That was how he knew she had fallen in love with him and although he no longer needed her, and wanted to end it, it was difficult to find the moment to tell her.

Despite it all, he had come to appreciate her feelings. She watched him with an intensity and a passion that he recognized as the same emotion he felt when he looked at Marienne, with the kind of need only someone who was lost and looking for something could feel. She often spoke of him leaving Marienne, as if in a trance, imagining them leaving town and settling down somewhere far away.

'My brother lives in Montreal,' she told him once, taking his arm and holding it around her waist. 'That's miles from here and no one would know where we went.'

'And what would we do there?' he humored her.

'Live together. We wouldn't have to hide it—we could grocery shop every Sunday. We could go dancing.' She had never sounded so excited or vulnerable before. He kissed her cheek and didn't say anything. 'We could get married,' she mused. 'We wouldn't tell anyone who we were or about our lives before.'

For a moment, he let himself consider the possibility of running away—not with Gina but alone. The temptation was always there, no matter how much he loved Marienne, to escape from everything holding him down. To stop fighting. He could rewrite his story, bury his old life in the vast country and never have to worry about it coming back. 'Promise me you'll think about it,' Gina said, moving on top of him. 'Promise me quickly.' He kissed her, goaded on by her enthusiasm. The idea was so tantalizing that he forgot about everything else and was certain he could do it. Marienne would eventually forgive him. She might be better off without him.

'I promise,' he said.

He wasn't sure how long he would have let his affair with Gina continue if he hadn't come home the next night to find Marienne back early from work. She was sitting on their bed reading, and when he came into the room, she turned over the corner of the page, running her finger along its fold, before closing it slowly.

'You're back.' The room shook with his silence and she had no choice but to fill it. 'The hospital was over-staffed tonight so I came home early.' He stayed near the door, the scent of Gina's perfume rooting him to the spot, making him unable to think of what to say. He took his time, undoing his shirt buttons slowly, playing out different stories in his mind.

'I went for a short walk,' trying to grin at her. 'I get bored when you're not around.' The lie came easily to him. It helped that she trusted him completely.

'You never said.' She patted the space beside her. 'I was worried.'

He pulled his shirt off, twisting it in his nervous hands and then throwing it into the farthest corner it would reach, sitting down next to her. When she leaned her head on him, he stiffened and stopped breathing but she didn't notice.

'I'm sorry.' Growing bolder by her obliviousness, he leaned back on the headboard and let her slip further into him. She was wonderfully hot against his hands. 'I thought I would be home before you got back.'

'Nice to get some fresh air?' she asked.

'Yes.' It took all of his breath to say that one word. 'But I'd much rather have been here with you.' She kissed his chest and then sat back up and opened her book.

'Me too, honey. Just let me know what you're doing next time, okay?'

'I will.' He got out of the bed, throwing his clothes off on the way to the shower.

He stayed for a long time under the steamy umbrella of water, enjoying the way it reached under his skin and burned him. He took his toothbrush with him into the shower, feeling the sharp sting of toothpaste that fell onto his chin. He moved the hairs of the brush slowly, in a strong, thoughtful motion against his teeth and when he finished, he turned his head up and opened his mouth, letting the water run into it; hot on his tongue and gums before he expelled his breath noisily and let out the minty stream. When he finished, he draped his towel loosely around his waist and leaned against the bathroom door.

He watched Marienne; the way her eyes flicked over the words of her book, fully settled now that he was home. Seeing her waiting for him had jerked him uncomfortably back into awareness; had made him remember how easy it could be to get caught. He climbed into bed, kissing her fast before moving as far away as possible from her, turning on his side so she wouldn't feel him shaking. She stroked his neck slowly with one hand, the other holding up her book, the glow of her light casting warm, red streaks behind his eyes. That was when he knew he would never leave her.

He told Gina the next day that the guilt was killing him. 'All this sneaking around and this fear—I can't do it anymore.' She lay, stone-faced beside him, staring up at her ceiling and he continued, trying to ease the blow. 'I don't want to end up hating you. You mean too much to me.'

She threw her silk dressing gown around her naked shoulders, wrapping it around her waist and sat up silently in bed, not facing him.

'This is about what I said the other day, isn't it?'

'No, no. It's not that.' He was glad she wasn't looking at him.

'Did you even consider leaving her?'

He shook his head. 'It wasn't an option, Gina. She's my wife.'

She stood up, pacing the small space at the foot of the bed, a nervous panic widening her eyes. She looked ready to claw through the wall.

'And that's why you've been coming here most nights a week, is it?'

'It's complicated, Ginny.' He couldn't tell her that he had never been attracted to her; that the reason this had started was because he had been drunk and out of control. That it had continued because she had given him something Marienne had stopped providing and now he no longer needed her. 'I care about you,' he said, choosing his words carefully, anxious that she might, at any moment, pick up the shiny black receiver of her bedside telephone, call the hospital and ask to talk to his wife.

'That's not the same thing.'

He tried to reach out for her but she was standing too far away.

'I think you should leave.'

'Ginny—'

She grabbed his arm with one hand and his jacket with the other. 'Get changed and leave.'

Once he was dressed, he came out slowly from the bedroom and found her sitting at her dining table. She had a glass of whiskey in her hands and it made him strangely reminiscent, remembering that night at the bar, surrounded by a whirlwind of snow and music. He watched the golden liquid glitter as it hovered above her lips before disappearing in one go into her quivering throat. He walked by her and opened the back door but turned around at the last minute. Watching her with her head down, slivers of moonlight falling onto her hair and creating strange shapes at her cheeks, he felt a sudden rush of empathy and wished he didn't have to hurt her.

'I know I have no right to ask this—' he paused and waited until she looked up. 'But please don't tell Marienne about us.' She laughed loudly and he was sure the whole neighborhood could hear it. She stood up quickly and the whiskey tumbler fell to the floor and bounced but didn't break.

'Just get out,' she said, pushing him onto the step before closing the door loudly in his face.

He saw the black shadow of her figure bend down to pick up the glass and she went to the kitchen sink to pour herself another drink. He watched the blue curtain swing back and forth and he wondered if he would miss her.

He spent the next couple of days watching the phone; rushing home with skipping breath and a stomach packed with nerves, sure that Marienne knew everything and was getting ready to leave him. Yet he was happily surprised every time to be greeted by his wife's smiling face; her fast kisses as she put on her earrings and pulled her hair back into a tight ponytail, her happy voice promising to let him know when she got back from work. When she was gone, he would sit on his porch, watching Gina's house and wondering why she had let him go so easily and quietly. He thought that maybe she found it romantic not to be able to have him. Maybe she had convinced herself that she had grown tired of him and thought of him as rarely as he thought of her. Or perhaps, just as he sat in the balmy night on the wicker swing outside his house, his feet dragging slowly beneath him, she might be at her dinner table under the green-black pattern of her lamp. She might have that same glass, choked tightly between her hands, which he was sure must have a small, sharp chip somewhere along its previously smooth rim, pricking her finger against it and thinking he would eventually come back to her.

And then she left suddenly, in the middle of the night, unaware that he was watching as she loaded her bags into the taxi before turning to look back at her house. She watched it for a moment and slid into a car, slamming the door behind her.

Once she disappeared, he stopped caring about her. He wanted her out of his life and she slipped unexpectedly easily from it, for a while becoming another shadowy secret to store away with all the others. There followed a few months of ease, temporary relief, before life took matters into its own hands, brought Frances into this world and everything changed.

23

Whitehorse, Yukon. December 1992

I am still shivering, wrapped in my blanket; the sting of the icy water still swimming within me. I blacked out at the river bank and when I wake up, I am in the infirmary, tucked tightly into white blankets. Sister Margret is hovering over me and I try to move my arms, try to explain to her that I'm sorry, that I'll never do it again and that it was a mistake. I am afraid she is going to expel me, that I won't have anywhere else to go because he won't let me come home.

Instead, to my surprise, her smile is as sympathetic as it can be and she asks if I'm alright. 'You gave us quite a fright, but the doctors said you're going to be okay. You were very lucky Joseph happened to be there.'

'Where is he?' I ask.

'He went home. It's late.' The clock reads almost ten o'clock.

'So I'm going to be okay?'

'Yes.' She pats my knee formally. 'They said you weren't in there long enough to get hypothermia or do any permanent damage. So just rest tonight and drink lots of hot liquid.'

An hour later, I'm in my bed, bunched up in the corner with

whatever covers I can find piled on top of me. But no matter what I drink or how many blankets I use, I can't get warm. Something colder and more terrifying than the water has tightened over my heart. Judy is sitting at her desk and every time I move, or grimace, she looks like she wants to say something, offer help, but when Victoria bursts through the door, she rolls her eyes and turns away.

'I should have known you were involved,' she says pointedly, but Victoria ignores her, pulling a face at me which I don't respond to. She jumps on my bed.

'Are you okay?' she asks, grabbing my hands. 'I was so worried about you.'

'Where were you?' I hissed. 'I was screaming for you guys,' lowering my voice, 'you weren't that far off. You must have heard me.'

She blushes. 'I'm so sorry,' flashing her eyes to the side to see if Judy is looking at us. She leans in closer and her breath stings my neck. 'He took me back to his car,' she bites her lip, and her apologetic look takes on a coquettish edge. 'I didn't realize—I didn't know you had gone.'

'Just forget it,' I say. 'I could have died, you know.'

I shouldn't be angry with her. It's not her fault but I hate how radiant her smile is; the gleam in her eye. She doesn't have to explain further; I know what happened in the car. I can feel the energy running through her, it snaps and burns me and shines too bright.

'I know.' She looks ready to cry. 'I feel awful. I'm so glad you're okay.'

'I'm going to get something to drink.' Judy leaves as if she can't stand being around us and once she is down the corridor, Victoria scoops up close to me, bringing her knees to her chest.

'I have something for you,' she says.

'What is it?'

She holds out a bracelet that is similar to hers; made of several colors of braided string. She takes my wrist without asking and puts it on. 'Just so you know how much you mean to me.'

'Thanks.' I take my hand back and let it lie in my lap.

'Forgive me?' she asks, and because I want to know what has happened with her and Leo, I nod.

'I'm just tired.' I wrap my sweater tighter around me and sink further into the blanket. 'What happened with you two?'

'He told me he loves me.' Her words are so excited they fight each other to come out first. 'I can hardly believe it.' She laughs, her cheeks stained pink. 'And then in his car—'

'I can guess,' I say, holding up my hand, but the image of the two of them stirs something in me and I push my knees together and close my eyes.

'Have you?' she hesitates and my look goads her on. 'Have you and Tom, you know,' she fumbles, unsure of whether she should say it.

My heart pumps in small, aching beats. 'Yes.' Even that small confession, no matter what she believes, makes me feel guilty and creates a deep knot at the back of my neck, holding me down.

'It's great, isn't it?' she throws her body back on my bed. 'It just makes you feel,' she waves her hand in the air, gesturing for me to finish her sentence but I don't know what to say. 'So full. Like everything is fixed—complete. Am I making any sense?'

I close my eyes. 'I want to go to sleep now.'

'Okay.' I know she wants to talk some more, but she hugs me again. 'I'm so glad you're alright.' She stands up and then turns back to look at me, lost in all the blue cotton. 'I'm leaving early tomorrow for Christmas break,' she says. 'I'm going to miss you.'

Tears sting my eyes. 'Me too.' I curl into a ball, facing away from her. 'Bye, Victoria.'

'Bye, Cee.'

As soon as the door is closed, I open my mouth and let it out; a ripping, choking sound. I'm crying because he hasn't called and I'm afraid. Because everything Victoria feels, I feel the exact opposite—I am broken and still waiting to be put together. Because her boyfriend loves her and no one loves me. I think of him but also of Joseph, who didn't bother waiting until I woke up to make sure I was okay, and I close my eyes and cry again and no matter how hard I try, nothing makes it stop.

24

Whitehorse, Yukon. December 1992

The black horse looks different up close; smaller and poorly drawn and I can see its teeth protruding from its reared mouth. The pub itself is empty and shut for the day and I continue down the empty street, hearing the crunch of untouched snow beneath my boots.

The Academy was empty when I left it this morning. Most of the girls have gone home for Christmas, as have most of the teachers. He never called me to ask if I wanted to come back, and although my mother did, I refused. Now, I make my way up the road and the shops fall away into rows of houses. They all look the same but I am prepared to wait outside each one until I find what I have come for. But I don't have to do that because I spot him in his white garden, building a snowman with his son. I stand apart from them for a couple of minutes, crouched behind a car and watch as Nova comes out onto the step. She shouts something at them but I can't make it out. Joseph stops his son by pulling him toward his knees. The three of them look at each other and seem perfect. I have come to thank him but something stops me from going forward.

He whispers something into his son's ear and the boy goes running clumsily through the snow and up the stairs. Joseph blows a kiss to his wife and she catches it in her fist before turning back into the house. He finishes off the snowman alone, flecking away extra bits of snow impatiently, sculpting it under his speedy hands. He is wearing nothing but a long-sleeved shirt and jeans and he doesn't seem to notice the cold. I tiptoe against the car, straining to see him. I will not speak to him today; I am happy just to watch him. In the three days since he saved me from the frozen river, he has been the only thing I can think about. The way his body moved down through the trees, in long and big gestures, the way only a man's can. I want to catch the curve-shape of his lips and steal away his smile and stash it under my pillow.

'Can I help you, young lady?' I gasp and turn slightly, bumping into a man standing right in my path, his arms crossed over his fat chest. His breath comes out strained, as if he has just climbed a flight of stairs after months of avoiding them. I quickly turn to check if Joseph has seen us. His back is to me and he is clearing the mounds of snow from beneath the snowman, flattening the area with the soles of his boots.

'No. I'm just a little lost but I'll find my way, thank you.' I try to get past him but he is blocking my way.

'Where are you going? Maybe I can point you in the right direction.'

'No, really.' I'm panicking. I don't want Joseph to see me—I'm not sure yet what I will say and I need time to prepare myself. 'I think I can figure it out.'

'Only if you're sure,' he pauses and I squeeze past him, through the space of his stomach and the car.

'Yes, thank you.' It's difficult to move quickly along the icy pavement and as the man slowly gets into his car, I can hear Joseph calling my name. I consider keeping on walking but that would only make me look suspicious. He jogs the last few meters toward me, his face crinkling in the sunlight.

'What are you doing here?'

'I'm just out for a walk,' I say. 'The house is empty and school is out for the holidays so there isn't much else to do.' His eyes regard me kindly. 'I also came to say thank you.'

'You know you didn't have to do that.'

'You saved my life.'

'It was lucky I happened to be walking Benson at that time.'

'Where is he?'

'Oh, he doesn't belong to me. I was walking him for a friend of mine.' He leans down to look at me closer. 'How are you feeling?'

'I'm better. They said I wasn't in there long enough to get hypothermia or anything.' I move my fingers and legs and grin. 'See? All working.'

He laughs. 'I'm glad,' and then he asks, 'Did you tell your parents what happened?'

'Yes, they were worried but I told them I was fine. They say thank you.' This is a lie. Sister Margret insisted on calling my parents the next day, but I told her I would do it myself. Instead, I sat in her office for half an hour, staring at the phone and willing it to ring, for him to call. Of course, he didn't so I picked it up, pretended to talk in case she was listening, and then left. No matter how much I missed him, I couldn't bring myself to dial the number.

'You're not going home for the holidays?' Joseph asks.

I shake my head and I'm glad when he doesn't ask me why. He turns to look back at his house and then asks if I want to join them. 'Nova is making a great spread,' he winks. 'Come on, we always have space for one more.'

*

She watches me over the table, bouncing Alex on her knees.

'Does someone know you're over here?' she asks.

'Nova.'

She presses the side of her fork to her egg, moving it back and forth, breaking it open and letting the center flow free. Then she pushes the egg through the yellow mess, covering it completely before putting it in her mouth. 'I just wanted to make sure,' she says. I smile a little at her uneasiness behind the piece of toast I am eating.

'Yes, I told them I was coming here to thank Joseph for what he did.'

She looks guilty when I say this. 'I hope you're feeling better.'

'I am, thank you.'

There is an earthy, natural spice that comes through in every bite of food and it punctures my tongue. It sits low in my ears and burns across my lips, instantly warming me. The high, whistling wind rattles the frame of the house, occasionally interrupting the comfortable silence around us. A door slams somewhere upstairs. Then the sudden ring of the phone gets Joseph out of his chair.

'I'll get it,' he says and is quickly gone. Nova straightens up in her chair, cleaning the crumbs off the table around her. Her body is tensed, as if it's getting ready to leap across the table and counteract anything I might do.

She asks, 'So, how are you finding the Academy?'

'It's fine,' I answer.

'Joseph was telling me you were having trouble fitting in.'

I bristle. I feel as if I am being reprimanded or judged. I wonder how much he has told her. If he has mentioned that night at the gate when my arms seemed glued to him and wouldn't let go.

'I was. But it's always like that in a new place, isn't it?'

'Yes.' She wipes away some of the mess from Alex's face and he tries to pull away. She holds him firmly with one arm around his chest. 'I suppose so. And you didn't want to go home for Christmas?'

'My parents have gone on holiday,' I lie. 'To visit my grandparents in Kingston, so it was just easier that I stay here.'

'Of course.'

She doesn't get a chance to say anything more because Joseph has come back and his mouth is turned down in a little frown.

'That was Janine,' he says, slipping back into his seat. Nova watches him with anxious eyes.

'Is everything okay?'

'She won't be able to make it today.'

'Why not?'

'She didn't really say,' he answers. 'Some sort of emergency...'

'What are we going to do now?'

I try to figure out what they are saying. My heart races a little with hope and I have to stop myself from interrupting. Not until I know for sure.

'I don't know. We could go tomorrow.'

'I can't do that. We promised and you know how important this is.'

'I can stay at home then.'

'I need you there with me.'

He puffs his cheeks out thoughtfully. 'Maybe I'll call Janine and ask her if she has a friend who can babysit.'

This is the moment to jump in. 'If you need someone to babysit, I can do it.'

Nova turns to me with a forced smile. 'No, that's okay. I'm sure we'll find someone.'

'I used to do it all the time back home.' My second lie. 'Alex would be in good hands.'

'I'm not sure the Academy would allow it,' she starts but Joseph interrupts her.

'I could ask,' he says. 'I'm sure they wouldn't mind.'

She stops side-stepping the real issue, impatient to find a solution that she wants. 'Just call Janine back and ask her if she has a friend that can do it.'

My face burns from the obvious rejection and I swallow down the urge to stay there and persuade her. I finish the last of my beans and stand up.

'Thank you so much for the breakfast,' I say, putting on my coat. 'But I really have to go now. I told them I would be back soon.'

Joseph glances at his wife but she is busy with her son. She looks up briefly and nods at me.

'You're very welcome.'

'Do you know how to find your way back?' he asks.

'Yes. I'll be fine.' I wrap my scarf around my neck and let him walk me to the door. He opens it and leans against the doorframe, watching as I step out into the quietness.

'Nice to see you're feeling better,' he says. 'Take care, Frances.'

'You too.' And I walk away from him and see that the last of my hope sits at his feet, near his potted plant, and it waves and sneers and chases me down the street.

I don't go straight back to the Academy. Instead, I wander down the main street which is long and deserted, piles of dirty snow pushed up against the curb. I pass a bank, a couple of cafes, and several hardware stores, all of them dark and empty. I imagine what the dead town would look like full of people; what it would be like to walk with them, to belong to them. I pass a theater with a gaudy sign arched on top. I pull the sleeve of my jacket over my hand and rub the window so I can look inside. The foyer is empty but if I look really hard and listen very closely, I can almost see the people crowded in it; families, lovers, friends, all gathered together, huddling in from the cold outside. They are laughing and talking, trying to be heard over all the other voices. *Easy with the popcorn, Ben, you don't want to finish it before the movie has even started. Did you hear what she said about me in school? I wonder if he's here—I asked him to come. Where are the tickets—honey, do you have the tickets?* I wish I could go in and try the door but it's locked. I keep on walking, the voices following, turning into images of people holding hands down the street, gossiping against car doors with their hats low over the ears and the collars of their jackets turned up against the winter chill. They turn and smile at me and say hello. They know me; receive me warmly into their daily lives and ask me how I am doing. They invite me home for dinner, their daughters beg me to sleep over. Their sons ask me out on dates and I say yes without hesitation, knowing that afterward, they will kiss me in their cars and fog up the windows. Here I am asked to babysit their children. I am trustworthy Janine.

No one is weary of me, always wondering about my secrets. In this life, I have none. I hurry on; accepted everywhere, I can go wherever I like. I wave and laugh, feel the giddy bubbles of it come out easily. I push my hair back and expose my face, straightening up and walking with squared shoulders. I want everyone to see me.

My father is absent; he doesn't fit in here. He hides in the shadows, always one step outside of my perimeter and I don't want to catch up. For the first time, I want to be without him. I want to know what it would feel like to be somebody else.

25

St Albert. April 1978

Frances. Elizabeth. McDermott. She was six pounds and an ounce of soft beauty with hard red hair, screaming up at him with closed fists and a blank mouth. He had been sitting on the small, floral printed chair in the corner of the hospital room when the nurse brought her in. They hovered near him but when he didn't reach out, the nurse placed the baby in the crib near the bed.

'She should be in very soon.' The nurse smiled at him, reminding him that if he were anyone else, if this were a different situation, it might have been the happiest day of his life. A new father, waiting eagerly for the mother of his child, having begun the satisfying process of completing his family.

'Thank you.'

She left them alone; him and his new daughter and he pushed himself to the edge of the couch, watching the slight movements of the baby through the spaces of the white bars of the cradle. Her soft sounds rose toward the ceiling, collecting in the corners and expanding across to him; rivers of milky, gentle sounds but he was in too much of a daze to hear them. He stood up and walked to her, hovering above the small body, struggling in its tight, pink blanket. He wasn't prepared for what she would look like and when she turned her face up toward him, her mouth opening and closing silently, he was taken aback. She was so different from how he had imagined and the sharp contrast between the baby lying in front of him and the one he had dreamed up forever in his mind made him feel as if he were sleepwalking; stuck and pushing through an oily dream. She wasn't smooth or white or perfect. She didn't have rosy cheeks or an even rosier mouth. Instead, her skin folded into itself; small crinkles along her unusually large forehead and her skin was chalky—covered in a thin, uneven layer of sticky white residue. The bottom of her full mouth curled downward, as if the muscles in it found it too heavy to support. She was new but she looked so old and yet, seeing her lying there on the clean hospital sheet, he recognized her almost instantly as his own. Perhaps it was the wide, half-open blue eyes that stared up at him and blinked in a flurry of dark-gold lashes. Or maybe it was that, when she started crying and refused to stop, he had to pick her up and discovered that she was perfectly suited to the shape of his hands; that despite her wrinkles, she was still crisp and clean and new. Most likely, it was because when he leaned down to inhale her vanilla scent, the dropping sensation in his stomach at the thought of what might happen when she was a little older, was lost; overwhelmed by a different, much stronger feeling mounting in his chest. His sense of responsibility as a parent, as a new father who now had a crying daughter to care for, outweighed the pull of those black cravings and caused his anxiety to drop away, replaced instead by a surge of delight. *I promise never to do anything to hurt you,* a silent promise he felt sure he would keep because just by looking at her, feeling her small hand grip his thumb, he was transformed into something bigger and stronger. So he folded away his secrets for the time being, safe in the knowledge that they belonged only to him and that he was better than them and he said it again, this time out loud. 'I promise never to do anything to hurt you.'

'Not like you did to me, you mean.'

Gina's tired eyes were staring up at him from a wheelchair at the door. The nurse started to push her further in but Gina held up her hand to stop her. 'Don't worry. My husband will help me from here,' she said, smiling up at the nurse who nodded and said, 'You have a beautiful baby. Congratulations,' before leaving.

James stood in the middle of the room, his baby cradled against his chest and he noted the resemblance of the pumpkin hair between Gina and the child in his arms. It had been the one thing he had truly liked about Gina and he was glad it had been passed onto their daughter.

'Well, are you going to help me or not?'

'Of course.' He put the now quiet baby back in the crib, tucking the loose edges of the blanket around her and then moving over to Gina. He pushed her toward the bed, pulling the sheets aside. He bent down to offer his neck to her eager arms. When he put her in the bed, her arms tightened briefly around his neck and he worried that she might try to kiss him, but then she let go and dropped her head onto the pillow. She hadn't yet looked at the baby, instead keeping her eyes trained on him.

'I'm not your husband,' he said finally.

'I know that.' Her head flopped lazily to the side and she watched him from the corner of her eye. 'But I've found that it's much easier to say that you are. Keeps people from asking too many questions.'

He was repulsed, watching her lying there on the stained pillow with stained skin. He had hardly thought about her since the day she had rudely pushed him out of her house and now he couldn't remember her. Their affair seemed like a distant, dream-like thing—a memory that didn't fit in with the rest of his life. She saw the way he looked at her and sighed.

'Try being in labor for the whole day and see how you feel at the end of it.'

He turned his eyes away. 'I'm sorry.' He didn't know what exactly he was apologizing for when she was the one who had ruined his marriage with an early morning phone call.

'Gave you quite a surprise, didn't I?' She grinned up at him and then looked over at the crib, her face falling. 'Well it was a pretty big shock to me too when I found out.'

'You could have told me earlier, Gina.'

'When? When you left me? When I left and didn't hear from you, not even once, to make sure I was okay?'

'I didn't think you wanted me to.'

She scoffed. 'That's a lie.' A bitter smile tiptoed across her face. 'How did Marienne take the news?'

He felt a sharp stab of guilt cramp at his side. He remembered the shock in her eyes when he told her about the baby, too taken aback by the news himself to be anything but blunt. He remembered the falling of her pretty face, but most of all it was her outrageous jealousy that stuck with him the most.

She had surprised him by making breakfast that morning, thick wafts of bacon and coffee wrapping around him like a warm glove that made him smile and rush down the stairs. She was waiting, just as he remembered she used to, by his chair in her cooking apron, her hair tied loosely back. She looked young and careless again, smiling sweetly at him as he came through the door. Spatula in hand, she moved back toward the spitting frying pan. He sat down and watched as she expertly scooped up the egg without breaking it, placing it onto a piece of toast before bringing it to him. As she put it down, she ruffled his hair and said, 'Good morning, darling.'

'Good morning.' He took her hand and kissed her wrist before she sat down beside him. 'It looks great.'

'I haven't made you breakfast in a while, have I?' She rubbed his arm and smiled again before picking up the newspaper and starting to read it. His heart broke open with joy and the blood flooded into it.

He took a bite, chewed slowly and let the flavors burst in his mouth. The sun shone through the kitchen window and the house seemed at peace. She put the newspaper down.

'I want to apologize,' she said. 'I know I've been acting a little crazy,' she hesitated and wrapped her fingers around his. 'It's been hard on you, and I'm sorry, but it's going to stop.' She swallowed. 'I've got to move on with my life now.'

'I'll be here.'

'I know.' She nodded and tears sprang to her eyes. She laughed; part out of sorrow but he also saw how much she loved him. 'I know that if I have you, I can get through anything.'

He wanted to tell her so much then; it was the most he had ever felt for her, but the high ring of the phone interrupted them from the living room. He was up before Marienne, pushing her down into the chair.

'I'll get it—you relax.' He walked out of the kitchen, his steps light and easy. He picked up the receiver. 'Hello?' He wasn't prepared for the loud, panicked voice on the other end and he had to hold the telephone away from his ear.

'James? Hello? Can you hear me?'

'Who is this?' He was tempted to put the phone down, annoyed at the interruption and eager to get back to his wife.

'It's Gina.'

'Gina?' His voice dropped and he spoke in a whisper, craning his neck to look back into the kitchen. Marienne was still reading so he knew she hadn't heard him; the slight shout as he said the name. He turned back to the phone and hissed, 'Why are you calling me?'

'I need you to come to the hospital.' She spoke quickly, breathless, as if it were too much of an effort for her to speak. 'Not Stolleri. The one in the city.' She told him the name and asked if he knew where it was.

'I do,' he said. 'But why do you need me to come? What's going on?'

'I'm having your baby.'

The ground dropped from under his feet and he had a strange sensation of falling forward even though he was standing still.

'What did you say?' He was angry now and the anger rolled out of him, wrapped in fear. 'Is this some kind of sick joke?'

'No, it's not.' There was something in her voice, a silver ring of victory, of having finally got her revenge on him for leaving her so selfishly, that made him sure she was telling the truth.

'I don't understand.' His tongue was numb and his eyes blurred so that all he saw was the white of the wall bleeding into the beige carpet, creating strange illusions and patterns that jumped out and laughed at him.

'Just get to the hospital and I'll explain it all. I just need someone with me.' When he didn't answer, she said, pleadingly, 'Please, James.'

'I'll be there as soon as I can.' He couldn't believe he was saying those words to her but he knew he had to go. He had to get her off the phone first, figure out what he was going to say to Marienne.

She hung up and he stayed rooted to the spot, the receiver growing warm from his sweating palms. A peculiar tickling had started up around the corner of his eyes, making them shake from the inside. It spread downward, filling his cheekbones and around his jaw, locking it painfully in place. A cold fear sneaked down his throat and grew hot in his body, melting at his knees so that he fell to the stairs, the phone dropping beside him. His chest was unbearably itchy with a million, prickly questions and he took short, half-breaths that never made it to his lungs. He was sure his heart would stop beating and that he would die and the thought came as a relief. When Marienne called out to him, she sounded distorted and far away and he had a scary sensation of leaking outside himself. Then she appeared and he heard her say his name from the doorway, louder and more anxious, before he felt the cool tips of her fingers at the base of his neck, cradling his head. His body jerked at her touch and then began to relax.

'Breathe honey, just breathe.' She pushed him up onto the staircase and forced his head down between his knees, rubbing his back in large, comforting circles. 'It's okay. I'm here. It's going to be okay. One, two, three,' she counted patiently and he breathed to the sound and rhythm of her voice. Slowly, the sensation started to return to him, starting at the soles of his feet and working its way up as his frantic breath struggled to fill his constricted chest. They stayed sitting like that for over fifteen minutes and when he finally fell back against the stairs, she asked him what had happened.

Exhausted and hurting to the point of dizziness, he told her the truth although he wished he could have made up a lie, stayed in her love for just a little while longer. He spoke with difficulty, still short of air, working his way around the vasectomy and starting from when he had met Gina in the bar during the snowstorm. Marienne stared at his lips as he spoke, as if she had to see the words form on his mouth as well as hear them. Her own twitched occasionally; it looked like she might laugh. She didn't quite believe him, perhaps thought he was still lightheaded and confused.

'We were having our problems and she was there—she listened to me. I just needed someone to talk to,' he said. 'But I never meant for this to happen. God—I never thought that she would—I mean, a baby,' he ran out of words then, fell short of any explanations. 'You have to believe me, Annie.' Marienne let go of his hand and stood up. 'Marienne.'

'Don't touch me.' They stayed apart, silent, each taking in the shocking news. When she laughed, it was dry and bitter. 'This is because I couldn't give you children, isn't it?'

'Of course not. I didn't want this. You know I didn't want this.'

She was crying, not listening to him, her own explanation solid in her mind. 'You told me it was going to be okay. That we were going to be okay.'

'I have to go to the hospital,' he said quietly. 'When I come back, we can sort all of this out.'

'No, please.' Her fingers had never been as strong as they were then, grasping at his arm. 'Forget the phone call ever came. You can't leave me,' her nails leaving half-moon impressions in his skin.

'I'll be back soon.' His head had cleared while hers had grown watery and he spoke steadily. 'I have to go and see her.'

'You said we were going to be okay, just the two of us. You promised me that.'

'It was a big mistake, Annie. I never meant for this to happen.' As ridiculous as it was, he looked to her for comfort; to help him unlock the dread that was still tied around his chest and wasn't letting go.

'Tell me when this happened,' she said. 'We were having problems but I thought that at the end of the day, you still loved me. What am I supposed to do now?' Her voice rose, coloring her neck and spreading to her cheeks. 'I was getting over it. I was getting better, James.' She almost shouted the last part.

'I know you were.' He felt a stinging misery, an enormous longing to erase the last few minutes of his life. 'I do love you, Annie, and this has nothing to do with the fact that you can't have children.' As he said it, he felt their old life slip away from him, disappearing like vapor into the air. 'I have to go to her. What else can I do?'

The phone call had left him too weak and unable to go after Marienne as she stepped away from him, grabbing the keys from the hook near the door. The action was a quick, horrible reminder of the life they had built together, the comfortable routine they had established; hanging the keys on the hook by the door every time you walked in so that you would always remember where they were.

'I can't believe you've done this to me.'

Those were the last words she spoke to him and more than six hours later, he stood above Gina with his daughter crying in the background and he looked from one to the other, knowing what had to be done. It didn't matter how she had come to be here or what might happen in the future, all that he was aware of was that she was wonderful and new and all his.

'She's beautiful,' he said to Gina.

'Really?' There was hope in her eyes that made him turn away and move toward the crib, looking down at his squirming daughter. He touched her brazen hair lightly. 'Don't worry,' he said, wanting to reach down and kiss her but he was still a little hesitant, disbelieving. Today, he was different; older and wiser and his life had weight and consequences to it. Everything around him seemed precious and vulnerable. 'I'll look after you.'

*

He wasn't used to sleeping alone and the bed was too wide for him; a sad, long stretch of loneliness. He sat up and moved to the smaller couch, spreading himself out to fill it. He carried a pillow with him, curling into it. He pressed his face into the soft material and was startled by Marienne's particular scent.

He had come home from the hospital to find her almost completely packed. She didn't acknowledge him when he entered the room and refused to listen as he spoke, his voice rising higher and higher with frustration. The nearly bare closet was dark and cold, gaping out at him miserably and he couldn't look at it.

'We have to at least talk about this,' he kept saying over and over again, following her around the room as she gathered up pieces and memories of their lives that had accumulated over the last few years. 'At least give me the chance to explain everything properly to you. You can't just walk out on me, Annie.'

'I'm not the one walking out. Don't you dare blame me.' She reached the dressing table and pushed her lipsticks and hairbrushes into a small bag with shiny bottles of perfume and a bracelet he had bought her for her last birthday. The small, heart-shaped charm swung carelessly in the air and it made him sad to watch it. She threw the pouch into one of her open, waiting suitcases, then stopped; her breath caught in her throat. 'Is it a boy or a girl?'

'Annie.'

'I want to know.' Her voice close to a shout; her back rigid and still. 'Boy or girl?'

He felt ashamed saying it; felt guilty for the rush of pride that flooded him. His cheeks burned. 'A girl,' unable to keep the pleasure out of his voice.

She caught the tears in the cup of her palm, sucking in deep breaths and falling to the edge of the bed. He was rooted to the spot, his own tears blurring his vision. She clutched the corner of the suitcase so tight, her knuckles turned white and hard. Her hair fell over her face like a thick, black sheet. She let out a low sound, so deep and painful, like a wounded animal, that he was immediately worried.

'Annie,' moving forward.

'I can't breathe.'

He went to her, put his hand on her shoulder and she turned around and let him take her in his arms, pressing her face to his chest. She bit down hard on his skin through his shirt. He felt the pinch shoot through him but held back his protest. Her shoulders shook and her tears were cold, burning holes in him. When she pushed him away, he had no choice but to let her go. She sucked in a few breaths, her face regaining its color and hardness. 'Do you want to know what hurts the most?' She turned to him fully. 'That you were so mindless about my feelings. That you made such a complete fool of me.' She blinked several times before continuing. 'That for all these years, I trusted you, when God knows what you've been doing behind my back.'

'I've always been faithful, Annie. I made one mistake. That's all it was. A horrible, huge mistake.'

'You shouldn't have made it then,' she spat out at him. 'No one forced you on her. No one forced you to get her pregnant!' Her hands were shaking and when she saw him staring, she pushed them into the pockets of her cardigan. 'And you let me work with her.' She'd had hours to think over what had happened and it didn't matter what he said now, there were things she had to say and she didn't want to listen to him. 'That was a clever trick, wasn't it?'

'What do you mean?' His heart sank and he tried to keep his face as neutral as possible.

'You know exactly what I mean. Asking her to offer me the night shift so you'd have free evenings to do whatever you wanted.'

'It wasn't like that.'

'Don't lie to me. Please, I can't take it anymore.' Her hands were working again, throwing things into the suitcase. Her fingers reached and hovered over their photo sitting high on the dresser, overlooking their bed, and she pulled away with a small choking sound before tipping it over and placing it face down so she wouldn't have to look at it. He wanted to say something, anything, but words escaped him as he watched her stride purposefully about the room yet with a look of utter helplessness across her face. She finished collecting what she needed, not bothering to double check if she had everything. She left without looking back or saying goodbye, forcing her way past him.

'Where are you going to go?' he asked, trying to catch her arm but she was too fast for him. 'I'll move out. You can stay here.'

'I don't want to be anywhere that reminds me of you.'

'Annie, please…' he felt a hot desperation build in his throat as the reality of her not being in his life anymore fully hit him. It sucked the words out of him so that he could only watch as she bumped her suitcase down the stairs, the loud thud echoing along the wall. He didn't try to help her and even when he begged, 'I just need to know that you'll be alright—at least tell me how I can contact you,' she refused to say where she was going. She was at the door, moving fast, but suddenly she stopped. He felt his heart rise, start racing with hope in his chest. But then she turned and he saw how hard her face was. How she suddenly seemed to have transformed from that ageless, bright girl he knew into someone lonely and sad.

'I just want to know why,' she said. 'After all these years we've been together, after how much I've loved you, why have you done this? You were the only family I had.'

He wanted to tell her something that would make her feel better; to let her know that it had nothing to do with her and everything to do with him. But it was impossible to articulate and he found himself shrugging helplessly. 'I don't know but I'm going to regret it for the rest of my life.'

'That's for you to live with,' she said. 'Don't put your guilt on me.' She pulled open the door.

He couldn't help but call out, 'I love you, Annie. Please don't leave,' but his declaration was met with a firmly closed door.

She had abandoned him to a room that was scattered and bare and broken; full of her absence and noisy with his desperation. It had grown dark by then but he hadn't had the energy to turn on any of the lights. So he moved blindly down the corridor, retracing her steps, feeling along the wooden banister. He made his careful way down the stairs, comforted by the velvet blanket of darkness that covered him. He was glad he could barely see around him. It didn't feel like his home anymore; nothing seemed right, as if the house had shifted off-balance without her.

He went to make himself a cup of tea, not because he wanted it but because he needed a distraction; the simple, calming pattern of the process. He noticed she had forgotten her favorite mug, left unwashed by the kitchen sink and he worried that she would miss it, wherever she was going. He picked it up and saw that it still had her lipstick stains around the rim from that morning and he poured hot water into it without rinsing it first.

He considered going back to the hospital, to spend the night there so at least he wouldn't be alone. He wanted to see his daughter again; to hold her and reassure himself. He smiled when he thought of her, knowing that it might be more difficult later on but also sure that now he had her, he couldn't live without her. Still, his world seemed empty and friendless without Marienne; like a black hole he was hurtling through and all he wanted to do was to hold her hand and steady himself. He finished his tea and the warm liquid tired him. He was heavy-lidded and worn out, but when he fell onto the couch, pulling the blanket up around his chin despite the heat, he was suddenly wide awake. He would have to bring Gina back to his house once she was ready to leave the hospital. She was still a stranger to him and the thought of having her here, in a home he had shared with a woman he had adored, one he had loved coming home to and knew every corner of, made him edgy. He closed his eyes, inhaling Marienne's smell; the images of her packing and leaving flashing against his eyelids. He started counting backward slowly from twenty, reassuring himself that he would find her tomorrow and fix everything, and before he reached ten he sank quickly into a noisy yet dreamless sleep.

26

Whitehorse, Yukon. December 1992

It's only six o'clock but the sun has already fallen asleep, shut its fiery eye. With the sudden darkness, something else is closing in on me. I am back at the Academy and already, the picture in my head has faded. I am filled with a restlessness I have never felt before. It jumps and pushes at me in frustration and I can't stay still. I think about how I could have become a possible fixture in their family; how that would have allowed me to grow closer to Joseph and how adamant she was in not allowing it. A sharp desperation pricks at me; I don't know how I will make it through the next three weeks with only this feeling for company.

I reach under my pillow and pull out a picture I have of him. It came in the post two days ago, along with a Christmas calendar and a pair of gloves. The photo was of him and my mother; they were standing in the park and one of them was holding the camera above their faces. She was wearing a dark green scarf and his hair looked grayer than I remember. I cut her out and kept his picture. It has already been folded and unfolded so many times that it's now beginning to split. I fall back onto my pillow and let his eyes roam over me. My fingers go over his mouth, and I feel its sting against my own. They travel down the shape of his shoulders and the need to put my arms around him; feel him solid and hot under me, so strong it takes my breath away. Then I hear a knock outside my door and I quickly slide the picture under my pillow and sit up in time as Sister Ann enters.

'Are you sleeping?' she asks.

'No.' I am aware of how suspicious I look; sat in the corner of my bed, shrouded by the fading day. 'I was praying.'

She smiles, pleased with my response. 'I hope I'm not disturbing you.'

'I just finished.'

She comes to sit on my bed. 'I didn't know you did that.' She pats my knee and looks around the room. I follow her eyes, feeling caught out. 'Prayed alone, I mean.'

'Sometimes. I've started to.' To distract her, I ask, 'Is it dinnertime yet?'

'No.' She crosses her legs and I notice again how womanly she is. Through the thin material of her habit, you can catch the occasional glimpse of her slim waist, the elongated arch of her spine that carries her softly straight. Those hands that always sit loose and light on her knees.

'You have blonde hair,' I say in surprise.

She tucks the loose strands back into her headdress and laughs quietly. 'More like a dirty brown,' she corrects me but she is wrong. 'Actually, I'm here because Joseph is downstairs.'

I don't know why he has come but when she says it, I involuntarily shrink into the blanket. 'I haven't done anything,' I say.

She looks at me, confused. 'He told me he ran into you today.'

'I went to thank him.' I'm not sure why I am so flustered. Sister Ann is oblivious to the way my body burns up, the beads of sweat that break out along my upper lip.

'That's good of you,' she says absently. 'He's here to ask you if you wouldn't mind babysitting his son tonight.'

'I'm sorry?'

'You don't have to but he's here to get you, if you want. I think it's a good idea.'

I don't know what to say. 'I'm not sure if—'

'It's fine if you're not comfortable,' she assures me. 'I can always get someone else.'

'No.' I stop her quickly. My head is giddy and I'm smiling so big, it hurts. 'I would love to.'

She stands up, straightening out the shape she has made in my covers. 'Great. Get your stuff and we'll go downstairs together.'

I grab my bag and slip my exercise book into it; it doesn't matter which subject. I won't be looking at it. I put a pen in as well, just for good measure. 'Okay.' I hitch my bag onto my shoulder. 'I'm ready.'

He is smiling in the foyer and I see him as I come down the stairs. I try to slow my footsteps but I crash into him at the bottom.

'I'm glad to see you.' He takes his hand out of his pocket and clasps my shoulder. 'Shall we go?'

'Yes.' I am grinning widely, skipping ahead of him.

'I'll drop her off when we get back,' he tells Sister Ann.

'Try not to be too late.' She smiles warmly at me. 'Have fun.' I grin and skip ahead and shout back over my shoulder that I will.

'I'm not sure about this. There's something about her, Joseph.'

I can hear them talking through the thin walls as I sit on their couch with Alex at my feet. I let him take hold of my shoelaces and he unties and ties them, making small, almost perfect knots. *And the bunny goes around the hole.*

'Who taught you how to do that?' I ask.

'My dad.' He smiles up at me. 'You want me to show you?' He has warmed to me so quickly; never having acknowledged my presence any of the other times I have seen him.

'Maybe later,' I pat the couch beside me. 'Let's just sit here for now and you can read your book.' I want him to be quiet, just until they have left.

'Nova, please.' His voice sounds deeper through the cracked pain. 'At least give it a chance.'

'I know you feel responsible for her after what happened at the river,' she is trying to keep her voice low. 'But you don't always have to be the hero.'

'I know that,' he says, a little sharply. 'Look, I talked to a teacher at the Academy. No one has any objections with her. She went through a rough time and she's come out of it.'

'I don't trust her. It just doesn't feel right. It's the way she looks at us—it makes me uncomfortable.' I look at Alex, as if he can understand what his mother is saying but, of course, he is oblivious and more interested in the pattern on my socks. My cheeks flush under the accusation and it hurts more than I thought it would to know that she doesn't like me.

'You're just worked up about tonight. Come on, come here.' I imagine him hugging her, gathering her up into the wide span of his body. 'You know I wouldn't have asked her if I didn't think it would be okay.'

Then they come into the room and Joseph kisses Alex goodbye. 'Be a good boy for Frances, now.' He puts him down and the boy holds onto his leg. 'You'll be alright?' He turns to me.

'Fine.' I smile, trying to reassure him even though I have no idea what I will do when they have left.

'And you've done this before?'

'All the time,' waving my hand in the air and meeting his eyes straight-on. 'I was the neighborhood nanny.'

He smiles at this. 'We're going to visit Nova's brother,' Joseph tells me. 'I've left the number by the telephone. In case you need anything, call us.'

'Thanks.' I force a confidence I don't have into my voice. 'There shouldn't be any problems, though.'

'He has to be in bed by eight thirty,' Nova tells me, kneeling down and pulling her son to her, her lips lingering on his cheek.

'Got it.' I shake my eyebrows at Alex, settling into the role. 'Hear that, little man? Eight thirty sharp.' He giggles and Nova relaxes a little. She kisses the top of his head once more as she stands. 'We'll be home around eleven,' she says, and her features slacken, letting the light soften in her eyes, prettying her features. 'Thank you very much for doing this.'

Her words send a firework of colors exploding in my cheeks and I hold onto the edge of the couch, bouncing my knee.

'Anytime,' I reply and when she closes the door behind her, I throw back my body and pump my fist in the air, shouting out in triumph. Alex, watching me keenly, stands up and does the same.

'Bet you can't catch me, bet you can't catch me.'

And he's right. A slippery, fast-moving six-year-old, Alex knows all the places to hide so that I can't get a hold of him. He crawls under his bed and every time I reach out to grab him, he slides further into the corner.

'Come on, Alex. You heard what your mother said about bedtime.' I press my face into the carpet and I'm met with wide, blinking eyes.

'I'm not tired yet,' he says. 'And Janine always lets me stay up until whatever time I want.' I remind myself to tell Nova this even though I know it might not be true.

'We don't have to sleep right away,' I say, stretching out my legs so that I'm lying flat. The carpet digs roughly into my stomach but I don't move.

'What do you mean?' I have caught him in my net of interest and he crawls nearer.

'I could tell you a story,' I say. 'If you promise to come out.'

'Tell me the story first.'

'I'll tell you half of it. If you like it, you can come out and we can finish the rest of it in your bed.'

'Okay.' He likes this deal.

I turn around, shifting my weight into the carpet to get comfortable and fold my arms over my chest. Tilting my head to the side, I look at him and for a moment, see someone else. A little girl with her chin in her hands, looking into eyes identical to her own.

'I'm waiting,' he reminds me.

Once upon a time. 'I've heard that one already,' he interrupts me.

'Not this one.'

'I've heard all the once-upon-a-times. Tell me something different.'

'Alright.' I close my eyes and it comes to me without being called. It's the story I have heard a hundred times before, with him under the luminous glow of my fake galaxy. He stopped telling it to me a long time ago but the words have stuck, like an old and broken piano tune. I blow the dust off it and start.

'This is a story only meant for the best little boys. Is that you?' I pause to ask. He nods, legs creeping closer to me, his eyes shining with interest. 'Okay, then.' The world fades out again. *It's a special story because if you're lucky, you might learn its secret.*

My father appears in the veiny light slipping under my eyelids, like a cracked picture that has seen too many years of sunlight. He is leaning over me and everything has disappeared into his smile; it is the only thing I see.

There is a magic house, not far from here, hidden in a magic forest, invisible to those it doesn't wish to show itself to. But I can tell you how to get there, if you like.

'Yes, yes!' I would sit on his knee and bounce against his chest and often, he would throw back his head and his laughter would rain down on me. Then he would stroke my hair, bringing me back down into the waiting shape of his body, molding me to him. His arms would always find their way around my waist, pulling me close, almost pinching.

There's a creek. The softest, lightest one you'll ever find; barely skimming the rocks and you'll have to listen very hard for it. You'll hear it because the air is so heavy and sweet that the river is in love with it and sings for it always. When it passes you, you might mistake it for a flash of light coming through the trees.

His voice took on a different quality when he told the story; it ebbed and sang and sounded easy. I could almost hear the river in it, traveling the channels of his blood. As he wandered this secret wood, his fingers would grow slack, like he had forgotten me. I had to shake him to bring him back.

'How will I know which way to follow it?' I asked.

Go in the direction it's flowing. But be wary; it's tricky and sometimes changes without warning, just like that. When you reach the end, there will be a clearing and you'll know you're there because it leads into a field. And in this empty field, there is only one tree. A pink cherry blossom.

'A tree like ours?' I climbed over him, always shocked at this; always eager to point out the uncanny coincidence. The tree was just below my window, spreading its cotton candy branches beneath me like a cloud.

Exactly like ours. And you have to tap on the tree's old branch when you get there. Only three times and only in this rhythm.

His fingers went to my neck, his forefinger and index pressed together like a doctor checking my pulse. *One, two, three,* he would tap and I would thrill at his fingers so close to the source of me. Bringing my knees up to my chest, I rested my forehead against him. He tucked stray hairs behind my ears and continued.

And then, if the tree wishes to show you, there it will be, sitting in the middle of the field, waiting for you to go in. Red door, blue shuttered windows; a valley of mountains as its gates.

'Who lives there?' I loved my part in the storytelling. Even though I already knew all the answers, I still waited eagerly for my chance to speak. Taking his body out from under me, he would put his hands behind his head. His throat bobbed as he struggled to swallow. I put my finger to the hard nub and he would hold my wrist there and smile.

A man and the girl he loves the most in this world; his daughter. The house is lovely when you go inside. The windows are always open and it's sunny all the time. The birds come and sit at the ledges and the air smells fragrant. They spend all their time there, in that house. They play and cook and tell each other stories.

He winked at me. 'Do they ever leave?' I asked once. His face darkened.

'No, they don't.' I asked him why not. 'Because they're happy there. They don't need anyone else.' The river in his voice turned stormy. I never asked again.

He has to hide her because of the townspeople. He's scared that someone might come and take her away. If that happened, he would be all alone with nothing but the birds and some squirrels for company. And if she went away, the river would stop flowing.

'Why would they take her?'

I stop at this new question. 'What's that?' I hadn't noticed Alex coming out from under the bed, sitting next to me, his crossed knees grazing my side. He is chewing thoughtfully on his thumb, his forehead creased in question.

'Why would the people want to take her away from her father?'

I lie quiet, my mind still in the grips of the magic house before I shake my head free of it. I don't have an answer for him because it's a question I never thought of asking. It only seemed natural that he would want to hide her, that she would want to be hidden, and now I feel unnerved.

'Come on, it's late. Let's get you into bed,' I say, standing up and helping him under the covers. He is already dressed in his pajamas.

'I haven't brushed my teeth yet,' he tells me.

'Do you want to?'

'No.' He smiles like we're sharing a joke.

'Then we'll leave it just this once.' I press my finger to his mouth. 'It'll be our little secret, okay?'

'Okay.' He closes his eyes and I stand over him until his breathing reduces to a steady rhythm and his body grows warm. I go to turn off the lights.

'My dad says you only hide something when you're doing something wrong.' He has flipped onto his side and is watching me. I turn the switch down, flicking the room into darkness. His night light casts peculiar shadows against the wall—streaking fish in the deepest part of the ocean.

'Go to sleep, Alex,' I say. 'Sweet dreams.'

I go downstairs and sit on the couch. Everything is unearthly quiet.

They'll let you in, if you ask nicely. Take some daisies with you, they're his daughter's favorite and they grow at the edge of the clearing, drinking from the water.

'How do you know they'll let me in?' I asked. He turned me over, his elbows by my ears, his mouth pressing fast and dry kisses along my nose and chin.

'Because they trust you,' he says simply. 'Because they know that you'll understand, when you see them, why they have to stay there. Because you can keep their secret.' He paused and our eyes met. He had stared at me countless times before, but never like that.

You can keep a secret, Frances, can't you?

I rouse to the sound of a key in the door. They keep their voices down as they come in and I reach the corridor just as the door closes. I'm not sure if it's a trick of the light that makes Nova's eyes look so red and her face so worn.

'Hi,' I say to them. Joseph rubs his hands and jingles them in his pocket for warmth. The cold has crept in behind them, stuck to their clothes, and I shiver.

'Hello,' unraveling his scarf. 'How was it?'

'Great.' I try to talk to Nova but she avoids my eye, slowly shrugging off her coat, absently staring at the shoe rack by the wall. 'He's a really good boy.'

'Is he asleep?' he asks.

'Yes. Eight thirty, just like you said.'

She sighs. Closes her eyes and sways slightly. Joseph is holding her by the waist.

'Thank you.' She walks, stumbles, and he catches her by the tail of her shirt. 'I'm fine,' she insists, brushing him off. 'Joseph will take you home,' she says. 'I'm going to go say goodnight to my son.'

'Try not to wake him,' Joseph calls to her in a loud whisper.

We stand in the corridor, facing each other. He rubs the back of his neck and smells sharp and clean, like air.

'Is everything okay?' I ask. There is something wrong with her, I can tell.

'Everything is fine.' He slowly removes his jacket. 'Look, would you mind staying the night? Nova isn't feeling well and we really didn't expect to be so late.' I'll call up the Academy and let them know, if it's okay with you.'

'Yes.' I say it before he's finished. 'Yes, of course.'

'The couch is a pull-out and we have lots of blankets and three pillows to choose from,' he grins.

'Any is fine.' I try to stop the bubbles of eagerness rising in my throat but they make my words choppy.

He glances up the stairs where Nova has disappeared. Everything is strangely quiet. 'You sure you don't mind?' he asks. I shake my head, not believing the luck of it all. 'I'll go get the stuff for you then.'

I wait for him by the couch as he goes upstairs to get a blanket and a pillow. I watch the clock impatiently, listening for him talking to Nova, waiting for her to change his mind. It seems to take an unusually long time before he comes back down with both items tucked under his arms.

'I've just spoken to Sister Ann and she said it would be okay if you stayed here the night and I dropped you back tomorrow morning.'

'Great.' I stop trying to hide my smile.

Handing the pillow and blanket to me, he pulls the couch out easily and it squeaks a little in protest. He pushes on it and I see the lines of his muscles move up and down as he checks the sturdiness of the mattress.

'Should be fine,' he says, throwing the blanket over it. It fans out and falls with a soft wisp.

'Thanks.' I put the pillow down, picking at a strand of loose string.

'Hey,' he is smiling at me. 'How about a cup of hot chocolate before you go to sleep?'

A warmth is starting up in me, circling my belly. 'That would be nice.'

For an extra treat, he grates a cinnamon stick and sprinkles a little on top of each of our drinks.

'Alex loves it this way,' he says. 'I have to hide it from him though somehow he always finds it.'

'He's a smart boy,' I say, thinking of our story time. Of how he lay looking at me sideways, his strange words almost sinister in the purplish glow of his night-light.

'Yes, he is.' Joseph takes a sip and licks the froth from his lips, holding the cup loosely between both hands. The slanting shadows of the kitchen make it look like its ready to fall but it stays steady, half-tilted. 'Gets that from his mother.' He laughs and then falls silent, putting the cup down and rubbing the heels of his palms over his eyes. 'Jesus, what a family.'

'Is she alright?' I ask again. Flecks of cinnamon stick to the underside of my teeth.

'She's fine,' he says. 'She just finds going to her brother's house a little difficult, that's all.'

'Why?' My curiosity licked, I am eager to know more about Nova.

'Money problems, love problems,' he waves his hand in the air. 'Things you are too young to be worrying about.'

239

'You think so?' I ask. 'Even love?'

'Especially love.' He nods slowly. 'It's a serious business and you shouldn't be wasting time on it at your age.' I let his words settle over me, sink into my brain. He notices my silence and slaps his hand down on the table. 'Anyway, tell me more about yourself.'

'There's nothing to tell,' I say nervously. This is dangerous territory and I navigate it cautiously, afraid I might let something slip.

'There must be something,' he says. 'Everyone has a story to tell.'

'Mine's boring.' I look down into my mug, brown foam sticky on the rim. When I glance back up again, his face is angled close to mine.

'Now if there is one thing I know about you, it's that you're definitely not boring.'

The way he addresses me, like he has done since the first moment I met him, as if there was nothing strange about me at all, makes me wish I could say something that would please him. But when I think back to when I was at home, all I can remember are those perfect nights. I had thought they would never end and now that they have, I realize that there are no other memories to my name. Everything else wasn't important enough to stow away, to pay attention to; whatever I did was tied to him—to the erratic pacing of his body, his sweaty palms gripping my shoulders. I raise the cup to my lips for something to do and find that it's empty.

Sensing my nervousness, he smiles at me and I am instantly warmed. 'How about I ask the questions and all you have to do is answer?'

'Okay.' The ugly feeling rising in me is quickly quelled.

'What's your name?' He looks at me with childish seriousness and we giggle softly together.

'Frances Elizabeth McDermott.'

'Good, strong name.' He nods with approval. 'Brothers or sisters?'

'None.'

'An only child. Lucky you,' he says. 'Growing up, I had to share everything with three sisters and a brother.'

'I like that,' I say. 'Sometimes it can get lonely being alone.'

'You don't say.'

We laugh again. Now that I have started talking, it becomes easier and I start to loosen up, throw my arms over the counter-top, adapting to his relaxed pose. 'Where are your sisters and brother now?'

'All over the place,' he says. 'Busy with their own lives.'

'Do you miss them?'

'All the time,' he nods. 'But we always make an effort to see each other. They all have children around Alex's age, so it's always a good time.'

I try to imagine what that would be like; to have such a full family. To love more than one person—it seems impossible to me but something about it also makes me desperate and empty.

'Another question?' he asks.

'Sure.'

He twirls his cup between his fingers. His body sits at a forty-five-degree angle, his legs sprawled out and touching the tip of my chair, always at ease.

'Do you like the Academy?'

'I've started to,' I say.

'I'm glad.' His eyes crinkle in the corners. 'It just takes time, doesn't it?'

'Yes.' I like the softness of his voice; how unforceful and gentle it is, yet so reassuring. 'It's a beautiful place.'

'It definitely is.'

'Especially the forest—there's something magical about it.' I find myself blushing as I say this; as if I have exposed too much of myself.

'That's why you were there the other day?'

'Yes.' I lie, thinking it could be true. 'Why were you there?'

'I love trees,' he says to me and when he sees my eyebrows wrinkle, he explains. 'I used to be a carpenter.'

'Really?'

'I made that chair you're sitting on.' He reaches out to touch it, tracing the old lines. 'And the table.'

'They're beautiful,' I say, because now, when I look at them, old and rough as they are, they seem faultless.

'Thank you.' His hand stops to rest in a groove, circling it. 'I only make sculptures now, and I usually go into the forest to collect wood for them.' We are silent and then he continues. 'It's the smell of the trees, I think, that really gets me. As if in all their years of existing, they've collected the entire world in their trunks.'

'And all the secrets.'

He looks at me and I think I've gone too far. Then he smiles in acknowledgment. He sits up straight, collecting the empty mugs. 'See, I told you, didn't I?'

'Told me what?'

'You're not boring at all.'

My stomach twists with painful happiness. Then I remember the things that he doesn't know about me; things that if he did, he would never look at me the same way.

He says goodnight at the stairs. 'Thank you for babysitting tonight.' He pats my head.

'If you need me to again…'

Time's pitiless fingers are closing over this moment. It will be over soon and I am gripped with a manic need to hold on to it.

'I'll know exactly who to call.' He starts up the stairs. 'Let me know if you need anything else,' he calls softly and disappears into the darkness.

I crawl into bed. Perhaps it's the strangeness of being in a new place, or the foreign sensation of being found interesting enough to talk to, to listen to, but that night my dreams are different. He is in them as always, but this time, he is made of wood; old and lovingly polished, smelling of turpentine. There is a vagueness to him that was never there before and the blurriness of his features are compensated by someone else's unflinching, tranquil ones; solid like a steady ocean that will never be tricked into changing direction.

27

St Albert. November 1978–October 1979

He thought he would never get used to her; a loud, almost bull-ish presence in his home. She disturbed the quiet equilibrium he and Marienne had established in their few years of being married. Now the house seemed to rattle and shake as she moved through it, rudely jolting everything awake. She was without any of the feminine sympathies that had made living with Marienne so easy and he thought it was no wonder her first husband had left her.

She made him wince as she tossed plates and cups carelessly into the sink, not bothered if they chipped or broke. He found coffee rings left to dry on the counters and tables and even though he tried to wipe them away, they never fully disappeared; only faded into a dull, ugly green. She never cooked nor showed any inclination to want to clean up after herself. She had moved all her belongings into the house without asking first and he found pieces of her scattered in every room. He couldn't seem to get away from her.

He bought a second-hand crib and put it in their room. 'You have that empty study,' Gina said to him. 'Why don't we convert that into a nursery?'

Something in him resisted; he didn't want a space where he would have to be alone with Gina. 'The book I've been reading said we should keep her with us at all times—at least for the first few months.'

He thought that having a baby would soften her, but it seemed to have the opposite effect. She went through the basic motions of feeding and cleaning their daughter but it was done in a mechanical, almost bitter way, only managed because she had to. Oftentimes, he would catch a look galloping across her face, reigning in the muscles of her mouth, as if she was trying to keep from screaming. It was a bright, caged panic he recognized in himself, clawing its terrible way through her and he wondered how they had ended up in this place, trapped together helplessly. He offered to call his mother for help, but Gina refused.

'I can handle it myself,' she said. 'I don't even need you. You don't have to keep us here if you don't want to, you know.'

'I do want you here,' he tried to assure her but sounded unconvincing, even to himself. 'Of course I want you both to stay.'

She rocked the baby against her shoulder. It looked unnatural on her—stiff and difficult and he remembered what she had said to him at the bar that day; how glad she was that she had never had any children. 'Then why don't you start helping me out?'

He could have refused—he could have told her to take a walk down the street and see which men helped change their children's diapers or burped their babies—that wasn't his job, but there was something keen in him, drawing him to his daughter even though he warned himself not to get too close.

Frances hardly seemed to move; she just lay in the cot with her knees bunched up to her stomach and her hands around her face, always with some noise cooing in her throat. She would hold up her closed fist and he would slip his hand inside and the happiness leaked from his mouth in a sad, little laugh.

'You can start by changing her diaper,' Gina told him one day, cornering him in the living room, baby in her arms.

'I don't know how.' It seemed wrong to him, to expose her like that.

'That's exactly my point.' Gina gestured for him to follow her upstairs. 'I have to go back to work sometime, so we have to share the responsibility.'

She handed Frances to him and he took her, his heart beating wildly against his chest. Sensing it, Frances started to cry.

Gina turned and saw him standing dumbfounded and paralyzed. She sighed. 'Just give her to me, will you?'

'I don't know why I have to do this.'

'Let me explain something to you,' putting the baby down on the blanket. 'I'm not like all those other women, not like Marienne.' She was furious, unbuttoning the cloth around Frances. He couldn't hear her anymore; her voice faded in what was being revealed. 'I expect you to help me out, do some of this.' All the clothes were pushed to the side now, just soft, white skin. 'Do you think I know what I'm doing? I'm new at this too.' She held the powder out to him. 'Now, come on.'

He went to her, half in a dream and took the bottle.

'Put some of it in your hand,' she instructed. The powder fell against his shaking palm; he was quiet, still trying to think of a way out. He must have stayed that way for a long time, white flakes falling between his fingers and onto the carpet, before she jolted him out of it. 'What are you doing? You have to rub it in, like this.' He closed his eyes, starting somewhere up near her shoulders. 'James!' She took his hand, roughly forced it down. 'Not there, here,' to where it was newest, the most beautiful folded skin. Moving his hand, covering the entire area.

'Enough. That's enough.' He pulled his hand away and the crying started.

'Ssh,' Gina hissed, leaning over the baby. 'Ssh. Let's just get this finished and we can get you to bed.'

'Is that it?' he asked, standing up. 'Are we done?'

'No.'

He didn't wait for her to finish. He just stood up and walked out. She would have known, if he had stayed any longer. She would have figured out something was wrong. Leaning against the door, he held his right wrist in his left hand, his fingers still holding the memory of her. The gravity of the situation hit him hard; the sounds of Gina and the baby becoming louder and more solid, planting their roots into the floorboards and etching themselves into the walls. *We're here to stay.* Since the day at the hospital, he had moved in a daze—perhaps the shock had numbed him, made him half-asleep, but now, with his daughter upon his hand, he could no longer run away from the truth. He would live his life now forever in fear and, unknowingly, so would she, skipping and dancing around the house, never aware that there would be danger lurking at every corner, ready at the slightest whim to snatch her up and destroy her.

It was a Sunday and she woke him up early. He sat up on the couch, massaging his neck and cracking it from side to side. He winced as a sharp pain shot through his arm.

'Maybe you should sleep in the bed, then,' she said from above him. He ignored her.

'What is it?'

'We're going out.' That was when he noticed Frances in her arms. It amazed him how much she seemed to grow in just a few short months. Now, her body was finding its rhythm and instead of moving in experimental jerks, it had direction—a determined purpose.

'Have fun,' he said, closing his eyes and trying to forget what he had just seen.

'You're coming with us,' Gina said and pushed Frances into his arms. She moved a little and almost started crying. He gave her a little shake. 'It's been nearly three months and we never do anything as a family,' Gina said. 'That's what we are now, I suppose.' The thought seemed to comfort her a little. She went to get the pram and he turned to his daughter.

'Morning, darling.' It was an instinct; the heat in his voice that came out when he talked to her. The spread of feeling in his chest; joy and pride that she was his. 'You want to go for a walk?' He placed her carefully in the pram, smoothing down her hair, electric on his fingers.

'Are you ready?' Gina looked at him expectantly, half-breathless as if she knew he was going to refuse to go along. And he nearly did, but looking down at Frances, the way she almost instinctively smiled up at him, it dawned on him that these were the few years that life would be easy for them both.

'I'm just going to have a quick shower and then we can go.'

The look of relief on Gina's face was evident. She nodded, breathing easily again. 'We'll be waiting.'

There was something about stepping out together, appearing as a family, that made him proud. He pushed the pram in front of him, Gina holding onto his arm and carefully stepping around the mounds of dirty snow. It crunched pleasantly under his boots.

'Are you sure she's warm enough?' he asked Gina.

'She's fine.' She sounded irritated that he had asked. 'We don't always have to be worrying about her. Can't we just enjoy this time out?'

He leaned over the pram; felt so full of pleasure that he couldn't stop talking. 'I'm just checking. Don't want my little girl freezing, now do I?' he grinned down at her and she gurgled a laugh back up and he thought he had never loved anything so fully nor so surely. He saw Gina wave to some women across the street. They gave her slight nods and then turned their backs to her and at once started talking. Gina pushed her hands into her pockets.

'Oh for God's sake. Surely there must be other things to talk about.' She looked ready to cry. 'I'm trying here, I really am. I wish everyone would just forget it and let us get on with our lives.'

'Stop being paranoid,' he said to her and then had to pull the pram to an immediate stop as their neighbor, old Mrs. Nolan stepped in front of them. 'Good morning, Harriet,' he said.

'Morning—haven't seen you in a while.' She stood before him on wobbly knees, dragging a shopping bag behind her.

'Work's been busy,' he said with a smile. 'Have you met Frances?' he gestured to his daughter. *Look! Look at how beautiful she is!*

'What a sweet thing.' Mrs. Nolan bent down as far as she could. 'Reminds me of my own granddaughter at that age.'

'Thank you.' Gina's voice was a little thicker than usual. It was the first time he saw a glimmer of pride in her eyes and he understood it. Mrs. Nolan ignored her. She straightened up. 'How's Marienne?' she asked.

It was unexpected, hearing her name like that, and he stumbled on his words. 'I'm not sure,' he said, feeling his previous light mood blunt a little.

'We all miss her around here,' looking at Gina, her old eyes sharp.

'We'd better be going.' Gina grabbed the pram from him and pushed it roughly down the street.

'Enjoy your day,' he said to Mrs. Nolan.

'She was a gem, that Annie,' the old woman called after him. 'She really was, I tell you.'

When he caught up with Gina, he saw that she had been crying.

'I can't take this anymore,' she said. He pushed her onto a side-street so no one would see them. 'Do you know what they're saying?'

'I don't care.'

'They're saying that I couldn't keep my own husband so I had to go out and steal somebody else's. They're saying we ruined Marienne's life, that she's miserable—'

'Stop it.' His voice rose, his anger stopped her.

'I can't do this.' Gina's eyes were wide and frantic, darting around as if the true, full weight of everything that had happened finally dawned on her. 'I'm going crazy staying at home all day with Frances and I can't come out because everyone talks about me. They treat me like I'm some sort of fucking pariah.' She twisted her hands in her scarf. 'This isn't what I wanted my life to be like. It's too difficult.'

'Well, I'm sorry.' He took the pram from her, pushing Frances out onto the street. He snapped, his own guilt and frustration turning to anger directed at her. 'But no one said it was going to be easy.'

It wasn't as if he never thought of her; he tried not to but sometimes, he would be sitting in his armchair and something would catch his eye. The silly lamp she got from a garage sale with beige tassels that continuously shed on their coffee table and over which they had their first fight. The quilt she had lovingly stitched for him when he had just started work and had hardly been home at night. He kept it on his knees always, tracing the inscription on the underside, *forever dancing to the beat of your heart*, and always felt the familiar twinge that came whenever he reflected on the past months, when he remembered everything he had been forced to let go of, everything he had done to Marienne. Then he would turn his face up and whisper an apology to the air and remind himself that she was better off without him.

He kept his distance from Gina, asking politely about her day and helping when she needed with Frances, but never venturing deeper than that. They lived two separate lives that joined briefly in the evenings, for dinner and vague conversation. He knew he should try harder; she was the mother of his child but every time he looked at her, he still saw the stranger that had stumbled her way to him through a snowstorm. The woman who had bulldozed his marriage and left him scarred and angry and had forced upon him the one thing he was determined to escape.

She had been there half a year when she attempted to take their relationship a little further. He had come home that night to her sitting in his armchair, the sound of a badly acted soap opera blaring out at her.

'Can you turn that down?' he asked her irritably. 'You don't want to wake up Frances, do you?'

'What does it matter?' she said, turning the volume down and looking at him. 'She'll be up in a couple of hours by herself anyway.'

He wanted to pull her out of his chair and remind her that this was his house but instead, he collapsed onto the larger couch, tilting his head back to rest against the pillows, glad for the support. His tie hung undone around his quivering throat, arms lax by the sides of his thighs. He wasn't sure how long he had sat that way when he felt Gina's hands on him, her fingers sliding into his collar. He jumped slightly but it felt good to be touched after so long, so he kept his eyes closed and his body as still as he could. She kissed his neck using her tongue, trailing it upward to his earlobe and biting down hard on the softest part of it. His hands responded without his assent, sliding up her shirt and circling her back tightly. She let out a quiet moan at the urgency of his touch and her head slid down onto his shoulder.

'I love it when you're angry,' she whispered, growing bolder and adjusting her knees on either side of him. When she pushed down, he came up to meet her, everything unfolding and coming loose inside him. In the periphery of his mind, something dark was creeping in.

Without opening his eyes, he grabbed her hair roughly and turned her over so that he was lying half on top of her. She wasn't small like Marienne and her body was still fleshy from the pregnancy. He took care to avoid these areas; her hips, her thighs, keeping his hands firmly on the sides of her face, or at the narrow space between her shoulder blades. She undid the buttons and zipper of his pants quickly and he pushed hard into her, feeling her legs come up and around him. He was in another time now, sometime in the future when her red hair was long and wavy. She was wearing a summer dress that had a flower pattern on it and her skin was soft and smelled like oranges. She was sitting on his lap and leaning back into his chest. He grabbed Gina's knees and pulled her closer to him; he needed something to contain him in case he decided to break free. Her small palms held tightly onto his lower arms, sweaty and light.

'Oh.' Gina's breathless exclamation as her body arched underneath his and he responded, stretching fully above her, his knuckles turning white at the windowsill above her head. She reached up to kiss him but he turned his head away at the last moment. Pushing his knees into the soft material, he thrust upward one last time, to the contorted faces in his dreams, his fingernails scraping against Gina's slick skin and losing their grip. He was losing his mind and letting it go and even when Gina stopped moving, he continued, afraid for it to end, afraid of what it meant. Her legs came off from around him and he collapsed against her, his breath wet on her skin. He never touched her again.

The rest of Frances's first year passed too quickly and before he knew it, the three of them and his parents were gathered around their dining table, looking at a cake with pink icing and one long, lone candle melting amidst the awkward silence that cloaked the room.

'Blow out your candle, honey,' he leaned over his daughter's highchair, kissing the top of her head. He was determined to make this a special day and he blew out the candle with an exaggerated breath *whoosh* that made Frances clap her hands giddily and both his parents laugh.

He cut the cake and plated a little piece for everyone, looking toward Gina, trying to encourage her with his eyes to help. To do something. But as usual, she sat stubbornly quiet at the head of the table, not bothering to get up and wish their daughter a happy birthday. He wasn't even sure she was aware his parents were in the same room as them. His father looked over at him and he shrugged helplessly.

'So, Gina, James tells me you're a nurse?' His father tried to make conversation.

'I used to be.' Her voice was indifferent and quiet and the three of them had to lean in to hear her. 'Not anymore, though.'

'Why's that?' his mother asked before he could stop her.

Gina's face jerked up, the corners of her mouth turned into a hard sneer. 'Because I'm the town whore.'

'Gina, come on,' he said warningly, but he couldn't help feeling sorry for her. She used to be so attractive, so well-groomed and assertive, but now she sat in front of him in a loose gray sweatshirt that did nothing to hide the baby fat she still carried and her face was sallow and bloated. The skin under her eyes was a startling murky color from lack of sleep; everything about her was lazy and uncared for. When she stood to pass him, he couldn't help but stare at her chipped toenails, overgrown and weak. He hadn't noticed up until that moment. He had been so busy with his daughter, spending whatever time he could with her, cherishing these simple days when she was still toothless and wild, when she meant nothing more to him than she was supposed to.

Once Gina had left the room, his mother said, 'I'm officially worried.'

'She's fine, Mom.' He scooped up a small piece of cake on Frances's plastic spoon, let her take it from him and watched in delight as she aimed for her mouth and missed. He laughed and wiped her face with her bib.

'I'm talking about Frances.'

He turned. 'What do you mean?'

'No one should grow up with a mother like that.'

'I'll fix it,' he said, standing to clear the plates.

'You're a good man,' his father said and James stood frozen in front of him, the plates balanced in his hands. One quivered and looked like it was about to fall. 'You're an excellent dad,' his father leaned back, exhaling and patting his stomach. 'Much better than I ever was.'

'That's for sure.' His mother took her husband's hand and they stared at each other, shining with pride.

And he forgot what he was holding, where he was going, and simply stood in front of his parents and asked, not for the first time, for their forgiveness.

After that day, Gina only became worse. She spent hours in bed, hardly touching Frances or ever looking at him. She became a ghost; as quiet as she had been loud, as sad as she had been so full of life, so he wasn't sure why, when she told him she was leaving, he was shocked by the news.

'I got a phone call from my brother a week ago in Montreal,' she said, her eyes darting impatiently toward the door. 'He said he knows someone who's directing a movie. He says they can give me a part in it.'

'I don't understand.' He tried to grab her and they tugged stupidly at each other until he finally relented. 'Everything was going fine. Where's this coming from?'

She laughed and he saw how his words made her face curl in disgust. 'For you it was fine,' she almost snarled. 'But what about me? Spending every minute with that baby, not being able to go out, not having any friends—I couldn't even go back to my old job after what happened.' She took a step closer to the door, as if she was afraid he would realize what she was doing and lock her in here forever.

'You can't just leave our child.'

She paused and he saw a glimmer of something at the edges of her eyes but it went away just as quickly. 'I owe it to myself to go and try out for this part. I'm still young—I have my whole life ahead of me.' When that explanation didn't suffice, she continued. 'I just need to sort things out, to get myself back to normal, then I'll come back and we can figure this all out.' But they both knew that once she walked out of the door, she was never coming back. 'Besides, she's your daughter too.'

'So you're just going to run off? Become an actress?' He had to laugh. 'You know that's not going to happen. Especially with the way you look right now.' He was shouting now and it was a mean thing to say, he knew, but he was afraid; not of losing Gina but of being left alone with his daughter, with no one to keep her safe. Gina pushed her bags down the steps wordlessly, not looking back at him. There was a cab already waiting.

'I want to start new. I'm miserable in this town and that will never change,' she said. 'I'm sorry, James. We only get one life and I'm wasting mine here. I didn't ask for this and it's not fair.'

'I hope wherever you go, you remember what you've done,' he called after her and didn't care if the neighbors could hear him. 'What kind of mother you were.'

She stopped, tilted her head to the side, pursed her lips and regarded him with some pity. 'That's exactly my problem,' she said simply. 'I was never any good at caring about anyone but myself.'

28

Whitehorse, Yukon. December 1992

I wake up to someone pushing at me. I groan and stir, wondering why Judy is back so early.

'Why are you sleeping on my couch?' It's a child, curious as he pushes his face against mine.

'What?' I roll over onto my back and pry my eyes open. It takes a few seconds before everything settles into order. 'Oh. Hi, Alex.'

'Why are you sleeping in my house?' he repeats, now up on the couch, looking at me with interest.

'I—' as soon as I start to talk, he changes the subject.

'Want to play?'

I push myself up. 'Let me wake up first.'

'Let's go play in the snow.' He is pulling at my arm, excited at this unexpected change to his usual mornings.

'It's cold out.'

'I want to make a snow angel.' He is looking at me adoringly, as if last night has made us the best of friends and I can't refuse him. He is sitting so close to me that if I wanted to, I could pull him down under the covers and hug him.

'Okay, come on.' I tumble out of bed and he hurries in front of me, shouting behind his shoulder. 'Ssh, quietly.' I catch him by the door before he leaves without a jacket. 'Hold on, let's get you into something warm.' It's difficult to get his arms into his winter coat because his body is so impatient, his eyes darting outside as if he is scared it will stop snowing at any minute. I zip him up and wrap Nova's scarf around his neck. Then I put on my own coat over last night's clothes and open the door. The morning air is a blast in our faces but he doesn't seem to notice, scrambling down the stairs and delightedly into the snow.

'Hurry up, Frances!' When he says my name, it gathers tightly in my chest and I want to hear him say it again. I run toward him, my body surging for this laughing child who has welcomed me into his life without question. I grab him and spin him around in the dappled sunlight, the snow glittering and dancing with us. He squeals with laughter and when I put him down, he falls into the new snow. His dark skin glows, wet with snowflakes and innocent excitement and his body moves like a sleeping jumping-jack. When enough repetitions are done and he's dug his way almost to the dead grass below, he holds out his hand.

'You have to help me up so I don't spoil it.' I take his small hand in mine and pull so hard that he comes up in a blur and I catch him by my side. He turns immediately to his snow angel to check that there are no footmarks around it and when he sees that there isn't, he throws his arms around my waist and screams.

'It's perfect,' I hug him back. 'Look how beautiful it is!' We stare at it together until he tugs at my hand.

'Your turn!'

I hesitate, already feeling the chill of winter under my jacket. 'Why don't you do another one?'

'You have to,' he insists. 'I did one and now it's your turn.'

I zip my coat further up, not wanting to spoil his happy mood. 'Okay, okay.' I get down slowly, wincing as the wetness presses against the back of my neck. He crouches down a little way away.

'You have to move.'

'Like how you did?' He nods, his hands balanced on his knees, leaning forward. The snow crunches and breaks apart as I move through it, falling into my face and clothes. I don't feel the cold; all I see is the eager way his head moves and the quickness in his voice when he says, 'more, more, faster, more.' The sun is shining into my closed eyelids and everything is still and soft. I never want to stop moving.

'You have to get up now,' he stops my arms.

'How do I do that without spoiling it?' I ask.

'Jump.' He demonstrates, leaping through the snow. 'Like that.'

I get up slowly, balancing on my heels and then projecting myself forward and out of the figure I have made.

'You did it!' He hops around me. 'Look, you did it!'

We stand together once more, looking at the strange figures. When I feel his hand crawl into mine, his cold fingers closing around my palm, I think I will burst from the feel of it.

'Good morning, you two.'

Nova is at the doorway, her dressing gown pulled tightly around her.

'We made snow angels,' Alex tells her.

'I can see that.' She looks at me and for once, it's without suspicion. 'They're beautiful, honey.' His hand struggles out of my tight grip and he goes to her where she receives him with a sweet kiss on the cheek. The gesture sends up a spark to my brain, it makes me feel nostalgic though I'm not sure what for. 'Come on, I'll make breakfast.' He disappears into the warmth of the house and I stand by our angels, already losing shape because of the falling snow.

'Come on, Frances,' she calls. 'You must be freezing.'

When I reach the doorway, she puts her arm around my shoulders. I stop, surprised, but then follow her as she guides me in, using her foot to slide the door shut and closing out the world behind us.

I stay with them all morning. Alex sits in my lap at breakfast and doesn't stop talking or moving, his eyes jumping around the room, taking it all in, forming a memory. Nova sits opposite us, sipping her tea and laughing along with him. She involves me easily in conversation, as if her son's adoration of me is all the confirmation she needed to trust me. I help her clean up and wash the dishes as Alex goes into the living room to watch T.V. and she keeps up a constant chatter, not minding that I don't say much. She doesn't mention anything about last night.

We are sitting together a few minutes later, Nova reading a story and Alex curled under her arm. I am lying on the floor and every time he looks up, I wink or laugh and I join in with the jokes and story, and the movements are natural and easy, as if I used to do it all the time. Then Joseph comes down. I hear his footsteps and my heart jumps to my throat. A low, hot awareness starts somewhere deep, churning its way up to my cheeks when I hear his voice from the stairs. My palms start to sweat and I keep my face turned away from the door, focused on the carpet, prolonging the anticipation of seeing him. I gather up the memory of our conversation last night and blush with the pleasure of it.

When he comes in, we all stop what we are doing. Nova smiles up at him as he comes toward her, kissing her lightly on the lips.

I wonder what it would feel like and touch my own mouth. He turns to his son.

'You're up early,' he says.

Alex points outside. 'We were making snow angels. Like how you taught me.'

'Is that right?' Joseph follows his finger and looks at me. 'How did you sleep?' he asks.

The simple question feels loaded with meaning. 'Good. Nice. Okay, yeah,' I mumble. I have never been nervous before—have never let anyone close enough to me for their words to affect me so much. If anyone notices, they don't say anything.

'Great.' He pinches his son's cheeks. 'Maybe we should always have you here if it means this little guy gets out of bed.' They all laugh but I don't because becoming a part of their family is so precious an idea to me, so beyond my reach, it seems cruel for them to tease me so easily with such a prospect.

'I should probably get going soon,' I say, even though I don't want to but it's difficult to sit here and not have his full attention; to watch them being so carefree. 'Are you sure they didn't mind that I stayed here?'

'No. In fact, Sister Ann said that if we needed you to babysit again, that would be fine. She thinks it's a great idea.' The three of them look at me, waiting for an answer, as if it isn't obvious already.

'Really?' I can't believe that they want me back.

'Of course,' Nova says. 'You were a big help yesterday.' She exchanges a quick look with Joseph.

'Great.' Joseph sits down beside Alex, dragging him onto his lap. The action makes my heart race uncomfortably and I have an urge to pull Alex away from him. I sit back down and shake my head clear. 'Are you alright?' he asks and I try to nod. 'Great. It's decided then.'

He doesn't take me back to the Academy until well after lunch, when the sky is beginning to darken and the road stretches ahead of us dotted in spotlights of yellow. Before we turn out of his driveway, I twist my neck back and see Nova and Alex standing at the doorway. I keep looking until they become two barely discernible dots and all I can make out is the back-and-forth movements of their wrists, waving goodbye, their voices ringing in my ears, shouting that they'll see me soon.

29

St Albert. May 1980

Summer was approaching; almost overnight, the trees had leaves again and people spilled from their houses, lying in their backyards and shouting at each other over their fences. At night, he would take her out onto the porch and sit on the swing, the unrelenting night pressing down upon them like a child's favorite blanket. The distant spattering of dogs barking and the hard vibrations of parties going on around the block were soft sounds in the background. He could smell hotdogs burning and hear the playful chirp of crickets in freshly mowed lawns; the croak of a frog serenading distant fireflies.

'There goes Mrs. Crawley,' he would say as a car flashed past. 'Probably off to her bridge game,' pushing his toes into the ground and then releasing his feet so that the swing rocked them gently. 'And there are the Pressley twins—God, they look different, don't they?' Still boys when winter had started, now they were sixteen and looked like young men. Limbs having shot up, forming muscle where before there was only fat, bringing a confidence with them, an excitement for the future. He had been that way once. He cradled his daughter to him. 'Promise me you won't grow up that fast?' he said, and then felt a terrible sadness and anger at the way the world kept moving relentlessly forward.

He was happy, despite everything that had happened. Life was simpler with Gina gone and Frances was a quiet and easy baby, never giving him any of the problems his friends had warned him about long ago. Very few instances of colds and fevers and maybe one or two diaper rashes, but other than that it had been smooth sailing and he didn't mind not having anyone else to help him. After six months alone together, they had found their rhythm which consisted of him waking up at six to feed her breakfast, dropping her off to a daycare a couple of blocks down from his work, and then hurrying back as soon as five thirty struck, standing by the glass door and always spending a few minutes watching her; the way she stumbled and straightened and crashed into the soft bean bags. The little gleeful laughs and the toys always gripped in her fists as a worker picked her up and spun her around. Then she would spot him and point and he would be called forward by that invisible bond between them and she would be back in his arms and soon after, back in bed, her cheeks red and sleepy.

He had moved her into one of the spare rooms, converting it into a nursery. He painted the walls himself, a swirling beige, and hung a mobile over her head that sang a soft tune for her before she went to sleep. And he would sit in the darkening room, staring and promising and loving her and wishing that he could have a little more time to grasp just how wonderful this time they had together was.

One night, during his soft commentary, he heard approaching footsteps. At first he thought they would go right by him; he had been so busy this past year that he hadn't had a visitor in a long time and he was surprised to hear someone coming up his porch steps. He had to blink twice before he remembered who the man was.

'Ben.' Thankfully the name came to him just in time. A man he had sometimes played poker with; quiet and sensible and had played that way, never winning or losing too much.

'Ridiculous heat, isn't it?' He came forward, looking down at Frances and James instinctively drew her closer.

'I don't mind it,' he said.

'Right.' Ben pulled at the fabric of his shirt, fanned it twice against his skin. 'I find it a bloody pain. Thank God for Jen—she bought two inflatable pools last week. Spends all day in them with the kids,' and then remembering the two women who had left this house, a sympathetic look crossed his face that James had fast got used to after Gina left. Ben looked around the garden, neatly trimmed and bursting with new flowers. 'I see you don't have one.'

'I don't really need it.'

'Well you're always welcome to come and use ours. Roxy is always looking for someone to play with.' He bent toward Frances. 'Hello, there.'

As if she knew she was being talked to, Frances squealed happily and held out her arms to this stranger. Her hair was caught up in the evening light and her pretty mouth opened in a gurgled laugh. Ben reached out for her but James held her tightly back.

'Is there something that you wanted?' he asked. He was protective over his daughter, so unused to having other people interfere with their nightly routine, that he was disconcerted and a little annoyed.

'Well,' Ben inserted two fingers into the collar of his shirt and tugged at it. 'It's Roxy's first birthday tomorrow and we're throwing a party.' He leaned back against the railing, his face shining with heat.

'So?'

Ben cleared his throat. 'The whole neighborhood is going to be there and I thought it would be nice if the two of you could come.'

'We're busy tomorrow,' James said, bouncing Frances on his knee, trying to get her to keep quiet. 'Thanks for the invitation.'

Ben insisted. 'I'm sure everyone would love to see you.'

'I said we can't.' The thought of all those people feeling sorry for him, wanting to hold his daughter, pet her and smother her, made him shake his head more forcefully. All those questions he would have to answer, those sympathetic glances he would have to face that would also tell him he deserved this loneliness, that he had brought it all upon himself.

'Okay.' Ben relented. 'If you change your mind, it starts at twelve and we'll be going all day. You remember how these things are,' he grinned, 'so you're more than welcome to drop by whenever you want.'

'Okay, thanks.' James turned back to his daughter, the man already far from his mind.

'It was good to see you,' Ben said. 'She really is gorgeous.' He reached out to touch Frances but before he could, James had sprung up from the swing, baby in one hand, forearm of the other pressed tightly against Ben's throat, shoving him down the stairs.

'Don't touch her,' he growled. 'Don't you fucking touch her.'

Ben's eyes grew wide as he stumbled down onto the pavement. He held his hands up to block any further contact. 'Hey, just calm down. I'm sorry.' He made a move to come back up, to apologize, but James forced him back down.

'Is that what you came here for?' his voice rising, a hazy anger clouding his vision. 'To look at my daughter?'

'What?' Fearful confusion creased Ben's previously friendly face. 'Look, I didn't mean anything by it—I was trying to pay you a compliment. What kind of fucking pervert do you think I am?'

Pervert. The word sent a rush of anger through him and a sickening feeling of shame pulled a growl from his throat. He released his hold on Ben's throat.

'Get lost,' he said. 'Don't come back. I don't want to see you near my house ever again.'

Ben turned and almost ran down the street, back to the twinkling lights of his house. He went inside and James heard him shout something to his family before the door closed behind him. James blinked a couple of times as the anger subsided and he held his daughter tightly to him.

Everyone kept their distance after that.

It was the middle of summer when his father passed away. A heart attack aggravated by a heatwave that left people in the town sitting by their fans or carrying cups of ice to rub along their necks. It was his new favorite thing to do with Frances; shivering as the ice fell down his neck and hearing her laugh at his expression, asking for a cube of her own. He gave it to her and loved the way it dribbled a pretty river down her chin.

His mother called him up early that morning, unexpectedly calm so that at first he thought he was dreaming. He drove to his parents' house that same day with Frances; it was the first time he had been back since he had got married and it felt strange to take her to the place where he had been as a boy. They held the funeral two days later, the entire procession shifting and sticky in their black clothes. He was sitting on a chair beside his mother, holding her hand tightly in his own with Frances gripped in the other. As he watched the coffin being lowered into the ground, felt it shake with the weight of his father, the hairs on his arms stood up. To be stuck in that box, under the smelly earth forever while everyone else got on with their lives seemed too cruel to him and he had a sudden urge to jump down and save his father from that fate. He jiggled his knee and tried not to move.

To distract himself, he scanned the crowd, picking up familiar faces from his childhood, all different but somehow exactly the same. His eyes came to rest on a small, perfectly still figure at the back. Her head was down and covered in a wide-brimmed hat but he was sure it was her; he would know her anywhere. She hadn't changed in the past two years—still as girlishly pretty as ever in a lace dress with her hands folded in prayer before her. *Marienne.* He said her name silently and as if she had heard, she looked up and saw him staring. She stepped back further into the throng of people. He wanted to go to her but the priest was speaking slowly, unbothered by the growing impatience of the crowd around him. *We therefore commit his body to the ground; earth to earth, ashes to ashes, dust to dust; in sure and certain hope of Resurrection to eternal life.*

The priest had barely finished his last words when everyone began to move; rushing to give their condolences, eager to climb back into the air-conditioned relief of their cars and hurry back to their own lives. James held Frances close to him and every time someone leaned down to tweak her nose or exclaim how pretty she was, he panicked and wished he could have left her at home.

He kept his eye out for Marienne but she never came forward; he saw her though, standing a little way away, watching them, before a group of people huddled around him and blocked his view. When everyone had left, with only two or three people standing over his father's fresh grave, praying for him or themselves, James couldn't tell, he stood up and went to look for Marienne. His chest beat erratically, and adding to the uneasy effect of the heat, made him lightheaded. It seemed like a lifetime since he had last seen her, so much had happened. But when he got to the tree she had been standing at, it was empty and he saw her walking slowly down the grassy slope to the street. She turned briefly before getting into her car and he lifted his hand in greeting, hoping she would see him and come back. She nodded and returned the wave. Then she slipped into her car and he sagged against the tree, Frances dozing in his arms, and watched as she drove once again out of his life.

Thoughts of her were distracting him, so he didn't hear his mother when she asked him, 'What am I going to do now, in this big house, without your father?'

'Did you see Marienne?' he asked, absently folding his father's belongings and placing them in an old suitcase.

'Where?' His mother pressed a shirt to her face. Her shoulders shuddered before she sucked in a deep breath and let it fall into the bag. He picked it up and re-folded it neatly.

'At the funeral, Mom.'

'Are you sure she was there?'

'Yes, I saw her. She waved at me.'

His mother frowned. 'I didn't see her. Maybe you imagined it—this heat is probably getting to you.' *Like it did to him.*

'No, she was definitely there.'

'Why wouldn't she come up and say hello?'

He looked over at Frances, sleeping peacefully in his parents' bed. Her cheeks were red with heat and her hair stood up. He wanted to lie down next to her. 'Why do you think?' he asked. His mother followed his gaze and sighed.

'She would have made a wonderful mother.'

'Yes, she would have,' he said, almost wistfully, letting go of his father's clothes and leaning against the bed frame. He opened his two top buttons and blew down his shirt. The heat was unbearable. He had received a letter from Gina just the other day, letting him know that she had landed a bigger role than expected in the movie. *I'm sorry,* she had written hurriedly, eager to get them out of her life, *but my place is here now. Take care of our daughter.* He had torn it up and thrown it in the trash and forgotten about it within the next hour. He hadn't expected anything else.

'You've done such a good job,' his mother was saying. 'Look at how happy she is.' They stared at Frances together and his mother reached up to curl a lock around her finger. He resisted the urge to slap her hand away.

'I wonder if she's living here,' he mused. 'How else would she have heard about the funeral?'

'I haven't seen her around,' his mother replied. 'Maybe she's living close by. I could try and find out for you, if you want to go and see her.'

'How would you do that?' A pulse of hope lit up in his gut. His mother smiled, lovingly running her hand over his father's favorite navy jacket.

'Why don't you keep this,' she said, handing it to him. He took it gratefully. Then she patted his hand and turned back to folding. 'Have you forgotten what a small town this is, sweetheart? If Marienne is here, there's nowhere to hide.'

He didn't have to go looking for her. She found him, which only made him miss her more.

He had taken Frances on a walk earlier that morning, wanting to show her the hill he had climbed every day to go to school;

the unmoving pond behind his house that the occasional burst of wind picked up and set back down again in sharp ripples. She was too young to understand any of it; he was doing it for himself. He wanted to remember something.

Brushing away fallen red needles of bottlebrush that dropped into the pram, he caught the scent of a particular tree he had never been able to identify it but had the peculiar, unforgettable stink of fish. He had always hated the smell but now it teased him, sparking off tiny bursts of nostalgia in his brain. He sat in the shade with Frances, listening to the murmur of water insects, surrounded by boyhood memories he thought he had lost.

'Sometimes it gets a little lonely, just the two of us, doesn't it?' He rocked her slowly in the stroller, putting his chin close to her face. She banged her fists against her legs and gurgled in reply. He touched her cheek and smiled tiredly from the sun that was already burning at his back. 'She would love you, you know. She would look after you much better than I ever could.' He stretched out his finger and she clasped it, biting down hard and then shouting out in what he had come to identify as her laugh. As always, he was astounded that she recognized him, that she understood what was between them, young as she was. He closed his eyes, pressed his forehead against the bar of the stroller and said, 'I would do anything for you,' before lapsing into a long silence.

He didn't hear the footsteps coming up from behind his house; they padded softly along the overgrown grass, so he jumped when she spoke.

'This always was my favorite part of the house.'

His head came up fast. 'Annie?' He squinted until she stepped out of the sunlight and into the shade of the tree.

'I'm sorry about your father,' she said.

271

'Thank you for coming to the funeral,' he replied.

'I wouldn't have missed it.' She came closer to him but didn't sit down, even though he shifted to make space for her. 'He was like family to me, you know that.' She bent toward Frances, stretching out her finger to tickle her belly. For the first time, nothing in him resisted letting someone else touch his daughter. He trusted Marienne, he always had. 'Hello there...' she was waiting for a name.

'Frances.'

'Frances,' she repeated, straightening up. 'That's unusual.'

'It seemed to suit her.'

Marienne cleared her throat. 'Where's Gina? I didn't see her at the funeral.' She said it casually but there was a trace of residual anger, worn away and blunt now but still there in her voice and tensed-up features.

'She moved back to Montreal to live with her brother six months ago and I haven't seen her since,' he said.

'She went without Frances?'

'I don't think she ever really wanted her.'

'I'm sorry.' Her hand fell to his shoulder and he closed his eyes when she squeezed it with fingers as well known to him as his own. He put his hand on top of hers.

'Have you been living here all this time?' he asked.

'I just moved back a few weeks ago.' She played nervously with her earring, tilting her head and rolling it between her fingers. Her hair hung perfectly straight over her shoulders and looked dark blue where it caught the light.

'Oh.' He wanted to know more; where she had been before, what she had been doing ever since she had left him, but he didn't have a right to know anything anymore. 'I've missed you. Nothing's been the same since you left.'

She pulled her hand away from his shoulder. 'That's not why I came here.'

'Whatever the reason was, I'm glad.' He grabbed her wrist. 'I want you to come back home with me, Marienne.'

After a long pause, she spoke. 'I waited for four years for you in this house, when you went away to college.' She smiled, picking up a leaf from the lowest branch of the tree. 'I remember coming out here in the evenings, wondering what you were doing at that exact moment—if you could tell I was thinking about you.' She started to rip the leaf to pieces, dropped down and sat beside him. 'You came to visit that one summer—a year before you were done. Remember you took me out on a boat on this pond, with dinner hidden in a picnic basket, and how beautiful it was that night?' He nodded, enjoying the feeling of being transported back, the swell of pleasure it evoked. The sense of infinite possibility that he had had back then, like all young people do. 'I thought you were going to propose that day.' She gave a sad little laugh. 'But you didn't, and the next day, you just left, like you did every year, and I told myself that that was it. I was done waiting—I was just wasting my time.' She stared down at her wringing fingers. 'But I couldn't leave. I loved you too much. I trusted that you would do the right thing.'

He turned away. 'I loved you too, you know. More than I ever loved anyone.' He looked out at the pond, remembering them as young as they used to be. He remembered how she had looked the day he had asked her to marry him. She was wearing a dark pink dress and her hair was in curls because they had just been to the fair and he had won her a pillow in the shape of a diamond ring. The real one had burned in his pocket all day. 'You were my best friend.'

'How did we get to this place?' she asked, looking over at Frances.

'I don't know.'

'I can't stay with you, James,' she said, her hand on his knee and her voice resolute. 'Not this time. I'm sorry.' She leaned in and kissed his cheek, pressing her forehead to the sweet circle of heat it left there. He could have trapped her face and kissed her if he had wanted, but he no longer had the energy and wasn't sure anymore that it would work. He caught the smell of her; lavender. He had forgotten and to remember it now was too painful.

'I wanted to give you this.' She pulled out a small picture frame from her purse and handed it to him. He turned it over in his hands. It was one of the four of them; him, his parents and Alison. 'I must have accidentally put it in my suitcase that night.' She stood up, pushed his hair back. 'Goodbye.'

It was only when she had disappeared back around his house and he heard the loud rev of her engine that he turned back to the photo. It had been taken only a few days before Alison had died and the glow in his mother's eyes made him smile even now. He had made the frame out of old bits of pasta and glue, while his mother lay almost dead upstairs with sorrow. She hadn't moved in the days following Alison's funeral and he had thought it would make her feel better. But she had hardly looked at it and so he went downstairs and put it on the mantle, sitting all night in front of it and asking God to forgive him.

When the tears came now, they were fast-flowing; muddled and confused and he wasn't sure who he was crying for. Perhaps he was mourning for everyone; for the time gone by, the mistakes made and the regrets accumulated. For the simplicity of that other time and for all that they had lost and could never get back.

That night, at dinner, he asked his mother if she wanted to come back home with him.

'Really?' She dropped her fork and her face sagged in relief. He felt guilty for not having thought about it before.

'Yes. I can't leave you alone here.' *I don't want to be alone there anymore.*

She turned to Frances, who sat in her highchair, bouncing. She was always moving now. 'Did you hear that, sweetheart? Grandma is coming to live with you.'

He tried to smile at the two of them. To have someone else's hands on his daughter—it was something he would have to get used to.

It took two weeks for them to pack up the house. Marienne never came back and he didn't try to find her. He didn't want to spoil her life any more than he already had. When they finally locked up, standing back to look at the towering, lonely house, the years of his adult life fell upon him. He couldn't recall how he had got to this point in his life, only that he had promised himself he never would.

'Are you ready?' he asked his mother, rolling the key around his hand. She nodded and leaned her head against his shoulder.

'I'm going to miss him,' she said.

'I know.' The key slipped into his pocket, the cool metal pressing against his skin through the thin material of his trousers. 'I'm going to miss him too.' He continued to stare up at the empty house. It looked heavier without anything in it. *Maybe now. Maybe after all of this, I can make it right.*

They walked over to his car, crunching feet over the gravel. They got in and he let his mother securely fasten Frances into her carseat. Then he turned the car quickly, pulling out of the driveway, staring back at the fading house in his rearview mirror until there was nothing there but air.

30

Whitehorse, Yukon. December 1992

I discover a missing childhood when I'm with Alex. A world in which everything is equally new and exciting—nothing is tainted. In his company, I color outside of the lines and marvel at my masterpiece. I spend hours watching talking ducks with lisps and gray rabbits dodging death. Nothing matters except what we are doing in the moment. His life hops along with a carefree loveliness that I seem to have skipped over.

'That's enough T.V.' Nova comes into the living room. 'Come here and help me with this cake.'

Alex jumps over me, grabbing my hand in the process and dragging me into the kitchen. The smell of the hot, waiting oven is a familiar one in this house. During the past two weeks, I have spent most of my time with them. Being here changes me; I become giddy and fun. I talk without reserve, never worrying that they will send me away. I am never quiet, always moving but calmer than I can ever remember being. Here there is nothing to worry about. Everything is simple, straightforward and right.

She gives me the icing to whisk and after a minute I scoop up a finger of chocolate mix and touch it to Alex's nose. He squeals and Nova laughs, shaking her head.

'That's to eat, not to play with,' she scolds us lightly but rolls her own finger in the bowl and drags a streaking line across her son's cheek. He yells and scurries under the table. Nova and I share a secret grin. Sometimes, I adore him as much as she does.

'What are you doing tomorrow?' she asks, taking the mixture from me and expertly whisking it, the chocolate light and giving under her hand where it was hard and stiff beneath mine.

'They're having a Christmas lunch at the Academy,' I say.

'You and the other five people left?' she smiles. There is a jest to her demeanor now that she trusts me. She teases her son and husband endlessly and has recently started doing the same with me.

'Exactly.' I stick my finger in the bowl, narrowly missing the whirring motion of the whisk and I steal some to eat. Like everything she cooks, the taste is hers alone. 'I could eat your food all day,' I say.

'Then come home for lunch tomorrow, if they'll let you,' she says. 'I'm making a feast.'

I purr at the invitation, never tiring of being included in their activities. 'Really?'

'Yes. You can even help me cook.' She glances at me from the corner of her eye. 'And by that, I mean wash the dishes.'

I giggle. 'Okay. I'll ask.' But I know, even if they say no, I'll find a way of making it.

'Great.'

'Is it just the three of you?' I ask.

Her hand movements slow down. 'This year, yes. I don't think my brother and his wife will be joining us.' She takes a napkin and rubs some margarine on it, coating the baking tray.

'What happened?'

The mixture bends and folds as she pours it in without spilling a drop or letting it touch the edges of the tray. She pushes it into the oven and closes it with her foot. Alex is playing with an imaginary plane that flies in between my legs and around our waists.

'When I was younger, I used to live on a farm.' She sits down, pulls out a stool for me. She catches Alex as he sprints around her, pulling her to him even as he tries to escape. 'Not so loudly, darling,' she murmurs. Then she turns back to me. 'It's not far from here—about an hour or so away. I remember once a month we used to come into the city for the Farmer's Market. My mother was the best saleswoman you ever saw. She could sell meat to a vegetarian.' She chuckles and I smile with her, afraid she will stop. But she is lost in her thoughts, letting the words fall and land where they will. 'When she died last year, she left the farm to my brother and me. He wants to sell it—well his wife does anyway.' Her chest heaves. She puts her head in her palm and tilts it toward me. 'But I can't seem to let it go. The more I think about losing it, the more I want Alex to grow up on it, like I did. Or at least to be a part of it.'

'That's why you're always going to his house.' I know they go there at least once every two weeks. Sometimes they stay there an hour or two, sometimes most of the night, but Nova always comes back altered; tired and snappish and lost in her own world.

She plays with a dishcloth. 'We used to be so close, but now,' her words fail. 'It's hard to be around him. Greed can do a lot of damage to a person. I hardly recognize him anymore.'

'That's why Joseph goes with you?'

'Yes.' At this, she smiles lovingly. 'He's very good with them. Keeps his cool when I can't. You know how he is.'

I feel an acute stab of guilt at this. *You know how he is.* Though I have come to like Nova, my feelings for Joseph differ; they are stronger and much deeper. When he is at home, I can hardly open my mouth to speak to him but always wait in the hope that he will address me. Invite me to stay for a cup of hot chocolate and look at me in that certain way of his, like everything I say is worth something. I shift in my seat.

'Do you want some tea?' I ask.

'That sounds like the best idea I've heard all day.'

I move around the kitchen as if it were my own; the wood cabinets and their large, silver knobs feel like home under my hands. I put two steaming cups in front of us. She plays with the string on the tea-bag.

'You've been a big help to me, Frances,' she says. 'I'm so sorry I was harsh with you before.'

'That's okay.' I feel guilty about my feelings for Joseph; she is being so kind to me and I have come to admire her, to care about their family in a way I had not expected. The tea sits uneasily in my stomach.

'So what are your parents doing for Christmas?'

It's been days since I have thought about him. He called me at the Academy a few days ago but I was rushing out of the door to meet Joseph and I told Sister Ann to tell him I would call him back. By the time I had the chance, he was already far from my mind. This growing distance between us saddens me but at the same time, there is a freedom in not needing to hear from him. 'They've gone to visit my aunt in Toronto,' I lie.

'You're not so homesick anymore,' she says, as if she can read my mind. 'I can tell.'

'I've gotten used to being without him,' and then hastily add, 'them'. I glance at her to see if she has caught my slip but she sees nothing odd in what I have just said.

'It's been a while since you've seen them.'

I nod. Talking about him makes me miss him again. Thinking of Nova's mother and her estranged brother, the sadness in her face as she spoke about him, makes me realize how much a part of me he is. I will never be able to get away from that feeling and I'm not sure I ever want to. 'It's been about four months.'

'I've made you sad.' She gets up to hug me. I press my face into the shoulder of her cardigan and clutch her arms, grateful for the comfort.

I pull away and try to smile. 'I really hope you get to keep your farm. I hope you and your brother stop fighting.'

She tucks my hair behind my ear, gathering it up into a neat ponytail and then letting it fall. 'Of course we will,' she says. 'He's family and if there's one thing we can never stop caring about, it's the people who were there with us from the beginning.' She pats my cheek. 'He'll realize it soon enough. Come on, let's go see what that little one is up to.' Then she stretches out her hand and I reach out for it, jumping off the stool and holding onto her so tight, I'm surprised she doesn't pull away in pain.

When I get back to the Academy, my head spins with joy when I see Joseph's car parked near the fountain. I wonder where he is and if I can catch him before he leaves. Maybe he is down by the river again, collecting logs for his sculptures. From one of the windows, Sister Ann leans out.

'Frances, you're back. Come on in—we're just about to start a game of charades if you want to join.'

Before I go in, I stop at the steps of the entrance and today, I look at the school in a different light. It looks like it's smiling at me, opening its wide door to welcome me in. It is no longer strange or scary to me, rather, I can't remember what it felt like to be out of place here, so sure are my feet on this paved driveway, my hand on the door handle. Sister Ann's words come back to me. *Pretty soon it'll feel more like home than home does.* Four months ago, I had scoffed at the idea but now I am stunned to see that she was right.

'Frances.' He comes down the driveway as I thought he might. He is holding some large logs and though they must be heavy, as usual, he doesn't look like he's struggling.

'Let me help you,' I say, almost running to him.

'Are you sure you can hold one?'

'Yes.' The wood is rough in my hands and again, I wonder how he made the smooth table in the kitchen, its perfect chairs, out of this plain, splintered piece of wood. I help him put them in his trunk and then he slams it shut and leans against it with a large exhale.

'I love the forest in the winter,' he tells me. 'Wet wood makes the best material.' He wipes his hands with that green rag that is always in his pocket. 'Where have you been?' he asks.

'At your house, baking a cake for tomorrow.'

'Nova makes the best cakes,' he says. 'Are you coming for lunch?'

'I'll ask.'

He ruffles my hair and I almost catch his wrist there. 'Great, I'll see you then.' He starts toward his car and stops. 'Oh, while I have you.' He takes something out of his pocket and hands it to me.

'What is it?' I turn it around in my hand. The wood is a myriad of different browns; soft and light all over but a dark, rich red within its swirling grooves. It's perfectly smooth; every line and shape unbroken so it looks like it was found that way, belying the obvious effort that must have gone into making it. It's a small sculpture of four bodies intertwined by their hands, forming a tiny circle, their heads bent low and close together.

'Alex and I made it.' He points at the two taller figures. 'That's Nova and I,' his finger falling to the shortest one. 'That's Alex,' slowly rising to one that is a little taller. 'And that is...' he pauses and my heart flutters in my chest.

'That's me?' My voice is barely audible.

'Exactly.' He looks so beautiful, grinning down at me, that it makes me wish away time. I want the world to close in on us here, to draw still, yet my happiness is tinged with the sad knowledge that the end of this moment is inevitable. Very soon, all the students will be returning. School will resume and I won't get to see them as often as I do now.

'It's so lovely.' I don't know what else to say. It takes my breath away and I slowly touch the figure that is meant to be me; me being a part of something.

'My pleasure.' His voice is deep and full. 'See you tomorrow.'

I watch him drive away and when he is gone, I can't resist pulling the statue out and looking at it again. Every time I touch it, it sets off a feeling so strong and good in me that I store it somewhere in the corner of my heart and tell myself never to forget it.

When I get to their house the next afternoon, Nova is laying the table. It's bursting with flavors and colors; pink cranberry, sweet potatoes that are orange and steaming and the turkey sits in the middle, a perfect golden-brown. She puts down a small vase of roses as the centerpiece. She is all about the small touches, that little extra something.

'Great, you're here.' She gestures toward the kitchen. 'Alex tried to sneak a little gravy and he's spilled some on his pants. Will you help him change, please?'

'Sure.' I love when she enlists my help; the wry smile we share whenever Alex has done something wrong.

I take him upstairs into his room.

'Did I spoil them?' he asks.

I open his cupboard, pull the second drawer out. 'Of course not. We'll wash it and it'll come right out. Just take those off.' I rummage through the pile and when I find a similar match, I turn around with them in my hands.

My heart catches in my throat. 'Alex.' I try to speak, but a throbbing shame burns my mouth. I wonder why, since I have done nothing wrong.

'Alex!' Nova is at the door, rushing at her son. 'I'm sorry, Frances,' she seems embarrassed as well, but not angry. Not upset with me. She pulls his underwear up, turns his face toward her. 'You can't do that, sweetheart,' she says to him. 'There are some parts of us we have to keep covered in front of other people. Remember I told you that?'

He looks ready to cry; his face has gone puffy and his lip trembles. I want to comfort him, but there is something that holds me horribly still. *There are some parts of us we have to keep covered.* There are some parts of us that are private, that can't belong to anyone. I hold onto the cupboard and breathe deeply. An idea is forcing its way into my mind but I don't want it there. I don't want to see. I'll never be able to go back if I do. I give Nova the pants and she helps Alex put them on. When he is finished, I kneel beside him.

'I'm sorry,' he says.

I take his face in my hands, pull him close to me. 'You did nothing wrong,' I say, trying to convince us both. I'm glad for his cheek against my mouth so she won't see the way it's shaking, the way my throat constricts and chokes, trying to hold my tears back.

'Let's go down, shall we?'

'Yeah.' I stand up, ruffle his hair, feel his cold skin against my thumb and forefinger. He goes back down, subdued, and I want more than ever to see that smile again; that bubbling excitement that causes him to be everywhere at once.

'Are you okay?' she asks me and when I nod, she puts her arm around my shoulder and pulls me close. 'I'm so glad you're here,' she says as we make our way down the stairs, side by side, and taking our time.

After lunch, Joseph asks Alex and me if we want to help him give Benson a bath.

'We went into the forest yesterday and he really got himself dirty,' he says to Nova. 'Leon is coming back tomorrow, and I think I should wash Benson before he comes to pick him up.'

'Where are you going to do it in this weather?' Nova asks him.

'In the bathtub?' The look he gives her is almost cheeky and she can't help but laugh. 'It's big enough to fit him.' He kisses her nose lightly. 'I'll clean up after, I promise.'

'If you promise.' Her eyes shine and she leans into the arm that goes around her. I look away.

'So are you coming to help me?' he asks both of us. Alex screams yes, Nova tells him to be softer. That is the beauty of a young mind; every five minutes, it's wiped clean and you can make new memories and never have to worry about the mistakes of the past. Though the food was tasty, I hardly ate, pushing the turkey into the gravy and pressing down on the mashed potato, hoping she wouldn't notice.

'Do you need any help in the kitchen?' I ask her.

'That's okay, sweetheart.' She stands up and starts piling the dishes onto each other. 'You can go help Joseph keep Alex in check.'

'God knows, I need the help!' Joseph has Alex in his grip, his arms loose around the small shoulders.

'Wait.' Nova grabs the two of us back and drapes cooking aprons over our clothes. 'There. Now come back in half an hour—dessert will be ready.' As I am leaving, she stops me. 'Are you okay? You hardly ate.'

She notices everything; she cares enough to pay attention. 'Cramps,' I lie, patting my stomach and making a face.

'There's so much left over, if you get hungry later.'

'Thanks.' Her kindness lifts my spirits and I feel lighter, taking Alex's hand and helping him with the apron, which is too long for him. He trips over it several times but doesn't notice because he is so excited.

Joseph takes us out into his shed. This is where he does most of his sculpting and the air is thick with sawdust; beige particles swimming in the air. Everywhere you look, there are sculptures. A few finished ones, but for the most part, they are only half-done. They lie on the long work table that runs along the center of the room, from one end to the other. Some are piled up in the corners, one on top of the other. The heady smell of varnish makes my head spin. I have never been here before and I am excited to see this special, important part of him; it makes me feel closer to him.

'There are so many sculptures here.'

'Nova is always scolding me for that.' He moves within the workshop, lovingly touching everything as if it is his first time in here too. 'But I can't help it—I'll start on one and then I'll get an idea for the next,' he shrugs. 'You know what they say about inspiration.'

I hear a bark from the corner of the room and Joseph brings over the Labrador. I give him a tight hug, feeling him strain and whimper against me. Alex hangs back, hiding behind Joseph.

'Come here.' I hold my hand out to him.

He shakes his head, grabs onto Joseph's trousers. 'I'm scared.'

'There's nothing to be afraid of,' I promise him. 'Look, I'll hold his head and you can just pet him,' I say, stroking the dog's face and turning it away from Alex. 'Come on.'

Joseph steps aside and gives him a little push. He comes forward on tiptoes, arm outstretched. He touches the dog's fur lightly and when Benson doesn't move, when his tail starts to wag, Alex pets him harder and faster. He laughs and Joseph laughs with him.

'See?' I glow, knowing that I have made them both happy and when Alex comes to me and holds my hand, I never want to let it go.

We trek back through the snow and, much to our amusement, Joseph gathers the huge dog in his arms and lifts him through the living room and up the stairs into the bathroom. I watch him, as I did that first day, moving swiftly and with ease, never faltering even when the dog starts to fidget and writhe in his arms.

Once Benson is in the bathtub, Joseph hands me the dog shampoo. He asks me to hold the dog still while he rolls up his sleeves, tightens Alex's apron around his neck and then checks mine. His hands touch my shoulders and burn through my clothes. I keep my eyes down and my heart is thundering in my chest. I pull away.

'I can do it myself.'

'Great.' Joseph picks up the shower head. 'Have you ever done this before?' and his gentle face eases the tension in my chest.

'Nope.'

'It's easy.' He turns on the tap and the water comes out in a forceful stream. He lets the water run over his hand until satisfied with the temperature. 'Come here, Alex.' He puts his son between his knees, lets him hold onto the shower-head and puts his large, steady hands on top to guide him. 'I'll wet him first and all you have to do is massage some shampoo into him.' His eyes are mischievous. 'It's just like washing your hair.'

'What are you trying to say?' I pretend to be offended.

He laughs at that. 'Ready?'

'Yes,' Alex and I say together.

And then all I am aware of is the water spraying in my face, the shampoo foamy between my fingers and the tough, golden fur, Joseph's hand showing me how to work it in. The way I accidentally catch onto his finger and it makes my heart jump but I also feel like it's wrong, and that seems right.

'Benson, no, stop it!' his voice is loud and commanding but then collapses into a laugh as the dog shakes out his fur and covers us all in a fountain of soapy water.

Later that night, I have borrowed some clothes from Nova; an old T-shirt and sweatpants and we're in the living room, watching *The Sound of Music*.

'It's not a Christmas movie,' Joseph protests.

'But it's my favorite and Alex loves the songs.' Nova turns to me. 'What about you, Frances?'

'I've never watched it.'

'What?'

They stare at me as if they can't believe it.

'What kind of upbringing did you have?' Nova teases. She must notice the look on my face, because she pats my hand and says, 'I'm only teasing. You're watching it now, so consider this a favor we're doing for you.'

And I take a sip of my hot chocolate and smile. 'Thank you.'

'So when you have children, you know what to show them.'

Children. It occurs to me that until she said it, I have never taken much interest in my future. I could never see my life outside of St Albert, apart from him. In my mind, we stayed this age forever and though the world might change outside, I never thought it was possible I would want to change with it. That was before I came here. Before I knew them. I look at the way Nova sits curled into Joseph's arm and Alex is playing on the floor with Lego. I see her hand always stroking his hair, tickling his ear; I see Joseph watching them, unaware of everything else around him. They are laughing at something. I remember being that way once, but the memory is so hazy, so pushed down, that I'm not sure it's me at all. It terrifies me to think that there might be other things I want. That no matter how much I love him, there could be something else I need more and for the first time, my bond with my father, that stronghold that has been the central force in my life, chokes me, and I have a furious urge to undo myself from him.

'I think you've scared her,' Joseph laughs, throwing a pillow at my head. 'Oi! Calm down. You're still young,' and they all laugh and tease me until I giggle and throw the pillow back.

When the movie is over, he doesn't have to ask me if I want to stay the night. I go upstairs and into the linen closet where I get the blankets and pillow myself. He has pulled the sofa bed out by the time I come back downstairs and Alex falls asleep beside me while Nova cleans up and Joseph is talking softly to her, sitting beside me. He is saying something about the farm but I don't pay attention to the details. I let his sound wash over me; a voice that has the whole world in it.

'Alex really does adore you,' Nova says, when it's time to go to bed. She picks him up, his head drops to her shoulder.

'The feeling is mutual,' I smile, sinking into the blanket. She bends to give me a light, warm kiss on the cheek and I close my eyes and let it heal me.

31

Whitehorse, Yukon. January 1992

The phone rings for a long time before he picks up.

'Hi.' I am questioning, tentative. I half expect him to hang up on me.

'Frances.' Instead, he sounds relieved but lighter. Like a different person. I wonder if he senses a similar change in me and it's painful and surprising to think that we are better off without each other. I push the thought away and feel for Joseph's statue through my clothes. I have carried it in my pocket since the day he gave it to me.

'How are you?' I want to tell him so much but can only muster those words.

'I'm alright. We miss you.' *We.* I don't mind that he includes my mother; being with Nova has diminished my anger for her. I almost miss her too.

'Sorry I haven't called.'

'There's no need to apologize.'

We both grow quiet, lost in our own thoughts. Perhaps he feels guilty for forgetting about me too. 'It's good to hear your voice though,' he pauses. 'I spoke to Sister Ann. She told me what an improvement you've made. That you've started babysitting for a family down the road?'

'Yes.' To hear him say it, so ignorant of the true nature of my relationship with them, makes me feel disloyal.

'I'm proud of you.'

'I haven't spoken to you in so long,' I say.

'I know.'

'That's why you sent me here, isn't it?' I didn't know it before talking to him but now it seems obvious. 'You knew this would happen.'

'Yes.' He waits for me to speak and when I don't, he asks, 'Are you okay?'

'I feel sad.'

I love him less now than I did before; perhaps because I have opened up some of that space for other people. Talking to him doesn't bring that familiar ache; it's a different one that hurts all over. The knowledge of something being lost, or slowly found out. I don't want to not love him—it's the only thing I have ever done truthfully.

'I'm sorry.'

'Why?' I ask. 'Why did you do it?'

After a measured pause, he says, 'You know why, Frances.'

And he's right.

I think of Alex again, of the way he stood, exposed and unknowing in front of me. I had done nothing wrong and yet the room suddenly turned dirty, every object in it leaning in and leering. *Don't look!* I had wanted to shout. *You have no right—he doesn't know. He doesn't understand, but you do. You do.*

I don't want to say it, but I have to. 'What we've been doing,' *what you've done to me,* 'it's wrong, isn't it?' I don't want to know the answer. I grip the statue and pray.

'Yes.' He takes a deep breath, as if he has been expecting this all along. It quivers and shakes in my ear. I choke back a sob. 'None of this is your fault.'

'Why?'

'Frances.' He sighs, long and drawn out, as if he is tired, and I try not to feel hurt; try not to expect him to sound guilty, sorry.

'Why did it happen? I don't understand.'

'Please, I'm sorry. I can't explain it all now but it was wrong of me. What I did, what I've done to you for so long, it's not right.'

I can't speak. I fall into a chair. My world shifts, as if it has been off-axis for fourteen years and has now only found its true course. Everything becomes a little bit clearer. I think back to my time at home, how I started to push myself at him, tried to seduce him in all the ways I had read about in books, copying the girls from school when they caught onto a boy they liked. I grow hot with shame—she must have known.

'You have every right to be angry with me.' I can picture him now, chewing his lip, his collar undone and his hair messy from a hard day at work. I will never know anyone else that way; as completely, like knowing myself. 'I just hope you don't hate me.'

'I don't hate you.' It's all too much for me—I can't take it in. Despite it all, he loves me. That much I am certain of and I hold onto that for now. 'I just wish it would all go away. I wish it had never happened.'

'We can forget about it.' He speaks hurriedly, as if he has been waiting to say this to me his whole life. 'When you get back, we'll put it behind us. You can come home now, if you want.'

'Not now,' I say. 'I don't want to come back just yet.' The statue's comforting presence burns into my side. It encourages me to go on. 'The reason I called is because I wanted to tell you I want to finish the full two years here.'

'Frances.'

'It has nothing to do with you.' I have never lied to him before. 'This is what I want.'

'Fine. I'll speak to your mother.' He sounds hurt but covers it well. 'You take your time. We'll start over when you get back.'

I want to believe him. I want so badly to believe that we can, that I can have with him what Joseph and Nova have with Alex but I also know I won't. Something dark has diluted our relationship. He is different to me now and I can't stop the sticky feeling of betrayal speeding through my veins. More than anything, I am afraid of what this change will bring about. How can I go back to him after all this?

'Okay,' I say. I have never been able to disappoint him. 'We'll start over.'

'Yes.' He sounds happy, speaks as quickly as an excited child. I have rid him of his burden but mine is twice as full. I feel more alone now that we don't share that.

'I should go now.' An ugly resentment is starting up in me and I don't want it to. Hating him would be the hardest thing to do.

'Alright.'

I start to put down the phone but he says, 'Frances?' and his voice is quiet. I know what he is going to say before he says it. *You can keep a secret, Frances, can't you?* 'You—you aren't going to tell anyone?'

'No.' I could never do that to him—the thought hadn't even crossed my mind. 'No, I'll never tell.'

'Thank you.' He hesitates before saying, 'I love you. You know I do, right?'

Tears spill over my eyelids. 'Yes.' The words feel wrong now; they burn like acid in my mouth. 'I love you too.'

32

St Albert. 1980–1983

She was standing in the driveway when he came down the street, returning home from work. Frances was on her hip, playing with her earring that glittered in the sunlight. He held his hand over his eyes and squinted, sure he was dreaming.

'Five thirty on the dot,' she said to him. 'Some things never change.' When he came closer, she kissed him shyly on the cheek. 'Welcome home.'

Overcome, he grabbed the back of her head and pressed his lips to hers, pulling the two of them to his chest. When he disengaged himself, he saw that she was flushed and he stirred with pride at the thought that she still wanted him.

'I can't believe you're here,' he kept saying. 'What made you come back?'

She took his elbow and guided him toward the house. She stopped at the bottom of the step. 'You took care of my roses.'

'Yes.' That first summer she had gone, and this one, he had carefully tended to her small patch of garden. This year, they were fuller and taller than the last; swirling, blood-red buds in a bed of dark, thorny green. It had made him feel better, less guilty,

knowing that there was something important to her he was helping to keep alive.

'This is my home,' she said. 'I planted those roses, we painted
that fence, do you remember?' and he said of course he did. 'You're
my family—so how could I stay away?'

He stopped her at the doorway. She was standing on the step
now and turned to face him, the top of her head just under his chin;
that wide-eyed, hopeful bride once again.

'Hold on.' He held onto her shoulders, his voice thick and pressing. 'Stay there.' He went back to the rose bush and picked one, held
the long stem carefully between his fingers. He held it out to her.
'Let's make a promise to each other here.'

She took it. 'What kind of promise?' bouncing Frances on her
hip; it was an instinct that came so naturally to her, she wasn't even
aware she was doing it. His daughter's head was lying on Marienne's
shoulder, her small hands tangled in the dark hair. It goaded him
on. 'That once we walk through that door, everything else gets left
behind. Our past, all my mistakes—we start again, just you and
me. Like we did six years ago.'

'It's different now, James.'

He was disappointed, had been hoping for a different reaction.
'You're right. I know you could never forget, but if you could try
to forgive me—'

She stopped him by taking hold of his chin and turning it up.
What she said next tore him up inside. 'That's not what I meant.
This isn't six years ago because we have a daughter now.'

He tweaked Frances's nose, saw her laugh and reach out to him.
He kissed Marienne again. 'Yes, darling, yes. We have a beautiful
baby girl.'

*

'The house has changed,' she told him over dinner that night.

His mother pulled a face. 'Say what you mean. It's a mess.'

He had stopped noticing. 'You get used to it,' he tried to defend himself.

'I've been trying to get him to clean up since I got here.' They shared a look of loving amusement. 'Maybe he'll listen to you.'

Marienne was feeding Frances, wiping her chin gently with the bib. 'I'll make sure he does.'

'Good thing I convinced you to come back then,' his mother winked at his wife.

He stopped eating, put his fork down. 'I don't understand.'

'Your mother came to see me,' Marienne said, putting the plastic spoon on her plate. 'Just after we spoke, a few days before you left Edmonton.'

'How did you know where she was?' he asked his mother.

'I was staying with an old friend of hers,' Marienne answered. 'I went to Toronto for a while after I left here, lived with my parents. But you know how they are,' she gave a short laugh. 'So when I found a job back in Edmonton, I didn't think twice. And Mrs. Buchanan offered me such low rent, it seemed perfect.'

'I've known Susan for years,' his mother said, referring to Mrs. Buchanan. 'I knew Annie was living there the moment she stepped in the house.'

'You should have said something to me,' he said.

'I thought I would leave that up to Marienne,' she told him. 'I know how much she loves you and besides, what does it matter now? Look at how well it's all turned out.'

'She reminded me that we're family,' the thin, elegant hand reaching under his, intertwining their fingers. 'How much we could have together.' Marienne spooned up some more food for Frances.

'I was hesitant at first but the more I thought about it, the more I realized that I didn't want to hate you for the one thing you've done wrong.' She kissed his wrist. 'I wanted to stay with you for everything else you've done right,' and he was sure he had never loved her more.

So the next day, a Saturday, they threw back the curtains and kept the windows open all day. He read the newspaper while they cleaned and dusted and steamed; made them sandwiches after they had covered the beds with new sheets and thrown away whatever items they found that weren't needed. He didn't know how Marienne felt, finding little parts of Gina around their house, but at one point, he saw her holding Gina's hairbrush over the trash-can, foot on the pedal and a mean, little smile on her face. He laughed when she dropped it in and said 'bitch.'

And then she clapped her hand over her mouth as Frances wobbled around her, looking up at him. 'I have to learn to watch my mouth.'

'No you don't,' he said, because they both knew she was one of the softest spoken people.

In the afternoon, Marienne decided to re-establish herself in the neighborhood. James went with her from house to house, daughter in tow, apple pie in hand.

'Marienne.' Lynn at the door, a three-year-old baby boy's fist clutched in her hand and another baby wailing on her hip. She looked haggard and drawn; long gone was that shiny-faced young woman who had dropped into his couch, expecting something much more but also a little less than what she had now.

'Hello, Lynn.'

'How are you?' She looked in surprise from James to Marienne and then her eyes landed on Frances, who was holding onto

Marienne's hand and smiling up at her. Lynn hesitated and Marienne pulled Frances closer.

'Is something wrong?' Marienne asked innocently, but there was a subtle pointedness to the question and Lynn quickly shook her head.

'No. Of course not.'

'Here's an apple pie. We really should get the children together some time.'

'Right.' Lynn took the pie and James tried not to laugh at her expression.

It was the same at every house; she greeted them like she had only gone on a long holiday and had now returned home. When they inquired how she was doing, their glances inevitably drawn to Frances, darting uncomfortably between the three of them, she shrugged and said she was doing fine, as if she didn't understand the reason they were asking. 'Just love spending time with this sweet angel,' swinging Frances's small arm. 'You have met Frances, right?' and if they hadn't, she held the girl up and let them shake her hand, knowing just as he did, it didn't take long to fall in love with their daughter. Her nonchalance, her stubborn refusal to say what they were all waiting to hear from her, made them shrug their shoulders and close their doors. And as soon as the first, hot, sweet taste of apple pie bit their neighbors' mouths, they were James and Marienne again, just as they had always been, and the silent agreement was accepted and understood. After all, no one wanted to dwell on the past.

Later, the four of them sat around the dinner table. They turned on the radio and drowned the house in music. They filled their glasses with wine and Frances's with apple juice, and heaped the delicate china plates they had received as a wedding present, with his mother's roast. Carrots, parsnips and new potatoes garnished the bird, all dressed in brown gravy and they shoved their forks in their mouths and waved them around in the air and kept talking even though they couldn't hear each other, and he saw that he had been wrong. Having a family was not about security; it was not about keeping him in check or protecting his daughter. It was not a superficial cover to put the rest of the world at ease. When he looked at the two women across from him, he knew it was about something else but he couldn't form the thought into words. Something that big, that precious, it would take lifetimes to understand.

The elasticity of a two-year-old mind astounded him. Malleable and willing, they snuck Marienne into Frances's past and established her there.

'Mother,' he said, pointing at Marienne every evening after work. 'What did you and Mom do today?' and Marienne stared at her hopefully and tried not to be disappointed when Frances went back to banging the flat of her spoon against the corner of the bowl.

'It'll take some time,' his mother tried to be encouraging. 'It took her two weeks to finally recognize me and even then,' she laughed, waved her hand, 'she calls me Bubbie, can you imagine that? I don't know where she got the idea!'

It was two months later when they heard it. It was snowing and they were going shopping. Marienne was buttoning up Frances's coat. 'Put your boots on, honey, we're going outside.'

'No.' Frances stamped her feet, her cheeks red and her small mouth pouted in determination. 'No, Mom.' The word was slurred and new but there was no mistaking it. Marienne's head jerked up toward him and his mother. *What did she say? Surely not, surely not,* all three of them open-mouthed and disbelieving. 'No Mom, no

Mom,' and Frances stamped her feet and looked right at Marienne when she said it.

By the age of three, he had lost his daughter to his wife. At dinner, in the car, she cried if they were even a person apart. He would come home to them lost in their own world; Marienne was always trying to teach her a new word, a new game, but even as Frances took her twentieth step, her hundredth step, Marienne squealed and celebrated along with the girl as if it was the first time she was doing it. 'Well done, my darling. What a clever girl you are!' grabbing her around the waist, lifting up the shirt, pressing her lips to the stomach, *brrrr*, vibrating her lips against the soft, white skin until Frances cried with laughter and tried to twist away. When they all settled in the living room after dinner, he would watch the news and Frances would crawl into Marienne's lap and fall asleep there, against her beating heart, and he would lean back into the couch, the world's problems forgotten and watch them together. The happiness he felt almost broke him.

Two years later, they took Frances to her first day at school. The three of them stood leaning against the car, crying and smiling as she waved back at them, her hair in a side ponytail and a brand new, neon purple, Ninja Turtles backpack hanging loose over her shoulders, and ran up the stairs into the building.

'Never afraid of anything, is she?' his mother had said when they slipped back into the car. James turned the ignition on and couldn't help smiling like a boy at Marienne.

'God, I love her,' Marienne said in a rush and they all laughed and agreed and turned to look back even though she had already gone.

Life continued to pass in this blissful, easy manner. He grew closer every day to Marienne and to his daughter whom he adored and did everything for. He taught her how to play baseball in the garden, as his mother and Marienne lounged, clapping and cheering and sipping their tangy lemonade. Sometimes, they asked their neighbors over, invited them to share in their happiness and it was on these endless summer days, when the sun refused to set and people lingered until early morning in his garden, that he truly felt complete. He watched his beautiful wife move in between people, her face tanned, a shine at her cheeks, and felt proud for what he had. He saw the way the men turned to look at her as she glided past, noticed how the women flocked to her, asking for advice and whispering silly gossip into her ear until she was reduced to loud giggles and exclamations of surprise. He saw that he wasn't alone in noticing the special bond Marienne and Frances had. The way, amid all those bodies, the girl always seemed to find that searching hand, pushing her tiny fingers into responding ones. The way she fit perfectly against Marienne's hip, her head cradled against the soft, black hair, thumb in mouth. He knew there was no way anyone could mistake the look on Marienne's face; the red blush of pleasure and gratitude every time Frances sought her out. And he saw the way people were touched by this, and how quickly the gossip stopped. Gina had no place in that garden; she had lost claim over this wild-haired child with the sea-blue eyes. Frances belonged to Marienne and eventually, people forgot that it had not always been that way.

Some evenings, mostly on weekends, his mother would babysit Frances and James would take Marienne out, sometimes with their friends and other times, alone. They would sit across from each other in candlelight, reminisce and tell each other stories they had told each other hundreds of times before. And he felt what he had always felt before; a connection so deep toward her, a lurch of gratitude swelling in his gut, for in her own way, she had saved him and given him what he had always wanted. And at the end of every date, he would stop her outside and give her a long kiss, hold her close and think that what he was feeling for her came closer to desire every day.

They threw Marienne a lunch when she turned thirty-five and invited the whole neighborhood. It was too cold in November to have a barbeque, so early that morning they pushed all the sofas and coffee tables in the living room to the side and used the dining table as a buffet table.

By twelve thirty, the whole house was full of noise; chairs scraping back and forth as people got comfortable, the occasional loud voice rising above the hum of all the rest, glasses being set down on tables as people stopped talking to greet each other. Marienne came down with Frances in front of her and he stood before them and couldn't believe his eyes.

'Here come the two most beautiful women in St Albert,' he had said.

'Mom let me put ribbons in my hair.'

'So I see.'

Her hair was done up in its natural waves and a blue bow pulled it back in a half pony-tail. It was how Gina had used to wear it; drawn back from her face and she looked more like her today than ever and he hoped Marienne, or anyone else, would not see it.

'It's old-fashioned, I know,' Marienne whispered in his ear, mistaking the look on his face. 'But it's what she wanted, and you know how she is about things she wants,' and they grinned lovingly at each other.

He tried not to notice that the dress, which they had bought three months ago, now fit her perfectly; the double straps on the shoulders sat taut against her soft skin and the hemline, decorated with white flowers, danced around her knees. A sneaky memory was fluttering its eyelids open and as she swayed from side to side, to show him the bell-effect of it, it stretched and smiled.

Marienne left them together and disappeared into the living room, where she was greeted by several shouts and someone's high-pitched, already drunken rendition of 'Happy Birthday.'

'Bubbie's calling you into the kitchen,' he said to Frances. 'I think she needs your help icing the cake.'

Frances was on her tiptoes, peering around him and into the crowd of people.

'Tell you what,' he turned her shoulders in the direction of the kitchen. 'Go and see what your grandmother wants and then you can come over there,' pointing to the drinks table, 'and help me out.'

'Okay.' She smiled; that brilliant, too-big smile that took up half her face and swallowed her eyes and she disappeared into the kitchen and he let out his breath. He hadn't realized he had been holding it.

By the time she came back to him, he was still unsettled and his fingers stung from making countless Bloody Marys.

'Smell my hands,' she said, and he did because she held them up to his nose; they smelled like oranges and something else beautiful. He had never noticed her scent before. He held her palm there for longer than necessary. 'Daddy! That tickles!' and he stood straight and dropped her hand. Feeling uneasy and a little sorry, he allowed her to drop the celery sticks into the glasses and take them, one by one and using both hands, to every waiting woman. She moved within the crowd, staring up in awe at the long-haired, lazy-spoken adults who wore sunglasses in the house and stained the furniture with smoke. They petted her like an animal, talked about her like she wasn't there and then handed her their empty glasses and asked for a refill. He laughed as she dragged her feet back, annoyed, her hair falling around her face in bronze wisps.

'I want to go and play with Oscar and everyone else,' she said. 'Can I?'

'Of course.' He shook the Tabasco sauce into a glass and when he looked up again to ask where they were playing, he scanned the room but she was gone.

They were under the stairs when he finally found them. He stood hidden, listening and smiling to himself.

'I told you, I put the keys over there.' Oscar was a big boy for seven years old and he had to sit hunched, hugging his knees to his chest.

'Well they're not here.' She was talking in an exaggerated, loud voice; it was her tone when she wanted something. He knew it made her feel grown up. 'But we'll help you look for them, won't we girls?' She turned to the other two girls sitting beside her. He didn't know whose children they were—they had just moved into the neighborhood. But that was Frances; she spoke to everyone she saw, always ready to share her toys, partake in other children's games and imaginations. The girls nodded and listened to his daughter and copied her as she got on her knees and slapped her palms on the floor, turning her head this way and that. 'Maybe the cat took them,' she suggested after a while. He had to hold his hand over his mouth to keep from laughing. She gestured to one of the girls. 'Caitlin, remember I said you were the cat?'

'Oh, sorry.' The girl got on her hands and knees. 'Meow,' she said.

'Bad cat.' Frances hit her lightly on the nose and everyone stopped to giggle. 'Bad cat,' she repeated. 'Did you eat Oscar's keys?'

'Meow.' The girl curled her fingers and slashed the air with her new paw.

303

'One meow for no and two for yes,' Frances said. 'Did you eat Oscar's keys, Caitlin? He has to go to work and he's very late.'

She was so serious, so innocent, and he had to sit down quietly, so overwhelming was his love for her. He wanted to gather her up in his arms and make sure she knew how adorable she was.

'Meow, Meow.'

'Good.' Frances held her hand out. 'Give them back to me.'

And the cat burped and opened her mouth and out came a fur ball and wrapped in it, shining and wet with animal spit, were Oscar's keys.

'Here you go, darling.' She said it *dah*-ling and dropped his keys into his waiting palm.

'Oh, thank you.' Oscar balanced himself on his palms and stretched his mouth out to reach her cheek. James saw this and quickly interrupted, pulling his daughter out from under the stairs, more roughly than he intended to.

'Daddy!' Her cheeks were red and he knew she had been waiting the entire game for that one moment; for that cherub-cheeked, blond-haired boy to get on his knees and push his face toward her.

'Cake time, come on,' and he practically lifted her up and dragged her into the living room.

They were all gathered around the dining table and in front of Marienne sat the two-tiered orange cake his mother had made. Frances pulled her hand from his grip.

'Frances,' he sighed but she ignored him and went straight to Marienne, who opened her arms and let Frances stand in front of her and lean against her stomach. The smile was back on his daughter's face. When the singing was done and it was time to blow out the candles, Marienne let Frances do it and she leaned forward and he averted his eyes, telling himself that the neckline was too low, that it wasn't his fault he caught sight of the white skin there and that he would never allow her to wear that dress again.

When everyone had left, he surveyed the damage they had done. A chipped glass, cigarette ash trod deep into his beige carpet, having taken on the shape of a hare, and someone's cardigan had been pushed into the cushions of the sofa. He was holding it, moving from the living room into the kitchen when he saw her.

She had kicked off her shoes after they had cut the cake and now without them, her legs looked longer, an unbroken, milky pink. Her head was tilted up to the ceiling and she swung her feet back and forth, kicking the leg of the chair every time she brought her heel down. In her hand, the silky blue ribbon was being twisted; she took the end of it and threw it into the air, watching as it came back down in delicate waves. He noticed the underside of her arm; how smooth it was and felt a strange, but familiar, pulse in his mouth. *Ah, yes, so you do remember.* The memory was fully awake now and it greeted him affably, stronger from years of sleep.

'Hey.' Marienne came to stand beside him and he jumped, blushed and turned to her.

'Someone left this here,' he said, trying to hide the sudden energy in his nerves but it made his hands twitch and she noticed.

'I think it's Diane's.' She took it from him, held his hand. 'Are you alright? You look flushed. Maybe you've caught what Elsie has—she had to go and lie down after we cut the cake.'

'Maybe,' he murmured. 'I think Frances is upset with me,' he whispered, grinning ruefully. Some impulse had pushed the name onto his tongue and saying it made him feel a little rush of pleasure.

'Why's that?' Marienne asked.

'I caught her and Oscar under the stairs—I swear he was going to kiss her.'

At this, Marienne laughed. 'That's our daughter—already a heartbreaker at five years old.'

'Did you have fun today?' he said, wanting to change the subject.

'The best.' She slid her arms around his waist and leaned against his shoulder. They stood watching Frances together and he hoped Marienne couldn't hear the fast, confused beat in his chest. He held onto his wife tightly, staring down into her dark eyes, like swirling pools, and let them lift him up and wrap him in their warmth. He felt a little sad as he held her, but forced it away. Something was coming, he knew that with certainty, and he wanted to enjoy these last few, truthful moments with her before it did.

33

St Albert. 1983

For a while, she was like a visitor in their house; a whirling dervish come to drive him mad. Nowhere and everywhere at once, he felt her laugh deep in his bones, those wide blue eyes swallowed him up in his dreams and the pink oval mouth spat him back out in the morning, sweating and gasping for air.

He was afraid to touch her, to even look at her, and when she reached up on her toes to climb into his lap, he pretended not to notice her and watched with a boiling need as she retreated, confused, to her mother. He sat in the corner and marveled at the way she had turned out; white skin made golden by an army of freckles, and when she smiled, it was a thin and long stretch of teeth and too much gum and it caught his heart in its grip and burst it.

No one noticed his behavior; they were too busy to see the change, and too content with the new family unit to want to. But he was different; altered in a permanent way. Marienne had been the temporary glue that held him together but Frances was his undoing and now he was broken and no one but her would be able to fix him. It felt strange to see his daughter this way; the little girl he had brought up with so much love. To see her as something else, something more—to ascribe desire to even the smallest thing she did. A twitch of her neck as she fell asleep in Marienne's lap, the way she couldn't stop talking when she was excited. Even a burp made him throb and shift in his chair. It had felt wrong at first, but the guilt wore off quickly. When you do something wrong often enough, it has a way of turning right in your mind and now he allowed himself to enjoy these new sensations; the fullness of them, the solidness. It was a feeling he remembered and he wondered how he could have ever let himself forget.

He grew more irritated and short with Marienne and his mother. Suffocated by their presence, judged every time they smiled at him or put an arm around Frances; she was his and he didn't want them touching her. So when he was sitting with Marienne one evening, watching Frances play with her dolls beside the television, he spoke without considering the consequences and said something that had been brewing in his mind for a while.

'I think you should ask the hospital for your old job back.'

She turned to him, confused. They had never discussed her going back to work and it was a rude jolt in their otherwise smooth life; a change when none was needed.

'Why?'

'Well, Frances is in school now and you hardly do anything during the day—I thought it would be nice for you since you're always saying how much you miss it.'

'They'd probably give me the night shift,' she said. 'I was really the only one willing to do it.'

It was so easy. She stepped gladly into the trap he opened up for her and he snapped her up. He looked at her almost sympathetically; she was so trusting, so unaware of what was going on inside him, and he almost told her to forget it. But then he heard Frances; she was lying on her stomach with her ankles crossed in the air. Saw the shape of her body under the white nightgown.

'The night shift is better than nothing,' he said. 'At least you'll be out of the house, interacting with people our age.' He tried to laugh, tried to make it sound like he was doing this for her; tried not to make himself sound desperate.

'When I met Tasha at the butchery the other day, she did say they missed me.'

'And why wouldn't they?' he pushed her hair back, leaned down to press his face to the tight skin of her neck. He opened his mouth against it and she sighed and let him stay there for a second before she pushed him away, giggling thickly.

'You really think it's a good idea?' she murmured against his ear.

'I'm just thinking of you,' he replied, dragging her toward him again by the collar of her shirt. He was burning up. 'You really were good at that job.'

'I'll talk to them tomorrow.' She gave him a kiss, slid her hand up his thigh and hooked her finger into the waistband of his trousers. 'What do you say we put Frances to bed and take this upstairs?'

Immediately, he felt a cooling in his chest; a hole opened up at the thought of not seeing her again that night. But he kept the smile on his face, took Marienne's hand and pulled her to a standing position. She picked up Frances and took her to bed and when she came into their room, he pushed her beneath him and lay his body down on hers and kissed her one more time, long and hard, to be certain she was persuaded. And he did it all intentionally, yet never truly allowing himself to grasp the concept of what it would mean once Marienne was gone, his mother sound asleep in her bed, leaving him and his daughter completely and terrifyingly alone.

*

The first night Marienne began her job, he stood at the window holding Frances's hand and they waved goodbye to her, watching as she disappeared into the darkness. Frances had been crying and he had to pick her up and bribe her with some candy before she stopped.

'Why is she going?' she asked him as they sat at the kitchen counter and she popped jelly coke bottles into her mouth, placing the tip between her closed lips and pushing in the rest using her finger. He took the bowl away.

'That's enough candy for you.'

'I don't understand why she had to leave me.'

'It's her job, Frances.' He was inexplicably annoyed with her. The sugar rush had made her eyes sleepy, her words fast and jumbled. She was agitated and so was he. After waiting so long for this moment, nothing about it was right. His heart hammered in his chest and his hands grew weak. He had to hold onto his teacup for a long time before he stopped shaking.

'But she always reads me a story,' Frances said.

'Bubbie can do that.' He stood, ready to leave her, relieved that it was so easy to walk away.

'But she's asleep.'

'Then someone can read to you tomorrow.' He took her hand and forced her off the stool. 'Let's go. It's bedtime.'

'I can't sleep without a story.' She dug her heels into the ground and threw her whole weight into his arm.

'Frances, come on. You're not a baby anymore.'

'I want you to read me a story.'

He sighed, turned back to his daughter. Saw the mass of curls spilling over her shoulders; the expectant gaze on her face. She had never been disappointed before and so to do it now, especially since she had done nothing wrong, would be cruel. 'Fine. Okay, I'll do it.'

She clapped her hands, jumped around in a little circle.

'But only a short one,' he couldn't help but smile.

Once he had her tucked in—she had a specific way she liked to have it done, tight around the legs so that they wouldn't move but looser up on top, in case she got too hot and had to free herself—he turned off the light and left a small one on her bedside table burning. He pulled up a small chair from her tea-party set and sat down gingerly. It strained under his weight and then settled.

'Which one do you want?' He held out two books that he knew were her favorites and had already opened the one she was going to choose before she had even done it.

'How did you know?' she laughed, her head tilted on her pillow to gaze up at him.

'Magic.' He winked.

Then he started to read; it was a story about a young princess who went on an adventure to save her handsome prince and he moved through the changing scenes; an old, stone castle, his voice dropping into the middle of a forest with trees so tall they blocked out the sun, hushed and breathless as it tiptoed up the stairs of the dungeon, a stabbing shout to send the guarding dragon to its death, and when he looked up to see if she was following, he discovered she had fallen asleep. Her chest rose and fell steadily and her mouth was slightly open. He closed the book and put it beside her lamp. The thundering in his chest was back. He stood up to kiss her then stopped, his hand hovering over the blanket, ready to pull it back from her shoulders. It would be so easy; he would be so quiet, so light to the touch, that she would never know. He stopped and dropped the blanket. It was his daughter—not someone else's. His flesh. To do something wrong to her would be the same as wronging himself. His hand refused to move and he felt a numbing sensation rise to his mouth and thought he would be sick. He quickly drew the blanket up to her chin and rushed out of the room and into the bathroom, dropping down beside the toilet. He gagged once, twice, and then the rush in his stomach settled and he lay down on the cool, tiled floor.

When he got into bed, he pressed his hands and eyes closed, turned his face up to the ceiling, through it into the starry sky. *Thank you, thank you, thank you,* and didn't stop praying until he heard the key turn in the lock and he sat up to welcome his wife home.

'It's just a weekend conference,' Marienne said over the dinner table a couple of weeks later. 'It's not like I'll be gone a whole month.'

'Where is it?'

'In Edmonton. Some Dr. Someone talking about something boring.' She rolled her eyes but he could tell how excited she was.

'A weekend is nothing,' he assured her.

'Exactly—that's why I was thinking that Elsie could come with me.'

His throat closed up but he kept his face calm. 'I don't know if she would be comfortable in a motel.' He spoke quickly before his mother could say anything.

Marienne turned to his mother. 'When was the last time you went back home?'

'Not since we left after the funeral.' She put her fork down, looked up at him. 'It really would be wonderful to go back—all those memories.' She was already lost in thought and he couldn't say no to her. 'I would love to see the house again.'

'We sold it, remember?' he couldn't help but snap.

'I'm sure the new owners wouldn't mind us taking a look around.' Marienne cast him a strange look. He was always so

patient and understanding that his sudden aggression had confused her.

He looked at Frances, her shoulders barely skimming the edge
of the table. She played with the peas on her plate, pushing them
back and forth with her fork and knife. 'Stop that,' he said and then
immediately felt chastised by the three faces looking back at him,
injured at his tone. 'Sorry.' He tried to collect himself. After that
night in Frances's room, he thought that the feelings he had would
go away, that he had stopped himself and with that action, killed
whatever darkness was swimming within him. But the next day,
he woke up to see that it hadn't; that although his conscience had
prevailed in that instant, it didn't mean that it always would. To
be left so alone with her for two days, made everything so much
harder to resist. 'I've just been so busy at work.'

'It'll be nice to have the weekend to yourself,' Marienne smiled
at him, thought she was doing him a favor. 'You can invite George
and some of the guys home for a few drinks.'

He looked at his mother's hopeful face, knew that if he asked
her to stay, she would, but he could see how much she wanted to
go and there was something goading him on to let her. He told
himself that nothing would happen, that he was stronger than that.
That he had done it before.

'Yeah.' He picked up his fork, cut into the slice of steak and pulled
it forcefully apart. 'It will be nice.' And even though everything in
him was in disarray, he smiled at the women in his life and they
relaxed and grinned back.

The weekend came too quickly. Saturday morning was sunny; clear
and crisp blue skies. He had been so preoccupied recently that he
hadn't realized it was already summer.

Marienne bent down to hug Frances and his daughter clung tightly to her neck. 'It's such a nice day today sweetheart,' Marienne said into her hair. 'Make sure you and daddy have a good time.'

'Okay.' The muffled voice against her shoulder.

'I'll miss you.' She kissed Frances and he envied her, not for the first time, for her clean and good feelings.

'Me too.' Frances retreated back to him and he held her against his knees. She blew a flying kiss to her mother and grandmother as they waved and slipped into the cab taking them to the bus station.

'So.' He let her go once they were out of sight. 'What do you want to do today?'

'I have homework.' She looked so forlorn, afraid almost, that he instantly wanted to comfort her.

'We can do that tomorrow.' He waved his hand in the air, speaking in loud, exaggerated tones. 'Mom's not here so we can do whatever we want.'

Her face lit up. 'Can we go swimming?'

And his face dropped. But now he had said it and she was running around the house, her mother forgotten, her energy found, and words were spilling from her mouth and there was no way to say no.

He took her to the local swimming pool, hoping that because it was a Saturday, it would be packed with families, that there would be someone there to distract him. But although it was early summer the weather was still unpredictable, leaving the place nearly deserted.

'One hour,' he told her, settling down on one of the beds. A floating device, towels, a beach ball, all came spilling out of his hands and onto the floor.

She pouted. 'Only?'

He could never refuse her. 'We'll see how it goes.'

'Okay.'

He tried to avert his eyes as she took her dress off; tried not to notice the way the bathing suit stuck so closely to her, it could be blue skin.

'Mom says I have to put the lotion on.'

'Good idea.' He leaned back and closed his eyes.

'She always does it for me.' She held out the bottle of suntan lotion and his whole body froze.

'I think you're old enough to do it yourself now.'

'But I can't reach all the places.' Her voice was reaching a whine; she was impatient to get into the pool.

He sighed, took the bottle from her. 'Sit.' His voice was rough and strained. She placed her little body between his knees and he shifted a little further away from her. He squeezed some of the thick lotion into his palm, placed two cold streaks on her shoulders that made her squeal. Despite himself, he laughed. He rubbed it in across the span of her back, reaching down to the part that was exposed. What was it about her skin that made it so different from Marienne's? It felt special under his hands, like magic. It hurt to touch but he never wanted to pull away. He knew that when she stood up, there would be a scar left upon his palm; that it would always feel empty, yearning, waiting for her to return.

'Done.' He shook himself out of his reverie, patted her skin and pushed her up. 'You can go now.'

'I need the floaters, Daddy.'

'Right.' His head was in pieces. He picked up an orange floater and opened it wide for her to slip her thin arm through it. He leaned down to blow into it, caught the girly scent of her, told himself that it was the flowers, the summer. That it wasn't possible for a human scent to stir those emotions within him. When he was finished blowing up both of the floaters, he sat back. 'Now go.'

And she ran, leaped from the edge of the pool, gathered up her knees in her arms while in flight and dropped like a bomb into the water. It splashed around her, a couple of drops reaching his face and he was grateful for the cooling effect. He slipped on his sunglasses and watched as she bobbed along the shallow end, kicked up her ankles, fussing the water, and he felt like a little boy again; all those feelings, childish and irrational, refusing to listen to reason, straining to fly and fulfill their needs. They were greedy and selfish and taking him over and he, sitting beneath the new sun, watching his daughter's fiery hair stretch thick and wet behind her like a mermaid's, settled back, opened up his body and let them.

She was in bed by six o'clock that evening. The swimming had tired her out and she had spent the rest of the day bleary-eyed and irritable and when he tucked her in, he was glad the day was over. It had been a long time since he had needed a drink but he was desperate for one now; a cold, liquid blanket to cover everything up. He went into the kitchen and searched through the cabinets, finding a half-full bottle of brandy, a remnant from Marienne's birthday party.

He took it out onto the porch swing and sat down. He drank straight from the bottle, running his tongue along the rim to acquaint himself with the taste before taking a full swig. It came up to the back of his eyes, pushing beads of sweat along his upper lip and dotting his hairline. He breathed heavily through his nose, feeling the unsettling presence of alcohol adjust in his bloodstream. The last time he had drank this way was at the bar with Gina and he reminded himself of what that had led to, told himself to stop. But then he remembered the wet, blue bathing suit, skin stained with chlorine, and he took another deep sip and the heat drenched his chest, pleasurable this time.

It didn't take long for his body to disengage itself from its surroundings as he felt the first effects of the brandy. He leaned back and sighed, letting it relax him to the point where he almost fell asleep and didn't hear George coming up the steps.

'Started already, did we?'

James opened his eyes, looked up at his neighbor and followed his line of sight to the almost empty bottle. He hadn't realized how much he had drank. And he had forgotten that he had followed his wife's advice and invited George home.

'It's been a long day.' He smiled crookedly, trying not to stumble on his words but they felt heavy in his mouth.

'First time alone with the kid?' George sat down on the swing, pushed his shoes into the wooden boards of the porch, letting go and leaning back as the swing rocked them back and forth. The world spun past him at lightning speed and he wanted to tell George to stop it but couldn't form the request quickly enough.

'Yeah,' he managed. 'First time.'

George took the bottle from him and he gave it up gratefully. 'Then I completely understand.' He sipped, slow and long, from the bottle. He scoffed. 'Listen to me—the way I talk, you would think I didn't love my children.'

'Do you?' He would never usually be that bold but the brandy was working, numbing him slowly.

'Of course.' George talked through the bottle. 'Sometimes, it's just too much, you know? I want to be sixteen again, smoking pot behind the school bleachers or making out with Kimmy Klein in my car.'

'Kimmy Klein,' James snorted. 'What a name.'

George laughed along with him, drained the last of the drink into his mouth. 'What a girl.' He paused, turned to James. 'Sometimes, it gets too hard, caring about other people.'

They sat in silence for a little while after that, the empty bottle somehow fell to the floor and rolled under the swing. He woke with a start when he felt George's hand on his shoulder. 'I think you should go to bed now.' George's large face looming over his. 'Need some help getting in?'

James stood, felt a sharp pain at the back of his head. He winced. 'No, I'm okay. Sorry—I forgot you were supposed to come over. Can we do this another time?'

'Of course.' George slapped him across the back. 'Good talking.'

He was hardly aware of his feet taking him back into his house, shutting the door and hearing George's footsteps retreat. He leaned against the door and gulped in some air. The room was spinning and he closed his eyes and let the world come up to meet him. He staggered further in, placing one foot in front of the other and finally, hauling himself up the stairs using the banister for support. He let his feelings guide him; it couldn't be helped. Aggravated by the alcohol, they took over and blinded him. He was lost. They held him by the hand, secret accomplices under the muggy cover of night, and led him quietly to her bedroom.

He had left the door slightly ajar and now he pushed it fully open. It was dark except for the luminous stars swirling on her ceiling, quietly vigilant over her sleeping body. The yellow lights from the rest of the street shone behind her curtains, slowly going off one by one as his neighbors turned their eyes away, rolled into their beds and left the two of them alone.

He went to her bed, knelt down on the carpet. Her hair was

still wet from her evening bath and her cheek felt overheated and tired.

'You're so warm,' he whispered. 'I'll just take this off for you,' pulling the blanket away, leaving just the sheet behind. 'Ssh. Go to sleep, honey.' And because she loved him and because she knew he would never do anything to harm her, she listened and soon he felt the steadiness of her breathing again.

The brandy was building on his tongue, clenching his stomach and rising to his throat. He clung tightly onto her blanket. 'I won't hurt you. I'm sorry, I'm sorry,' leaning down to kiss her cheek but then he couldn't stop and he traveled down to the palm of her hand, pressing his lips to the bone at the ankle of her feet, *so perfect, how come everything about you is so beautiful?* He picked her up and she stirred. Said something but he couldn't hear her anymore.

'Don't be afraid,' he pressed his face again to her cheek, nuzzled her hair, her neck, 'you smell wonderful, my baby. My beautiful, baby girl,' and pulled her down onto the floor with him.

The next day, in the late afternoon, he took her to the park.

'It's always the most beautiful here at the beginning of summer,' he told her. 'The leaves are all new, the flowers are coming up,' he said, breathing in the air. It smelled different; like how he had always imagined it would. 'I just love it here.' They sat down on a bench; he curled his hands under her armpits; felt the hotness of her beneath her red sweater, lifted her up and then slid her close to him. She put her head against him. He took the hot chocolate she held in her small hands. 'Don't drink all of it—it'll make you sick.'

'Sick like how you were yesterday?' She turned her face up to look at him and he took his arm out from around her. He knew it was coming, but now she had asked it, he panicked and didn't know what to say.

He had woken up last night on the floor of her room; she was sitting beside him, pushing at his shoulder. She had been crying and he tried to calm her as he struggled to sit up. The alcohol had drained away, leaving him with a pounding headache, a dry mouth and a sense of something having been lifted off him only to be placed back with an extra load.

'Ssh.' He stroked her hair, guided her back to bed, pulled the blanket right up to her chin. He was glad for the darkness because he couldn't bear to see her face. 'I'm okay, it's alright. Daddy is just feeling a little sick, that's all. Go to sleep now,' and he sat beside her until her eyes fell shut and she got lost in her dreams.

He had sat up all night with something hot running in him; his body refused to keep still but it wasn't the guilt. He hadn't had these kinds of feelings ever; they were strong and all-encompassing, not something sad and watered down. They made the world take on a different light and for the first time, he saw how splendid everything in it was. It made him regretful for what he had missed out on for so long but also excited that he had discovered it. He hadn't hurt her—had barely touched her and he convinced himself, before he fell asleep, that he had done nothing wrong.

But now she stared up at him and he couldn't face her. 'No, not sick like daddy.'

'But you're okay now?' she asked him.

'Yes.' He took a sip of the hot chocolate; it got stuck in his throat. 'Everything is okay. Everything will be okay.' There was something thick on the tip of his tongue. He didn't want to say it, it made him sick to his stomach to say it, but he had to. 'Let's keep this a secret from mom and Bubbie, okay? Let's keep it just between us.' He tried to smile at her; tried to make it sound like a game they were playing. He felt like a monster.

'Why?' Her eyebrows crossed in confusion.

'I don't want mom to worry,' he said, turning her shoulders and looking at her more urgently now. He realized how easy it might be for him to get caught. 'It's very important that you don't tell her, Frances.'

'Okay.' She didn't want to disappoint him but he knew she was only a young child, that she might let it slip. But he also knew that she was too young to understand what had happened yesterday, that she might say he had been sick, that he had acted strange, but no one would think twice. It terrified him more to think how easy it could be to get away with.

He gave her the hot chocolate back and let her finish it.

'I like this place,' she said. 'Can we come here every day?'

He tilted his head down to press his cheek against the top of her head. 'We can come here whenever you want.'

That night, he lay beside her as she fell asleep, turned his face into the pillow and found it easier this time to hide his sounds. He lay there for what seemed like an eternity, hearing her tiny snores, falling in love with her again and again, before he heard the doorbell, went downstairs and let the real world come rushing back in.

34

Whitehorse, Yukon. January 1993

After the phone call to my father, I go slowly back up to my room. I pass the full-length mirror Judy and I share and I stop. I say my name, hushed at first and then louder, until it becomes something solid. I touch my shoulders and arms, trail my hands down my waist, leaning over to wrap my forefingers around my toes. The running length of my calves, the slight ankle bone where my legs meet my feet, the hair that tickles my knees, all come to life. They feel real and strong and for the first time, like they belong to me.

'Miss me?' The loud voice pulls me quickly to a standing position and Victoria bursts through the door, invading the quiet circle I have created for myself. Her skinny arms wrap around my neck. I haven't thought about her in two weeks and now, standing so close to her, with her breath on my cheek, I feel strange and uncomfortable and want her to leave.

The girls have slowly been filtering back into school since the beginning of January and the constant sound of cars pulling up, excited chattering and suitcases being hurled up the stairs, is too loud for me. I have got used to having the building mostly to myself and I find the noise and congestion irritating; it turns the building back into the cold, unwelcoming place I first came to. And with the starting of school tomorrow, rules have been reinstated and I'm no longer free to do what I want. Joseph took Nova and Alex to visit his sister and I haven't seen them in almost a week and I wonder if they feel as empty as I do.

'I had the best holiday ever!' She pushes me into the corner of my bed and lies down beside me, folding her hands behind her head. She kicks up her legs, fussing with my blanket. 'Aren't you going to ask me what I did?'

'What did you do?' I ask it automatically, hoping it will satisfy her and she will leave soon.

'Spent every minute of it with Leo.' She hasn't stopped smiling since she came into my room and now she tells me that he would pick her up every morning and they would spend the whole day together.

'My parents didn't like it but they couldn't stop me.' She waves her hand in the air proudly. She says he took her to museums, to different restaurants every night, describes how he would sneak her into the coolest clubs because he knew 'practically everyone' and how much time they spent in his car.

'We couldn't go to my house because of my parents and he lives in a basement with three other guys.' She laughs at the memory. 'It never got boring though,' she tells me, flipping onto her side. 'And everyone loves him.'

'And he loves you.'

'He told me he wants to marry me one day.' She holds out her hand and shows me the ring he gave her; old and the underside has already turned brown with rust. 'It's a promise ring.' She looks closely at me. 'Don't you like it?'

'It's pretty.' I turn back to my books, hoping she'll get the hint.

'I have a favor to ask you,' she says instead.

'What's that?' I have lost interest in her; my mind is full of Joseph and his family and all that matters to me is when I will see them next.

'He said he would come see me on Thursday.'

'So what do you need me for?'

'I'm going to sneak him in and I need you to help keep watch.'

'Victoria,' I shake my head. 'If we get caught—'

'Please.' She grabs onto my arm. 'He'll only be here for twenty minutes, tops. They never check on us during free time anyway.' She pouts. 'Please, please, please,' and bats her eyelashes, thinking that because it works on him, it will work on me. It does. I feel myself relenting, unable to say no.

'Don't we have hockey that day?'

Once a week, in the afternoon, we play a sport and the class is held in the old gym near the pavilion.

'Exactly.' She nods. 'I'll say I'm not feeling well and I'll come back here to meet him.'

'What about Taylor?' I ask, referring to her roommate.

'You know how she is—she's always in the library. But I would feel better if I knew you were watching out for me—you know, in case she decides to come back or if one of the teachers feels like doing a search.' She takes my hand. 'Nothing's going to happen, but just in case...'

'Fine.' I say it so that she will leave and stop distracting me. 'I need to do some homework now.'

'Classes haven't even started.'

'I didn't do so well last semester so I'm giving myself a head start.'

She is too happy to think that anything else is wrong. 'I have to go unpack anyway.' She gets up. 'See you tomorrow?'

I nod and she closes the door, briefly letting in waves of sound before shutting out the noise from the corridor, leaving me to my daydreams.

I am supposed to meet Victoria the next day after classes to 'plan project L' she giggled into my ear and she is waiting for me on the veranda, swinging her leg impatiently against the wall.

'It's about time!' she says when she sees me. 'Where were you?'

'Sister Ann wanted to see me about something,' I lie. After classes, I had gone out the back entrance of the building to look for Joseph but I hadn't found him. Now, I drag my feet toward the bench and sit down beside her.

'We only have a few minutes left before dinner,' she says.

'I can't help that she wanted to talk to me,' I snap.

Victoria lapses into an angry stony silence. I scuff the heel of my shoe into the floor.

'What's with you these days?' she asks me. 'I come back and it's like you don't care about anything anymore. I thought we were friends.'

'We are.' I close my eyes and put my head back. She sounds so dejected; the warmth is gone from her voice and I don't want to be the one to spoil her excitement. 'It was hard being stuck here alone.'

'I told you to come home with me.'

'Frances.'

The voice is warm and low and smashes into my heart. I turn fast, my breath racing and almost can't believe it when I see him smiling down at me, hands in his pockets. Calm as always. I have to sit on my hands and cross my legs tightly to stop myself from running at him.

'Hi.' I'm smiling so wide my teeth hurt. I introduce him to Victoria and he greets her with that charming tilt of his head and she blushes, despite herself. It's somehow comforting to know that I'm not the only one who feels that way about him.

'Nice to meet you,' he says and then turns to me. 'I've just spoken to Sister Margret—I've asked her if you can come home with me tonight for dinner.'

The blood rushes to my head. It is wonderful to think that as I was looking for him, he was seeking me out purposefully, wanting to see me as much as I wanted to see them. 'Did she say yes?'

He laughs and nods. 'Yes, she did. I'm heading over there right now—do you want to come with me? I didn't realize you might be busy.'

'No.' I stand up quickly and then remember Victoria. 'We can talk tomorrow.'

'Sure.' She looks confused and I know that when I get back, she will be waiting to ask me a hundred questions and I resent her presence here, soiling the moment.

'Great.' I turn to him—almost reach out my hand to hold his but I keep it tightly held behind my back. 'Then I'll come with you.'

He says goodbye to Victoria and then puts an arm around my shoulders and leads me down to the car.

'I'm glad you agreed,' he says as we slip into the car and feel it jump to life beneath us. 'Nova is making her famous vanilla cake and trust me, you don't want to miss it.'

And he twists the dials on the radio, turning the music up loud and we sing and laugh all the way home.

They tell me the news after dinner. We sit down in the living room and Nova hands me the slice of vanilla cake with the most icing as if that will make it better. The three of them sit on the long couch, Alex in the middle, and I sit opposite them, in the recliner with my legs curled up beneath me and the sweet burst of flavor on my tongue.

'This is amazing,' I say.

'I'm glad you like it.' Her voice is unusually soft and gentle. 'We're so happy you came today. We've missed you.'

I want to say it back to them but the words are too precious and even if I do let them out, they will never understand what I'm really trying to say. 'Everyone's back at the Academy now.' I make patterns in the icing with the small fork she has given me. 'So we're not really allowed to leave whenever we want anymore.'

'You must be happy to have everyone back.' She is talking for the three of them and when I look at Joseph, his eyes look a little sorry.

'Yeah.' I chew slowly, choosing my words carefully. 'But it's noisy and I miss my space already.'

'You have good friends though here, don't you?' He is speaking now. 'That girl, Victoria, she seems sweet.'

I don't want to talk about Victoria right now; I don't want to talk about anything outside of this room, outside of us. 'She's nice. Why are you asking me all these questions?' The way they are looking at me has started to make me uneasy.

'We just want to make sure you're happy,' Nova says. 'We care about you.'

I put the bowl down; there is no room in my body for it anymore. Her words fill me and lift me up. 'Thanks.' They look at each other; she gives him a slight nod. I realize that tonight, even Alex seems subdued. 'Is everything alright?'

'Frances,' Joseph sighs, sits up straight. 'There's something we have to tell you.'

I prickle immediately even though I know I have done nothing wrong. Perhaps it's an instinct from doing terrible things my whole life, from keeping such a closely guarded secret. I wonder if I will feel like this my whole life and I hope that I won't. 'What is it?' I ask. But I am still too content, too comfortable, to make anything of the way his forehead crinkles into an upside down V, the way he rubs his palms on his pants.

'Nova's brother has decided to give up the idea of selling the farm.' The words come out in a rush and at first I'm confused. And then I remember what she told me that day we made a cake together. How sad she had looked and I smile now.

'That's great.' I reach for her hand and she takes it, squeezes it.

'Thank you. We're so excited. He's decided he wants nothing to do with it so he's given his share to us.'

My smile is beginning to waver; I think I know what they are about to tell me but I don't let myself imagine it. Suddenly I want to be anywhere but here. I can't speak, so Nova carries on talking.

'Remember I told you,' I start shaking my head, *no, you can't say it. Please.* But she carries on regardless. 'I told you that I want Alex to grow up on the farm like I did.' My eyes go to Joseph and he is watching me sympathetically. 'So—'

'You're leaving.' I say bluntly.

'Yes.'

We sit that way in silence and when I look at them again, I see it. They are a family; the three of them. I'm just an outsider who has been lucky enough to be invited in, asked to sit on this couch and be near them.

'When?' It's all I can do to keep calm; asking the mundane questions, hoping that the real issue will disappear.

'We're going to start moving everything in a couple of weeks, so perhaps by the end of the month.'

'What about your job?' I ask Joseph.

'I gave in my resignation today.'

'That's why you went to see Sister Margret.'

Strange that this little fact that he went to see her for something else, that I was just a side thought, should be the thing to hurt me the most.

'Yes.'

I can feel myself getting angry but remind myself that I have no right over them; they are not mine to keep. Not mine to love. 'That's wonderful for you.' I speak through the blockage in my throat.

'We're going to miss you,' Nova says. *It's not enough.*

'Me too.'

'It's getting late.' He shifts on the couch. 'You have school tomorrow, don't you?'

'Yes.' I speak through a painful daze; he looks distorted and angular. His voice seems menacing. It doesn't suit him and it scares me. There is a black pool of fear spreading like spilled ink in my chest, coating my organs with poison.

'Let me drive you back.'

'I'll walk.' I get up.

'Frances, it's dark and cold.' He has come closer; he is clear again, his eyes are concerned. 'I'm driving you back.'

At the door, I hesitate with my jacket hugged close to me.

'We'll see each other before we go,' she pulls me into a hug. 'You can come over on the weekend. Help us pack.'

'Okay.' I ruffle Alex's hair, he says goodnight to me and I bend down for him to give me a kiss. We all laugh, joined together in our affection for him, and this solidarity makes me feel more lonely.

'Let's go.' Joseph ushers me out. 'I'll be home soon.'

And I see her, with Alex held against her body, looking just as she did the first day I saw her; but now we smile at each other, she tilts her head and waves, *goodbye, honey,* before the door swings shut and she is gone.

'Are you alright?'

The question makes me jump out of my reverie; my head is leaning against the window and I stare out at the speeding tarmac falling beneath the wheels. Slowly being destroyed, car by careless car, and it doesn't know how to escape.

'What?'

His eyes are trained on the road. 'I know we've all gotten pretty close recently.' The profile of his face, half-lit by light, part in shadow, gives him a devastating sharpness. I want to trace my finger down the dangerous slope of that cheekbone, travel all the way down to the slender neck.

I turn away, reminding myself that it's wrong to think of him that way. 'Yeah. We have.'

'And I know it's sudden—this move,' he shrugs apologetically. 'But with it being the beginning of January, it just seemed like the perfect time for a new start. Before we lost our nerve.' He shakes his head, gives a strained laugh. 'Change can be a terrifying thing,' he says. 'I've lived here all my life—I can't imagine myself without it.' He pulls up outside the school, turns off the ignition.

'So why don't you just stay?' I try to compose my voice.

'Alex,' he says. 'Nova has always wanted him to grow up there, to go to the school she went to. She's a romantic.'

'What about you? Aren't you scared to leave your home?'

He shifts onto his side so that he is facing me. I can't bear to look at him so I continue staring straight ahead. He exhales through his nose. 'Life won't stay the same way forever, you know. Something is bound to shift and that's the beauty of it. You grow up, you get married, you have children,' he pokes me on the shoulder. 'You meet unexpected people.' I can't help but smile and his grin grows wider. 'We're here now, so change can't be all that bad, can it?'

'No,' I say, finally facing him.

'You're a wonderful girl, Frances,' he says to me. 'Don't forget that.'

When my body starts to lean in to him, I think at first that I am going to kiss him, but instead, my arms go around his neck and I hug him tightly. My chin rests on his shoulder; it is a warm but formal embrace. There is such goodness in him, such kindness, that I can't bear to ruin it. I don't want to do something that will compromise him, that he will end up feeling guilty for even though I know he would push me away and it wouldn't be his fault. I love him in so many different ways that it pains me to have him so close and know that he can't be mine, but something in me is also calm in the face of this fact—it feels right that it's this way.

'Thank you,' I say. I don't want to think about them leaving. I still have a month. 'For everything.'

I pull away and open the door but just before I leave, I turn back once more. There is something in his eyes that tells me no matter what hasn't been said between us, he understands all of it.

35

St Albert. April 1989

She had grown tall; he could feel the way her toes grazed his shin. She had never been able to reach there before. And her muscles felt hard in some places, rigid and uninviting.

'How old are you now?'

'You know how old I am, Daddy.'

They were lying side by side on the picnic blanket Marienne had set out for them two hours ago, staring up into the sky. He looked straight into the sun until his eyes watered and his line of vision was nothing but tilting, dancing spots.

'Eleven in a couple of weeks.' Marienne sat down next to them, let her daughter's head fall into her lap. He tried not to feel jealous. 'What shall we do?' She pretended to think, tapping her bottom lip. 'I know. Let's have a party.'

Frances sat up straight. 'Really?' turning to her mother, 'Like a real, grown-up party?'

'Ask your father.'

'Well?' He heard her voice from above him but kept his eyes closed, his voice even.

'What does a grown-up party even mean?'

'It's one where there are no parents.' She poked him in the stomach. 'You have to stay upstairs. Or in the basement, whichever you prefer.'

He didn't like it when she was like this; when she acted like he was nothing to her. 'Why would you want that?' he asked, trying to hide his snide tone. 'Is there a boy you like?' It was childish, he knew, juvenile and beneath him but he couldn't help the way he felt.

'No,' she blushed, confirming what he had long suspected. She had been acting strange recently, always hovering near the phone, waiting for it to ring and when it did, she would pounce on it and there would be a momentary seizure of panic and then her face would relax. 'Hello?' he would hear her say in her practiced voice; in the slow and careful way Marienne spoke. And then someone would ask for him or Marienne and her face would drop and she would hand them the phone almost grudgingly, telling them not to take too long. And when they were finished, she would wrestle past them and go back to watching it. She took longer than usual to get ready for school and every time he drove her, she would fidget and play with her skirt, push her fingers through the roots of her hair.

'You're too young to care so much about the way you look,' he told her once.

'You don't understand, Daddy,' is how she replied and he hated the thought of this growing distance between them.

She had been secretly his for six years. He knew every inch of her; that scar from when she had been riding her bike and it flew over a bump and she ripped her skin on the tarmac, or that beauty spot hidden in her scalp. He knew her from what she said, what she might say next; and he knew that her hair seemed longer at night, tangled around his wrists.

She asked him once, at the beginning, what he was doing when she was facing the wall and her back was to him.

'What do you mean?'

'You make funny noises.' And the bluntness with which she had spoken had hurt him and he hadn't touched her for three days. But then, when his guilt wore off, as it always did, he found himself back in her bed, holding her tightly and explaining.

'Do you know what a snore is?' he asked.

'No.'

'It's the sound most men make when they're sleeping. Because of this, here,' he took her hand, pressed it to his Adam's apple. 'Sometimes we find it hard to breathe.' Lying was not difficult anymore.

The only difficult part of it was worrying that Frances might let something slip, that Marienne might catch on. He knew she would never believe it—how could she when he hardly believed it himself? 'Remember, don't say anything to mom and Bubbie about this,' he would always whisper before he left her room. 'It's our secret, right? I'll be very upset if you do.'

'I won't tell,' she would say as she fell asleep. 'I promise I won't tell.' and he knew she wouldn't because she didn't understand what was happening. Because he always held her on top of her clothes; it was a barrier he refused to cross. Yes, he loved running his hand over her smooth arms, touching his mouth to her neck, but he never went further than that. He pressed her against him, feeling the fabric of her nightdress against the thin material of his pajamas and it was enough.

But at ten, she was forgetting him as soon as he left her room. It was as if she didn't think twice of what he was doing; perhaps she didn't want to. Perhaps she loved him too much, trusted him implicitly and wouldn't allow herself to know what was happening.

'So, what's his name?' Marienne asked, making a face at James. He had his sunglasses on and pretended not to see her.

'Sam.' She covered her face with her hands, gave out a squeal. 'I'm so embarrassed. Stop talking about it.'

'Is he your friend?'

'He's on the dance team with Kylie.' She couldn't stop smiling.

'Well, you have to invite him to the party,' his mother said.

'There isn't going to be a party,' he interrupted.

'Of course there will. He's just teasing,' Marienne rubbed Frances's shoulder.

'No.' He raised his voice; straightened his spine. Declared it loudly. 'I'm not comfortable with the idea.'

'James!'

He ignored his wife. 'Sorry, Fran. Maybe next year, when you're older.'

And they watched as she got up and stormed to the car, crossing her arms over her chest and trying not to cry. She had never been able to argue with him.

'Come on, honey.'

'I'm sorry, Annie. I said no.' He got up, started clearing up the plates. He didn't care that they were upset. The birthday would come and go and eventually they would forget about it. 'Come on, let's go home.'

Two nights later, she said to him, 'I don't want to have the party anymore, anyway.'

Marienne had already left for work and his mother was asleep. They could hear her sounds from the room next door and he was glad for the thin walls.

'Why are we still talking about this?' he said, annoyed, but then turning to her and seeing how her eyes dropped, how disappointed she was. 'What's the matter?' he asked.

'Sam doesn't like me,' she told him.

He felt a rush of relief. 'I'm sorry. But I'm glad. I don't want you spending time with any boys.'

'I'm eleven, Dad. You can't pretend I'm going to stay a child forever.'

He looked at her face; the bones bending, forming and starting to fit into her features. 'No,' he said and his voice changed. 'You're definitely not a child. Look at you; at how beautiful you are.'

She blushed at his tone. 'You think so? Sam said I wasn't his type.'

'Sam sounds like a silly boy,' he murmured, but had forgotten all about him already. His hands went to her hair, thick and strong in his fingers. 'He's obviously talking about someone else.' He turned on his side so that they were face to face. 'You have the most beautiful face.' His fingers traced the freckles across her cheeks. 'Those eyes are the bluest I've ever seen and this nose,' pinching it slightly and she giggled. 'It's the nose of a queen,' moving closer, moving her closer with his words. 'And this neck,' sliding his hand down to the hollow space there, pressing lightly. 'And these shoulders, and these knees,' she started to laugh as he tickled her behind her knee caps. He lowered his voice. 'There's nothing about you that's ordinary.'

'You think so?' Her voice was hushed, pleased.

'I know so.' He smiled, his hand dropped from her. 'Now come on, give me a kiss.' And he offered up his cheek but she went for his mouth. It was something that terrified and excited him and the shock of it made him pull away. She was wide-eyed.

'I'm sorry, was that wrong?'

And he had the chance to do the right thing. He put his hand back up to her cheek and the words swelled in his chest and he felt an incredible and surprising pity for her. But the feeling of her on his mouth was lingering and strong and he couldn't speak. When she did it again, it was long and sweet and clumsy and it changed everything.

She acted strange with him in the days following. Every time he looked at her, her face became pinched and her eyes turned messy. She couldn't speak to him without blushing. When he went to her room at night, he discovered she had started wearing lipstick.

'What's that for?' he had asked, her lips plump and clownish.

'It's lipstick. Mom wears it all the time.'

He gave her a tissue, couldn't look at her when she was like that. 'Please take it off.'

'I thought you would like it.' She looked ready to cry.

'You're gorgeous, just the way you are,' he said to her. 'You don't need crazy colored lipstick to make people see that.'

'I love you,' she said. Not *I love you, Daddy*. Just, *I love you*, and it sounded strange but also true. As if she had plucked the confession straight from his heart and recited it back to him.

'What do you mean?'

'You make me feel special.' She said it and then buried her face in her pillow, kicking her legs against the mattress. He put his hand on her back to stop her.

'That's because you are.'

She tilted her head up to him. 'Do you love me?' she asked, almost breathless.

'Of course I do. You know I do.'

'No,' she hesitated. Stammered. 'I mean, like a boy loves a girl.'

And it wasn't until she had asked him; it was only because she pointed it out, that he realized he did. That she was the one he could say anything to, do anything with. That around her, he wasn't afraid—she knew the worst he had done and still she stayed. Still, she looked at him with those adoring eyes and despite everything that had happened between them, she made him feel clean. But she was his daughter and even if she didn't know it, he knew it was wrong and the right thing to do would have been to tell her no, that he could never love her like a boy loves a girl because that wasn't right. Instead, overcome, he nodded. 'Yes.'

'Me too.' She spoke in a rush, jumped on him and his arms captured the length of her waist. There was no going back from this.

It could have gone on forever; it could have finished in a day. That was the nature of their relationship; no one knew about it and so it was as if it didn't really exist, or existed in another dimension that belonged only to them. It was their secret and they were in charge of it. She was a good actress; an even better liar than he was, and they could have probably carried on deceiving everyone if it hadn't been for the flu epidemic that came sweeping in that winter. The stuffy noses, the sore throats and feverish skin, forcing everyone to their beds. Everyone but his mother. Instead, a heavy head and a burning throat led her to get up and go downstairs, into the kitchen, in search of an aspirin.

It was a Saturday, which meant that Marienne stayed at the hospital for longer than usual. She came home around midnight, sometimes later, so he didn't force Frances to button up her collar, didn't take out the arm that was wrapped around her chest, tightly encased in her nightgown. He was curled up into her, his face buried in her neck. He must have been telling her a joke because she laughed but he couldn't remember what it was because of what happened after. In the next ten minutes, Frances had fallen asleep.

She grew hot against him and he pushed in closer to her, saying *I love you, I love you,* and then he heard the footsteps but it was too late.

The door swung open quietly before he could pull away, and a beam of yellow hit his face and froze him. He saw his mother, watched her squint, but then she backed out and it was dark again. He wasn't sure if she had seen them; was certain that she couldn't have missed it, and he lay paralyzed against his daughter, his breath so short, he might not have been breathing at all. He wanted at once to forget that she had been there; if she asked him tomorrow, he could just pretend it had been a trick of the light, that she was getting old and seeing things. He could even get Frances to admit that she had snuck a boy into her room. But he had to know now and this urge pushed him out of the bed, even though he thought he was going to be sick from the fear. He buttoned his trousers with shaking hands, pulled on his T-shirt and then without thinking, opened the door and let himself into his mother's room.

'Mom,' he said, without looking at her.

He knew she was sitting on the bed, glass clutched in her hand, a small white pill in the other. 'What were you doing?' she asked. When he looked at her, he saw that her eyes were still hopeful. She was waiting for him to dispute her assumption, to explain it away with a laugh and a joke.

'It's not what it looks like.' At the point where it mattered most, he found himself unable to lie. He had been overtaken by a sudden compulsion to tell the truth.

'Then what was it?' her voice quivered. 'What were you doing, James?'

'She had a nightmare.'

'That doesn't explain why your hand was in her nightgown. Why you were half dressed, for Christ's sake!'

He kept quiet, staring down at the carpet. He held himself tightly against the wall and seemed, even to himself, like a monster.

'What were you doing?' close to a shout this time. 'Oh my God, oh my God,' holding her head in her hands and he went quickly to her, afraid someone would hear, be alarmed and come over. 'Don't touch me,' she yanked her hand away. The water splashed from the glass and into his eyes. She let it go and it dropped onto the carpeted floor with a dull thud. He reached for her again but she slapped him hard. Her fingers stung his cheek and vibrated in his head. She stepped back, scared of him.

'Please, just listen to me.'

'She's your daughter,' she said. 'She's just a child.' She grabbed him by the shirt, shook him. The hastily closed buttons came undone. 'I can't believe this. Tell me this isn't happening.'

'Let's go downstairs. I don't want to wake her up.' He maneuvered her out of the door. It was easy to do—she was as limp as a baby. His mind was racing with lies but they all reached dead-ends. There was nowhere to go from here but to tell the truth. He felt surprisingly at ease.

He put her in his chair, sitting beside her on the coffee table. She rocked back and forth, moaning something he couldn't comprehend, so he waited.

'You were,' she started, but choked on the image. 'Before I came in, were you...'

'Yes.' He helped her, tried to be kind and finish her sentence, cringing at his own answer.

'Why?'

He shrugged, not because he was nonchalant but because the question was too big, too vague to answer. It had started for a certain reason and was continuing entirely because of something else. Reasoning wouldn't make it better for her. 'I can't say.'

She was angry now, disgusted, and when she spoke, flecks of spit formed at the corners of her mouth. 'What do you mean, you don't know?'

'It's just,' something shut down in him, clamping him up. 'I've never hurt her. You know I would never do that.'

'How is this not hurting her?' she gestured to him without looking and he saw that his zipper was undone. His face burned with shame; he hated her in that moment. She was taking everything that was precious to him and turning it into poison. 'Just tell me why and we'll get you help. You need help.'

'No, I don't. I'm not a monster.'

She was trying to understand; he saw it in her eyes. The same disbelief, the same disgust he had felt about himself so long ago. 'Was it my fault?' Her fingers dug into his palm, hurt him, but he didn't pull away. 'Did I do something?'

'Of course not.'

'Your father.' Her face sagged. 'Your father—was it him? Please tell me that you didn't, that you weren't—'

'No,' he said sharply. She wasn't listening. 'It's not that. It's none of that.' He thought about telling her about Donna, of when it had first started, but that seemed irrelevant right now. He spoke with surprising calm, as if he had just woken up from a dream and come back into the real world after a long and tired sleep.

'There are people like you,' she said, suffocated by her words and he saw that what he had said had pushed her away forever. 'Who are in jail.'

'I'm not like them.' He was growing impatient with her, furious at her accusation.

'I didn't say—'

'At least I tried,' he exploded. 'I spent a long time fighting it—at least I have a conscience. I never hurt her and I never would. Don't I deserve some credit, some sympathy for that?'

'What are you saying?' she asked. 'Listen to what you're saying. How can I forgive you for what you have done? How can God forgive you for it either?'

He was up and over her in a second, a scream in his throat. 'This is what he made me,' a rage in his voice that shook the windows. 'This is not my fault. It's not my fault.' He released his grip on the sofa and stood back from her, his body clenched and waiting for a fight. 'I told Marienne I never wanted children. I never asked for this—it was forced upon me.'

She stood up to leave and he caught her.

'Where are you going?'

'Leave me alone.'

'Are you going to the police?'

They struggled but she was too weak for him. 'You're going to report me?' He was incredulous, beside himself with panic.

'I'm going to do what's right.'

'No.' He pinned her arms behind her, forcing her back down. 'No, please, you can't do that to me. I'm your son!'

'What about my granddaughter? What about Annie?'

'And what are you going to tell Marienne?' He cocked his head, was astounded at the sneer in his voice. 'You're the one who convinced her back into this marriage. Are you going to apologize? Are you going to make up for the thirty years she's lost? For everything she's going to lose after you send me away to rot in a jail cell?'

She started to shake and he took her hands, softening his voice. He put his head in her lap even though she tried to pull away.

'We're family, you can't do that to me. Please, I'm sorry. I won't do it ever again.'

'Get off me.' A choked sob. 'Please,' and with one last shove, she pushed him to the floor and stood up. 'This can't be real,' reaching out to shake his shoulders. 'How could I not have known this? You're my son—it can't be true.'

'Then let's forget it happened. I told you, I'll never do it again. We can move on from this.'

'How can I trust that's true? After all this, how can I believe that?' She straightened out her nightgown and this time, he didn't have the energy to stop her as she stepped away.

'You're going to the police.'

'No.'

He turned his surprised eyes to her, couldn't help but ask, 'Why?'

'I won't ruin two other lives because of what you've done.'

'Thank you.' Relief washed over him; he felt weak. 'I never meant to hurt anyone. I'm still your son—I'm still the same person.'

'Don't think I'm doing any of this for you.' She started walking to the stairs. 'You stop this right now. And you tell her it's wrong—you fix her.' He felt a fleeting panic at the thought of never kissing the back of her ear again; never telling her another story and watching her eyes brighten with interest. But he nodded. 'And don't expect me to ever believe anything you have to say again,' she told him. Her face had darkened, closing him off for good. 'I'm only protecting you because of the two of them. Because they need you and because I'm the one who brought Marienne back.'

He stayed silent and she felt a compulsion to keep talking. 'He was so proud of you, you know. We both were. You were everything to us.' Her voice was hard, emotionless. 'I'm glad he's not here to see this. To see what you've become.' And those were the last words she ever spoke to him.

He didn't watch her leave. Instead, he went back to his chair, sank into it and pulled his knees up to his chest, cradling himself, swinging back and forth slowly, looking out of the window and watching the night stretch on. And though he stared and searched, he knew it was hopeless. No matter how hard he tried, a young boy once again, wishing his life and luck away, he would never be able to find the point where the darkness ended.

36

Whitehorse, Yukon. January 1993

The wide, open room gathers up the sound of my rapid footsteps, collects them and throws them back down so that my ears fill with them. I run with all my might, pushing my heels off the floor, head-on, using the power in my shoulders, dodging in and out of girls. I hear someone calling my name, *Frances, pass it here, over here,* but I ignore them and keep going. My thoughts are being left behind, discarded, and they cannot catch me. The stick is simply an extension of my hand, the ball just something to toy with; someone comes in my way and I charge right through them. They fall to the floor, a loud whistle and finally I stop; red-faced and panting. I see that it's Victoria on the floor; she is clutching her wrist and looking up at me in surprise.

'That's enough.' Sister Ann drops the whistle around her neck. 'Okay girls—go get changed.'

She is staring at me and I know it's because she is wondering why I am so active today, having never shown an interest in playing hockey, or any other sport, before. But I find it helps with the anger, the panic that is under construction in my body, that will be complete by the end of the month when I watch them drive away from me. But right now, it is watered down, parts of it exiled through the sweat forming at my neck and running down my spine, drowned out by the exertion of my heart.

'Are you okay?' I ask Victoria.

'I've done something to my hand.' She tries to move it in a circle but winces. 'Shit, that hurts.'

Sister Ann comes up to us. 'Everything alright?'

'I think I've done something to my hand.'

'Let me see.' She gets Victoria to stand up, gently easing the pained wrist into her palm, massaging it around the bone. She pushes the palm up and Victoria grimaces.

'That really hurts.'

'Sister Margret has a first aid kit in her office—let's go get you a bandage. It's probably just a small sprain.' She starts to move toward the front door. 'Come on.'

Victoria stands completely still, holding her wrist to her. 'I'm sure it'll be okay,' she says. 'It feels better already. It's probably just a bruise.'

'Still, it's better just to make sure.' She looks at me. 'Well done today, Frances.'

'Thank you.'

'I didn't know you played.'

I shrug. 'It's just one of those days, I guess.'

'Come on, Victoria.'

Victoria has no choice but to follow her. She cannot argue anymore without raising suspicions. She looks back at me and I nod to reassure her. *I will keep him safe until you come back,* and then I turn and go out the back door, instantly swallowed up by the four o'clock darkness.

I find him already there; sitting on Victoria's bed, tapping his foot up and down nervously.

'Hi,' I say and he jumps in surprise.

'You're not Victoria.'

'Really? I hadn't noticed.'

He smiles at this. 'I wasn't sure I had the right room.'

'Who says you do?'

He laughs. 'You're funny,' he says. 'Frances, right?' And I nod. 'Vic never mentioned that about you.' There is a lilt in his voice, a slight teasing, that draws me closer, makes me lean against the bed frame.

'What did she say about me?'

He slides closer; his eyes are long-lashed and feminine. They are out of place on his otherwise large, muscular frame. 'Wouldn't you like to know?' He looks me up and down, brazenly, and when his eyes hold mine again, they are on fire. 'Definitely not how pretty you are.'

I stir under the attention. It has been too long since someone has looked at me that way, and it starts up an old emotion in me that I have missed. That I thrive on. I sit down next to him; have to press my leg against his thigh because there isn't enough space between him and the end of the bed. I know I shouldn't. I know how much Victoria likes him; how hurt she would be if she were to walk in right now, but I need him more than she does.

'Where is Vic?' he asks.

'She hurt her wrist so she's gone to get it checked out.' I put my hand on his thigh, feel his leg jump. I move it further up.

'What if she—'

'She won't.' I am tired of this talking, overcome by hot desperation.

'I thought you had a boyfriend.'

'Not anymore.'

And I don't have to say anything else; my head is jerked back, his mouth is on top of mine, over-eager and searching. It is a natural state for me to have someone's body on top of mine, their hands

347

covering me and it feels safe. His hands go down to circle my waist, they pull the ends of my shirt out from my gym pants. 'Someone might come in,' he says breathlessly and I'm saying that I don't care, falling on top of him, trying to drown myself in him. Trying to feel something for this boy who is good looking and smells nice—who is my age and who is attracted to me. But his tongue is too clammy and his fingers too clumsy, too young. There is no depth to him and I start to pull away but I'm too late.

The door has already opened. I hear a girl shout something and I am scrambling off the bed, pulling my clothes around me, saying, 'Victoria, Victoria, I'm sorry, sorry,' but then I turn around and it's not her. I see thick black glasses and teeth protruding from thin lips. Library books hugged to a chest.

'What are you doing in my room?'

'Taylor.'

At first, I am relieved, but then her eyes dart to the bed, where Leo is smoothing out his hair and her face curls in disgust. 'You're not allowed boys in here.'

'Look, let me explain.'

'And this isn't even your room!' She is backing out. 'You're not allowed boys in here, it's the rules,' she repeats and I chase after her, grab her arm, but she pulls away and I'm struggling to fix my clothes.

'Taylor!'

She runs down the stairs, shouting as she does, 'there's a boy here—Frances has a boy in my room!' and I'm sprinting after her, still hoping that I can shut her up, that no one has heard what she is yelling, but by the time I reach the foyer, she has disappeared into Sister Margret's office. Leo skids to a stop beside me.

'Got to go,' he says, pulling his leather jacket on. 'Shit, what a mess,' pausing to hold my eyes. He isn't even apologetic. 'Tell

Victoria I'll call her,' and he has pulled open the door and is running back to his car.

And I stand in the middle of the foyer because there is nowhere else to hide and I wait for the voices to stop in the office. Hear the chairs scraping back, the loud bang as the door is thrown open. See the thunderous face of Sister Margret. Victoria and Sister Ann are behind her. Taylor is red-faced and pointing at me. Sister Margret tells her to be quiet and we all stare at each other. I don't look at Victoria.

'Frances, Taylor told me you have a boy upstairs.'

'You can go and check if you want.' I will not admit it. She hasn't seen it herself; she will never know the truth for certain. I can convince her. I have to convince her.

'She's lying.' Taylor's voice is high-pitched and warbling. I have caused ripples in her clean, religious mind. Disturbed the waters there. 'She was on the bed with him. They were—' she blushes. Stops. I have to laugh at her expression.

'You think this is funny?' Sister Margret turns to me.

'No.'

'What were they doing?'

'Kissing.' She hisses the word. 'More than kissing.'

Victoria gives a little gasp; her eyes grow wide. Up until then, she thought that Taylor simply walked in on Leo and me in the room. In her mind we were probably just sitting beside each other, making conversation to pass the time until she showed up. Sister Margret turns to her. 'Did you know about this?' she asks.

And Victoria looks at my face and knows everything I have done because I cannot hide my guilt from her. She stands straighter, her face goes blank. 'She's been seeing him for a while.'

'Victoria,' I start toward her, but am stopped by Sister Margret. 'That's not true!' I'm shouting, wildly glaring from one to the other.

'She said she was going to try and sneak him in,' her lie is smooth, unbroken. She doesn't even pause to blink. 'I told her it was against the rules. I warned her and thought she would listen. But obviously she didn't.' She meets my eyes straight on. *You deserve this. It's all your fault.* 'His name is Leo.'

I hear a breath being sucked in behind me. I turn around. A group of girls has gathered behind us, watching with interest. Judy is at the center of them. She has recognized the name—she knows who he belongs to. I hope that she will step forward and tell the truth and save me. But she doesn't want to get involved—doesn't want to spoil her reputation with the teachers and so she keeps silent.

'You know the rules, Frances,' Sister Margret says. Everyone falls silent. They don't believe she'll do it. It has never happened before; no one has ever got caught. Sister Ann moves forward, touches Sister Margret's shoulder.

'Surely we can talk about this—decide an appropriate punishment,' but she is stopped as she is shrugged off, dismissed.

'You're sure about what you saw?' Sister Margret asks Taylor.

'Yes.'

'Go and pack your bags.' She is addressing me again. 'You leave tomorrow morning.'

'Please.' I am close to crying now. I don't want to go home—I can't go back. 'It was a mistake. I'll never do it again, I swear. Please don't kick me out.'

She turns to the group of girls. 'Everyone back to your rooms.' And eyes travel over my body, my disheveled hair, my swollen lips. I hear snickers and whispers, all saying the same thing, *it's over. There's no choice. You'll never see them again.* And Victoria passes me, hisses in my ear.

'You bitch. I can't believe I trusted you,' and I see the pain I have caused her, the broken heart she will now have to live with because of me and I put my head in my hands and cry. When I look up again, Sister Ann is waiting to take me to my room but everyone else is gone. I am already a part of this place's past.

I leave early the next morning, before classes start and I am ushered quickly down the stairs, not even given the chance to turn around and say goodbye.

'You can't do this,' I keep saying. 'You can't just kick me out in one day!'

'You broke the rules. There's nothing else I can do.'

'And my parents? They've paid for the full year—this isn't fair.'

'I spoke to your father last night and he said he would be more than happy to have you back home.'

I resist the urge to grab onto her habit. To fall on my knees and beg. 'Two more days,' I say. 'Give me a couple of days at least to say goodbye.'

Last night, I wanted to sneak out to see Joseph and his family but Sister Margret stayed with me. She sent Judy to someone else's room and sat up all night, watching me. She wasn't taking any chances, she told me. Not this time.

'I tried,' she said. 'No one can say I didn't.'

It would be easy to tell her the truth, to convince her that it was Victoria's plan all along, but I have hurt her and I owe her this. I lie on my back, my eyes are hot and dried up, my throat parched but I have no energy to get up for a glass of water.

'I didn't know it was a crime to be in love,' I say bluntly.

'What you were doing with that boy was not love.'

'How do you know?' I ask, sitting up, swinging my legs over the bed. I sneer at her. 'Were you there?'

'Taylor told me what she saw.'

'Taylor is a dried up, pathetic virgin.' The words burst from my mouth before I can stop them.

Sister Margret's mouth twitches but she says nothing. There is no point reprimanding me anymore. I have failed her and she will not waste her time. 'You're young still,' she says, uncharacteristically patient. 'You'll see in time.'

'See what?'

'That lust is not love. It's just an old impulse, reserved for animals and Godless people.' She has moved into preaching mode, her face shines. 'To feel something here,' gesturing quickly to the place between her thighs, 'is not to say it means anything in here,' lightly placing her hand at her heart. 'This place is pure and you have to be clean and good to experience what it has to offer. You'll understand in time,' she repeats. 'But I'm not going to be the one to teach you.'

And now she is pushing me toward the car, and I peer in, hoping it's him but it's not. She throws my suitcases in the trunk. 'Gerald will take you to the station,' she says and all of a sudden, her face has become gentle. It looks old and weary and I see that she is a little sad to be doing this. 'Here's the train ticket.'

'I don't want it.'

'Take the ticket, Frances.'

'I said I don't want it. I'm not going home.'

She slams the door shut and hands it to the driver instead. 'Make sure she gets on the train,' she tells him, loud enough for me to hear her. 'Walk her onto it if you have to.'

'Yes, Ma'am.'

'Goodbye, Frances,' she says. 'I'm sorry it had to end like this.'

'Fuck you,' I say and she steps back as the car turns into the driveway, leaving the Academy in a squeal and skid of tire.

The car edges slowly along the driveway, reaching into the forest from where I will disappear forever, when I see him. Striding through the thicket of trees, logs in hand from his morning search. Our eyes meet, his eyebrows cross in confusion and I think he says my name. Through the fog, he walks to Sister Margret and I turn, following him with my eyes. She points at the car and says something. My body leaps into action. I grab the driver by the shoulder, 'Stop the car!' I'm shouting. 'Stop the car, I want to talk to him!'

'I can't do that,' he pushes me off. 'I'm sorry. Please sit down.'

'I have to say goodbye to him! I have to explain what happened.' I move to open the door but we're traveling at too fast a speed and he is quickly disappearing from my view and I don't want to miss him. I pound on the back windshield, I scream his name until my voice turns hoarse and the tears blur my vision, and when it clears, the Academy is long gone and I can no longer see the tall, gently imposing profile of him but I will always remember how it stood, unwavering and steady against the pearl-white backdrop of a harsh and implacable winter.

Gerald walks me to the train station. He looks uncomfortable asking the guard if he can watch me get on the train and I tell him he doesn't have to do that. That I have to go home because no one else will take me.

'Unless you'll let me stay with you,' I laugh almost manically.

'I'm just following instructions,' he says and stands apart from me.

And the conductor helps me onto the train, shows me to my seat. He smiles and tells me that it will be a long journey. That if I need anything, I should ask him and I ask if he can mend a broken heart, and if not, can he take away my memories? But he is no longer listening, already walking down the carriages.

And ten minutes later, we are moving. I watch out into a sea of white and patchy brown, as the train rocks and shakes, further away from them. Something catches in my throat. *Don't worry, you'll forget about them soon enough.* I almost laugh at my own naivety. I could try for years; I could sit on this train and travel the world and it would never be far enough. Because when you fall in love with someone, as I did with all three of them, that love follows you around like a stubborn shadow wherever you go, tripping and blinding you—it doesn't matter where you step, it's always in your way.

37

St Albert. January 1993

It's late the next day when I get home. It's so dark that I can hardly see where I am going as I step off the bus that drops me only a few blocks from my house. I walk slowly, dragging my feet against the pavement. It's jarring to be back here so unexpectedly—to not want to be here. There is a throbbing in my head and my mouth is dry. I haven't eaten in what seems like days. I reach the white fence closing off my house, rub my knuckles over the cherry-blossom tree on my way in and its trunk seems worn and tired.

I stop at the front door, watch the pale lights behind it, and my heart lurches. It squeezes until I think it will stop; it might break and empty out of me and I wish that it would. I knock and he pulls it open almost instantly so that I almost fall into him. He catches me, *Frances, are you alright?* and his voice is sharp with worry. I feel the momentary thrill of his hands on me—it's a reflex his touch always stirs, it can't be helped. 'I'm so glad you're back. I was worried.' He crushes me to him.

'Where's Mom?'

'She's at work. She doesn't know you've come back.'

'You didn't tell her?'

He helps me in, puts me down on the couch and grazes the back of his knuckles against my cheekbone. The action is menacing in its tenderness, perhaps because of it, and I shrink away. He stops; drops his hand. 'I wanted to see you alone first. I thought we could talk.'

'There's nothing to talk about. I was expelled.'

'I know. Sister Margret called last night.' He pauses. 'She told me what happened with that boy,' and when I don't offer an explanation, he says, 'we can talk about it tomorrow.'

'I told you, there's nothing to say.' Tears form at the corners of my eyes; salty and stinging along my skin. I pull my sleeve over my hand, wipe it over my eyes and feel the cotton grow heavy with the tears. 'It's not even true.'

He sits down next to me, holds his hand out and lets it sit there, palm up, asking. I put my fingers in his and he wraps them up tightly. Binds me to him.

'I don't care if it's true or not. I'm just glad you're home.'

There are lines in his face that I don't remember; marks and features that never belonged to the man I've known all my life. The roughness of his skin no longer feels like a silken comfort; it's coarse and scrapes my hand painfully.

'I need to know why this happened,' I say to him. Despite my exhaustion, I am adamant. It's the first time we have spoken since that phone conversation and now, being forced back here, I have to find my answers.

'We can talk about this another day, when you aren't so tired.' His eyes dart from one corner of the house to the next. He looks uncomfortable.

'That's why you didn't tell Mom, isn't it? That's why she's at work—because you knew I might ask.'

'You aren't thinking straight, Frances. We'll have this discussion when your head is a little clearer. A lot has happened in the past two days.'

'I want to talk about it now.' A part of me is emboldened, self-righteous, but I am also frightened. So many things have changed and I'm not sure I can handle anything else.

'Do you remember when it started?' he asks me. He is wrestling with the confession; it doesn't want to leave him.

'No.' My first memories of him are vague. I don't remember when it began, only that it has always happened.

'I didn't think you would. You were very young.' He trails off, lost in thought. 'It wasn't meant to carry on for this long. I thought no one would find out—I really believed I could stop it.'

He puts my hand in his lap, strokes my limp fingers. I draw them back, wishing I could fold up my entire body that way and disappear from this terrible place that is slowly caving in on me.

'So why didn't you?'

'I wasn't strong enough.'

'That's not an excuse.'

He touches my shoulder, drags his touch, feather-like down my hand. 'Frances,' his voice throaty and thick, weighing me down.

I pull away, shaking my head through the tightening revulsion in my gut. 'Don't do that. You can't bully me that way anymore.'

He draws back, indignant. 'Is that what you think I do?'

'I know you're used to getting what you want.'

'That's not fair,' he starts to protest.

'I trusted you.'

The words hang between us. He stands up and faces the still, black street outside. I see something, a coyote perhaps, darting down the street and over someone's fence but other than that, there is no movement. 'Not anymore then,' clenching and unclenching his jaw, biting down hard on his teeth.

'That's what you wanted, isn't it?' I ask. 'For me to understand all of this? That's why you sent me away, so it would stop.'

'Yes.' He half-laughs, tears springing to his eyes. 'You don't know how hard it was—not calling you or seeing you. There were so many times when I wanted to.' When I don't respond, he continues, 'but I should have listened to your grandmother and done it a long time ago.'

'Bubbie knew?' I had always suspected it, known it, but I want to hear him confirm it.

He nods. His throat moves tightly up and down and the action catches a fleeting memory in my brain, sends it down in a pool of blood to my heart. Even the smallest thing can make you ache if it has been lost to you for so long.

'I promised her I would stop when she caught us. It was just before you turned eleven.'

'I don't remember.'

'You were asleep when she came in.' He shudders at the thought, the recollection becomes too real. 'She never spoke again after that night.' His head hangs. 'And then she found out that we—that I was still...' he gestures helplessly, unable to find the words. 'It was the night before she died. Do you remember that?'

I say I do. I remember the way he flew off me and landed silently at the door, crouching down, listening. *Someone's there,* he had said and I had laughed it off.

'That's why she killed herself.' He doesn't have to say anything else. The way his face contorts gives me confirmation.

'I told her. I tried to explain that I lived a long time being scared, fighting something inside me that I believed was very wrong. Until you—you changed it all.'

'What was it?' I ask. 'What were you fighting?' He doesn't want to tell me and I am left to formulate my own answer, watching his mouth curl at the side, his head dropping further. 'With me—it wasn't the first time?' I wasn't expecting to hear myself say this and it astounds me. Leaves me breathless; strangled by the rapidly unraveling threads of truth.

'No.'

He looks so old and exhausted, leaking his poisonous past onto my lap. Hearing him talk reminds me of what Sister Margret said the night before I left the Academy. About lust and love; cleanness and Godless people. She said I would come to understand someday but I hadn't expected it to come this soon. I had been so sure of his love for me; it had been the only thing that allowed me to forgive him. But now that I know there was someone else, the fact is blaring and loud and sullies everything.

I stand up and he moves to stop me. 'You know no one can find out about this.' He looks afraid, as if it has just occurred to him that the secret is mine as well as his. That the choice to keep it or not belongs to us both. 'You aren't going to tell anyone, are you?'

'I don't know.'

'You can't,' his voice rises, becomes child-like and desperate. 'Do you know what would happen if you did? What they would do to me?'

What about what has happened to me?

'You knew how wrong it was, all this time,' I say. 'You knew and you never stopped me.' I am shouting now, betrayed, drowning in my helplessness. 'You should have stopped it.'

'I know.' He looks ready to reach out for me again and I hope he won't. I don't want to have him on me; the thought makes me feel

359

dirty and sad. 'I'm so sorry but please, she can't find out. It would ruin everything.'

He is referring to my mother and for a brief moment, I contemplate what would happen if I were to tell her, if I could find the words to explain to her exactly what he had been to me; and even if I said them, would it make anything better? I can't shake the feeling that once our secret has been exposed, given new life, I will never be able to escape it.

'What do we do now?' I ask him, a burst of desperation from my throat. 'I can't lie to her anymore. I don't want to.'

'Listen to me,' he says, 'if anyone finds out, it could destroy all of us. They'd take me away—how would you survive? Where would you live?' He is wild-eyed. 'What I've done is wrong and God knows how I regret it. But I've looked after you—I'll always look after you.' His words peter out. 'Please, Frances. You can't do this to me, please.' His fingers squeeze my cheeks and I can't get away. 'I love you, you know I do. I'm sorry, promise me. Promise me you won't tell.'

I take his wrists and drag his hands away from my face. 'I don't want you to touch me anymore.'

'Frances.'

I close my eyes. I can't look at him when he is looking at me that way. 'Please. Don't say anything else.'

My words and tone offend him but he doesn't protest. He only puts his hands under his thighs and nods slowly. 'If that's what you want. Whatever you want—I just want you to be okay. The only thing I've ever wanted is for you to be happy.'

'I have to go to bed.' I can't listen to him anymore. I think I might burst from emptiness.

'I can help you with your things.'

'No.' I shake my head firmly. It is the first time I have refused him and the declaration comes out wavering and loud. The thought of him following me to my room roots me to the spot and it dawns upon me that I will never feel safe here again. 'I'll do it all tomorrow.'

'And you won't say anything,' he is at the bottom of the stairs, his foot on the first step, clutching the banister. His face is swallowed up by the darkness, 'to anyone?'

'I won't.'

And he breaks out into a smile, cannot hide his relief, and I have never felt lonelier.

'Thank you. I'm glad you're back. Things will get better, you'll see. I'll make it better for you.'

I don't reply. I won't tell him about Joseph, about all that he has shown me. My father is still hopeful for the future; it looks brighter and better now that he is confident our secret will remain hidden and I don't have the energy or the strength to spoil that for him just yet.

38

St Albert. January 1993

Three weeks later, I stand at the kitchen sink on my tiptoes, the curtain pulled back slightly. He is shoveling snow in our driveway, muscles like tightrope between his shoulder blades. Every movement he makes sets off a series of sparks in my nerves, as if I am made for him and out of him, as if I cannot survive if he is gone—that I will no longer exist once he stops being this to me. He is so familiar that I know he is going to wipe back the hair that falls into his eyes before he does it. Its color catches the midday heat, made more golden by sweat and sunshine. It hurts me to watch him this way, concealed by blue-flowered lace, especially now that I know what I'm guarding. I drop the curtain and sit down next to my mother. She is bent over something, her hands moving two big needles clumsily.

She had come home that night I returned and I heard them talking downstairs as I pretended to sleep.

'She was so miserable there,' I heard him tell her. 'Maybe her getting expelled was a good thing.'

'How can it be a good thing?' She doesn't sound angry, only worried. I wanted her to come upstairs, to put her cool hand on my forehead. I dreamed that she asked me what was wrong and that I told her and she took everything away and made me light. But instead, I lay in bed and tried to suppress the wave of feeling hitting against my chest. It shocked me to realize how much I missed her, how long I had missed her for. 'We sent her there for a reason, James,' she says. 'We wanted her to change the way she was acting. To learn that how she was behaving was wrong.'

'She has learned her lesson, Annie. I think it's time we were a family again.'

'I just want what's best for her,' she replied. 'I hope you're right, James.' I could tell she was hugging him because her words were muffled.

'Let's not make a big deal out of this,' he said. 'She knows what she did was wrong. Let's just move on.'

'I'm just glad she's okay. I love her.' And the words carried up, settled over me and gave me some small bit of comfort before I fell asleep.

'Has it always been this quiet here?' I ask now.

'I'm surprised you're just realizing that,' cocking her eyebrow at me.

I had never had any need for other people. I preferred it when they stayed away but now my life seems as empty as that blank street outside; no pedestrians, no noise, no traffic. No one except him, shoveling at my heart and pushing everything else out.

'What are you doing?' I ask.

'Knitting.' She grins ruefully. 'Some of the ladies do it at the hospital when it's a quiet night and I just sort of picked it up.'

'Looks like fun.'

'I could show you,' she says, treading carefully. 'If you want.'

'Yes.' I smile slowly. 'I would like that.'

'Great.' It's almost a shy look she gives me, a flush of pleasure in her cheeks. It makes me blink in surprise. *She really does love me.* I don't know how or when I forgot that, lost in all my violent feelings for him.

'Do you want to go for a walk?' I ask in a rush, worried she will say no. Instead, she puts her knitting down.

'Sure. Shall we tell your dad?'

I put my glass in the sink. 'I think it'll be nice for us to spend some time together, alone.'

She rises, unable to contain the grin that splashes childishly over her face. 'Let me get my coat.'

I suggest that we go to the park, the one he always used to take me to. The small pond has frozen over and I wonder where all the ducks have gone and if they will come back. I can almost see him there; blurred against the cold sunlight, calling out to me, and I turn away. We find a bench and she brushes away the snow with her glove and sits down, holding my hand and bringing me down with her.

'I talked to the principal at Crawley,' she says, referring to my old high school. 'They said they would be willing to take you back next week, granted you pass a standard test.'

'I hope I haven't missed too much.'

She pats my hand. 'We'll get through it,' and I bring my head down to her shoulder and thank her. There is a pause; I copy the rise and fall of her shoulders, the soft pattern of her breathing. It loosens the truth in my gut, pushes it upward until it is at my throat, hovering on the tip of my tongue and I sit straight, convinced I will tell her. I am tired of holding onto it and I want her to help me. But she speaks first.

'I want to tell you something,' she says. Her eyes are down-cast; she plays with a loose thread in her glove, tugs at it until the material knots up and shortens. She takes it off and pushes it into the pocket of her parka.

'What is it?' I am hesitant to ask, hoping she doesn't know what has happened with my father. She is the only person I have left and it would be too hard to know that she had a part in it too. She takes a strand of my hair and turns it in her hand.

'Everyone must tell you what a beautiful color this is.' She smiles a little sadly and when I raise my head to look at her, her beauty crashes into my eyes. Her pale cheeks are stained pink from the cold and her eyes, when they look at me are simple and easy; a peaceful black, eyelashes that graze the bottom arch of her eyebrows. 'Tell me, do you ever wonder why you have red hair?'

'Bubbie said I got it from her side of the family.'

'What about the freckles? The height?' She stops playing with my hair, turns her fingers down to my cheek. 'Do you ever notice how different the two of us are?'

'I never really cared.' That's not true. I spent a long time wishing I looked more like her; cursing the color of my skin, the lankiness of my frame compared to her toned, small one. My hardness compared to everything that is soft about her.

'That's probably because you're so pretty.' Her hand falls back into her lap and she takes a deep breath. 'Frances, what I'm about to tell you, you should know first that your father and I kept it from you because we thought that it was the right thing. We didn't see the point of telling you because we loved you so much and we didn't want you to suffer.' Her face crumples. 'I know it's not an excuse, but I don't know if you remember—you were so young—we used to be so happy. And I didn't want to spoil that.'

'I remember,' I say, because somehow I do. I remember this look in her eyes, the pulse of love in her voice. I remember how much she used to mean to me and I can feel it now, rising up in me again.

'I'm not your real mother.' She says it quickly and when she finishes, she is panting, bright-eyed with shame. She chews down on her bottom lip, pulls at it between her teeth. 'Oh God, I'm sorry. I—'

'What do you mean?' It is so far from anything I ever expected to hear from her that I almost don't believe her and respond with a strange calmness. Almost nonchalance.

'Your father and I were married for four years when we had a rough patch—that's all it was. Just a point where we were confused about the things we wanted. It was the first time we had really disagreed on anything and he...' she shrugs helplessly. 'Maybe I should have been more aware of what it was doing to him.' She heaves the blame onto her shoulders, doesn't want me to think any less of him. 'Anyway, none of that matters. What matters is that your real mother's name is Gina Baker.'

Gina. I let the name sit in my brain, settle on my tongue. I accustom myself with it but when I try to imagine what she looks like, I only see the woman sitting next to me.

'What happened to her?'

'Your father said she left when you were a baby.'

'Why?'

She takes my hand, turns to face me fully. 'I don't know, Frances. Maybe she wasn't ready to have you or maybe she wasn't cut out to be a mother but it wasn't your fault. And none of it matters because I'm here and I'm so glad that I'm a part of your life.' Her face clenches. She even looks pretty when she cries. 'I loved you from the first moment I saw you.' She looks terrified at the thought of losing me and I want to comfort her.

There was a girl at the Academy who discovered she was adopted close to the time I arrived. I remember the way she fell to the floor in my room, having come to talk to Judy. I remember the way all the other six girls there dropped down around her in a tight, comforting circle. She was crying and saying she didn't belong anywhere, that her 'fake parents' were liars and her real ones deserters. She didn't know who she was anymore, she said, her eyes going around the circle, pleading for help and they reached out and stroked her shoulders and told her that no matter what, they were her family. I had watched as she stood up suddenly, stepped out of the circle, looked at me with blood-shot eyes.

'I'm going to find her,' she had announced. 'I have to know who she is. I have to find my family.'

That is not the way I feel. Gina is a strange name of some strange woman I can't even picture. Although recently I have been angry toward my mother, she has never been a stranger to me. She has always been there, hiding in the shadows, waiting patiently for a time when I need her. Like the time I was eight and fell off my bike and she was there to drag me into her lap, sing a song and make me chocolate-chip cookies. Or the time Freddie Keating called me 'spotty face' and I tried to scratch my freckles off, came home with bloody cheeks and she turned me to the mirror. 'Do you know why they're all different shapes? Because they're telling a story about you,' she had said. 'This one here,' she pointed to a misshapen one on my cheekbone, 'it says how funny you are,' tickling me until I giggled. 'This one,' touching the largest one near the bottom of my ear, 'tells me how big your heart is.' She wrapped her arms around me and brought me close to her and her voice swallowed me. 'You should never be ashamed of any part of yourself.'

'So you came back after she left?' I ask her now.

'Yes. Your grandmother convinced me, reminded me of how much I always wanted a family.' She takes a long breath. 'I'm sorry it's taken so long for me to tell you. But I want to be honest and I think you deserve that. You're old enough now to know the truth.'

'Thank you.' I hold out my arms around her and bring her close to me. It's a shock to hear her say it but all I feel is mild, indifferent surprise. 'I'm not upset,' I assure her.

'You don't hate me?'

'How could I?' I pull away. 'You came back to look after me even though I wasn't yours. I love you.' I say it with all the truth I can muster; with all the affection I have held back from her for so long. I say it, pushing the guilt deep down inside me; she has been honest with me but I cannot afford to do the same with her, even though I was ready to only moments before. Our family has been built on a volatile foundation of secrets and it is slowly crumbling. The only thing that is keeping us together is the biggest one of them all, and if that should come out, none of us will survive it. So instead, I tell her that there are worse things people can do to each other, that eventually I may want to look for my biological mother but that will never make me feel any less for her and that the time is not now. I'm happy here, with my face against her neck and her scent heavy in my nose. I like the sound of her bracelets running down her wrist as she strokes my hair, the pacing of her heart; it's strong and steady and reminds me that no matter what, as long as she is there, I will never be alone.

There is a resistance between us; I feel it more acutely every day, whenever he comes near me. The other night, I asked for the key to my bedroom.

'Why do you need one?' he asked and I felt a surge of annoyance.

'I want my privacy.' Truth was, it made me uncomfortable knowing he could come and go as he pleased.

He didn't want to give it to me but my mother persuaded him. 'She's old enough now, James,' she said.

'I'll have to look for it,' he grumbled and the look he gave me was so reminiscent of our past that it almost made me relent.

I start back at my old school and everything feels different. No one is as hostile as I remember and it's a little easier to get along with them. Having opened myself up to Joseph, it's simple now to do the same with other people.

I find a job at the local video store to keep me out of the house for as long as possible and the distraction proves useful; I am slowly starting to forget what he means to me. I am leaving the store late one afternoon, a slight flutter in my nerves when I think of what I am returning to. Distracted, I accidentally run into someone.

'Whoa.' Arms reach out to steady me and I look up into a wide, friendly face. 'Sorry about that.'

'No, it was my fault.' I step away, recognizing him from my school. 'Frances, right?'

'Yes.' I play nervously with the strap of my bag. It shocks me that he knows who I am. 'Sorry, I don't know your name.'

'Darren.' He holds out his hand and I take it tentatively, pulling away almost immediately in case he can tell they're clammy.

'I've seen you around school,' he says, his hands deep in his pockets, a little self-consciously.

'Math class,' I help him. 'I think we're in the same one.'

'That's right.' He nods, tilting his head at me and I look at the ground. 'You work here?' Pointing up with his thumb to the sign on the door.

'Just on weekends.'

'Do they let you watch videos all day?' he asks in a teasing tone.

I laugh. 'They keep me pretty busy.'

'That's too bad.' He holds my gaze for a long time and when I blush, he breaks it. 'Well, maybe I can come by sometime. Rent a couple of videos. You can tell me which ones are your favorites.' There is a look on his face that creates a sudden coldness in my gut. The keen interest hiding within his pupils reminds me of the way my father used to watch me; daring and hopeful. It flatters and scares me and I try to tell myself that he isn't my father, that it's okay to be doing this—that there is nothing to be afraid of. But I cannot stop the hammering in my chest or the cold sweat that breaks out along my neck. The unprovoked resentment I feel for this boy.

'I have to go,' I say, starting to walk backward, turning to run down the street. 'I'm sorry, I have to go.'

When I turn the corner onto my street, I slow my pace, bending down over my knees and sucking in deep breaths of cold air. My chest hurts but not from the exertion. It's from that boy's curious, bronze eyes. His lips red and cracked from the cold, stretching to smile sweetly at me. The chance I may have just passed over and all the opportunities I might miss in the future. I automatically reach into my pocket and there it is, where I always keep it, unbroken and waiting. I run my fingers over the well-known lines of it, the four heads, four pairs of hands joined together. I can picture them now; they make me smile and laugh with their dark, glowing faces and their voices are soft and loving and good, easing the tension that runs in my veins. *Give it a little more time. All you need to forget and move on is just a little more time,* reminding me that despite everything, there is still the possibility of something better.

*

A few days later, she is leaving for work, waving goodbye to me in the darkness. *See you soon.* A prick of anxiety stings my gut; a new sensation that overcomes me now whenever she leaves. *Please come home quickly.* I stay outside for a long while, sitting on the stoop, finding a twig and drawing in the snow. From my position, I see him moving within the kitchen, fixing dinner, and I feel an acute stab of sorrow; a sympathy for him although I'm not sure why it's there. At times like this, I wish I had never discovered the truth because now I see something soiled in what I had always believed to be perfectly beautiful. It makes me worry that all the other things and people I love, or might come to know, might be that way too.

He opens the door and comes to sit beside me, exhaling loudly, his breath coming out in a fog. He puts his hands into the pockets of his jacket.

'Has she gone?' he asks.

'Yes.'

'This came for you today.' He pulls something out of his pocket. It's a slim, white envelope, crisp and uncreased. My name is written in shaky letters on the front. I take it slowly, running my hand over the smooth manila, turning it in my hands. 'Do you know who it's from?' he asks.

'Friends.' I recognize the immature handwriting immediately and although I want to open it, I refrain from doing so.

'From the Academy?'

'You could say that.'

He knows from my tone that I don't want to tell him anymore and he leaves it alone, changing the subject.

'Your mother told me you've been asking about other boarding schools.'

'A few.'

It's a much-needed comfort to stare at the thick, inviting pages of a brochure and imagine myself within the vibrant possibility of them. To remind myself that I don't have to stay here—that there are other places I can escape to.

'You told me you were never going to leave. Do you remember how adamant you were that you couldn't bear to be away from me?' His eyes meet mine but I don't hold them for long. With the silver reflection of the street lights in them, they don't look like his. 'Don't you feel that way anymore?'

'A lot has happened since then,' I state simply.

He closes his eyes. 'It feels like a lifetime ago.'

And we sit together, lost for words and uncomfortable in each other's presence for the first time.

'Is she safe with you?' I ask finally, needing to know and feeling guilty that I'm already thinking of abandoning her. That she will never learn the truth about her life.

'Your mother? I would never hurt her.' He is offended that I could ask. 'I love her.'

That doesn't mean you aren't going to—I can't say it; thinking it is one thing, but to have the words pressing and real on my tongue, is entirely something else. 'You've done it before.'

'And look at how much it's cost me,' he answers. 'Look at what's happened to us.' He is spitting out the words now.

'How come you can control it now, after everything that has happened between us?' I ask stonily.

'You were always there,' he tells me. 'I couldn't get away from you and every time I saw you, it just became harder and harder. But now that you're going, now that I can avoid them,' he is referring to our neighbors' children and to hear him speak it so simply, so truthfully, makes me cringe in disgust, 'I can almost pretend it's not there.' He sighs, puts his head into his cradling palms. 'It's easier to remember what's important.' And then he adds quietly, 'Look at how much it's taken from me.'

And as I look at his too-long hair falling into his eyes, the way his shoulders sag—with relief or failure, I can't tell—I believe him. It's time to move on, for both of us.

'I'm sorry I had to ask.'

He stands up. 'Dinner is ready,' he says in a way that is distant and makes me momentarily regret asking him. He goes in and I follow him.

'I'm just going to put this away,' I say and run upstairs. I open my bottom drawer, push aside the piles of clothes until my fingers graze at the brochures I have there and I take the statue out of my pocket and place it on top. I hold the letter up to the light, let it sink into the spidery letters of Alex's writing and then put it down with the statue, wanting to keep it closed until a time when I really need it.

As I am leaving, about to turn off the light, I hear the laughter of a little girl and it makes me turn around. I see her dancing within these walls, the overflowing ink of her happiness staining every corner. I see the man with the golden hair and permanent smile, who at one point, meant the world to her. They ignore me, trapped in their horrific happiness, and it hurts because it's always hard to say goodbye to something that has given you joy, even though you have no use for it anymore. Even though you no longer want it and find it ugly.

I turn the lights out on them; cast them into the smoky shadows of my past. Whether I am ready for it or not, whether it is right or wrong, everything has changed irrevocably by the time I step out into the brightness of the corridor. When the door swings firmly shut behind me and I can't hear them anymore, I am finally free to take a step in the direction of the only place to go from here; away from this decrepit space where it all began—forward and without him.

Acknowledgments

First and foremost, I would like to thank the four most important people in my life: Nasoor, Nilufer, Safia and Mishal—my parents and my sisters. It is because of your unfailing belief and constant patience that this novel has seen life beyond my desk drawer. Words will never be enough to express everything I feel for you.

Thanks to everyone who read the various drafts of *In Between Dreams*, in particular Jonathan Myerson for believing in me and his always insightful comments, Lucy Caldwell and everyone on the MA course at City University, without whom this book would not have been possible. Thank you to Mihir Shah, for all the advice, the countless brainstorming sessions and encouragement while I was writing and to Tamiza Rasul, Shaloo Manesh and Rehana Virjee for their endless support and wonderful friendship. Thanks to Rahim Kassam, Amit Shah, Fatima Hussain, Vicky Patel, Kushal Sanghrajka, Shivali Kamani and Sandhya Dulashia, among many others, for their constant enthusiasm and excitement. Thank you to my grandparents for their support and for teaching me the meaning of unconditional love.

My gratitude goes out to my agent, Janelle Andrew, for, among countless things, her passion, commitment and delicate editing.

To Charlotte Van Wijk for believing in this story as much as I do and for treating it with such care and understanding. A big thank you to my editor, Rosalind Porter, whose advice I trusted instantly and for her dedication to making this novel the best it could be. Finally, a big thank you to everyone at Peters, Fraser & Dunlop and Oneworld Publications for turning my biggest dream into a reality.